A Degree of Truth

MURIEL BOLGER

HACHETTE
BOOKS
IRELAND

First published in Ireland in 2019 by
HACHETTE BOOKS IRELAND

First published in paperback in 2020

1

Cataloguing in Publication Data is available from the British Library

ISBN 978 1 4736 9147 6

Typeset in Book Antiqua by Bookends Publishing Services

Printed and bound in Great Britain by
Clays Ltd, Elcograf, S.p.A

Hachette Books Ireland policy is to use papers that are natural, renewable
and recyclable products and made from wood grown in sustainable forests.
The logging and manufacturing processes are expected to conform to the
environmental regulations of the country of origin.

Hachette Books Ireland
8 Castlecourt Centre
Castleknock
Dublin 15, Ireland

A division of Hachette UK Ltd
Carmelite House, 50 Victoria Embankment, EC4Y 0DZ

www.hachettebooksireland.ie

A Degree of Truth

Muriel Bolger is a well-known Irish journalist and award-winning travel writer. In addition to her works of fiction, she has also written four books on her native city, including *Dublin – City of Literature* (O'Brien Press), which won the Travel Extra Travel Guide Book of the Year 2012.

@MurielBolger

ALSO BY MURIEL BOLGER

Consequences
Intentions
The Captain's Table
The Pink Pepper Tree
Out of Focus
Family Business

This book is dedicated to friendship –
whether it's the kind that endures and lasts a lifetime,
or the sort that intersects at different stages,
to nourish, uplift and sustain us.

PART ONE

COLLEGE DAYS

PART ONE

COLLEGE DAYS

Chapter One

The mass exodus for summer was accompanied by many goodbyes, hugs and kisses, and promises to keep in touch during the holidays. From the first day that Tansy had crossed the threshold, she had felt connected with the university in a way she could never have imagined. She'd definitely miss being here over the next few months. And if she was feeling a little directionless, Phyllis was on the verge of tears.

'Our second year over already. It's gone by far too quickly.'

'And you know the scary part? When we finish, we'll be considered educated,' Mags said.

'When that time comes, we'll have our bits of paper to prove that somebody thinks we are,' Tansy said. 'My biggest worry right now is can I manage to keep paying the rent with the summer job falling through? If I don't get anything this week, I'll be heading home to try my chances there.' And I can spend more time with Ross, she thought.

Gina said, 'I told you not to worry about that. My folks are happy to pay to hold the place for us till September.'

'While you're off in Spain – not that I'm even the tiniest bit jealous or anything, but I thought we were supposed to be all grown up now, not depending on handouts from our folks,'

Phyllis said, then she laughed. 'Oh, who am I kidding? It would definitely make life easier if I had wealthy folks like you two.' She put her arms around Gina and Mags.

'We'll manage, somehow,' Tansy said, following them.

'Yeah, yeah, yeah. But we can still have aspirations … like …' Phyllis slowed down as they passed the notice board in the university entrance hall. The notices on this had played an important part in opening their eyes to college life, to its culture and its sub-cultures too.

'What is it?'

'Look, Tans. There's a job for you.'

A large handwritten notice, which neither of them had seen earlier, had been secured behind the glass in the case, obliterating at least five others. It was written in bold red marker.

Urgent. Student, literate, intelligent and fluent in English, required for three months to transcribe manuscript. Start immediately. Will be paid. Must be punctual and interested in anthropological perspectives. Interviews 12.30–2pm today in Room 207. Professor Sean Pollard.

'I'm an arts student. I've never even heard of anthropological perspectives. What the hell are they?'

'I don't know but, Jaysus, Tansy, how hard can that be – transcribing a manuscript? And you get paid.'

'It was obviously written in a hurry, probably by someone hoping to take advantage of a penniless student. The payment is probably a pittance.'

'Anything is better than nothing. What would you have made in the coffee shop? In the summer – with all those students coming in to use the Wi-Fi – and not leaving tips? Go for the interview. Now! You've nothing to lose.' She looked at her watch. 'It's a quarter to two.'

'When did you become so bossy, Phyllis Martin? I can't go for an interview when I know zilch about the topic.'

'Go in and wing it – tell him you're willing to learn, that people are your thing. I think that's what anthropology is about, isn't it, studying people and their traits?'

'I think so, but ...' Phyllis grabbed Tansy's arm and steered her back to the quadrangle. 'What about Mags and Gina? They'll be wondering where we got to.'

'I'll text them. Have you any credit on your phone? Mine's dead.'

'So's mine.'

'I rest my case. We need you to get the job!' She laughed.

Phyllis was on a mission and no one and nothing was going to stop her. Two men were waiting in the corridor outside Room 207 when they turned the corner.

'This is a waste of time,' Tansy whispered, 'they're probably graduates.'

Phyllis ignored her and went straight over to them.

'Hi guys, are you here for the gig? You'd better be good. You've stiff competition here. My friend is just back from Peru, where she was working with some doctoral candidates in the field over there. Isn't that right, Tansy?'

The men didn't have a chance to react to Phyllis's revelations because from the open door behind them a generously tattooed girl emerged and shook her head at them. On her heel, a tall man followed and without preamble said to Tansy, 'In that case I'll take you first.'

She felt her face redden, her palms sweat and her mouth dry

before she realised the drumming was not someone practising for a rock concert, but the blood pumping through her veins.

'You, yes, you, come through,' he ordered, turning back to the room.

She wanted to run. She was vaguely aware of one of the other fellows walking off, in disgust, anger or defeat, she wasn't sure which, and of Phyllis's two hands on the middle of her back propelling her towards the door.

'So, you're a bit of an expert,' he said. 'I rarely meet young people with so much experience. How old are you? Twenty-three? Twenty-four? Where did you study?'

She couldn't even think of a plausible lie and stammered, 'Actually, I'm —'

'Let me explain the project. I'm Sean Pollard, Dean of the Faculty.' He launched forth before she could confess. So addled was she that she scarcely heard a word of what he was saying.

'... And hand written, that's why it's imperative that it's error-free.'

Hand written? Error-free? Had she to handwrite a manuscript? What had to be error-free? She'd kill Phyllis when she got out of this room, which seemed to be closing in on her, making her very aware of the professor's presence. He seemed to fill the space. His melodic voice was authoritative yet pleasing to her ear. She felt herself flush under his scrutinising look of intensity. Focus, she told herself, thinking his floppy hair made him look more like a student than a professor. A mature student. Focus.

'You've no holiday plans, or other jobs, I hope.' He paused, making it sound like a question that needed an answer.

'No. I had something lined up, but I —'

'Good, because I need total commitment until this is finished. The university has come up with funding at the eleventh hour and has put another room at my disposal. That's where you'll be working. It's right next to my office if you have any queries, but I'd prefer not to be bothered every five minutes, so I think structured times to meet and discuss these would be less distracting for both of us.'

'I'm not—'

'I hope you are not going to tell me you're not interested.'

'No. I am. It's just … I was just going to say—'

'Good. I like to get going early. I am usually here from seven, but I can see from the look on your face you think that's too early. How would an 8 a.m. start sound to you? You'll be free to leave at four and that'll give you a chance to work on your own papers.'

'I feel—'

'Oh, by the way, you'll be properly rewarded. The funding covers fairly decent remuneration, which, in light of your experience, is a good thing.'

In light of my experience … The sum was almost three times what the coffee shop was offering, with tips. 'And if we finish before our deadline, there'll be a bonus in it for you.'

'That sounds very—'

Again, he cut her off before she could tell him that she was a fraud, a fraud with no experience whatsoever.

'I wish I had more time to talk this through, but I'm running late already. Give me your phone number in case I need to contact you and I'll give you mine.' He scribbled his down on a piece of paper, stood up and put out his hand.

'Welcome to the team, Tansy.' She was out the door before she really knew what was happening.

One of the guys was still waiting outside. Phyllis was like an excited puppy. 'Well? Did you get it?' she whispered.

A voice came from behind her. 'She did, and I'm afraid, young man, I won't be needing your services,' Professor Pollard said to the other candidate, 'but thank you for coming along. I'll take your details in case this one doesn't work out.' He turned and went back inside.

'Jaysus, those walls must be paper thin or else he has ears like a bat,' Phyllis said. 'Oh, by the way, that was Noel. He's doing philosophy and he's going to join us for a drink.'

That was no surprise at all. Phyllis was like a magnet attracting specimens of humanity in all guises, large and small, glittering and dull. She'd make a good anthropological case study herself, Tansy thought.

'I'm sorry,' Tansy said to Noel when he returned.

'No need to be. The best person got it and, to be honest, I haven't a clue what the project involves.'

'Neither have I. Phyllis, I need to talk to you, privately,' Tansy said.

'Sure, but let's go and meet the others first.'

They found their friends frantically trying to hold on to a table in the student bar. Noel was introduced. It was a good hour before Tansy managed to get Phyllis on her own, in the toilets.

'What were you thinking, doing that, lying through your teeth? Not only have you landed me in it, Phyllis, but you cheated that poor Noel guy out of a job. He might need it more than me.'

Phyllis laughed. 'Don't be like that, Tans. All's fair in love, etc. What's the pay like?'

'Very good, but I'm not taking it. I can't bluff my way into something I know nothing about.'

'Well, you must have managed it at the interview.'

'I didn't get a chance – he overheard you spoofing and assumed what you said was true. He never asked me one question about my experience. He just took it as a given.'

'Oh.' She considered. 'That could be a little awkward all right.'

'I'm going to ring him and tell him the truth.'

'You can't do that. Look at the alternative. I mean, apart from being close to Ross, do you really want to go back home to the country for the summer and leave all this behind?' She waved her arms dramatically around the dingy washroom, with its pockmarked mirrors, purple doors and orange walls. 'Well, maybe not this exactly, but you get the picture. Besides, those profs are all buddies and you'd be labelled "unreliable".'

'And a liar. Thanks to you.'

'But if you didn't spoof him, he can't tell them you did. You didn't lie. It was he who jumped to conclusions, not you. So that makes it his problem, doesn't it? Brazen it out if he makes any accusations. Getting the job in the first place has to mean he thinks you have potential. Give it a try and see what happens. What have you got to lose? If you're out of your depth, you can pretend your granny in Timbuktu needs you.'

Tansy replied, 'I'm not happy about it.'

'It's not like you to be negative.'

'Negative? I'm not being negative! As for you … Well, it's just like you to be bossy, but I suppose I do need a job.'

'Then stop stressing and playing it safe. Give it a shot.'

'I just hope it doesn't all end badly.'

'What's going on in here?' asked Mags, coming into the toilets at the end of this conversation. 'What might end badly?'

'This one's summer job, which I got her, and that's going to pay her a shedload of money and set her up for next year. Just sayin'. She should be thanking me and buying me a drink. Instead she's having second thoughts. I give up. I should have gone for the interview myself.' Phyllis flounced off and Mags looked at Tansy.

'Not now. It's a long story. I'll fill you in later.'

'We have to head back to the flat and help Gina pack.'

'She won't need any help. She's the most organised person I know.'

'I just want to make sure she isn't taking my best clothes to Spain with her.'

'I doubt she'll want any of mine, Mags. You know what a label whore she is,' Tansy said. 'And I've just had a thought. Maybe now I'll be able to buy something that hasn't been previously loved and comes from a charity shop. And maybe, just maybe, I'll be the one heading abroad next year.'

Chapter Two

By the time she left on Friday to go home to visit her parents in Dunmoy, Tansy was still suffering pangs of indecision. Her mother was waiting to collect her from the bus. As they drove, she said, 'The town is really suffering since the new shopping centre opened on the bypass. And now the cinema's closed down. It's such a shame. Your father and I used to enjoy going there.'

'So did I.'

Tansy found herself looking at what had once been the epicentre of her universe. It seemed to shrink with each visit. It only took a couple of minutes to drive through it and, despite knowing every bit of it, that still surprised her. Each time she returned it felt smaller and more contained and looked so – she searched for a word to describe it – so flat. That was it. It seemed flat.

The church was the highest building in the place. After that came the parochial house, which was close by, an austere, dull, old, pebbledash three-storey, a window on either side of the hall door, with symmetrical ones on the floors above. The bank ranked next, with its stone facade and grandiose corner entrance on one side of the market square. Mary McLaughlin's general draper's and outfitters on the opposite side added a little bit of balance before a row of mismatched shopfronts led them back into the country.

She knew what was happening as they drove past Dunfy's field, with its donkey standing like a dishevelled sentry guarding a few outhouses that had seen better days. It was what her mother feared most when she went off to college. She was outgrowing Dunmoy and she didn't know where that would lead. What would happen if after college she didn't want to come back from the city to spend her life here? Ross would never leave. He was firmly rooted, and she had told him she'd never leave him either, but that didn't stop her wondering.

'Ross, you'd love Dublin once you'd got used to it. I know I do. I love the old tall houses in Rathmines, where we live,' she had told him enthusiastically shortly after starting college. 'Each one is a warren of high-ceilinged bedsits, and grand elegant stairways. They must have been beautiful when they were the homes of wealthy families.'

'I think I'd feel smothered.'

'I don't think you would. Ours is right in the centre of student flatland. It's very cosmopolitan.'

'And noisy and crowded. No, thanks. Give me the wide-open spaces anytime,' he had replied.

As though reading her mind, her mother remarked, 'I suppose you've got used to the city by now.'

'I have and I'm really happy there. It's so alive. There's a great busyness to the place. I love the ethnic shops – they sell things I've never heard of and can't pronounce. And there are lots of charity shops, where we go rummaging for bargains.'

'It certainly seems ideal,' Peggy said.

'It is. We're close enough that we can walk into town and save on bus fares if we want to. There's even a twenty-four-hour mini-market at the end of our road.'

'I don't think Dunmoy's ready for that yet.' She laughed, amused at her daughter's enthusiasm. 'It's great to have you home, though. It's not the same without you around.'

'Well, I'm here now, until Sunday.'

'I've made an apple tart. We'll have a cup of tea and you can tell me all your news. I miss our chats. You know your father's not one for small talk or gossip, and I want to hear everything before you go swanning off with that boyfriend of yours,' she said, turning into the driveway.

Her mother seemed incapable of calling Ross Doyle anything other than 'that boyfriend of yours', and for Tansy those four words adequately summed the whole gamut of emotions Peggy felt towards him.

They encompassed her opinions that he wasn't good enough for her only daughter, and that was not because they had expected more for her. True, Peggy would have preferred Tansy to have hooked up with Jim Murty, the doctor's son, or Maurice Daly, the solicitor's second lad. Both Jesuit boarding school educated and destined to take over family practices locally. It wasn't the social status they enjoyed that drove Peggy's attitude to Ross. There was bad blood over a land title between her family and Ross's, going back to her great-grandfather's time. In small communities, it took aeons for such memories to fade.

Tansy had long given up defending her choice. She had fallen for Ross when they met at a local disco. He was her knight in shining armour. Her first love, all-absorbing and passionate.

Whenever she thought about him, she smiled. Leaving him to go to Dublin was the hardest decision she'd had to make until then.

In a kind of way, they'd known each other all their lives. He went to the boys' school in the next town. His family kept horses and lived on a fair-sized farm, just two miles away from Tansy's parents. As a result of marriages, Ross's family also owned several businesses and ran the main grocery store in town and the undertakers too.

'You really do love those horses,' she said to him at a local meet where, despite his youth, he impressed her with the way he seemed to be able to converse knowledgeably on equine matters with the trainers and jockeys. Someday I'll be confident like that, she thought.

He had been a tall, gangly kid, whose straw-coloured hair made him easy to spot anywhere. That had now darkened as he had filled out, and his popularity had increased with his sporting prowess.

'College isn't an option for me. I hate book-learning and study,' he told her. 'Anyway, I probably wouldn't get the points because I am decidedly average academically.'

'It's not the be-all and end-all of everything,' she said, holding his hand. She told him, and Peggy, that his tenderness and affinity with humans and animals were attributes that she deemed to be more valuable than brains.

Grudgingly her mother agreed with this logic, countering it with 'Yes, although they won't pay a mortgage or put food on the table. I suppose there'll always be the family businesses to fall back on, although I never saw you standing behind a counter serving your betters.'

Tansy laughed. 'And you won't either. Ross wants an outdoor life, one that doesn't deal with death or slicing rashers.'

'We'll see. I told your father to be back for tea. You know what he's like – if there's nothing needing to be done, he'll find something.'

There was no point telling her mother to stop fussing. That was Peggy Nugent's nature.

Even though it was warm outside, Tansy's favourite spot was, and always had been, the kitchen. Nothing much ever seemed to change in here, although the big wooden table was now covered with a spotted oilcloth, instead of the one they'd had when she left. It had been patterned with bunches of cherries with a blue stripe around the edges. The bills and letters still had a place of their own on the second shelf of the dresser, along with her grandmother's never-used collection of blue and white crockery jugs. When she said she thought they were very old-fashioned, her mother had chided her. 'They came from your father's home and they mean something to him. Someday you'll understand.' Tansy didn't believe she ever would.

'When I have my own house, I'll have plain white everything and purple napkins,' she once told her other nan, 'and everything will match.'

'Oh, you innocent wee dote.' She laughed. 'That's what we all want. Everything matching and in its proper place, but life isn't like that. You'll learn soon enough that sometimes even the cracked cup has a place in someone's heart.' She had looked at her intently through her thick lenses and said, 'You haven't a clue what I'm talking about, Tansy, have you?' And she hadn't.

Now sometimes she recalled conversations like those that she had enjoyed with her nan before dementia robbed her of her cognitive abilities. Since Tansy moved to Dublin, she was beginning to understand the desire to hold on to bits of childhood, to keep things with sentimental attachment, things that had always been there, with all their imperfections. She would love to have been able to tell her nan that she was now grown up enough to admit to herself that the big range and the smell of brown bread or scones baking in the oven, and the chats with her and her mother in this room were an intrinsic part of what made her who she was. And that someday she intended to visit the places she'd promised her she would. Some ditty they used to recite together had a line 'Morocco, Mauritius and Malta' in it. She couldn't remember anything else about it, apart from her nan showing her where they were on the globe she'd bought her and telling her, 'I've never seen any of those places so you must go for me instead.' Tansy vowed then that she would, some day.

'Everything that happens of significance, and of none, has been discussed around this table,' her dad said when he returned to find his women sitting there. 'And it's heard its fair share of balderdash over the years too.'

Tansy laughed and hugged him before enquiring about Gappy Jim.

'The poor old fellow's not too good. He's getting on and he's as deaf as a stone now. He spends most of his time watching racing on the telly.'

'I couldn't image him not being around the place. He's such a part of it,' Tansy said.

'Aye, that he is. He's moved in with Little Jim now. He wasn't looking after himself properly.'

Although Gappy Jim was one of the farm workers, he came

inside every day for tea breaks and lunch. He earned his moniker because he was missing a few teeth, and he walked with a limp after an altercation with a horse at the local racetrack when he was young. There was nothing little about his son, Little Jim. In his forties and at six feet four, he now towered over everyone in the church at Mass each week.

'The old boy is a frustrated jockey,' her father had told her. 'He knows everything there is to know about horses. If he'd had money, and maybe a little more education, he'd have made a great trainer.'

'Enough of that. We can talk about them anytime,' Peggy told her husband. 'We want to know all about your exciting life in Dublin, Tansy. Did you get another job, or will you be coming back to us for the summer?'

'No, Mam, I won't because I've got something else. I'll be doing a bit of work for someone in the university. I only found out about it on Wednesday, and I wasn't too sure if I'd be up to it at first,' she replied, admitting to herself for the first time that she was willing to give the job a try. 'The pay is much better than the coffee shop too, so I'll be able to save, if it works out.'

'What will you be doing?'

'Working on some anthropological research papers for one of the professors.'

'That sounds very fancy.'

'It'll probably be boring as hell, but I'll give it a go.'

Tansy could see her mother's delight at this piece of news. Peggy would just have to let people know how well her daughter was getting on in the capital.

'Please don't go telling everyone about it, Mam.'

'Now don't go getting above yourself, Tansy. I know you're

getting the chance to go to university, which is more than your father or I got, but never forget who you are. Having letters after your name won't make you better than us,' she cautioned, 'although there are some who think they do. Like those Ferguson girls. So rude to poor Mary in the shop.'

Tansy stopped herself saying they were probably trying to halt Mary's inquisition. Mary had no filters when it came to personal questions.

'It's not that. It's just that I can visualise Mary McLaughlin telling everyone – "I hear the Nugent girl is working for a professor, no less, up in Dublin. What do you make of that?" You know what she's like.'

Her mother laughed. 'Indeed I do.' No other shop in the town had its window displays changed as often as McLaughlin's. Because of its location on a corner, her drapery shop provided a lookout in two directions. That gave Mary a bona fide reason to keep an eye on everyone's comings and goings, and somehow she felt she had a duty to share these with many a willing, and the odd unwilling, ear.

'She's harmless, really.'

'That's not what Dad thinks, is it?'

'Who are you telling?' he replied, casting his eyes skywards and they both laughed. By now everyone knew the story. A few years previously, Gappy Jim and her father had business in the bank down the street from Mary's shop. Pat Nugent, who never put a bet on anything in his life, was seen ducking into the betting office, dragging Gappy Jim after him to avoid an inquisition by Mary. She had been casually observing their movements and had come outside ostensibly to inspect her window, but in reality to intercept and interrogate him.

He'd muttered something about trying to avoid 'that old gossipmonger' to Gappy Jim. He, a regular in the bookmaker's, misheard and said, 'Put a tenner each way on Gossip Column for Pat here and one on Annaghmakerrig Dawn for me.' Pat's horse was a rank outsider and romped home first after a pile-up eliminated the favourites shortly after the off.

By the time Pat returned home, Mary McLaughlin had already phoned his wife to congratulate her on their fine win.

'Knowing your father's aversion to gambling, I didn't know what to think when she told me she'd seen him leave the bank and go straight to the bookies with Gappy Jim!' her mother reminded Tansy, and they laughed at the memory.

'You never forgave her for that, did you, Pat?' Peggy continued, without stopping to take a breath. 'He'd have liked to surprise me with the unexpected windfall; instead he had everyone coming up to him for weeks afterwards, asking how much he'd won. You'd swear our numbers had come up on the Euromillions and, Lord knows, he doesn't even approve of me having a flutter on that.'

'And you wonder why I don't want you talking about me,' Tansy said.

'Indulge me. It's natural to want to tell everyone about my only child when they're all talking about theirs.'

She gave in. 'I'm going to get ready for Ross.'

◆

'Hi, gorgeous. You look cool,' Ross said, grabbing her in a bear hug, 'and you smell delicious too. Hi, Peggy, Pat,' he said, grinning at them when he'd released their daughter.

'Where are you off to?' Peggy asked.

'We're meeting some of the guys from the club, then we'll head to the gig in Ryan's.'

He drove out of the yard, away from watchful eyes, and pulled over. 'I've been looking forward to this,' he said, taking her in his arms and kissing her passionately. She responded eagerly. She loved his touch, his smell and his taste. The sound of an approaching vehicle saw them pull apart.

'God, I've missed you, Tans,' he said, kissing her when the car had passed.

'Me too. I've been looking forward to this all week.'

'I have too, but we'd better head. The others will be waiting.'

Even though it frustrated her that they got so little time alone, she liked that he was so popular that everyone wanted to be around him.

'Well, what do you think about the job. Am I mad starting it?' She'd told him about it on the phone.

'No, you're right, so long as it doesn't stop you coming down to see me,' he said, leaning to kiss her.

'Keep your eyes on the road! You might even see more of me as I'll be able to afford to do it more often, although I want to save as much as I can.'

'And become a woman of means with prospects.'

'Are you after me for my money?'

'Not yet, but it's beginning to sound promising.' He laughed as he turned into the car park. He was spotted immediately by some of his GAA mates and she knew she'd have to share him for the rest of the evening.

They left before the end of the gig, and when they had stopped for a goodnight kiss and cuddle, she asked, 'When are you coming to Dublin to meet my friends? They think you're a figment of my imagination.'

'I'm actually going up tomorrow, with the horses. There's a meet in Leopardstown.' He sighed. 'You know I hate the city. I'm a country boy at heart.'

'And I'll be here.'

'Typical. The gods are conspiring to keep us apart. If it's not too late when I get back, I'll call you. Now I'd better get you home,' he said, releasing her. 'I've an early start.'

They next day Tansy visited Gappy Jim before going to the new shopping centre a few miles away. She missed not seeing Ross and wished he had less demanding and more normal hours.

On Sunday the smell of roast pork and vegetables filled the kitchen when she'd come back from walking through the fields with her dad. They sat and chatted over lunch.

Tansy always hated leaving her parents. If she'd had siblings, it might have been easier, but she felt the burden of being a one and only child at times like this. Her parents were mad about each other, but she knew her mother craved female company and chatter, while her father relished peace and quiet. She had only managed to snatch an hour with Ross at the stables earlier in the day and he had told her he would be working over the next two weekends, so she had promised to come down the following one.

'Try to come up and see me in the meanwhile,' she said.

'Babes, you know I want to, but you know what it's like here. I miss you so much when you're away, but I'll see what I can do.'

'It's gone by far too quickly,' her father said. 'You could take the later bus.'

'No. That's always packed, and I have some things to do.'

'You'll need to be ready for the new job. Don't forget to take those bits I baked for you.' Her mother fussed.

'Thanks, Mam. Phyllis will be thrilled when I turn up with cake. Mags isn't eating carbs this month and with Gina away, there'll be more for her!'

'That one is like a knitting needle as it is. It's fattening up she needs, not all that no-carb nonsense. Take that and buy yourself a new top or something suitable for work.' She pressed some twenty-euro notes into her daughter's hand.

'Mam, I don't need that, and you can't afford to be giving it away either.'

'Stop that now. You'll have to look smart. Mixing with those university types. I don't have much chance to spoil you any more. I miss that and you.'

'I can't believe I'm hearing this after years of complaining about the music blaring at all hours! It's not so long since you thought I'd never grow up and leave. Now you're telling me you miss it.' They laughed.

Her dad started the engine and she hopped in. He didn't say much in the car. He never did and, unlike the times she spent with her mother, neither felt the need to talk. He wished her luck as he took her bag from the boot and hugged her. She waved goodbye again from the bus window.

Just wait until I'm settled in the job. All the way home this ran through her mind. Who was she fooling? Certainly not herself. She had no choice now but to turn up in the morning and see what happened, although she was under no illusions about that.

She would have liked to have gone away to Spain with Gina to au pair for the summer, but she didn't want to leave Ross for that long.

'You're mad, girl,' Phyllis had told her. 'Don't put your life on hold for any man. What's he going to do when you go off for your Erasmus year?' She hadn't answered.

'You never told him you were considering that, did you?'

'It wasn't the right time.'

'I give up,' her friend said in exasperation. 'Mark my words. It never will be, Tansy. It never will be.'

'Maybe not, but look at it from my perspective. He's totally involved with the GAA, with training as a player and a coach, never mind his horses. When Ross's dad realised that he was serious about turning his back on the family businesses, he ensured wheels turned within wheels to have him taken in at the local stud farm. Now that he's there, he's trying to make a name for himself and get noticed. He's working flat out to be successful. I can't begrudge him that, don't you see?'

'What I see is that if he's so busy, he wouldn't even notice you were gone.'

'That's not fair. He sees things in black and white and just doesn't understand why I'd want to go further afield to study when I can do that here,' she added, almost as an afterthought. 'He has to follow his path and I'm following mine. I'm quite happy with that.'

'Well, you shouldn't be,' Phyllis said. 'You're sacrificing your ambitions for his. Do you love him enough for that? Does he love you enough to let you do what you want?'

'Of course we do, and he never tried to stop me doing anything,' Tansy said.

'Could that be because you don't tell him what you really want? You can't live your life like that. You have to reach your own potential and that means you can't hold back for anyone. If you do, you may spend your life regretting it. Just sayin'. Now, did you mention something about cake?'

Tansy didn't reply, but Phyllis had hit a nerve.

They joined Mags, who was resisting the carb temptation by staying in her room, sorting out a suitable 'work wardrobe' for Tansy.

'You can have these. I'm paring down,' she said, tossing an armful of almost new items on the bed.

'You mean you want to make space so you can buy some more,' Phyllis said.

'I know,' she said, laughing, 'but I can't resist a bargain. None of them cost very much anyway.'

'That's a matter of perspective. When your old man is minted, like yours, nothing is expensive. For me, going to Penneys is a spree.'

'Don't exaggerate, Phyllis,' Mags said. 'Let's get you organised, Tansy. I saw this woman on the telly one morning showing how to build a capsule wardrobe.'

'What in God's name is a capsule wardrobe?'

'Basics in neutrals, like jeans and black trousers, a few shirts, a cardi or jumper or two and a jacket or blazer like this one,' – she took one off a hanger and laid it down – 'and then you add extras to mix and match, like so.'

'There's a label on that,' Phyllis said, holding up a polka dot top, 'and on this. Half of these have never been worn. Mags, you're such a spendthrift.'

She laughed at her friends. 'They're not all mine. Gina left a load of her stuff behind and you know she never minds us wearing them.'

As the piles grew in co-coordinating colours, Tansy said, 'This is such a waste of time. I'll probably be back home tomorrow before either of you is even up.'

'Then you'll be the best-dressed anthropological disaster in history!' said Mags.

Chapter Three

Professor Sean Pollard was at his desk when Tansy arrived, ten minutes early. Tucked away in a part of the campus that she didn't usually have any reason to visit, she wanted to make sure she knew exactly where she was supposed to be. She never remembered being so nervous.

'There's no need to knock,' he announced as the door swung open. 'Come on in and take a seat. I just have to reply to a mail, then I'll be with you.'

As he tapped the keyboard, she looked around. The room was enormous, and it had a masculine smell of old books and wood, the sort of space she'd expect to find in a gentleman's club or a barrister's office.

His desk was enormous too, filled with neatly stacked piles of paper. The walls were lined with bookshelves right up to the high ceiling and there was a set of library steps on either side. As she took in the air of gravitas, she wondered who used the other two desks. She was sure he'd said she'd be working next door to him. She hoped he hadn't changed his mind and that she'd be sitting here, under his watchful eye. One of the desks was messy and there was a knitted scarlet cardigan draped over the back of the chair. At the other one, the seat was tucked perfectly under the tidy desktop.

In the quiet, the professor's sigh almost startled her. He closed his laptop and said, 'Sorry about that. The blasted internet means there's no such thing as being away from your desk, no matter what hour it is. There's always something that someone thinks is so important that it can't wait.'

She nodded.

'I know this place looks disorganised, but it's not. Trust me, it's ordered chaos. Each pile is there for a reason, so whatever you do, don't move or remove anything in this zone,' he said, waving his arms about. 'Your space is next door. I'll come in and explain what you'll be working on as soon as the other two arrive.'

She didn't know who 'the other two' were, or if she would be working with them, but she hoped they'd get there sooner rather than later, before he had a chance to quiz her about her non-existent experience. She didn't have to wait long. Trevor turned out to be a quiet final-year philosophy student. Linda was quite the opposite. The professor summed her up by saying, 'Linda here is working towards a degree in behavioural studies.' Tansy figured she had picked the right career path if her attire was to be taken as a reflection of her personality. She was wearing a floaty mustard top, patterned palazzo pants, orange Doc Martens and a lilac gypsy scarf.

'We're all part of a team, but we're involved in different projects. That's another reason for not moving things about and for keeping everything catalogued and cross-referenced as you go along. These two share this space with me. Now let's get you set up next door.'

With an economy of words that she'd come to recognise as his style of delivery, he synopsised the project. So far so good. It didn't show any major obstacles that would trip her up in the first hour. Her task was to transcribe essays and field study results for a manuscript due for publication the following year. She had to check sources, cross-reference them and ensure they were correctly credited.

'Is that all clear?'

'Yes. I think so.'

'As I told you, I don't wish to be disturbed every five minutes. If you've any queries, write them down and you can interrogate me when we have our allocated discussion time.'

With a nod that made his hair flop over his face, he was gone, and she exhaled. She hadn't been aware she was holding her breath.

◆

'I wasn't expecting him to be so amenable, friendly almost,' Tansy told the girls later. 'He'd been so brusque the other day, I was ready for more of the same.'

Phyllis wanted to know if he had quizzed her on her experience in Peru.

'Not yet,' she answered, and she explained how he had left her to find herself. 'I think he just assumes I know what it's all about, but he did say if I had any problems I was to ask. He's allocated me fifteen minutes each morning for queries and the same in the afternoon. Other than that, I'm not to disturb him, and I quote "unless it's life-threatening" or he's "in danger of being sued for plagiarising someone's work".'

'He sounds like a pompous git, granting audiences,' Phyllis said.

'Or a bit on the compulsive side,' Mags argued.

'Possibly. He's just terrifying. He gives off that air of knowing everything. He's so efficient and organised, but at least he's not checking up on me every minute, although any time my door opens, I'm expecting it's him to tell me he's cottoned on to the fact that I shouldn't be there.'

'Maybe he'll never find out.'

'I doubt that. I'm surprised he hasn't done a background check already. Anyway, I intend to keep my head down for as long as I can.'

'Did you get a lunch break?'

'Three-quarters of an hour and a voucher for subsidised meals in the canteen.'

'You jammy wagon! You'll be minted by the end of the summer,' said Phyllis, who was always skint.

'That's not the best bit. I don't have to buy coffee either. He has a fancy machine in his office. Needless to say, I wasn't going to keep traipsing in and out, but by eleven I was suffering withdrawal symptoms. Then he appeared at my door with a cup for me. He did tell me not to expect him to do that again, though, that I'd have to help myself in future and bring him the occasional one when he was bogged down.'

'I bet he did,' said Phyllis. 'Chauvinist.'

'What's chauvinistic about that? That's what we do all day in the restaurant,' Mags said.

'But we get paid for doing that,' argued Phyllis.

'Maybe that's included in what she's being paid to do.'

'"She" is here. Hello? I'm being paid for doing a job and if that includes carrying a cup of coffee across a room occasionally, I have no problem with it,' Tansy said. 'I thought it was a nice gesture – it made me feel less in awe of him.'

'So long as he doesn't start offering you tips ...' Phyllis replied. At the looks she got from the other two, she retreated. 'Just sayin'. That could be construed as personal services.'

'Jesus, Phyllis, are you mad?' Mags said. 'Getting him a coffee is not the same as stretching out on a casting couch.'

'Get a grip,' Tansy told her friend. 'There'll be no casting couch or anything like it. He has two others working on another project with him and they couldn't have been nicer.'

'Are they both women?' Phyllis asked.

'Would it make a difference if they were?' Mags enquired.

'No, I was just curious. I know he's old, but you can't deny the Prof is very dishy. If he's surrounding himself with young women, he could be going through a mid-life crisis.'

'I don't think I'd call him old,' said Tansy.

'And if they were young men – would you have an anthropological category for that?' Mags enquired.

'You both have very creative imaginations,' said Tansy. 'There's one of each. Now I'm going to get out of this module of my capsule clothing collection, or whatever you called it, and go for a run. I need to work off some of this stress. Do you want to come?'

They decided to join her. None of them worked on Monday nights. They set off along Rathmines Road and turned right to run along the canal. They weren't the only ones with that idea. The fine weather had forced everyone out of doors. Just as they jogged on the spot waiting for the lights to change at the bridge, other runners caught up on them.

'Don't overdo it – I don't want you to be late in the morning, Tansy' was what they heard as a trim and toned figure passed them by and sprinted ahead of them.

'If it were politically correct to wolf whistle, I'd be tempted. Who was that?' asked Mags.

'My professor.'

Chapter Four

At first, she felt very self-conscious going next door to help herself to coffee so she started taking a mug with her after her allocated slot for her audience with the Prof. Trevor and Linda had no such inhibitions. They started taking theirs to drink in Tansy's office.

'I just told him we needed a change of scenery to keep us stimulated,' Linda said. 'I think he's probably glad to get rid of us for a bit. He can't even make a personal phone call with us in there.'

'She actually said that to him. No, I'll correct that,' said Trevor, whose humour, Tansy was beginning to realise, was very sharp. 'She actually told him "we're moving out to give you a chance to call one of your lovers".'

'How did he react to that?' Tansy asked.

'With resignation. He just laughed and said it was very thoughtful of her.'

'But he gave nothing away,' Linda added. 'He never does. He must have women falling at his feet. He's very attractive, especially when he smiles.'

Tansy agreed. He *was* very attractive, even when not smiling.

'He doesn't have the same effect on me, yet I have to listen to that every day,' Trevor said, 'and about how great he was with them all when he took them on a field trip together last year.'

'Pay no attention to him.' Linda laughed. 'Sean never notices me. Not in that way anyway.'

Tansy didn't want to ask, but she was curious about his personal life. Was he married, divorced, desperately seeking?

'It doesn't stop you flirting with him, does it?'

'He loves it. All men love being flattered, don't they, Tansy?'

'I suppose they do, although I don't think that applies exclusively to men,' she replied.

'I'll have to try harder, so,' Linda said.

'As if a man of his standing would risk his career carrying on with a student,' Trevor said.

'I don't know. It kind of adds to the mystique. Is there a law against it, I mean an official ruling about teacher/student liaisons?'

'Use your loaf, Linda. It wouldn't be ethical. How could someone who is involved in that way be deemed to be impartial when it comes to correcting papers and exam results?' said Trevor with a sigh. 'There are around sixteen thousand students at the university, and probably the majority of them are male. Why don't you focus your efforts on one of them instead?'

'Because I find guys of my age too juvenile and ... limited,' she said, as though dismissing him. She turned to Tansy. 'How's the work going anyway?'

'Now that I know what I'm supposed to be doing, it's making more sense,' Tansy replied. She hadn't told them how she had ended up as their colleague. Perhaps she would when she knew them better, assuming, of course, that she hadn't been caught out first.

'It does, but sometimes I wish Sean wasn't such a bloody perfectionist. He's doing my head in,' Linda whispered, for fear he'd hear her. 'He's substantially changed the wording three times already and we're only on a preliminary draft of the first paper.'

Tansy was almost at the end of her second week and could never see herself getting to the point of calling the professor 'Sean'.

'Thankfully, the stuff I'm working on has passed that stage. It's already been proofed a few times when it reaches me.'

'At least Sean sets the same standards for himself as he does for us. You have to respect him for that,' Trevor said. 'And it seems you've made an impact, Tansy. He was singing your praises earlier. You spotted some errors or something.'

'It was no big deal. Anyone would have seen them,' Tansy said.

'Obviously someone didn't.'

'We'd better get back,' Linda said, taking their mugs with her.

'I'd like to be working in here,' Trevor said. 'You can get some peace hiding away.'

If only Trevor knew how close to the mark he was. Tansy felt she was hiding away and was about as invisible as Pliny's proverbial ostriches. She'd come across them while researching the uncle and nephew for an essay she'd been writing on familial authors in history. She couldn't remember now whether it was the Elder or the Younger Pliny who had written about them, but whichever it was, it started the myth that ostriches buried their head in the sand and believed that no one would see their long spindly legs and huge shaggy body sticking up like a beacon.

Good God – she was beginning to think like a nerd after only two weeks! She laughed out loud before she realised the door had opened and the Prof was standing there.

'I'm glad you find my work so amusing. May I know the cause of such merriment?'

'Oh, it's nothing. It just reminded me of something.'

'Something you came across in Peru, perhaps?'

She felt the blood drain from her face. 'No, definitely not, not Peru. I was just trying to remember something about Pliny.'

'The Plinys were Roman – they were a long way away from Peru.'

She could visualise Phyllis telling her again and again that if he broached the subject to brazen it out. She had made no claims and could be accused of nothing.

'They certainly were, although I don't know much about Peru. I've never been there,' she said, relieved to confess at last.

'Really? I was under the impression you had been there working on some anthropological perspectives.'

'Whatever gave you that impression?' she asked, avoiding eye contact by shuffling some pages on her desk.

'Something I overheard the day I interviewed you.'

'Oh. What was it?' she asked innocently.

'I don't remember the details, but it was enough to persuade me to hire you. Have you had any experience in this area at all?'

'Brazen it out! Brazen it out!' she could hear Phyllis's voice in her head. It had been easy for her to say that. She wasn't sitting behind the desk with her inquisitor towering over the other side.

She swallowed.

'I don't recall you asking me anything about my experience

at all. I thought it was because you seemed to be in such a hurry to be somewhere else. Has my work been unsatisfactory?' she asked him, thinking, Phyllis would be so proud if she could see me now.

'Anything but,' he replied. 'I've been quite impressed by your dedication and diligence and the way you take initiative. I've had language students work for me before and they couldn't punctuate a three-word sentence, never mind read through a dissertation and paraphrase it.'

His answer surprised her, not only because he didn't seem fazed by her admission, but by the fact that he knew what she was studying.

'I respect honesty,' he pronounced gravely. This was it. She sat waiting for the axe to fall. He paused and she couldn't bear the suspense any longer. He was about to fire her and a sense of relief washed over her. The pretence would be over.

'And you want me to leave?'

'As I said, I respect honesty. And you didn't try to bluff your way in – it was your friend who spun the tall tales to scare the competition away.'

'You knew?'

'Since about ten minutes after you left. A colleague of mine was waiting to talk to me when the two of you arrived and he filled me in on the charade.'

'Why did you let me start? You had my number. You could have called and told me not to come in.'

'And you had mine. You could have called me and said you wouldn't. Why didn't you?'

'I needed a job, and I like a challenge,' she said defiantly. 'And now you're going to fire me.'

'Whatever gave you that impression?' he replied. 'I actually came in to give you this,' he said, handing over an invitation. It was to a lecture he was giving in Dublin Castle.

'Don't feel you have to go. You could bring a friend along, if you like. You won't be fired if you don't,' he said with a glint in his eye. He turned and walked out before she could reply.

She sat looking after him, smiling. She felt that a weight had been taken off her. She couldn't wait to tell Mags and Phyllis what had just transpired.

◆

'He knew all the time and he strung you along. What kind of twisted git is he?' Phyllis was incensed. She was running around in a bathrobe, looking for her hair straighteners, getting ready for another busy Friday night at the restaurant.

'I actually think he sounds decent,' said Mags, who was dressed and ready to go. 'At least he gave you the benefit of the doubt and a chance to show if you were up to the task. And you're still there, so you must be. He could have decided not to do that.'

'There were two fellows outside when we arrived for the interview, and I do remember one of them walked away when I was called in. I thought he was just annoyed at being passed over. That was obviously his colleague,' Tansy said.

'Or his spy. Do you think he had him there as a plant to hear what everyone was saying about him, or about themselves?'

'Phyllis, your imagination is going to land you in trouble someday,' Mags said. 'He knows everything, she's still there, and he didn't fire her, end of story. So, tell us, Tansy, what's this lecture going to be about?'

'It's part of an international conference on nomadic peoples and the future of their cultures in modern society. I know it sounds heavy, but I think it could be interesting.' She took the invitation from her bag and showed it to them.

'It says there's a reception beforehand,' Phyllis said. 'That means free wine or champers.

Mags raised her eyes skywards before asking, 'What do you wear to such an event?'

'Does it matter, Mags? It's not the Oscars. There'll hardly be a red carpet.'

'Of course it matters. It always matters,' Mags insisted.

'You can count me out. I don't think I want to socialise with him. I'm not sure I'd like this Professor Pollard very much,' said Phyllis.

'There you go again, making snap decisions, Phyllis,' Mags said. 'There'll probably be hundreds there and you won't even meet him. I'd love to come, Tansy, but wouldn't you rather bring Ross with you?'

It hadn't even crossed her mind that he might like to go. When she asked herself this question, and she did so over and over again, the answer was always the same. He wouldn't be the slightest bit interested. Not for the first time was she concerned that what they had was slipping away slowly as they forged their own paths. Their interests were pushing them in opposite directions. Could their relationship survive another few years? She'd have to make an effort to ensure it would.

'I'll ask him, although I'm not sure if he could get away from the stud for an overnighter right now.'

'If he can't, I'd love to come. I'm curious to see your professor and make up my own mind whether to like him or not.'

'That's great, Mags. I'd be glad of the moral support. I can introduce you to Trevor too. And it'll be a chance to hobnob with people who are not scruffy students.'

'Oh, how grown-up you've become in a few weeks. I hope you're not including us in the scruffy student part,' Phyllis said. 'Remember, we live with full access to Mags's and Gina's wardrobes.'

Tansy laughed at them. 'Do you two never stop bickering?'

'We're not bickering. Are we?'

'I don't know what gave her that impression,' Phyllis said.

'If you're not ready in five minutes, I'm going on ahead.'

'If you hadn't hogged the shower, I'd be ready.'

They were off again.

'You'd both better get a move on or you'll be late.'

'C'mon, Mags. Friday night is good tips night.'

'I'm the one waiting for you. I've been ready for ages.'

Tansy just laughed as they went down the hallway.

Peace and quiet at last. She rang Ross. She was used to his telephone manner by now, although it had taken a while. In the early days, she always felt he was looking at a screen or doing some other task that stopped him being fully engaged while he talked. She now accepted that he just wasn't a telephone person. To him, it was simply a tool for quick communication. Like her father, he didn't do small talk. She was about to learn that he didn't do lectures either.

'Babes, if I was going to swing a night in the city, it wouldn't be to sit listening to some old codger spouting on about fossils and the like.'

'He's not an archaeologist and he's not that old.'

'Whatever. He sounds like he should be. Why don't you skip it and come down here instead? I miss you.'

'It's midweek, Ross.'

'Exactly. I love you.'

'I love you too, and I suppose it's a no, to the lecture I mean.'

''Fraid so, Babes, but I'll see you soon and we'll do something special, OK?'

She hoped they would.

◆

She emailed Gina, writing her a long missive to fill her in. A little later she heard a reply come in.

That pair will never change. They are the best of friends and the worst of friends, but they'd walk through fire for each other too and then argue about whose fault it was that the fire started in the first place.

I miss all that, although I absolutely love it here. I never thought au pairing would be so luxurious! The house is fab. It's a restored mill with an orchard, a tennis court and a wood with a stream running through it. The Señora is an interior designer so the place is decorated with all sorts of eclectic stuff, half of it, I suspect, she bought for clients who hated it and it ended up here. I mean, who wants a pair of matching giraffes, which are at least nine feet tall, in their hallway? I can't begin to imagine what their house in Madrid is like if this is their holiday pad.

The girls are great. They're eleven and twelve. Their English is really good and I'm not allowed speak any Spanish to them at all. They've been teaching me some, though, and I suspect it's not necessarily what would be accepted in polite company.

The cook (yes, they have a cook!) has totally converted

me to proper tapas, and I'm even getting used to dining at the ridiculous hour of half-ten at night. The kids are still up then too.

I'm being called – have to dash.

Love and hugs to you all, regards to the elusive Ross, and go easy on your professor!

Gina

xoxoxoxo

Tansy smiled. 'Elusive Ross and my professor indeed,' she said out loud, closing her laptop. The phone rang a little later. It was her mother.

Tansy told her, 'Yes, Mam. I've survived. I can't believe it's two weeks already.

'I'm delighted to hear that. Sure I knew you would.'

'Not half as much as me,' she said. 'It's a great feeling. Any news from that part of the world?'

'Nothing much at all except that Gappy Jim took a turn and is in hospital. It's not looking too good.'

'Aw, Mam, I'm so sorry to hear that. I hope he's not in pain. Please give him a hug for me and send him my fondest love.'

'I would, but I don't think he'd be aware of that, although he was thrilled to see you when you were down.'

'Let me know if anything happens.'

'Of course I will, but I think it's a matter of when rather than if, at this stage.'

'Dad will really miss him. So will I. He's always been such a part of my life and he's the nearest thing to a grandfather that I've ever had.'

◆

The following week Tansy went to work in a different frame of mind than on the previous two Mondays. She had nothing to hide from Professor Pollard and she smiled when she thought about the way he let her know he knew. She was beginning to feel comfortable in her surroundings and more at ease going in and out of his room. Half the time he was so engrossed in his work that he'd just incline his head in acknowledgement and say nothing.

There was usually a query or two that needed attention during her 'audiences' with him. As the days went on, she found she felt less intimidated in these one-to-one sessions; they didn't seem quite so formal any more. He'd even asked her opinion on a quote he was considering using in his lecture.

'Oscar Wilde or G.B. Shaw?'

'If your topic is serious, I'd stick to Shaw. If the content is dull and boring, then Oscar's your man,' she replied. 'He can always lift the mood.'

'Now why didn't I think of that?' he replied, raising one eyebrow. 'Thank you for that considered reply, but for the record, my content is never, and I quote, "dull and boring".'

'I can only offer my considered opinion on that after I hear your lecture.' She smiled and was about to go back to her room when he said, 'You'll be glad to hear that you'll be rid of me on Friday. I have to go to Galway for an award ceremony.'

'Great, Sean. Let's hope you're giving one this time, because you're running out of wall space for the accolades,' Linda said, waving her arms about. Perched behind a tower of volumes and manuscripts, Tansy thought her black and red ensemble with matching spotted bandana made her look like a giant ladybird.

'Sorry to break it to you, but I'll be on the receiving end again this time.' He grinned.

'Congratulations. Are you going to tell us for what, or is that information embargoed?' Trevor asked from behind his tidy desk.

'Not at all. It's for my paper on the influences of the corresponding yet separate calendars used by pre-Columbian cultures and adopted by Mayan civilisation.'

Trevor replied, 'My father has all sorts of theories on why the Mayans didn't project a future for the world beyond the twenty-first of December 2012. He called it their millennium bug. Do you have any views on that?'

'Several,' Sean replied.

Tansy sat there feeling hopelessly inadequate as words like 'Tzolkin', 'Haab', 'Ahau' and 'Cumku' peppered this exchange. She would have to look up the Mayan calendar later. She knew she shouldn't be surprised at such knowledge. It was his area. He was Dean of the Faculty, and he hadn't got that far by passing his time playing snooker. It was Trevor who impressed her with the confident way he conversed with the Prof and by the fact that such topics were obviously up for discussion in his home. She felt a little guilty making such comparisons, but she could never imagine such a conversation taking place across their kitchen table in Dunmoy. She wasn't even sure if her mother and father would know any more about the Mayans than she did. And Ross. Would he be any better? She knew he wouldn't. But then she knew precious little about horses and wasn't that keen to learn any more. She dismissed these thoughts. It wasn't fair to make such comparisons. Wasn't that what education was supposed to do? Open your mind to new ideas and worlds?

And wasn't that exactly what her parents were giving her the opportunity to do?

'Tansy.' Sean's voice interrupted her train of thought. 'You wanted to ask me something.'

'Yes. There seems to be an anomaly in this section,' she said, spreading some pages on his desk. 'I've found two accreditations for the same source material, and both had been cited as the work of two different authors and in different volumes. I've checked and rechecked, but I haven't managed to solve the puzzle.'

After listening to her concerns, Sean scribbled a few notes before saying, 'Well spotted, Tansy. I shouldn't be at all surprised if the second piece has been plagiarised by that so-called Spanish expert. I've never quite trusted his work. I've had occasion to question elements of it before, but he always manages to present it in such a way that there's a degree of doubt as to whether he really copied the whole lot or it is a happy coincidence. Leave this with me and I'll follow it up on Wednesday. I can't get around to it before that.'

'Of course. You have your lecture. I am going to go, and I'm bringing a friend,' she told him.

'That's good. You might find it interesting as there's a bit of a crossover with what you're working on right now. If not, and you're bored, you can always slip out a side door,' he quipped.

'You never know,' she replied, smiling. 'We might!'

She grinned as she went back to her room.

Had she almost flirted with the Prof?

Chapter Five

'I've never been inside before,' Tansy told Mags as they walked up the steps of Dublin Castle, the city traffic still buzzing behind them.

Tansy led the way to the reception desk where she was asked for her name. She saw Trevor's right below hers and wondered if Linda might have changed her mind and decided to come along too. It would be nice if they all met each other, she thought. Then they'd know who was who when they were mentioned in conversation.

'We came here in transition year, but I hardly remember it. There was a boys' school on a day trip at the same time and I fancied one of the guys, so history wasn't really high on the agenda.'

Tansy laughed. 'Why are you whispering?'

'I don't know,' Mags whispered back. 'Why are you?'

'It just feels right somehow. Hallowed halls and all that.'

'You're nuts, Tansy. Let's have some wine and see if we know anyone.'

'Isn't it beautiful? I'm definitely coming back to do the tour. I want to see it all.'

'I'd love to do it again too. Now where's this professor of yours? Can you see him?'

She couldn't, but she recognised a few faces, lecturers from college. They stood in the circular room under the ornate, domed ceiling. Dwarfed by pillars, they surveyed the scene. It was peopled mostly by suited men and women, many from abroad. One woman in a brightly patterned, long skirt with a matching top and an amazing headdress stood out like a beautiful butterfly against a mainly monochrome crowd. Tansy found her gaze drawn back to her again and again. The woman looked across, smiled and came over to talk to them.

'I didn't mean to be rude, staring at you, but you and your clothes are so beautiful,' Tansy told her.

'It's my traditional dress, for special occasions. I'm glad you like it,' she said, introducing herself as 'a professor of anthropology in Durban, originally from Nigeria'.

'The headdress is amazing and looks so intricate,' Mags said.

'Most of us learn to arrange these from our mothers or aunts,' she said, laughing. 'They're called *geles*. May I ask what is your involvement in the conference?'

Tansy told her and she smiled. 'Ah, I know Sean well. We had dinner together last night. I met him in Owerri a few years back. He's a very talented man.'

'I'm afraid we're monopolising you,' Tansy said, spotting Trevor.

'To be honest, some of these people are very boring and, believe me, there's nothing as boring as a boring academic. Ah, here's another old friend, Professor Emeritus Ernest. He's not one of the aforementioned.' She laughed again.

'Lewa, you're looking resplendent, as always. This is my son, Trevor.'

'And this is my old man,' Trevor said to Tansy.

'And this is my flatmate, Mags.'

'Less of the "old man"! It's a pleasure to meet you, both. Sean told us to look out for you.'

Before Tansy registered the comment, a bell rang. People began to migrate towards the doors. Ernest said, 'We're going to have a bite afterwards with Sean. Would you like to join us and we can talk then? You too, Lewa.'

She replied, 'I'd like nothing more, but protocol declares I dine with the ambassador and his wife.'

Tansy was unsure. She looked at Trevor, wondering what to do. Had they only been asked out of politeness? He smiled at her, nodding his head, but before she could respond, Mags said, 'We'd love that, wouldn't we?'

'Good. We'll see you afterwards. I believe a table has been reserved somewhere. We'll meet you here in the foyer later.'

'What were you thinking of?' Tansy asked her friend, after they had found their places. 'You do know we can't leave now, even if we're bored.'

'I know.' Mags grinned. 'I'm having a ball. I won't want to leave. You never said how cute Trevor was. You kept that very quiet.'

'Trevor? Cute? I never thought of him like that, but now that you mention it, I suppose he is, in a serious sort of way.'

'I can't wait to meet your professor now. If Phyllis raves about him, he must be hot too.'

'Keep your voice down. His wife could be here.'

'He's married?'

'I haven't a clue and I didn't ask him. Please don't either. This is all very awkward. I've never seen Trevor outside the office and I know precious little about him. And I don't know if the Prof will be very comfortable with me hustling in on his night. I'm completely out of my depth and I'm beginning to regret coming here, never mind bringing you with me. Please behave.'

'Relax, Tansy. I will.'

She wasn't too sure, but she was aware of the sumptuous settings and found her eyes wandering over the portraits and wondered what they had witnessed over the centuries in this very place. A round of clapping heralded the arrival of the speakers and they waited for the opening addresses to conclude before Professor Sean Pollard was introduced.

As Sean took over the microphone, she was impressed by how confident he was, standing there in front of his peers – some of whom were probably more knowledgeable – yet speaking with authority and conviction. She was completely drawn in.

No one sneaked out of the room during Sean's lecture, nor was there a sound, a cough or any shuffling. He spoke with a fluency and clarity that held his audience's attention. His delivery was natural and he often brought a touch of humour to his topic. Tansy looked around her. He owned the audience. She felt ridiculously proud of him, and secretly excited at the thought of dining with him later.

At the end, he got a prolonged standing ovation, which he acknowledged with a bow and dismissive gestures. He left the podium and shook hands with a few of the other VIPs and delegates who were sitting in the front rows. Then he left the hall.

'Well, what's your verdict?' Tansy asked Mags.

'That was fascinating, and I have to say he's very impressive. I thoroughly enjoyed it.'

'So did I. He came across as being much more affable than I expected.'

'Affable! What a strange word to use. It sounds so old-fashioned,' Mags said.

'Well, he is, a bit, isn't he? What would you have called him?' Tansy asked.

'Ask me after the meal. Come on. They're waving at us, over there by the exit.'

'We're meeting Sean at the restaurant,' Ernest said.

'Are you sure we're not gate-crashing his evening? We won't mind ...'

'Of course not. He knows you're coming.'

Sean was waiting at the restaurant when they arrived, and Tansy introduced Mags to him.

'You'll have to stop calling me Prof. It's Sean from now on.' She found it strange at first but by the end of the evening his name slipped off her tongue quite easily, as did Ernest's.

'I have to confess,' she told him at dinner, 'that I have never had the slightest interest in nomadic peoples and their future in society before listening to you tonight. Now I feel the need to fill in the enormous gaps in my education and learn more about their origins.'

'Tell that to some of my undergraduates, the ones who yawn their way through lectures, when they bother to turn up at all,' he replied. 'We might even get you interested in those Peruvian Mayans,' he said with a wry smile.

'That's the beauty of learning – it never has to stop,' Ernest said, oblivious to the inference.

Tansy listened as the conversation ebbed and flowed, absorbed in a new world. She had never been to such a fancy restaurant. The price of the wine would have exceeded her mother's grocery bill for a week. Would she be expected to pay for Mags and herself? Surely not. If so, she would just have to pretend she had forgotten her purse and offer to pay Sean back the next day, even if it meant raiding the utilities jar in the kitchen. She was fascinated by so much; by the way little snippets of facts were dropped eclectically into conversations and how topics merged into others, punctuated by stories and anecdotes. At some stage she became aware that Trevor and Mags had their own show going on. She had never seen him so animated, jolly even.

She was also aware of Sean in a way she had never been aware of anyone before. She could sense when he was looking at her, even before they made eye contact. He addressed her by name and engaged her in conversation. He made her feel special and important. She was falling under his spell. By the end of the evening, Mags had a date with Trevor, who had to leave with Ernest and Sean to go on to another colleague's house where they were expected. Somehow Sean had managed to pay the bill for them all without anyone noticing. Mags and Tansy took a taxi home, also courtesy of Sean, who told her he had enjoyed the evening and was delighted they had come and that she needn't worry about the taxi fare. 'That'll go on the expense account. Tip included,' he said, handing the money to the driver.

'It's been unforgettable,' she told him.

His reply, 'I know', wasn't what she had been expecting to hear.

Back in the flat, they were still discussing the evening when Phyllis came home from her shift at the restaurant.

'You missed a great night – Sean took us to dinner after the lecture, at Piaf, and I have a date with Trevor!' Mags gushed as soon as she came through the door.

'With nerdy Trevor, who works with you?' Phyllis asked Tansy.

'I never said he was nerdy.'

'You didn't have to. I joined the dots. And who's Sean?'

'Sean Pollard – Tansy's professor!'

'So it's "Sean" now, is it? Tell me, what's he like and is he married?'

'I haven't a clue.•Trevor's dad is a widower, but there was no mention or suggestion of a Mrs Pollard at any point,' Tansy replied.

'Is he as pompous as he sounds?'

'He's not pompous at all. He's funny, attentive and affable too.' Mags looked at Tansy and laughed. 'Isn't that right?'

'I suppose Mam would describe him as polished. Ernest too, that's Trevor's dad. He was with us as well. They've seen so much of the world. I could have stayed there listening to them all night. They were great company.'

'Did you learn anything interesting?' asked Phyllis.

'Loads. I discovered that the Roma gypsies originated not in Romania, as I had always thought, but from the military in northern India; that the Maoris are not indigenous New Zealanders, but Taiwanese instead. And I also discovered that I love scallops and *îles flottantes* too.'

'So I take it the night was a success.'

'Definitely,' said Mags, 'and they know how to treat a lady, unlike some of the yobs I've gone out with.'

◆

Years later, whenever Tansy looked back on her life, she would pinpoint that night as a shift-changer. It was the night that she grew up. The night she knew she was shedding her skin, like a snake that had outgrown it. She had felt herself being physically impelled onto another stage, a stage that would see her leaving her country girl persona behind and, even then, she had been acutely aware that there'd be no going back. It was the night she started seeing life in other colours.

Instead of getting a glimpse into a world that was new to her, she had experienced it at first hand. She wanted to be part of this other sphere, where conversations were stimulating and football, rugby, GAA, drink and girls were not the only things males talked about. Where people had experienced things she never had, and where they moved in diverse social and cosmopolitan groups.

It was the night too that she first realised that Sean Pollard was much more than a professor. He was a very attractive man, and when he looked at her, she felt herself unable to hold his gaze for fear he could read her thoughts. And she wouldn't want to share those with anyone.

It was the night she noticed the faint lines around his eyes and how blue his irises were. It was the night she noticed how there were threads of silver hair at his temples. It was the night she noticed his beautifully manicured hands and how his voice was so melodic and seductive. Yes, that was then, she'd sigh. That was the night everything changed.

She would also recall how she had been brought back to earth with a bang that night just as they were going to bed.

Tansy noticed the light flashing on the old-fashioned answering machine in the flat. The messages were from her mother, saying she'd tried a few times to reach her on her mobile, but Tansy had turned off her phone for the lecture and had deliberately left it powered off in the restaurant.

'I didn't really want to tell you this in a message, love, but Gappy Jim died late this afternoon.' There was a catch in her voice as she added, 'He'll be buried on Friday. I realise now that with your job it could be difficult for you to get down, but I know you'll do what's right. And we'll collect you from the bus.'

Ross had phoned too. 'I'm sure you've already heard, Tansy. I'm so sorry. I'm sure I'll see you over the next few days, Babes. If you need anything, lifts, etc, just shout. You know where I am. Love ya.'

With those calls, the buzz of the night vanished.

'I'll miss him. He's been part of my life since ever I can remember,' she told the girls. 'He put me up on a donkey for the first time, and he let me sit in the tractor with him. We often collected the eggs together. He loved his spuds, swimming in butter and drizzled with salt. I'm surprised he didn't die years ago from heart failure.'

'He sounds like my grandfather,' said Phyllis. 'We used to do things like that together.'

'In a way, he was the nearest thing I had to one,' she reasoned. 'I'm so glad I went to visit him when I was home last time.'

But a funeral, on Friday, and her mother's utterances about doing what was right carried an implication that not to return home for his burial would be an unforgiveable transgression.

'Can I realistically expect to get time off when I've scarcely been there three weeks?'

'I think Sean will understand. He seems OK. If he gets shirty, you could offer to make the time up – do an extra hour a day. The worst he can do is say no,' said Mags.

'If he doesn't, you could always pull a sickie. Now, I'm wrecked. I've been on my feet all evening, not dining in Piaf like some I could mention, but waiting on ungrateful punters who tipped really badly. Will you two please go to bed and not stay up nattering all night?' Phyllis said, heading for the bathroom.

'Tansy, I'm sorry you got that news after such a fab evening. Thanks so much for bringing me along and for introducing me to Trevor!' Mags hugged her friend.

Tansy wondered if effervescent Mags and serious Trevor would have a lot in common, but she couldn't answer that, not with the thoughts she had been having about a country girl and a suave professor …

She tossed and turned all night, crazy thoughts whirling around in her head, people dancing, women with exotic head ties, debonair men, wine waiters in white gloves, and even in this half-asleep state, she knew she would never see her world in quite the same light again.

She must have dozed off because the alarm clock shocked her into the new day. She couldn't believe how awful she looked when she saw herself in the mirror. She did what she could to make herself presentable and alert. It didn't have much effect.

She arrived at work early and waited until after half-eight. By then she knew he'd have had a chance to deal with urgent emails before she disturbed him. Sean's words of greeting when he saw her were, 'If I didn't know any better, I'd think you'd been out on a binge last night. Or did you go on somewhere?'

'I didn't sleep very well ...'

'Not something you ate, I hope?' He sounded concerned.

'Not at all. The food was wonderful, but I need to ask you something and I know I should wait until our conference time ...'

'Well, it's obvious that you have something on your mind. Out with it.'

'First, I want to thank you for inviting me to the lecture and for dinner afterwards. Mags and I really enjoyed every minute of it.'

'It was my pleasure and you thanked me last night, I don't know how many times. So let's move on to second ...'

'Second, I was wondering if I could take Friday off?' She hesitated.

'Is it important that you do?' he asked.

She explained.

'Of course, you must go. There are things in life that take priority over everything else, especially work.'

'I will make up the time.'

'There's no need. I'm sorry you went home to such bad news after a lovely night. Well, it was for me.' He cleared his throat. 'Now, I have to crack on as I'll be missing tomorrow too.'

She couldn't believe how easy that had been. Trevor winked at her as she left the room.

'Dinner at Piaf's! Well, you have him wrapped around your little finger, haven't you?' Linda said when they came in for their coffee break.

'I had to tell her about last night. She actually coerced me into it after eavesdropping on your conversion with the Prof. How is Mags this morning? Did she really enjoy the night?'

'She did, very much. We both did.'

'Why didn't I pay more attention when he told us about that bloody lecture?' Linda complained. 'I could have been there, having dinner and sipping wine with him. Maybe he'd have noticed me and seen me for what I am.'

'And that would be as what, exactly?' asked Trevor.

'As a cool, sophisticated chick, that he'd like to spend more time with.'

'Shouldn't that be – with whom he'd like to spend more time?' he asked.

She turned to Tansy in exasperation and said, 'I blame the parents, really I do.' And they all started laughing.

Tansy was daydreaming when Sean came into her room. She was aware of his presence in a way she hadn't been previously. His gaze unnerved her and for a millisecond she saw something in that look. Something she couldn't identify. A look that seemed to penetrate her very being. She felt herself redden and turned away.

He seemed unusually thrown and, when he regained his composure, he fanned out a sheaf of papers. 'Eh, I've checked those references that you queried and you were right. The Spaniard has plagiarised the second citation.' He sat on the edge of her desk and pointed to the relevant passages marked in red on the pages. She noticed his woody cologne as he outlined what appeared to have been stolen and what didn't.

She inhaled as she listened, her mind wandering. She had to concentrate very hard to keep on track.

'Would you like to look over the section again when I've removed it?'

'Can you give it priority? I'd like to show it to some of my colleagues. We need to take action to stop this guy. He's the sort who destroys all our credibility.'

'I'll get started on it straight away.'

He thanked her and left. That was awkward, she said to herself. I acted like a teenager with a crush on my teacher. Before she figured out how to act as a grown-up, the door opened again and he popped his head around it, neither in nor out.

'Just a thought, Tansy. I'll be driving to Galway tomorrow night, and I will be passing through Ballinasloe. I could give you a lift for that funeral on Friday. You can let me know, unless you have already made other plans. That's all,' he said and was gone.

'That's a bit of luck,' her mother said when she told her that evening.

Sean said he'd leave at six and arranged to meet her at the college car park. Part of her was looking forward to the drive, being with him for a few hours, getting to know him better. But she was apprehensive too. Something inexplicable had happened the previous morning. Had he been aware of it too? Instinctively, she knew he had, even though it had only lasted a blink or two.

He probably had that effect on everyone, she told herself. There's poor Linda suffering from unrequited love for him, undoubtedly only one of the many women who had fantasised about him over the years. She was sure he and some of the other professors and lecturers had a great laugh over such groupies when they got together. Some probably even thrived on the adulation.

She had no intention of adding her name to his list of groupies.

Chapter Six

On Thursday she packed a few things and took her bag to work with her. She'd have a bite in the canteen, do an extra hour at her desk and be waiting at the car park at the appointed hour.

Sean was already there when she arrived and waved at her. He hopped out, took her bag, put it in the boot and opened the door for her. Ross never did that.

He eased his way effortlessly into the city centre traffic and, after asking her if she minded the window down a little, he remained silent. There was an operatic aria playing on the radio. She recognised it but couldn't name it. If she asked, would he think she was unsophisticated? He was probably *au fait* with all sorts of classical music. She wasn't, so she said nothing. She figured that was the best strategy. The piece of music ended and she blurted out, 'I really appreciate the lift, Sean.'

'Think nothing of it. It's not as though it's out of my way, and I'm glad of the company too.'

'So am I,' she replied and wondered if that had sounded wrong. Before she could agonise over it any further, he asked, 'Are your folks native to the west?'

'They are, both from Galway, from a little place called Dunmoy.'

'My grandfather came from a remote farm near Maam Cross. When I was small, I was sent down to stay there with my grandmother every year for my summer holiday. The big adventure. I loved it because I have no brothers or sisters. There I had cousins to play with and we were allowed to run wild and get up to all sorts of mischief. I loved the freedom. It was such a contrast to my life in the city.'

'And I used to go to Salthill or Bundoran for my seaside adventure,' Tansy said.

'What made you pick Dublin for college?'

'I wanted to broaden my horizons a little.' She laughed. 'Doesn't that sound parochial?'

'Understandable, really,' he replied. 'And have you? Broadened your horizons?'

'I certainly hope so. I love city life. It's never dull. A lot of my year picked Galway, but I wanted to go to the capital,' she said.

'We all have to start somewhere.'

'There's so much world out there ... I had hoped to go abroad for the summer but I never ...'

'Don't tell me – you have a boyfriend?'

'Well, yes, I have.'

'And let me guess – he didn't want you to go.'

'No. It isn't like that. I decided not to – this year.' She felt a little awkward speaking so personally to him.

'Is he studying too?'

'No. He's not into books and study. Horses are his thing.'

'Is he older than you?'

'Just by a year.'

'Take a word of advice, and you can tell me to mind my own business if you like, but I'm going to say it anyway. Don't let him hold you back. You're a very bright young woman. Don't get tied down with responsibilities yet or you'll spend your life regretting the places you didn't see and the things you didn't do.'

'It's not like that. Ross didn't ask me not to go …'

'He didn't have to, did he? You decided for him. I've seen it happen again and again.' He took his eyes off the road and looked at her. 'I've said enough, Tansy.'

Annoyed at the way this conversation had gone, and emboldened because of it, she asked, 'And you, Professor, have you spent your life regretting things you never did?'

'*Touché!* And I'm "Professor" again, am I? Yes, there are one or two opportunities I missed out on. Just a few but, hell, I'm not that ancient. There's still plenty of time to rectify most of those. It's the ones that come along only at certain times in our lives, when we're commitment-free and fearless, like in our student days. They're the ones we never get back again.'

She could hear the wistfulness in his voice and wondered what his regrets were.

'It's not too late, though, is it?' he asked. 'Tell me, you do intend doing your Erasmus year or a term at least?'

'I'm not sure.'

'What do your parents think about it?'

'My parents aren't too keyed into university life. Neither of them had those opportunities. Dad just took over the farm as expected when he was old enough and Mam worked in the family village shop and helped mind her grandmother at home until she married him. They're delighted that I'm getting opportunities they didn't have, although Mam's always worried that I might get "notions above my station" hanging around with all those "university types". She makes sure I stay grounded.'

'I'd better stay out of sight when I drop you off, so,' he said and they both laughed.

She couldn't believe they'd been more than an hour on the road. The journey was flying. The ice was well and truly broken and the silences didn't seem so awkward any more. He suggested they stop for a coffee or a bite to eat and they pulled off the main road. She tried to pay, but he wouldn't hear of it. While they ate, he asked, 'How are you enjoying working on my papers?'

'Very much. Reading through them has made me realise how little I know about anything.'

'Don't let them intimidate you. I've spent almost twenty years getting to this stage.'

So, he's at least twenty years older than me, she thought. He's closer in age to my folks than he is to me, yet it doesn't feel like it. Maybe being around young people all the time had that effect.

'Where do you see yourself that far forward? And don't tell me as a wife with a few kids.'

'Would that be such a bad thing? Being a mother is a precious calling. It's also one that's denied to over half the world's population because they are men.'

'Touché once more! I wasn't implying it's a bad thing and it's not, if it was all you ever wanted from life. If not, it could be a waste of talent, a loss of potential and the avenue to regrets.'

'What's stopping me having a career and motherhood too? Lots of women manage both very successfully.'

'Your personality, I'd say, and before you give me a slap across the face for that, let me explain myself.'

'I'm not sure I want to hear it.'

'I'd like to tell you anyway. Trust me, college days are for exploration, experimentation and new discoveries, and those discoveries include getting to know yourself. In my experience, for what it's worth, there are waiters and there are doers in this world. The waiters hang around waiting to see what their friends, families, boyfriends, whatever are going to do, and the doers get on with it – living and enjoying life to the full. They're the ones who are most likely to have it all. You have potential, Tansy, and I'd hate to see you become one of those people who looks back on these important years with regret. You'll never get them back. We'd better hit the road again or your folks will think I've kidnapped you.'

Again, he opened the car door for her. She buckled her seat belt and asked, 'Professor, I'm curious to know what gives you the right to assume any of this? Do you analyse all your research assistants? It's just that I hadn't realised that you were such an authority on everything. And I don't think you realise how pompous you sound.'

He raised an eyebrow at her. 'Have you finished?'

Emboldened with rage, she continued.

'No. For someone whose life's work is based on facts, such sweeping generalisations seem at odds. You don't know me at all, yet you feel you can pigeonhole me. What makes you think that I will conform to one of your stereotypes?'

'The fact that you're making choices because you're assuming you know what your boyfriend wants or rather, doesn't want,' he said.

'I would hardly have equated an Erasmus stint with something life-changing.'

'I would have to disagree with you there. Don't hold back on your education because it might make your boyfriend feel inferior to you.'

Was that what she was doing? She didn't answer, but sat in silence, seething, as the countryside flew by, the late evening sun dazzling them as it sank lower in the sky. He had exposed a nerve she didn't know she had. He pulled down his sun visor and reached across to do the same at her side. She didn't know how long the quiet lasted until she became aware of the road sign stating 'Ballinasloe 7 km'.

'We're almost there,' he remarked.

'I appreciate the lift,' she said.

'But not the advice. I won't take it back, Tansy, and I won't mention it again, but think on it. It's not too late to change your mind. I could pull a few strings if you really wanted to get on the programme next term. I think it would do you good to go abroad for a while.'

'Thank you,' she replied, his suggestion awakening possibilities that she had deliberately not entertained in depth before. What was it about this man? He seemed to be able to read her better than she could read herself. By closing off options that were open to her to explore, would she really be shutting out opportunities and building up regrets? She wished, and not for the first time, that Ross was a bit more engaged with her plans and expectations. Perhaps she wasn't being fair to him. Maybe if she shared them with him, he might be. She'd make sure she'd have a chance to talk to him about them over the next few days.

Chapter Seven

Her parents were waiting at the appointed rendezvous, Peggy dressed in her good black funeral coat, Pat in his dark suit. Tansy hadn't expected to see Ross standing beside them.

'The welcoming party,' she said lightly to Sean, attempting to break the tension, which was now palpable between them. She didn't want to leave him on that note. 'Come and meet my folks.'

She hugged her parents, holding her father for a moment or two longer.

'Dad, I'm so sorry. I know how close you and Gappy Jim were. You'll miss him.'

'He was an uncomplicated man with simple values. It was his time. He wouldn't have wanted to linger.'

'Pragmatic as always, Dad,' she said and he smiled.

'Now who have we here?' he said as Sean took her bag from the boot and her mother rushed forward for a closer look at the professor and thanked him profusely for giving Tansy a lift. Ross waited until they had finished. He kept his arm around her proprietorially after greeting her with a kiss.

'Sean Pollard, the professor I'm working for this summer.'

She made the introductions and Sean shook hands with them. 'And this is Ross, my boyfriend,' she said as he took her rucksack from Sean.

'Ah yes, the one who is interested in horses.'

'That would be me, but it's a little more than being interested in them – that makes me sound like a gambler. I'm not – those beasts are my livelihood.'

'So I hear. And Tansy is not working *for* me. She's working *with* me, on an anthropological research project on specific surviving tribes and their customs. She's a bright spark and will go far if she's not held back.' Then, looking at each in turn, he said, 'I think it's time I headed on. It was nice meeting you all and I hope the next few days go as well as they can.'

'What a lovey man, isn't he?' her mother gushed as he drove away. 'He's so – so ordinary. And he thinks you're a bright spark, who'll go far. No airs and graces about him.'

That's a matter of opinion, Tansy thought.

'He's only a glorified teacher, not God,' Ross muttered, and Tansy hoped her mother hadn't heard him.

'I wasn't expecting you all to come to meet me.'

'If I'm perfectly honest, I didn't just come for you – and for Gappy Jim, of course,' Ross said. 'Babes, I have a bit of business to attend to here before I go home, but I met your folks at the funeral home and they told me when you were arriving, and hey presto, here I am. I couldn't stay away.' He pulled her closer. She was disappointed. She would have liked to have spent time alone with him that evening. She needed time with him. Apart from the sadness of the occasion, there was too much going on in her head, things that the security of time in his arms might fix.

'I have to run now, but I'll pick you up in the morning for the funeral,' he said, kissed her and left. She joined her parents and heard all about the removal and how Mary McLaughlin was going to keep her shop closed until after the requiem Mass, 'out of respect'.

'There's no "out of respect" about it, although, like everyone else, she was fond of the old fellow,' her dad said. 'He'd be surprised at how well liked he was. Peggy, you know Mary's only afraid she'll miss something and that's why she's closing her shop, so she can get all the gossip outside the church.'

Tansy and her mother just smiled at each other, a smile they both understood. He'd never change his opinion of Mary.

Back in the kitchen, her mother had already prepared and baked enough food to feed a battalion. Tansy forced herself to eat even though the edge had been taken off her appetite by the scone she had eaten on the way, and by the tone of the conversation that had accompanied it.

'It's good of you to have everyone back here afterwards. How many are you expecting?'

'It's hard to say, but Gappy Jim spent more time on this farm and in this farmhouse during his life than anywhere else.'

They checked and double-checked that they had set out enough of everything for the expected influx the following day. Her dad went off to look at a sick animal and Tansy wondered how long it would be before her mother's questions started.

'Is he married, the professor?'

'I don't honestly know, Mam. He never mentions a wife or family and I never ask him. Things like that don't come up in conversation. He didn't have anyone with him at his lecture the other night, and I presume he's off to this award ceremony on his own too.'

'What a waste. A lovely man like that. Maybe he's widowed or separated, or looking after an aged parent.'

'You're incorrigible, never happy unless you're match-making.' She laughed.

'Well, speaking of which – can you see Ross and yourself making plans in that direction? He was pretty keen to see you earlier on when we met him.'

'Definitely not, Mam. I want to travel and maybe study overseas somewhere.'

'How does Ross feel about that?'

'I don't know,' she replied honestly.

Tansy couldn't believe this was the second time this topic had come up today. Why should Ross's opinions be so important?

'We actually haven't discussed this in any great detail, but it's my life, and it's about what I want too. Is it a crime to make my own decisions about that?'

'Of course not, but it's good to have a family when you're fit and young.'

'Ross is trying to make his way in a very tough business,' Tansy said 'And he's not ready to settle down yet.'

'I would have followed your father anywhere.'

'And what if I want to do more with my life than bury myself in a backwater?' As soon as she heard herself utter those words, she knew she had offended her mother. 'I didn't mean it like that, Mam. I meant …'

'I know what you meant, Tansy. I've seen it happen to the O'Dwyers, and the Tanners, and the Fergusons and others too. They all saved and scrimped to educate their children and once they had their degrees, they were too important to come home to live and work with their own. It was what I feared most about letting you go up to the city, but I didn't think you'd be like that. I thought you'd be happy here.'

'Mam, I never said I wouldn't come back …'

'You didn't have to. I saw it in you the last time you were home. There's a restlessness about you that wasn't there before. This place is too small to contain you. Believe me, I do understand,' she said, putting her hand over her daughter's. 'I can't pretend to like it, but you have to follow your head, Tansy, as well as your heart.'

Tansy was confused. What was her mother trying to tell her? She had never questioned her about her feelings on living her whole life at the edge of the village where she had been born and raised. It had simply never come up, but somehow it seemed the right time now, when reminiscing and remembering the times spent over the years with Gappy Jim.

'There are so many things to see and do and I need to know that I can be free to be part of them. Didn't you ever feel like that, Mam?'

'Of course I had feelings like that. Everyone has those "what if" moments, if they're honest. I think maybe I wasn't as brave as you, or your friends. But circumstances were different then too. Once I fell for your father, nothing else mattered. We always knew the farm was his destiny and I suppose we planned our lives around that.'

'That's true,' her father said, coming in from the back porch and going to the sink to wash his hands. 'She knew what she was getting into when she took me on.'

'And it worked.' She laughed.

'There's a part of me that's afraid that if I step outside, I'll lose what I have here, and maybe Ross too, and I'm not sure I'm ready to find out yet.'

'Let things take their course. Life has a way of sorting out the big stuff,' her father said. 'I'm sure your mother often wonders what would have happened had she married that Ayleward fellow from the bank, although she'd never admit that to me, would you, love? He was always trying to take her from me. Now he's a bigwig in finance in Brussels, isn't that right?' he teased his wife.

'Don't be taken in by that smokescreen.' Her mother laughed, swishing him away with a tea cloth. 'Ask him about Rose Rankin – the district nurse who used to visit his mother and make sheep's eyes at him all the time. He might have fathered her ten children if she'd had her way.'

'Rose Maloney – formerly Rose Rankin – with all those kids?'

'The very one. And a looker she was back then too. Still is, despite carrying all that brood.'

Tansy looked at them. Her parents were actually flirting with each other and that didn't happen very often. Would she and Ross be like that in twenty years' time?

'You have to do what you feel is right for you,' her father said.

Peggy agreed, adding, 'Ross is another matter. If you love each other, that will endure long enough for you to spread your wings and find out what you really want. Trust your instincts.'

Tansy needed to talk to him, to hear his voice and his reassurance, but it was too late to phone. Ross rose at the crack of dawn to exercise the horses and wouldn't relish being woken at this hour. It was a clear night and she didn't close the curtains. The sky was studded with stars. Gappy Jim had taught her the constellations and together on several occasions they had watched spectacular meteor showers that seemed to go on for hours. She missed seeing clear skies like this when she was in the city. There, their beauty was eclipsed by light pollution from the street lamps and neon signs.

The quiet unnerved her. She had got used to the hum of urban traffic, the frequent sirens of an ambulance or fire engine making its way to some emergency and to the noises from the other flats, with the comings and goings of their occupants, even her own flatmates. At first, she had found it difficult to sleep through any of that, but gradually city life had become her normality. Tonight, it was the reverse. She couldn't settle. Her mind spun like a washing machine, working its way through the cycles, fast for a few minutes, then slowing, then gaining momentum again as she replayed the conversations of the day.

What was it Sean had said? She shouldn't hold back developing her talents and ambitions because she thought they might make Ross feel inferior to her. That had really annoyed her, yet it niggled too. Was that really what she was doing? Not everybody could be academic and, although he hadn't got a decent Leaving Cert, his talents lay in other directions. And she loved him.

She had never let herself think about how he'd feel when she was qualified, with her BA, her H Dip, her fluency in a few languages. She had always avoided such discussions. She'd never want to make him feel inferior. Was that what Sean meant? Would she grow to be embarrassed by her achievements, downplaying them so that Ross wouldn't feel any less than her? Would that cause her to feel resentment?

Sean had told her to think about what she wanted from life, where she would see herself in twenty years. She lay there thinking about this but found it impossible to project. Try as she might, she couldn't see herself in Dunmoy.

Before she finally dropped into an uneasy sleep, she had made her mind up on two things. She was going to take up Sean's offer of help to try to get a late Erasmus placing, but first she was going to talk to Ross about it.

It was a conversation she needed to have. It was time she stopped pussyfooting around these issues.

Chapter Eight

It was the following evening before she got her chance. It had not seemed appropriate to bring these things up first thing that morning when Ross arrived to take her to the funeral, and with so many people back at the house, she had been busy all day. By late evening, when all but a few of the neighbours who were helping to put dishes and tableware away had left, he suggested they go for a walk.

It had been an emotional day, and she was conscious that it was the closing of a chapter that spanned her whole life. Her first experience of death too, with its conflicting feelings. It was a beautiful evening, the sun caught the surfaces of the fields and the stony walls and painted them in a rosy golden hue. She could just imagine Gappy Jim coming over the horizon, his dog at his heels, and she realised that was a sight she would see no more.

'You're miles away,' Ross said, taking her hand. 'We need to talk.'

'That's never a good opening for any conversation,' she replied. Surely he hadn't picked up on her newfound doubts too? Was she that transparent?

'I know, but a few things have been happening while you've been in Dublin.'

She felt her heart sink – he's going to tell me he's met someone else. Don't let it be that.

'Don't look at me like that, Tansy,' he said. 'It was bound to happen. We've both done a bit of growing up since we met and it's only natural that we'd change.'

She didn't say anything. She didn't know what to say. He continued holding her hand. 'And it's far better if we get the wanderlust out of our systems before making any commitments.'

This wasn't at all what she had been expecting. Relieved, she said, 'Then we won't have any regrets later on.'

'You're amazing. I didn't think you'd take it as well.' He stopped and stood in front of her, looking into her eyes. 'I only told my father this morning. How did you find out?'

'Your father? What has he got to do with this?'

'Isn't that obvious? It affects him too if I'm not going to be here for two years.'

'Not going to be here for two years? I haven't a clue what you're talking about.'

'The meeting I had last night, in Ballinasloe. I was offered a two-year contract with one of the biggest studs in the Emirates and I've accepted. I'm off to Dubai.'

'Without consulting me?' she heard herself say.

'I didn't think I needed your permission,' he replied.

She couldn't believe what she was hearing. To think she had been willing to sacrifice her own plans so that he wouldn't feel excluded from her life – and here he had been, making his own all along, as though she had not even existed, never mind been of any significance in his life.

'You're right, you didn't, but it would have been nice to have been told or had some discussion about it. This is the first mention you've ever made about going anywhere, let alone overseas. It hardly all happened last night. Surely you must have been thinking about it for a while. You'd have had to set up meetings, interviews and the like and all that time you never thought you should tell me?'

'You know I'm not good with words and I'm not great at small talk on the phone.'

'I'd hardly call going to work halfway across the world, for two years, small talk.'

'When you put it like that, I suppose it isn't. That's why I wanted to have this talk now.'

'And if I hadn't come home for Gappy Jim's funeral, when would you have told me? When you were at the airport?'

'Don't be like that, Tansy. It's a great opportunity and you're away anyway.'

'A hundred and fifty kilometres down the road hardly compares with around eight thousand, does it?'

'I suppose not, but that's why I feel it's better to end things between us, before I leave. I wouldn't expect you to wait for me. You never know who we'll meet in between, now that you're hobnobbing with your professors and I'm going out foreign.'

'When is this all happening?'

'I'll be off once my work permit comes through. I've filled in all the necessary forms and just need a medical report to complete the red tape.'

She didn't answer. She was too stunned.

'Aren't you glad for me, Tansy? It's a one-in-a-million chance.'

'I'll tell you what makes me glad about it. That I now see you for what you are, and that's a conniving, selfish user. You've been stringing me along. You've never once mentioned looking for a job abroad.'

'I didn't—'

'No wonder you never asked me about my plans. They really didn't matter to you, did they? And you were too busy making your own, while I put off making mine. You're right about one thing, Ross. We've changed. We're different people.' She turned and started walking back to the house. He began to follow her.

'Don't even think about coming after me. Or anywhere near me ever again.'

'But my Jeep—'

'You can pick it up tomorrow. Just stay away from me and my home.'

Unshed tears blurred her vision. She couldn't fully grasp what had just happened. How stupid had she been to think they would ever have had a future together? They had nothing in common apart from a juvenile infatuation, puppy love, which had now evaporated. She could accept his reasons and grudgingly admit that her own feelings were probably running along similar lines, but she would never have dumped him the way he had dumped her.

And for that I had been willing to give up on my own dreams and expectations, she thought.

I'll never do that again, she promised herself. I will never do that again.

Chapter Nine

Ross's four-wheel drive had been moved from their yard before Tansy got up on Saturday. All day long she expected to hear from him, but these expectations came to nothing. No apology, no explanation, just an inexplicable silence. It was almost as if it were he who had died, not Gappy Jim. She kept busy helping her mother get the house back in order after the influx the previous day.

All the talking and figuring out. She told herself she had really got it wrong. Her parents were furious – her father had wanted to tackle Ross, while her mother's tight-lipped expression spoke much more than the words she uttered. 'I never was his biggest fan. You knew that all along, Tansy, didn't you? But I never credited him with being so underhand and low. I don't want to say I told you so but ...'

'You don't have to, Mam. I know I'm better off without him, but it hurts. It really does.'

Her father drove her to the bus on Sunday afternoon, laden down with cakes and goodies. When she protested, he just laughed.

'You should know you're talking about the woman who invented comfort food. I used to be trim!'

It'll take more than tea-brack and pear and almond tart to comfort me, she thought. I need a change of scenery, an adventure of my own, as far away from Ross and Dunmoy as I can go. No more playing it safe.

The journey back to Dublin only gave Tansy more time to build up another head of steam before she broke the news to her flatmates. She had a pain in her chest. Whether it was from grief, hurt, disappointment, anger or a combination of all of them, she didn't know. But the hurt was tangible. Phyllis offered some creative solutions as to how she'd deal with Ross, while Mags kept telling her, 'It's better to find out what he's like now than wasting more time on him.'

'I know, Mags. And I'd be grateful if you wouldn't mention this to Trevor. I don't want it discussed at work. I'll tell him myself.'

Tansy didn't mention the conversation with Sean that had triggered her change of heart about looking at the possibility of an Erasmus stint. That could wait. She needed to sound out Sean first and find out if it was really a feasible option so late. She knew how coveted such places were and she wasn't even on a waiting list anywhere.

◆

Tansy settled at her desk, vowing to put Ross and the awful weekend behind her. She usually liked these first hours in the day when it was quiet and there were no interruptions. She was surprised when Sean came in.

'I think I may have spoken out of turn the other day, Tansy, and just hope I didn't offend you or your parents. That wasn't my intention.'

'You needn't worry; no one even noticed,' she replied.

'That's good. No harm done, so,' he said and was just leaving when she blurted out, 'Eh, your offer to help me get a late placement on an Erasmus programme – is it still there? Because if it is, I'd like to try.'

'So you talked to the horse man and made him see sense.'

'That's not how I would have put it, but he has absolutely no objections.'

'Well, that's a positive development. I've a bit of work to catch up on this morning – leave it with me for a couple of days.'

'I'm sorry, I never even asked how the award ceremony went.'

'Very well, if a bit tedious. Trust me, there's nothing as dull as a crowd of academics trying to outshine each other.'

When he left, she felt marginally better, although still wiped out and a bit rudderless. She was resigned to the idea that her half-formed plans may come to nothing. There was no guarantee that Sean would be able to do anything for her, and if she told her flatmates, she might just jinx any chance she had of him succeeding.

That night, to try to keep Ross out of her thoughts, she went to an awful sci-fi movie at the cinema with Mags and Trevor. They were really getting on well and she felt a pang of envy watching them banter and laugh so easily together. The following day after work she defrosted the fridge and cleaned out the food cupboards; she even ironed, a task she hated.

'You're like a whirling dervish about the place, and it's not that I don't like this clean-machine mode, but it's unnerving,' said Mags. 'Will you sit down and relax, read a book or something.'

Two days later Sean told her, 'I may have news for you.'

'Oh. Fantastic.'

'Let's not get exited just yet,' he replied.

'That's easy for you to say,' she told him.

'I'm afraid I've had no joy with any of my French contacts.'

'Oh,' she uttered, feeling her optimism fade, but he continued, 'So it's a matter of Hobson's choice. I know you're reading Spanish too and it turns out you could be winging your way to Spain – to Alcalá de Henares in January for six months, if you wish. You might even be able to stretch it for a few more months with work over the summer if you wanted to.'

'That's fantastic. How did you manage that?'

'I can't really take any credit. Just before I approached a friend who is involved in the selection process, a coup in some South American country meant the diplomatic families were recalled for their safety, and fortuitously one of them had a son who was enrolled at the university so this has freed up a space. It has your name on it now, if you want it. The downside is that they want an immediate answer, or it will be put back on the list tomorrow.' She was stunned and before she could reply, he urged her for a response. 'Well, what are you thinking?'

'I'm thinking, it's time I stopped playing it safe and is this really happening? I didn't dare hope that it might. And yes, I'll take it, wherever it is.'

'I'm glad to hear you say that.'

'How can I thank you?'

He raised an eyebrow at her and she sensed he stopped

himself from whatever he was going to say. She reddened and looked down at her hands.

'No need for thanks. I'll ring my contact and let her know. The rest is for you to follow up on. And, Tansy, I'd appreciate if you kept my name out of this when telling your friends. I oughtn't be interfering when you're not one of my students. You can mention the coup freeing up the place, but no more. I'm not supposed to get involved in things like this.'

'I understand. I can't thank you enough.'

'You can, by not letting me down. Can I ask how you managed to talk the horse man around to letting you go?'

'I used my powers of persuasion,' she lied, forcing a smile and looking him in the eye. Whatever feelings she thought she had for Sean had vanished along with any kindly disposed ones towards the male population in general. She had no inclination to tell him what murderous intentions she had to keep pushing aside every time she thought of Ross making his own plans, dumping her and heading off to Dubai. Nor would she admit how easily she had forfeited her opportunities so that he wouldn't feel diminished for lack of them. She had to keep focusing on her mother's words – 'he wasn't worthy of you'. Maybe he wasn't, but that still didn't stop her berating herself for her gullibility and stupidity.

She wasn't going to let infatuation for the likes of Sean Pollard skew her equilibrium.

They chatted a little longer and she found herself relaxing and smiling for the first time since Friday, as she tried to visualise herself abroad. She didn't know what to expect, but saw herself somewhere sunny, on a history-steeped campus with arches, pendulant wisteria and bougainvillea and the smell of jasmine in the air.

Over the next few weeks, she found it difficult to concentrate on her job, her mind hopping from one thing to another. She threw herself into her work and felt very proud of herself when she finished the last reference in the index and was able to hand over the complete printed bundle to Sean with two back-up copies on memory sticks.

'I'm impressed, Tansy. I suppose you wouldn't like to come and work for me permanently, would you?' he asked.

'Afraid not, Sean. I have places to go and things to do,' she replied. He smiled and she flushed.

On her last morning, he brought her in a coffee and took up his position on the corner of her desk. 'I know it's short notice, but if you're free this evening I'd like to take you out to dinner, to say thank you for your work. I have to tell you, despite your lack of Peruvian experience,' he said, grinning at her, 'your work ethic and attention to detail have really impressed me. I never thought I'd have those papers ready for submission on time and, if it hadn't been for your diligence, they would not have been.'

Had he just asked her out to dinner? Had she heard him properly?

'I know it's Friday and possibly you have plans, but Trevor and Linda are both free, so will you join us?'

She felt a wave of disappointment sweep through her. For an insane moment, she had thought he wanted to take her out on her own. But of course he didn't. What had she been thinking? She wanted to decline, but the opportunity of spending an evening in his company was too appealing.

Despite telling herself that she had no feelings, no feelings whatsoever, for Sean, she was unable to deny them. Her heart leapt when he came into her room to discuss the project's progress. And when he'd perch on the edge of her desk, his long legs dangling, she found it impossible to concentrate on what he was saying.

She had mixed emotions about the fast-approaching new term. With her contract up, she would have no reason to spend any time with him and, strangely, she wasn't looking forward to that. She knew she'd miss it.

'That sounds great. I'd love to.'

'It does, if that pair can stop sparring for a few hours. I'll let you know when I've booked a table. Somewhere Spanish seems appropriate.'

'It sounds fabulous. I'd love that.'

He took them to a small restaurant off Wicklow Street, which she had passed so many times, but which was way out of a student's price range.

Linda was the last to arrive. Sean did a double-take.

'You look different tonight.'

'She always tries to look different,' said Trevor, 'and she usually succeeds.'

'You pair make me laugh,' Tansy said.

'I know he loves me beneath it all,' Linda replied. She had added pink dye to her hair in two long streaks and had plaited them from ear to ear, fixed in place with a big, pink, floppy flower. She had a long, floaty skirt, in pink, and a white, scoop-necked top. 'I know from that look, Trevor, that you have an opinion.'

'I always have an opinion. Sometimes it's more prudent not to offer it.'

'But I asked. Honestly.'

'You honestly want to know, or you want to know honestly?'

'Why do you always have to be so arcane?'

'Because that's who I am. I like precision and, since you're so persistent, I'll tell you what came to mind on your entrance. I thought marshmallows, pink and white marshmallows. And I was instantly transported to cub camps and toasting them, the marshmallows not the cubs, over the campfires!'

'I give up,' Sean said, laughing. 'Remind me never to ask what you think.'

'And that goes for me too,' Tansy said.

Sean ordered cava while they perused the menu. There were so many things there that she'd never tried before – fried baby squid, *patatas bravas*, anchovies served in vinegar, fried peppers, prawns sautéed in peppercorn sauce, *chorizo* cooked in cider.

'At least I'll know what they are when I come across them in Spain.'

'That's partly why I chose this place; the other reason is because I usually find myself looking at everyone else's meal in restaurants, wishing I had chosen what they had. With *tapas*, you get to try everything, so feel free to order whatever you like and we'll all share.'

Linda said, 'I always thought *tapas* was a specific type of cooking.'

'No. I believe it got its name from the word for "lid", *tapa*. Farm workers used to put a piece of bread over their glass of beer or wine to keep the flies away. Then they'd eat the bread with olives and probably some cheese. Gradually these little snacks became more creative and now come under the umbrella of *tapas*.'

Tansy was falling under his spell again, listening to his melodic voice, remembering the previous dining experience with him after his lecture, what great company he was and how knowledgeable he was about so many things.

'That's amazing, Sean,' Linda said. 'I'd never have known that. I need to hang out with you more often.' The others laughed.

'We're going to miss having you around,' Sean told Tansy as they said their goodbyes outside the restaurant.

'You can always drop in for a coffee at lunchtime when he's gone for his constitutional to the Green,' Linda suggested, nodding towards Sean. 'Can't she?'

'So long as she doesn't distract you from your work.'

Trevor said, 'As if she needed an excuse. I'll walk home with you. I told Mags I'd wait till she gets home after her shift.'

'Ah yes, Sean, I hear you're a matchmaker, bringing those two together. Can you do anything for me?' Linda asked in that coquettish manner she used on him frequently.

He laughed. 'I think you credit me with too much. I don't think my talents extend in that direction, Linda, but I'll keep a lookout.'

He hugged Tansy warmly. 'It's been good having you on the team.' She felt her eyes well up. She didn't want to think how she would feel not seeing him every day. 'I wish you all the best, and remember, I'll be keeping an eye on your progress.'

He released her, kissed her on the cheek, turned and, with a wave, walked into the neon-lit street. She looked after him until he was obscured by a crowd of late-night revellers.

Chapter Ten

Tansy waited a bit before she told her parents about Spain, knowing her father was feeling a bit fragile now that his old friend was gone. And her mother hadn't stopped raging about the way Ross had treated their daughter. The dispute over the land and every bit of scandal ever known about his family had been dredged up and picked over by Mary McLaughlin and herself. When Tansy did break the news, it gave them the chance to move on to something new. Now when they met, their chats had a different focus.

'Tansy going abroad to study? But you must be fierce proud of her altogether, Peggy.'

'Of course we are. To think she'll be going to a foreign university and will be talking in a foreign language. Who'd have thought, and her father and I both leaving school at sixteen.

'Sure, Mary, we thought we were doing well if we could say our prayers in Irish, and if there was a farm or a shop to inherit or an apprenticeship to be got, we thought we were made up for life.'

'You're so right, Peggy. I suppose it's their time now and they'd be mad to let these opportunities pass them by.'

Peggy replied with a sigh, 'Moving away to Dublin was one thing, but Spain. I blame my mother – filling her head with romantic notions of foreign lands when she was a tot. They used to spend hours looking at places on a globe.'

'Let's hope that she doesn't fall in love with a foreigner and stay over there.'

'Oh God, Mary, don't even put that thought into the ether. Gappy Jim had a great expression. He used to say, "Don't bid the devil good morrow until you meet him", so I'll try and live by that and hope it will never happen.'

'Sound,' Mary agreed.

•

The new term began and Tansy found herself wanting to cross the campus to Sean's office, but any excuse she could come up with sounded lame. On the rare occasions when they did bump into each other, he always seemed genuinely pleased to see her and enquired about her studies and her preparations for her sabbatical.

The last time that had happened was a few days before Christmas, in Grafton Street.

'Have you time for a coffee?'

'I'm heading home this afternoon on the bus, so it'll have to be a very quick one,' she answered, aware of all she still had to do, but not wanting to say no. 'The later one will be packed and I don't fancy standing all the way to Ballinasloe.'

'OK, let's make them expressos rather than espressos!' he said. Taking her arm, he guided her through the crowds into the nearest café. They could hardly hear each other above the din. Christmas tunes wafted in and out over the chatter. Sitting across from him, it really hit her how much she missed seeing him. How special that summer working for him had been. She loved listening to his voice and would quite happily have stood on the bus, after all, the whole way to Ballinasloe and back to have another coffee with him.

'You'll be glad to hear our manuscript is with the publishers.'

She laughed. 'I'm flattered at you calling it "ours". And by the way, everything's in place for my Erasmus adventure.'

'You must be excited.'

'Excited and scared too. It's my first time going somewhere where they speak a different language. I hope they'll understand me!'

He laughed. 'I have every confidence in you.'

He kissed her on the cheek and she got a whiff of his familiar woody aftershave. He held her arms for a minute before he vanished into the crowds again. She felt an emptiness envelop her.

Chapter Eleven

With new luggage, a new haircut and a new passport, the first week of the New Year saw Tansy enrolled in the Universidad de Alcalá. She had had to look up Alcalá de Henares, but had found it quite easily.

She felt a great degree of satisfaction at having negotiated her way through Madrid-Barajas airport and finding the right connection to take her to Atocha. She had been apprehensive about flying. Would she know where to collect her baggage: what if it got lost? She had felt bamboozled deciphering the countless direction signs, some with recognisable place names, others distinctly foreign and obscure to her.

You did it, girl, you got here, she told herself with pride when she spotted the university representative with some other people. She was the last to be dropped off the bus, the others being deposited at a student hostel. As they navigated the medieval part of the city, the driver pointed out so much that she found it hard to take in. A few streets from the medieval centre, they stopped outside a secluded villa with shuttered windows.

◆

'Aqui estamos,' he announced, hopping out to get her bags and open the gate for her. She lifted the heavy knocker and almost immediately heard the sound of footsteps on the tiles.

Pedro and Rosa Torres welcomed her warmly, ushering her inside. The smell of something distinctly foreign and mouth-watering filled her nostrils and she realised she was starving.

Everything was so different to home. The furniture was large and dark, the rooms were bigger too, and reminded her of an antique shop she passed every day when walking to college. There was scarcely a patch of wall surface that wasn't hidden by a gilt-framed painting of some shape or size. An eclectic mix of bric-a-brac inhabited every surface and corner, as though the occupants had been collecting for years.

'You must regard this as your home while you are with us,' Rosa told her as she took her to see her room, where a large, high bed with an excess of pillows and cushions dwarfed everything else.

The main window overlooked a garden with a courtyard that was partially covered by a pergola. Bare stems and branches, which she thought must be vines, twisted and rambled over the structure. In a deep alcove off one end of the room, she discovered a book-lined space, housing a large desk in front of another window with an aspect to the side. She had her own bathroom next door with a large, claw-footed bath and an enormous, old-fashioned, brass shower head.

'Leave your unpacking until later,' Pedro urged her, coming in with her large suitcase. 'Rosa has dinner ready for us.'

'I'll be down in a minute,' she replied, pleased that she could easily understand what they were saying.

Tansy came downstairs carrying one of her mother's porter cakes and a plum pudding.

'I like this *madre* of yours too,' Rosa said with a grin.

'Wait until you taste them before you make any judgements,' she replied.

She phoned home later that evening and faced a barrage of questions.

'They couldn't be nicer, Mam. They really made me feel special. It's obvious they're used to hosting students …

'They raved about your baking …

'Yes, the room is terrific. It's huge and very Spanish … It's like having my own apartment …

'No, I'm the only one here. I'm not sure if that will change. It's a big house …

'Yes, they do both speak English, very good English, but they've told me they won't be practising with me. It's *español* all the way now …

'Yes, they promised to show me around tomorrow.'

When she finished that call, she typed an email to Phyllis with more of the same and cc'd it to Gina and Mags.

Well, girls, you'd be proud of me. I made it! Got on the right plane, train and bus. A bit scary, if I'm honest. Loved flying! First impressions – very good. Great welcome. Gorgeous home. Gi-normous bedroom. Nice family. Señora talks mucho. Señor quieter. Unpacking now. *Hasta mañana.*
Buenos noches a ustedes tres.
Xxx

She pressed 'Send' and looked around her, deciding what to put where. Her laptop pinged a message. It was from Phyllis.

Knew you could do it. But good God, woman, you're not even there a single night and you're talking in one and two-word sentences like English was your second language!! I'll let you away with it for tonight, but I want more than that next time! Details, details. Remember, I'll be living the experience through your eyes – as we can't all afford the luxury of being there ourselves.

Your replacement is moving in tomorrow. It'll be strange having a male in our girlie zone. I hope he has some hot friends and doesn't have smelly feet! Will advise you on both. Miss you.

Phyllis

Xx

Tansy smiled. She wouldn't get away with anything when she had Phyllis as a friend.

'*Miss you too. Will do better next time!*' she typed, suddenly realising how tired she was.

◆

On a scale of affluence, Tansy's family was definitely at the bottom of her flatmates' league. But for the fact that she had no siblings to be paid for and put through college as well, and for a small legacy left when her grandmother died and the village shop was sold, Tansy would certainly not be here now, settling in as a foreign student.

Phyllis had no such trips on the horizon. She was the fourth of six. She depended on her earnings and tips from the restaurant to keep her afloat while she studied, taking on extra shifts whenever they were available.

'I have one go at this so I'm not going to flunk my exams or bunk off lectures,' she'd told them when they'd moved in together, that first year. 'And don't look at me like that. Financially, repeating is not an option for me. I intend to enjoy my student years, but they are the means to an end, and I have to remember that. Don't worry, I'm not a swot and I won't be in bed by ten every night.'

'Thank God for that,' Mags had said. 'I thought we had a cuckoo in the nest.'

Although Tansy knew a chance like hers was not likely for her friend, she also knew that Phyllis was genuinely happy it had come her way. That's what she loved about her, her generosity of spirit and her sense of self. They had a special bond and it didn't bother either of them that Mags's family was loaded, and Gina's was close behind in the financial stakes.

Tansy had read everything she could find about the university, one of Spain's oldest, but even that hadn't prepared her for the beauty of the ancient buildings. She could imagine the Cistercian monks of old walking around the courtyard, with its tiers of arches on three levels, as they contemplated and prayed, possibly even singing the same Gregorian chant that she had sung at school.

A quiet air prevailed in the cloisters behind the baroque façade that separated the realms of academia from the bustling town square on the other side.

'I love it, I love it, I love it,' she said to herself as she walked around, discovering the narrow cobbled back streets where the locals lived, peering into courtyards and through archways. She thought of Sean and, for the umpteenth time, was grateful for whatever string-pulling he'd managed to do to magic up a vacancy in this historic place. She had a few days to familiarise herself with her new surroundings and get her bearings before her lectures began. She'd write and let him know, but that could wait until she'd seen a bit more and could be specific.

Phyllis wasn't the only one living the experience with her.

'Have you made any friends yet? What about your hosts? Are they nice to you? What's the food like? Is it very foreign?' Her mother's bombardment made her smile. She'd only ever been 'on the continent' once. That was before Tansy was born. It was on a parish pilgrimage to Lourdes and Peggy had been a designated helper. She still talked about the group from Holland who served cheese and cooked meats to their invalids – for breakfast! 'Imagine that,' she used to say. 'Cheese and cold meats – for breakfast!'

'Yes, Mam, it's very different to what we eat at home. And here we don't have our dinner until ten o'clock at night.'

'And you go to bed with all that food in your stomach? That can't be good for you.'

'That's how they live over here and it doesn't seem to do them any harm. It's their culture. They don't finish work until around eight in the evening, and by the time they get home and prepare food, it's very late. I don't find that as strange as having an enforced siesta. Everything, and I do mean everything, closes from one to four, then they go back to work again.'

'It sounds like a very long day and not a very efficient use of time.'

'It is, but I'm told that when the weather gets warmer, I'll be glad to go into hiding too.'

She loved hearing from the girls and kept them posted.

It's been surprisingly easy to settle in, even though it still feels strangely alien without you two, Mags and Phyllis, squabbling all the time and you, Gina, organising my life for me! I feel sorry for the new flatmate. He doesn't know what he's let himself in for. I'm getting used to the Spanish accents and their funny ways, but I miss you lot! Mags – how's Trevor?

No, Phyllis! I never heard from Ross and I hope I never do! I've put all that behind me. And, no! No romances – yet. The social life looks promising, though, and I'm enjoying it all.

Tansy was struck by how remarkably well turned out and polished the students were. She told her mother, 'Even though they dress casually, they look a lot smarter than our lot – as though their clothes were ironed after each wear and lived on hangers!'

She wrote to Phyllis:

I've made some new friends. There's a coffee shop in the square where we hang out together. Prof keeps in touch weekly. Short missives. He's so thoughtful. I'd never have expected this outcome when you forced me into that interview last summer. Isn't life funny? Write and tell me all the gossip.

She had kept her feelings about Sean to herself. Her flatmates would have dismissed them as a student crush. Phyllis would have disapproved; she wasn't his greatest fan although Tansy didn't really understand why, and with Mags and Trevor being such an item, she thought it better to keep it to herself. She didn't really know what 'it' was, but it was something more than a student crush. Of that she was sure.

His mails, no matter how short and non-committal, made her feel insanely happy and she had to hold back from letting that show in her replies. She wrote:

> There are storks' nests all over the place. They are big woody clumps of sticks and twig, perched precariously on the cathedral's bell tower, and all sorts of turrets and spires around the square. I'd never seen storks before. When they're getting ready to fly, they align themselves, like swimmers about to high dive, heads out, legs extended. I envy them. They look so graceful soaring above. I'm fascinated by how they land on those hazardous nests. Of course, you've probably seen them loads of times, but I think they'll always be an abiding memory of Spain for me.

His reply made her smile each time she read it.

> And it seems to me as though it's not just the storks who are spreading their wings and taking flight. Your enthusiasm is infectious, Tansy. Don't ever lose that.

Chapter Twelve

When Tansy looked back on her life, she remembered this interlude in Spain for so many reasons. It was a period of self-discovery and when she really grew up. Moving to college in Dublin had been the start. Getting her summer job had been a continuation. The night of Sean's lecture and the dinner afterwards would always stand out, but moving to Spain had raised her to another echelon altogether. As her confidence grew during her time there she realised she was quite capable of achieving whatever she wanted from life. She had conquered the fear of facing the unknown and she was doing it on her own too. As Sean had put it, it hadn't only been the storks who had been learning to fly. She had too.

That first flight from Dublin to Madrid was only the beginning – the beginning that saw her wanting to conquer the world, to explore and see as much of it as she could. The exposure she got to different nationalities and cultures in Alcalá de Henares fuelled this hunger.

She hadn't any idea what she wanted to do with her life after she finished university, but she knew it was so much more than her earlier ambitions of marrying Ross and living near Dunmoy.

She still couldn't shake the feelings of betrayal and disbelief she felt whenever she remembered the cold-hearted way he had let her down. It made her feel she had been used and it wasn't a nice feeling.

As she matured, she realised she hadn't yet come to appreciate just how important friendships were, especially the ones that endured.

She didn't meet Álvaro on the campus, but dancing around the bandstand in the main square one night. He was with some students she'd got to know. They'd talked into the small hours. He'd called to the Torres the next day to apologise for keeping her out so late and assured them it wouldn't happen again. They liked Álvaro and knew of his family. Rosa immediately saw a romantic entanglement developing, but Tansy knew that wouldn't happen. She didn't see him in that light at all.

Chapter Thirteen

'I had hoped you might be coming home for Easter.'

'I wasn't planning on it, Mam,' she said, knowing her mother would have been looking forward to her return.

'I've a bit put by to cover your air fare, if that's what's stopping you.'

'You're too kind, but that's not it. I want to stay and see the Holy Week festivities.'

'I thought you saw all that before Lent, at the carnival.'

'That was different,' she explained to Peggy. 'The events for Holy Week, or *Santa Semana*, as they call it, are much bigger and more ritualistic. There are processions and parades to beat the band, and the celebrations go on for days. Apparently, there are all sorts of mysterious brotherhoods and societies here and they compete with each for the best pageantry and displays.'

'It sounds a little over the top – irreverent, even. Don't get mixed up in anything peculiar.'

Tansy rolled her eyes. That was so typical of her mother.

'I've made a simnel cake, but I didn't put the almond paste on. I thought you'd like to do that when you got back. I suppose I'll just have to finish it and send it to you for your Spanish family. Do you think they'd like it?'

'That's very thoughtful. I'm sure they'd love it.'

When she put down the phone, Tansy's conscience pricked her. For as long as she could remember, it had always been her job to shape the marzipan decorations for their Easter cake. Eleven perfectly round balls, supposedly one each for the twelve apostles minus Judas, and a single white one representing Jesus. It was yet another object of dispute between Mary McLaughlin and her mother. Mary insisted it was a cake for Mother's Day and not Easter Day and that the balls should number thirteen, Judas included. Peggy and Mary argued about this every year, and they never reached a conclusion.

Was she being selfish? Should she go home, or was her mother just doing what her mother was very good at doing – reminding her that she was her little girl no matter who she became, or wherever she was? She swung between guilt and a sense of needing to be independent. The latter was one of the driving reasons why she was here. She thought about it for a few minutes and then she did what she always did these days when she needed a second opinion. She consulted Phyllis. After a while, when she couldn't reach her, she figured she was probably doing a shift at the restaurant and sent her an email instead.

She asked Rosa.

'Of course your *madre* would like you to go home for Easter. That's natural. But she'd also like you to enjoy your experiences here, don't you think? You're not home ill, Tansy, are you? It's a long time to be away, especially for the first time.'

'Home ill? Oh, you mean homesick,' she said and she laughed

out loud. Realising her mistake, Rosa said, 'Of course I mean home sick.' And they both got a fit of the giggles.

◆

Phyllis's reply was waiting for her when she got home.

> Are you mad, woman? Stay for Easter. Squeeze every scrap of life out of it you can while you can. If I win the lottery, I'll come over and join you. The only thing that would make me tell you to come home would be the fact that we'd get your room back from your successor and that would mean no more of his beard trimmings around the taps in the bathroom and no more half-washed dishes in the sink. He seems to think that there's a fairy who comes in when we're out and does them for us. He also seems to take up much more space than you ever did! As for his choice of TV programmes, and the volume ... don't get me started ...
>
> Saw your professor today. Exchanged pleasantries. He's growing on me! Your Álvaro sounds like fun ... Those pics were great. There's no one on the scene here, although there was a really fanciable guy in the restaurant the other night, at a family celebration. He didn't ask for my number, though. I think I'm destined to be an old maid, or "an unclaimed treasure", as an old neighbour of ours used to say about the spinsters of the parish.

Tansy chuckled and read on. Phyllis liked everything tidy and tied up with ribbons. Of course there was no future with Álvaro, but it wasn't up to her to share that yet, and certainly not in an email. She was just at the end when a window popped up alerting her to an incoming message.

That warm feeling flowed over her – the one she always got when she imagined Sean at his desk writing to her.

I trust you continue to enjoy and benefit from your time abroad. I just wanted you to know I'll be in Alcalá for a few days in April.

He – Sean – was coming to Spain – to Alcalá!

I hope you'll find time to show me around when I'm there and maybe fit in a dinner with me on one of the evenings. I'll let you know more when it's been firmed up. It would be lovely to see you. My good friend, who orchestrated your place there, has asked me over to discuss a project with her. She's also extended an invitation to me to attend the Cervantes Prize-giving. You probably know more about that than I do. See you soon.
Take care.
Sean

He's coming here – and he wants to spend time with me, she thought. She felt excitement surge. Don't be ridiculous, she told herself. You can't read anything into that. Of course he'd look you up when he's here, in your university, wouldn't he? He'd do that in the line of duty. He did say he'd be delighted to see her, though. And she'd be delighted to see him.

In all her thoughts, she had never imagined that the next time they'd meet, it would be here.

Stop acting like a lovesick puppy, she told herself and laughed out loud as she realised she'd never seen a lovesick puppy or knew what one looked like. Act like a grown-up. He's just a colleague of sorts. Would he notice how she had changed, matured, even? She felt she had come a long way from the timorous girl who was physically projected into his office by Phyllis the day of her interview. She owed him a lot. He'd given her a chance even when he knew she was a fraud. And he did put his professionalism on the line to get her here ... She composed herself and replied.

> That sounds lovely. I'll gen up on Cervantes in the interim, so as not to let you down. I look forward to seeing you and filling you in on everything. I hope the current research project is going as planned and look forward to seeing you here.
> Best regards,
> Tansy

Once she'd hit 'Send', she looked up the event he'd be attending and wrote to the girls:

> Guys – newsflash. Sean's coming over here to go to some prestigious event at the university. The King will be there. He's taking me to dinner. Not the King. Sean! I would have thought that the royals coming to the university was a big deal, yet I haven't heard mention of it before now. I'm obviously moving in the wrong circles. I want news.
> Miss you all, lots.
> T xx

She knew she was in Cervantes' birthplace. She couldn't avoid that. His home was at the end of the Plaza de Cervantes, which was named in his honour, and the main meeting place in town was at his statue. There he stood decked out in frills and flounces with a quill in hand. Locals affectionately referred to it as '*El Monigote*' – the stick man.

Don't bother reading Don Quixote, girls. I'm an authority on
it now. I'd never read it and had every intention of doing so
before Sean arrived. I made the mistake of mentioning this
to my tutor, who has a remarkable resemblance to the stick
man (with a less manicured beard and pointier nose) and
immediately regretted it. He's a Cervantes nut and virtually
gave me a page-by-page summary. He never paused long
enough for me to interrupt. By the time he'd finished, I felt I
was the one who was four hundred years old.

When their timetables allowed, she spent a lot of her free time
with Álvaro. They talked about everything from politics to art,
lecturers and food to his girlfriend, Elena. She was pursuing her
studies in Philadelphia for a year, in fine art and art restoration.

The following day Tansy wrote to Sean:

I've never seen anything like it. They really go in for this Santa
Semana with an over-zealous fervour that defies description.
I found parts of it quite graphic and grotesque, almost
sinister. Some of the ornate floats were led by men, at least
I presumed they were men, togged out in white robes with
pointed hoods covering their faces – they reminded me a
bit of the Ku Klux Klan. Bands played, candles flickered, the
statues were dressed in the most elaborate costumes. It was
surreal and bizarre. But I'm glad I saw it.

Chapter Fourteen

'It's a big occasion being taken home to meet someone's family.' Rosa fussed and almost reverently added, 'Especially the Lopez-Cabellos.'

'It's not as if Álvaro's bringing home a prospective daughter-in-law,' Tansy assured her before he picked her up.

They drove for about half an hour into the countryside. The sun bathed the fields in a golden light.

He told her, 'Don't let them intimidate you. The aunties will swamp you with questions. My mother won't. You'll probably be seated next to my grandmother.' He grinned as he turned abruptly into an imposing entrance. It was flanked by a pair of tall, ornate gates with a crest in the centre of the arch above them. These opened onto a long driveway, olive trees in neat rows stretching in all directions. The house came into view and Tansy gasped when she saw it. It was a mansion.

That was her first experience of serious wealth. Old money wealth. A couple of sleek low sports cars were parked on the golden gravel alongside a variety of top-spec convertibles, and when he saw her looking at them, he said, 'They're my father's. Cars are his thing.'

The hallway was enormous, pale marble, with mirrors and family portraits in heavy gilded frames. A wide staircase with carved wooden balustrades wound its way upwards in a gentle curve and the biggest chandelier she had ever seen hung from the ceiling. Her jacket was taken by a uniformed maid, while another offered her a glass from a tray of drinks.

'I think everyone is in the drawing room,' Álvaro said, taking her hand and leading the way. 'Let's face the music!'

'I'm sure it won't be that bad. It's not the Inquisition!'

'Oh yes, it is!' He smiled. 'You're the first girl I've ever brought home for Easter lunch. You've no idea what they'll read into this. They'll think the dynasties are under threat and that I'm being unfaithful to Elena, but they'll be too polite to say that! Come on. Let's have some fun.'

It was obvious that apart from Álvaro being the heir apparent to the family name and fortune, he was much loved too. He was greeted affectionately by his parents, sisters, aunts, uncles and cousins, two of them aging priests. Tansy immediately forgot all their names.

Somewhere in the distance a gong sounded and Álvaro's father, Álvaro Senior, said, 'I hope you are enjoying your time at our university, Tansy. It is a very ancient one and our family has had a long association with it. If you have any complaints, let me know. I do have some friends in high places.' He grinned.

'Thank you, I'll remember that, but so far everything's been great and I'm really enjoying it. It's a very enriching experience in so many ways.'

'That's good. We'll talk later – now enjoy your lunch.'

Everyone and everything oozed taste, style and class. Tansy couldn't believe she was here. It was so far removed from

Dunmoy. She almost gasped when she walked through the double doors where a row of servants, capped and aproned, stood waiting to seat the guests. She figured that this room alone would have dwarfed the downstairs of her family home. There were at least twenty-four settings on the wonderfully polished table. Cut glasses glinted and the matching cutlery was polished to perfection. Tall, themed flower arrangements were spaced precisely along the centre, high enough not to impede vision or conversation flow from either side.

What followed was a succession of *tapas* and fish, fowl, game and meat and a medley of colourful dishes, some of which she recognised, others were new to her. All were paired with wines from the family vineyards.

◆

'This lamb is lovely and tender, Peggy,' Mary McLaughlin said, helping herself to a second plateful. She always came to the Nugents' for Easter lunch. She and Peggy were distantly related and Peggy could never bear to think of anyone being alone at Christmas or Easter.

'You're right there, Mary. You can't beat a bit of spring lamb and mint sauce. I wonder if they're having that over there in Spain with their peculiar traditions and foreign food.'

'Probably not,' she replied.

'You'd miss Gappy Jim all the same, wouldn't you, Pat? He was very partial to a bit of lamb,' Peggy said to her husband. 'Little did we think last year ...'

'I was just thinking the same thing myself,' he replied.

On the sideboard beside a vase of nearly opened daffodils, the first to appear in the yard, stood the traditional simnel cake that Peggy had decorated with the customary twelve marzipan balls.

At least that was the same as last year.

◆

Tansy was amazed at how long the lunch lasted. It went on for hours and the noise level increased as time went by.

'That was quite an experience,' she told Álvaro later. 'Your father wasn't at all what I expected. I thought he would be stern and autocratic, but he was exactly the opposite. But I did find your grandmother a bit intimidating.'

'She has that effect on most people. She's used to getting her own way and she usually does, because it's easier just to give in to her.'

'I like Elena's father. It's a pity she couldn't be here. I'm dying to meet her.'

'And she, you.'

'Do you see yourself taking over the family businesses?'

'In the future, yes. I've been brought up knowing where my duty lies. My family is set in tradition. They lined up Elena for me when we were in our prams. That was, of course, before they knew I was gay.'

'Does she have any say in the matter? Doesn't she mind about that?' She thought that sounded crass and said, 'Sorry, Álvaro, that's very impertinent of me. I didn't mean to …'

'It's OK. She knows the score. Has done for a long time. It's different with our families. It's never openly discussed. In Spain, we are still very good at hiding certain things – things that are considered unsavoury. Legally, homosexuality isn't a crime, but culturally we're still a very macho culture. It's going to take some time before most parents – fathers and grandfathers, in particular – will openly discuss having a gay son or grandson. But that's changing. Being seriously rich has its responsibilities and marrying well is one of them. Elena knows we'll be expected to have children and if she has affairs, they have to be discreet. As will mine.'

'I'm not sure how I'd deal with that. I thought arranged marriages were a thing of the past in this part of the world.'

'Admittedly, they're not common any more but they're not as unusual as you might think.'

'But is it legal if you're forced into it?' she enquired.

'But we're not being forced into it. We both consent. Elena knows what she's signing up for – respectability, position and security for the sake of her family. There are no males to take over their winery and vineyards and her father has been letting things slip as he's got older. This way the *bodega* will be returned to full efficiency, jobs will be secured and the name will continue.'

'And what will you get?' she asked.

'All of the above and a beautiful wife, hopefully children and the knowledge that I'm providing a future for my family and the estate workers too.'

Tansy hesitated before continuing. 'Can I ask – do you like each other?'

He laughed. 'Actually, we do, very much as it happens, and we have a lot in common – friends, interests, lifestyles. Psychologists say those things are more important and more enduring in a relationship than lust and physical attraction, although Elena is a beauty too. I've got my business and law degrees, and will finish my master's in the autumn, and when my father wants to retire, as the only son, I'll be ready to step into his shoes.'

'What if you refused?'

'I won't.'

'I still think I'd like to marry for love.'

'There are many kinds of love, Tansy, and it's not as though I'm going to be catapulted into a terrible existence, is it? It's a pretty good life and it's one of enormous privilege, so I'll be a dutiful son and husband, as is expected of me.'

She smiled. 'When you put it like that, I can see where you're coming from.' She leaned over and kissed him on the cheek. 'You're a good guy, Álvaro. That's far more important than anything else.'

'Not everyone is like you, *querida*,' he replied. 'I can't wait for you to meet Elena. I know you'll get on. And it's wonderful being able to open up to someone like this.'

'That's what friends are for,' she replied. 'And mine back home are going to be so jealous when I tell them about today. Thank you for inviting me. It was wonderful, and so were your family.'

Vineyards and mansions in Spain to a small holding in Galway and a shared flat in Rathmines – their worlds were poles apart, yet in Álvaro she felt she had found an unlikely kindred spirit.

◆

In Rathmines, the new flatmate sat staring at his laptop.

'You're hogging the only hotspot in the flat,' said Mags. 'Are you going to sit there cogitating all night? Because I need to go online.'

'So do I,' said Phyllis. 'You know the rules.'

'Indeed I do. Because you keep telling me. I'll be another half hour – less if you'd stop wittering on about this Tansy bird and let me get on with it.'

The girls looked at each other and Mags nodded in the direction of her bedroom. They left him in peace.

'"This Tansy bird" – I ask you. She'd put him in his box if she were here.'

'He's winding you up, Phyllis, because you made him clean the bathroom earlier. Don't let him get to you.'

'I'm sorry. But I'm a bit down in the dumps. There's you with Trevor, happy and in love. There's Gina already making plans for the summer to go au pairing again, and as for Tansy, well you can see her star is in the ascendant – the rapidly ascendant. I just don't seem to have any focus any more.'

'Maybe you're working too hard. Drop a shift or two at the restaurant and we'll have a night out.'

'I have to get my degree. I can't afford to repeat. Don't get me wrong, Mags, I'm delighted for Tansy, I really am, but a little bit of me is jealous. Is that a terrible admission to make? At the moment, everything she touches seems charmed.'

'I think it would be abnormal if you weren't just the teeniest bit envious. I know I am when I read about how and what she's doing. Don't get me wrong. I love Trevor, but he's so focussed, it drives me mad sometimes. When he's in study mode, there's no distracting him and he's quite happy to stay there until he's achieved his goals. I have to practically bulldoze him to take time off, and when he does, it's magical and it's worth the wait.'

'I suppose we're all different.'

'You can say that again, Phyllis.'

A loud knock, followed by 'I've finished', ended their chat and Phyllis suddenly felt much better.

Chapter Fifteen

Sean Pollard was at his desk as usual at 7 a.m. He liked to get a head start on the day and answer his mails without interruption. He checked the time again. It was 7.15 – 8.15 in Spain. He would wait another fifteen minutes before calling Tansy. There was something about her that appealed to him, something he could never quite put a name to. He was intrigued by her. Was it her curiosity about life, her genuine interest in everything, the way she wanted to embrace new experiences, or the fact that she was out of bounds? He couldn't say, but whatever it was, he found her beguiling.

He picked up his phone and dialled.

'Hi, Tansy, I just thought I'd touch base. It's less impersonal than mailing. As I told you, I'm going to be in town for a few days next week.'

'And I'm looking forward to seeing you,' she told him.

'I just wanted to let you know that I'll be tied up on the first of these with meetings, etc., and on the second with the award ceremony.'

'Oh, what a pity. My hosts, Rosa and Pedro, have been looking forward to meeting you.'

Was that disappointment he heard in her voice?

'They sound like lovely people – of course I'll make time to meet them. Tell them I'm looking forward to that too.'

'They'll be delighted.'

'I'm hiring a car for the duration and thought if you'd like to bunk off on Friday, we could do a bit of sightseeing together, that is if you don't have anything more exciting in your diary. Chalk it up to cultural experiences.'

'That sounds wonderful,' she replied.

'As I'm partly responsible for you being there, I can't let you spend six months in Spain and not visit the Prado and the Reina Sofía museum to see Picasso's *Guernica*. That would be like going to Paris and missing the Eiffel Tower, the Louvre and the *Mona Lisa*.'

She laughed.

'That sounds wonderful, Sean. I was planning on spending a few days in Madrid before I come home, but I'm still hoping a summer job will materialise here so I've held off on making any arrangements yet.'

'Don't commit to any job before you check the average summer temperatures. It's insufferably hot in Madrid and most unpleasant. Try to find a placement on the coast somewhere,' he advised.

'That never entered my head,' she replied.

'Well, I'm glad to be of some use. Now I'd better get back to work. I'll ring you when I arrive.'

'Take care,' she said.

'You too.' And he pressed 'End call', beginning to look forward to this trip.

◆

Tansy may not have heard much about the royals' annual visit previously, but suddenly the college was buzzing in preparation. The gardens and planters were being tidied and watered, the windows cleaned and the paintwork refreshed. This Cervantes Prize was universally rated, but for Tansy it was the arrival of Sean that was foremost in her mind. His phone call had further ignited her excitement at his impending visit. When he had rung off, she thought, if she was like this after hearing his voice, what would she be like when she saw him?

Later that day she was surprised to be summoned to the Dean's office. There was another woman there whom Tansy had seen around campus.

'I'm sure you're wondering why I sent for you.' The Dean smiled at her.

'I am. I hope I haven't fallen behind on my assignments.'

'On the contrary, you've been doing very well, exceptionally well, in fact, which is why we wanted to talk to you.' She nodded in the direction of a stunningly beautiful woman with glossy black hair and amazing green eyes. She reminded Tansy of an exotic animal, a big cat. 'Professor Cortez here oversees the Cervantes Prize ceremony, and after some discussion we thought you might like to come along on the day. Not to the actual solemn ceremony in the Paraninfo, you understand. That's reserved for previous winners, invited guests and academics, but each year the royals meet a group of selected students. We thought it might add to your experiences here to be included among those.'

'Wow. Me? Of course. I'd be honoured. Thank you.'

'It's always a notable occasion. I'm sure you'll enjoy it,' Professor Cortez said. 'And it will be a nice memory for you to take back to Ireland.'

'There's no doubt about that. One of the professors from my university is attending the actual event.' They nodded at each other. This was obviously not news to them and Tansy wondered if it was Professor Cortez whom Sean had contacted to get Tansy her placement there. He had never mentioned a name, nor had she asked. Had he something to do with this unexpected invite too?

'What do I wear?' she asked, laughing and feeling foolish. 'I've never met royalty before.'

Professor Cortez handed her a printed sheet. 'You'll find all you need to know on this. Just don't be late.'

'Oh, I won't be,' she assured them.

As soon as she could, she phoned her mother.

'Is everything all right? You don't usually ring at this time,' Peggy asked when she heard Tansy's voice on the line.

'Couldn't be better, Mam. I've something to tell you that you can boast about to Mary McLaughlin, and to everyone else in Dunmoy. I'm going to meet the King and Queen!'

She had to hold the receiver away from her head as Peggy responded.

'My God. Are you serious? Why? When is this happening?'

She explained.

'Twenty-third of April. It's on the same date every year.'

◆

Phyllis's delight was almost as feverish as Peggy's had been.

I've just turned a delicate shade of pea green with envy. Hobnobbing first with the aristocracy and now with royalty. Is there no stopping you? As regards what to wear, Tans, what about one of Mags's dresses that I made you pack – the black and white stripe that you said was too posh for you? That's elegant and sophisticated and shows off your waist. (Don't forget to take the label off it!) Or that lovely lemony one with the sash that you thought was too demure.

She had forgotten all about the dresses Phyllis mentioned. When she had first arrived, she had put them on hangers at the back of the cavernous wardrobe. They were still in their zip-up bags. She had considered them too stylish for her and was sure she'd never have any occasion to wear them. She decided to take them out and have another look.

While unzipping one of the bags, she heard Rosa come home. Still holding on to it, she ran down the stairs to share her news.

'But that's such an honour. Have you told your *madre* yet? She'll be delighted.'

'I did and she is!'

'Have you got something to wear already?' she asked, eyeing the bag.

'I'm not sure. Maybe you could help me decide.'

They went to her bedroom and she showed Rosa the options.

'Put them on and let me look.'

After she had changed, the black and white got a 'Perfect'.

'Now let me see the other one.'

When Tansy had tried on the lemon dress, Rosa said, 'You could wear either. Let's see about accessories before deciding. Pedro tells me I have enough bags and shoes to open a shop.'

And she had. They mixed and matched and ended up with two complete outfits before agreeing.

'Definitely the first one is the best for the big occasion. Keep the other one for your dinner with your professor.'

♦

Yes, Gina, I feel a bit like Cinderella being prepared for the ball. And you were so right about those dresses, P., Mags, don't throw anything away, ever. I'll take all your cast-offs and impulse buys from now on. I actually look and feel nice in them. I think I was born for this high life.

Mags, how's Trevor? Delighted things are still going well there. Have you managed to put manners on you-know-who, or are you still finding pizza boxes on the drainer and beard stubble in the sink?

Luv you all. xxx

Chapter Sixteen

'Just wanted to let you know I'm here,' were Sean's opening words when he rang Tansy. 'I'm at my hotel but am committed to a faculty dinner this evening.'

He was here. She couldn't help grinning as she heard his voice. She had been waiting for this minute for what seemed like hours.

'It's lovely to hear from you.'

'I'm looking forward to seeing you in the morning, and hearing all about your adventures.'

'That'll take all of five minutes,' she said, laughing.

'Then we'll have to find something else to talk about, won't we?'

She slept restlessly, with a headiness she hadn't experienced before, feeling a sense of excited anticipation knowing he was close by. Dressed and breakfasted, she watched the big clock in Rosa's kitchen crawl its way slowly to ten o'clock. Seconds after it had chimed, the doorbell sounded and she had to stop herself jumping up to answer it. Sean was here, on her doorstep, in Spain. They embraced and she kissed him on both cheeks. 'The Spanish way,' she said and laughed.

'Well, you look as though it's agreeing with you, Tansy,' he said, hugging her warmly, then holding her away from him and looking at her closely. She didn't want him to let go.

'You don't look so bad yourself,' she said. She'd forgotten the effect that great smile of his had on her. Rosa and Pedro hovered and she made the introductions. Tansy was amused at how like Peggy Rosa was, fussing over him.

'It's a big day for Tansy.'

'And for me too, I assure you. Invitations to events like this don't land on my desk often either,' Sean said.

While he talked to Rosa and Pedro, she had the chance to study him. He certainly looked very distinguished, togged out in an impeccably cut grey suit, crisp shirt, silk tie and handkerchief with a yellow and grey geometric pattern. She had deliberately dressed casually with her hair tied back. It would be a while before she had to go and glam up and that was exactly what she was planning to do. She'd show Sean Pollard there was another side to her.

'Tansy tells me you've made her very welcome here.'

Before anyone could say anything, the doorbell rang again. Tansy took delivery of an enormous bouquet of flowers. There was a little box and a card tied to it with a matching ribbon.

Again, Rosa fussed as the men looked on. Tansy opened the crested envelope and read 'A little memento of this special day. Enjoy it. Much love, Álvaro xxx'.

'Isn't that thoughtful of him?' she said to no one in particular. She opened the little velvet box and found an intricately crafted silver chain with a disc attached, nestling there. This was engraved with an image of the Cervantes stick man statue in the square.

'I'm overwhelmed,' she said in English and laughed. 'I can't even think of the word in Spanish now. I'm so emotional. It's really beautiful. I'll wear it today.'

'From a secret admirer?' asked Sean. Did she detect a little hint of something there or was that wishful thinking on her part?

'Secret? I don't think I'd call him that exactly,' she said, giving nothing away. He drank a coffee before he left. She told him as she walked him to the door, 'I'm so happy you're here today, Sean, because only for you, I wouldn't be.'

◆

'You never told us he was so handsome,' Rosa said. 'He's very congenial, although I don't think he was too impressed by Álvaro's contribution to the occasion.'

'Really?' Tansy replied, trying to sound indifferent, but secretly thinking she couldn't have orchestrated that surprise better if she had planned it herself. She hoped it had made him feel the tiniest bit jealous. No! She wanted him to be insanely jealous – the way she was when she thought of him being with anyone.

She had hardly recognised herself in the mirror in Mags's black and white striped dress, black patent pumps with tortoiseshell buckles and a matching clutch that Rosa had loaned her. The new silver necklet shone where it caught the light. She had let her hair fall softly to her shoulders, catching one side back with a tortoiseshell clip. She wasn't sure about the shorter length when she'd first got it cut, but now she loved it. She came down the stairs with newfound confidence.

'Has this elegant and sophisticated butterfly been hiding in my house?' Pedro asked.

'Perfectly beautiful,' said Rosa.

Tansy hardly recognised her peers either, all spruced and polished as they waited, talking and laughing nervously. The award ceremony over, two liveried pages in crested tunics and velvet plumed hats opened the closed doors. The royals and a procession of dignitaries followed. Then Tansy and four others who had been chosen for presentation were beckoned.

Professor Cortez did the formalities. Again she reminded Tansy of an exotic cat. She looked very regal in a moss green dress that matched her eyes perfectly. After shaking hands, each student had a few minutes of private conversation with both King and Queen. Tansy was oblivious to the cameras clicking, but was totally aware that Sean Pollard was somewhere among the assembly in the courtyard, watching her. She sensed his eyes on her and turned to see him at the edge of the crowd. He raised his glass a little and smiled. She smiled back, ridiculously delighted to have someone with whom to share this special moment. No, not someone. Him.

'I was so nervous.'

'It certainly didn't show. You look really stunning, by the way, and as relaxed as though you were born to it.'

'You must be used to this sort of thing.'

'Nothing quite so glamorous. Let me get you a glass of something. Bubbles or flat?' he'd asked as a waiter juggled a tray through the throng.

'I think it has to be bubbles.'

'I absolutely agree.' He handed her a glass, clinked his with hers and toasted, 'To us.'

'To us,' she echoed.

'Did the occasion and the royals live up to expectations?'

a voice sounded from behind her. She turned and saw it was Álvaro's father.

'Oh, hello. Yes, it surpassed all of them.'

'And they looked as though they were enjoying meeting you too,' he replied.

'You flatter me. And I'm so excited, I've forgotten my manners. Have you two met? This is my friend Álvaro's father, Álvaro Lopez-Cabellos Senior, and this is Professor Sean Pollard from my university in Dublin.'

'We have met. We were actually chatting inside earlier, but I didn't realise that you knew each other,' said Sean.

'It's a curious old world, full of coincidences. I'll leave you to enjoy the rest of the day,' he said. 'What a pity you're here for such a short visit, Professor. We could have had lunch together. Nice to see you, Tansy, and you look wonderful. Do come and visit us again soon.' They shook hands and he went to mingle.

'Do you know who he is?' Sean asked.

'Of course I do. He's Álvaro's father, moneyed and very influential.'

'He's also the Marqués, after whom the new modern languages buildings here are to be named. His family paid for much of the restoration of the Archiepiscopal Palace of Alcalá de Henares, which suffered a disastrous fire in 1939, during the Spanish Civil War. The King mentioned him in his speech earlier.'

'I'd no idea.'

'I'm honoured you're still talking to an ordinary mortal like me,' he teased.

'I always imagined – no, that's a lie. I never imagined any of it, because I never, ever in my wildest dreams saw myself knowing a Marqués, or actually talking to a King and Queen of anywhere. They are all so nice and ordinary.'

'Are you free for the rest of the day, or do you have plans with your Álvaro?'

'No. No plans at all,' she answered, deliberately ignoring 'your Álvaro'.

'Then maybe you'll do me the honour of coming down off that cloud and sharing your time with me.'

Her – do him the honour! This day was just getting better and better.

She'd stay on the cloud for as long as she possibly could.

Chapter Seventeen

En route in his car they discussed her course and his work, and she felt elated to be with him again. She'd forgotten just how stimulating and hypnotic she found him. And how attractive and at ease he seemed to be in any situation. He removed his tie and jacket and tossed them onto the back seat.

'My good friend Ernest sends you his kind regards. I believe Trevor and your friend Mags are quite tight.'

'That's right, ever since they met at that lecture of yours in Dublin Castle.'

'I get blamed for everything.' He laughed. There was a pause, which she didn't feel the need to fill. She would have been happy to have driven around all day with him.

'This Álvaro, is he your boyfriend?'

'No, he's not.'

'Is that because the horse man back home is waiting for you, or because you just don't fancy him? If I were a betting man, I'd say the guy with the title would win hands down.'

That jolted her. She had never told him how things had ended with Ross and she didn't want to spoil the day by talking about that. He looked over at her, waiting for an answer. She didn't give him one.

'Have I said the wrong thing?'

'You seem to make a habit of getting me into your car and feeling that, because I am a captive audience, you can say what you like about my life. Is it just me, or do you do that with everyone? Whichever it is, it's not a nice trait, Professor,' she said.

He laughed out loud. 'Well, that's a new insight into my character.'

'I'm glad you find it amusing, because it has the opposite effect on me. What right do you have to make pronouncements on my friends and associates while you sit there giving away nothing about yourself or your relationships?'

Why did he have to ruin a perfect day? Why do his opinions matter so much to me?

'*Touché*. I stand chastised. I was just interested. Feel free to ask me anything you want and I'll give you an honest answer.'

She waited a few minutes before turning towards him and saying, 'OK, so tell me, have you a wife and/or a family? If not, are you in a relationship with anyone now? Are your parents alive? Have you ever —'

'Whoa there. One question at a time and then you'll answer mine. Deal?'

She nodded. She wanted to ask if he'd ever had relationships with any of his students, or his research assistants.

'I don't have a wife or children. I was married, briefly, a long time ago.'

That wasn't what she had expected to hear. She didn't know what to say.

'I fathered a baby, a premature little boy. He hadn't a hope of survival. He only lived for a couple of hours. We called him Ivan Peter.'

'Oh Sean, I'm so sorry. I shouldn't have asked. It was none of my business.' Her voice had caught and he put his hand over hers and squeezed it to comfort her. It was as if an electric current had connected the two of them and coursed through her.

'I want to tell you, Tansy, I married the mother, who was one of my students, but after we lost our baby that was annulled. She later moved to Canada and we don't have contact any more.'

'I really am sorry for intruding on your privacy.' She had put her other hand over his. 'You needn't say any more.' That little gesture closed the gap between them – both in rank and in the nature of their relationship.

'Don't be upset. I asked for it. Sometimes I fall short on the social graces. It comes from living alone, I think.' He withdrew his hand to change gears as they rounded a bend.

'I was pressured into "doing the right thing" and get married for respectability's sake. If Ivan had survived, I'm not sure whether we would have stayed married. Probably not. None of it should ever have happened. It was after a wild party up at the Hell Fire Club on Halloween and I don't honestly think we'd ever met more than three or four times before that. I didn't see her again until she told me she was pregnant.'

'That must have been a very tough time.'

'It was. Her family, naturally enough, were furious. And to top it all, she flunked her end-of-year exams that summer and dropped out. My parents didn't hold back either. Their only son, whom they'd waited for years to arrive, had let them down and disgraced the family name.'

'You didn't turn out too badly in the end, did you?' She smiled at him. He took her hand again. It seemed the most natural thing in the world. It felt safe somehow, a gesture of trust between them.

'That's a matter of conjecture. It still comes back to haunt me occasionally. It's hard to shrug off a reputation in a small community and that's exactly what a university is – it's like a small town where memories are long and tongues sharp. If the baby had survived, no one would have paid any attention to us, but because of the tragedy it became very public.

'And that brings me to your next question. Am I in a relationship? No, not currently. I suppose I'm not really good material for relationships. I tend to get too immersed in my work. What was next? Oh yes, are my parents still alive? My father died some years ago, but my mother is still very much alive. She's a formidable woman, with an iron will and a very judgemental nature. I've always fallen short of her expectations.'

'I'm sure that's not true. She must be very proud of you, your successful career, your books, your awards.'

'But not at my failure in finding a suitable wife, or in the non-provision of grandchildren. No. I'm afraid I'm still being measured and falling short.'

'Aren't you very hard on yourself?'

'I don't beat myself up over it, but you haven't met my mother. She has this knack of making me feel like a naughty child, her naughty child, no matter what I do. Now that I'm in my forties, you'd think I'd have gotten over that, wouldn't you?'

'You don't look that old.'

'Being in your forties is not *old*!' He laughed.

She realised that she never thought much about his age, and now that she did, it didn't seem to matter at all.

'I'm not sure if it's possible for our parents ever to see us as grown-up. Maybe it's just that they're not capable of seeing us as others do. We're always their unfinished works, still needing a bit of honing and refinement,' Tansy said. 'Or maybe we're just incapable of behaving normally around them and we still try to be what we feel they expect. What do you think?'

'I think, Tansy Nugent, that's very profound, from one as *young* as you. You really have grown up. But you may have a point or two. Now, is there anything else you'd like to know? Because I think I've answered everything.'

Lots, she thought. I'd like to know lots more about you, but she shook her head.

'Then it's your turn. How is the horse man dealing with your being away for so long?'

'I have no idea.' She filled him in on what had happened between them.

'The little bastard. And I agree with your mother. You deserve better than the likes of him.'

'Maybe not. Maybe he's just doing exactly what I am – finding myself and my place in the world. He could have handled it better, though!'

'I agree with you there. And this Álvaro of the silver necklet. Is that serious?'

'No, we're just friends, very good, genuine friends. That was him being his kind and thoughtful self,' she answered, reaching up to feel the chunky silver disc at her neck.

'Good. So, I'm not treading on anyone's toes by monopolising your time over these few days?'

'Would it matter if you were?'

'That sounds like a challenge, and no it wouldn't!' He laughed.

'I'm indebted to you, kind sir. Now, where are we going exactly?'

'You'll see. I hope you'll find this as interesting as I do. During the Spanish Civil War, a group of families moved into the cellars of the old castle in the hills over there.' He pointed to some sprawling ruins in the uneven landscape ahead of them. 'They survived there practically in darkness and in appalling conditions for almost three years while Franco's republicans waged their reign of terror all over the country.'

'It sounds horrific.'

'It was, but what makes this so interesting is that these people were on opposing sides, yet they put their differences aside for their survival. They lived and pulled together to get through and to give their children some hope and a future.'

'I know very little about that time,' she confessed.

'I don't want to bore you.'

'Bore me!'

'This is what brought me to Alcalá. The survival rate was higher than in other places, because of this phenomenon. That whetted my appetite and now it seems that a lot of papers and photos have been unearthed and donated to the university and they're interested in doing some further studies on these people.'

'And they want some input from you?'

'That's the plan. What interests me is what traits, if any, made some groups work together like these, hanging in there, while others just surrendered or joined the oppressors to survive, slaughter or be slaughtered.'

'You won't find out much in an afternoon, will you?'

'No, but I will get an idea of the geography and a sense of place. If I agree to working on their research, it could mean coming over, possibly for an extended period of time.'

'But wouldn't that affect your PhD students and your undergraduates?'

'Not at all. Wheels don't turn that quickly in academia. This project is only at the embryonic stage right now.'

A little further along, he said, 'This looks like the place', slowing as they drove through a sleepy medieval village where red geraniums added bursts of colour to the dusty streets. A white-haired old woman, dressed completely in black, sat watching them from the seat outside her house as Sean reversed into a parking space. She smiled a gummy smile and gave directions when he asked her where he would find the town hall. He stooped down and took her gnarled hand and kissed it. She beamed toothlessly back at him. He had made her day.

And that was the moment that for some reason Tansy's mind captured with the clarity of a camera – an image that would remain true in colour and essence and never fade. Sean, tall, debonair and charismatic, in a town somewhere in Spain, whose name she didn't know then, charming a nameless, toothless old woman.

Tansy stumbled on the uneven cobbles as they walked away and she inwardly cursed her high heels. So much for trying to look cool and sophisticated. He took her hand to steady her and didn't release it when she regained her balance. She liked this feeling of being cherished.

'I didn't know you spoke Spanish,' Tansy said.

'That wasn't on your list of questions, was it?' he asked,

grinning at her before adding, 'There are lots of things you don't know about me, Tansy Nugent. Nor I about you.'

That was true. There were. Lots of them, and she wanted to know the answers to every single one of them. She was definitely beginning to sense that the attraction was not as one-sided as she had thought.

Chapter Eighteen

Later, when they were driving back to Alcalá, he said, 'I've really enjoyed spending this time with you, Tansy.' She knew he meant it. The barriers had come down. 'I've booked a table for dinner at my hotel, although I didn't know if you'd be free or even want to join me.'

For a second, she wondered if he had someone else lined up to be his companion if she hadn't been free.

'It's a *parador*, and it just happens to have one of the best restaurants in the city. It's within walking distance of your house, so we can both enjoy a glass or two of wine without having to worry about getting home safely.'

Once inside, he asked if she'd like to freshen up. He led the way. There was a life-sized statue of the Virgin Mary in the corridor by his door.

'I wasn't expecting that!' she said and laughed on seeing it.

'These *paradores* were all former convents, monasteries and castles that have been turned into luxurious hotels. There are no prizes for guessing what this one was.' Behind the bed hung a giant tapestry showing nuns working in a garden. 'I'm not sure if they are there to keep me chaste, to protect me while I sleep or to cover up crumbling plasterwork!'

The room was quiet, so quiet she could hear his breathing and her own. They stood there for an awkward moment. He seemed to be about to say something but changed his mind.

'I'll leave you to it. I'll see you downstairs in the bar.'

She found him in what had formerly been a cloister. It was now covered by glass and divided up into more intimate spaces by oversized terracotta pots. Some giant ferns bowed towards each other, mimicking the graceful arches in the architecture.

'It's like an old Hollywood movie set with these statues and religious paintings, especially here in the bar.'

'There's nothing fake about them. They're the genuine article.'

'Would you mind if I sent a picture to my mother? She'll never believe such places exist.'

The waiter offered to take it and snapped the pair of them, Sean with his arm draped casually behind her shoulders, a glass of bubbles in his other hand.

'I don't recognise half the things on the menu,' she told him when they were seated at their table.

'That's because these places specialise in traditional dishes with local ingredients.'

The food didn't disappoint and, as she waited for their coffees, she reached out and stroked the velvety petals of one of the flowers in the little centrepiece.

'Aren't they flawless? I can never remember what they're called, though.'

'They're gerberas, from the daisy family. The Egyptians believe they are happiness flowers.'

'I can see why. They make you want to smile.' Tansy had

never been as happy in her life. She didn't want the day to end, but nature was fighting her on this and it was winning.

'I can call a taxi, if you'd like,' he said.

'Can we walk? I love the way the city comes alive at night.'

'I'll be honoured to be seen with you on my arm.'

'I think you've had too much wine.' She had laughed as they'd linked one another and set off.

She thanked him again at the door of the Torres' house and he stepped closer and gave her a goodnight kiss. She was acutely aware of his warm breath, the smell of wine and a familiar woody-scented aftershave. Neither moved for what seemed like several minutes. He brushed his lips against her cheek, pulled away and said, 'Get your beauty sleep, Tansy. I'll see you in the morning.'

She hadn't imagined that. She knew that whatever she had felt, or thought she had felt on other occasions, something tangible had definitely just happened between them. It was the same thing she'd sensed that day he'd come into her office and sat on her desk the summer before. *Get a grip, girl*, she told herself. *I must have had too much to drink*. She went in, closing the door quietly, not wanting to disturb Rosa and Pedro.

She hadn't phoned her mother to report on her encounter with the royals, or Álvaro, as she had promised to do, and she had no intention of emailing her friends tonight. There was too much to think about. She just wanted to get into bed and reflect on every single thing that had happened that day. Their intimate revelations in the car, the hand holding, the awkwardness in his hotel room. And their goodnight embrace.

Chapter Nineteen

By the time Sean came to collect her the next morning, she had phoned home, providing all the details her mother needed to know to impress Mary McLaughlin and her other cronies: what she had worn; what the Queen had worn; what she had said. Had she really spoken to the King too? Had she any photos?

She'd talked to Álvaro, thanked him again for his gifts, and told him how she had felt so privileged to have been part of the university's special event and about her outing with Sean afterwards. She'd told him she was wearing the necklace.

'I'm so glad you like it. Enjoy Madrid and the Prado and you can tell me all about it when we meet.'

'I'll look forward to that,' she answered, and she really meant it.

With those two things ticked off her list, she set about writing a very sketchy synopsis of the royal event and emailed it to Phyllis.

Amazing day, spoiled rotten by two good-looking men – and that doesn't include His Majesty! Felt like a princess in your dress, Mags, the b/w one. Chatted to my new best friends, the King and Queen. Drank champers (cava). Spent the rest of the day driving around the countryside with Sean, who loves my 'new look'. Almost came to blows with him in the car. Do I hear you say, 'So what's new?' Sorted that out. Told him what happened with Ross. Had dinner together afterwards at his hotel. Took me to his room to show me his tapestry!! Off to the Prado with him shortly.

Xxx

She checked herself out in the full-length mirror in her room for the umpteenth time. She was wearing tight denims, which seemed to elongate her legs, a crisp white shirt and a pale blue sweater draped around her shoulders. Sean arrived just then. He was more casually dressed today, chinos and a soft leather jacket. Noticing the inspection, he said, 'Well, do I pass?'

She flushed. 'I'm sorry, yes, of course you do. I didn't mean to be so rude.'

'I'd pass you too. In fact, I'd give you a straight A. You look very grown-up and classy. Now let's hit the road. I have tickets booked for twelve-thirty, but thought we could have a stroll around the Retiro Gardens before that, and maybe grab a coffee somewhere first.'

On arriving in Madrid, they parked the car and walked towards the Crystal Palace, along an avenue of statues, the trees showing off their delicate blossoms. New leaves were about to burst open and provide shade from the unrelenting sun of the months to come. Others had already shed their pink blossom petals and two gardeners were busily sweeping these into little piles and scooping them up. She wanted to tell them to leave them there – they looked too pretty to disturb.

She took out her phone.

'Another Kodak moment?' he teased.

'Phyllis insists – she's living my Erasmus semesters by proxy.'

'Let's send her a selfie and see what she makes of that,' he suggested.

'You must find me very gauche. You know this is the first capital city I've been to apart from Dublin,' she told him. 'And I want to see loads more. I can never understand why some people keep going back to the same place again and again for holidays, even at home, instead of trying somewhere else.'

'Now that would make an interesting research topic. It probably has something to do with a fear of stepping outside their comfort zone.'

Tansy enjoyed listening to his theories, the musicality of his voice and the diversity of his knowledge.

'This place is vast. I'd no idea. And the queues …' she said as they approached the Prado.

'Wait until you get inside.'

'We had a print of that in our school, and although it always gripped my attention then, it doesn't compare with seeing it in reality,' she remarked, after standing for ages studying Velásquez's *Las Meninas* or 'Maids of Honour'.

'I love the richness of colour and textures and the way the light falls on the little princess. It's magical.'

'Let's see what you think of the Goyas, then,' he said.

She studied each one intently and pronounced, 'Not much. I find them too dark and sombre, disturbing almost.'

'Let me show you something else of his that'll make you change your mind,' he said, leading her to the *Clothed Maiden*. This had quite a crowd around. Beside it was Goya's other version

– *Unclothed Maiden*. Their guide told them their original owner, a mayor of the city, had hung them both in his house, one on top of the other. That way he could change them over by means of a pulley mechanism whenever he wanted to conceal the nude.

'Clever old fox,' Sean remarked, standing close beside her. 'They are stunning, though, aren't they?'

'They are, intriguing and rather beautiful and very different in mood,' she told him. The more aware she was of him, the more uncomfortable she felt with the subject matter, though. What was he thinking? The naked model reclining, unabashed, on her frilled pillows seemed to be gazing right at her, defiantly. Tansy turned and moved in the direction of the next room.

'I never expected there'd be so many people here,' she said.

'If you've seen enough, we can leave.'

'Oh, I have to see the Picassos, even though I really don't get him.' She wished she'd been a bit more grown-up. How did others react to looking at nudes for the first time with someone about whom they were having the most unexpected thoughts? She didn't know. Perhaps he was having them too. Surely there must be an etiquette for that somewhere.

'They're not here,' he explained. 'They're in another museum dedicated solely to twentieth-century art. I didn't book that because I thought you might be galleried out by now. We could finish up here, have a bite of lunch and see what the queues are like, if you still have the stamina then.'

They went to a small café he knew at the back of a *charcutería*. She was mesmerised. Cured legs of ham and hindquarters hung from the rafters on hooks. Festooned behind the counters were garlands of countless varieties of sausage, their pungent garlicky smells permeating throughout.

The waiter kept replacing their dishes with more until she couldn't eat another morsel.

'You haven't tasted these *pimiento* olives,' Sean said. 'They're really good.' He took one from the little dish and held it up to her mouth. She opened it and bit into the salty flesh, and as she did so he looked her straight in the eye. Could this moment of intimacy mean he returned her feelings? She couldn't say why, but she knew for certain he did. She felt he was looking right into her soul, reading her thoughts. She couldn't hold his gaze and looked away. He said nothing.

What was wrong with her? Had she really become one of those silly students who'd developed a crush on her teacher? Who fantasised about him and who would contrive 'accidental' meetings just to get a smile in return? Yes. She had. On more than one occasion last term she had found herself walking up and down Grafton Street at lunchtime in the hope of a chance encounter with him, either on his way to or back from his daily stroll through St Stephen's Green. It hadn't happened, though.

But that had changed. She had changed and so had he.

What she hadn't expected was this well of emotions to bubble up and consume her. She definitely had very adult feelings for this man who was much too old for her. She'd be twenty-one in the summer. Who are you kidding? You're still twenty! Over twenty years of an age gap. That's insane, she told herself. Once he leaves, you can bury these notions about seeing him in that light.

But it was too late for that. She had already fallen for him. Sometimes when he looked at her a certain way, she knew he was having the same thoughts. It was as though, without any warning, there was a force that triggered an inexplicable current between them. Something that was completely out of her control and that she knew, no matter how strong it was, could have no future.

'You're miles away, Tansy. What are you thinking?' he asked.

'Just that I love it here,' she lied. 'You've shown me such a lot in a short space of time, but instead of feeling I've learned so much, it's made me realise how much I don't know.'

'Don't think of it like that. You've just had your curiosity awakened and you have years ahead of you to satisfy it. Are you still up for queueing for the Picassos, or are you tired out?'

'Let's give it a try.'

They walked the short distance to the Reina Sofía museum and found that they had avoided the earlier rush. They stood in a short queue and joined a tour.

◆

As the guide started explaining the story of Picasso's *Guernica*, Sean found himself engrossed in watching Tansy. She had remarked that she always thought this work was overrated and decidedly uninspiring. Now he watched as she became absorbed in it. He could sense that she suddenly got this artist; got where he was coming from and what he was trying to tell the world in this painting. He could see that she was feeling the fear of the people and of the bulls and the horses as the German bombs had rained down on a village going about its market-day business, destroying everything in their range.

He was watching a young student become a young woman in front of his eyes, with all the possibilities and promise that could entail. And she was out of his reach. For now, anyway.

'That needed to be painted in monochrome,' she told him as

they walked away. 'It was the day colour died for those people in Guernica.'

He put his arm around her shoulder and hugged her briefly, thinking, *and today you've put it back into mine*. He didn't tell her that, though. Instead he said, 'You are a very perceptive young woman. Do you know that? Most of my students couldn't tell a parsnip from a Picasso.'

He was glad he was going home the next day, before he did or said something stupid, yet he didn't want her to move away. He liked the heat of her body next to his. She was irresistible. Then he surprised himself with a suggestion.

'Why don't you call your friend Álvaro and ask him to join us for dinner this evening?'

He saw a look of bewilderment cross her face before she replied with a laugh, 'I didn't think I'd ever be able to face food again after that enormous lunch. It's just as well you're not staying any longer. You're bad for my figure.'

He knew she wasn't fishing for compliments. Her figure was perfect.

'We won't be eating until half-nine or ten. That'll give us time to get back home, have a bit of a break, work up an appetite and freshen up. I'll collect you about nine. How does that sound?'

'Great. I'll call Álvaro when I get back. I'm sure he'll be delighted.'

They were both very quiet on the drive from Madrid. He felt he had been ambushed. He knew there'd been an attraction. It was only now he was beginning to realise how strong that was. When he drew up outside the Torres' house, she kissed him on the cheek and said, 'It's been another magical day. I'll never forget it, Sean, thank you so much.'

'Neither will I,' he said, cupping his hand over hers for a few seconds. 'Neither will I.'

She hopped out of the car and gave him a wave.

•

Tansy appraised her appearance in the long mirror and nodded in approval. The lemon dress was perfect. She didn't know about the evening ahead, though. Why had Sean decided to invite Álvaro to join them? She'd have preferred not sharing him with anyone.

'Take some photos,' Rosa said.

'She should have married a photographer,' said Pedro. 'Take that, take this. If it moves, if it stands still ...'

His wife ignored him good-humouredly. 'Not many people can wear that colour, *querida*, but with your chestnut hair, it's beautiful. You're beautiful.'

And she did feel beautiful that night and she liked the transition. She also liked the lifestyle that went with wearing 'fancy frocks', as her mother would call them, and the people who moved in the circles where occasions to dress up were commonplace. A fleeting moment of unease made her acknowledge that perhaps her mother's fears about her leaving her hometown had been right. She would have to be shoehorned back in if she was ever to fit into Dunmoy again, and perhaps what was more disturbing was the knowledge that she didn't mind one little bit.

'You look stunning,' Álvaro said when she entered the room. Sean's verdict was the same when he arrived. If she had entertained doubts at all about the night being a success, they had been needless. Both men got on famously and chatted about art and military service, university life, family vineyards and lots besides. When they left the restaurant, Álvaro headed off and Sean asked her, 'Taxi or shank's mare?'

'Shank's mare,' Tansy answered, wanting to savour a little time alone with him. He tucked his arm through hers and they walked in silence for a bit.

'Are you straight back into lectures next week?' she asked.

'Yes, and it'll be mayhem from here on. The exams are on the horizon and some of those who really want to pass are panicking, those who never bothered to turn up for lectures are panicking and the ones who've cruised along pretending they didn't care are panicking, and they all think an hour or two of my time is going to solve their problems, and it's not.'

'So that's the way you professors look at things.'

He didn't seem to have heard that. He seemed distracted the closer they got to her house.

'Well, Tansy, this is it. I'm sure we'll meet up sometime before next term. Good luck with your studies and the exams, and congratulations on doing so well thus far.' He sounded like the professor she first met, a teacher talking to a pupil, and not even one of his own.

'Have I said something to upset you?' she asked, puzzled at the change of tone the evening had suddenly taken. 'This is me, Tansy, not an exam paper with a number. Remember me – the one you told your secrets to in the car yesterday. What's wrong, Sean?'

'This is. I can't do it, Tansy. I can't be around you.'

'What do you mean, you can't be around me?'

'Exactly that. I can't promise to act as I should and there's too much at stake for us both. I don't know how you feel, but I'm getting deeper and deeper into this relationship and it's wrong on so many levels. I'm mad about you.' He took her hands in his. 'I'm not imagining you have feelings for me. Am I?'

'No, you're not,' she said quietly.

'I knew it. I sensed it long ago, and now I'm certain. That's why I asked you to bring Álvaro along tonight. I couldn't have trusted myself to be alone with you. I wanted to take you to my room and make love to you, all night long.'

'Didn't you think that maybe I didn't want you to trust yourself?'

'You've no idea how much willpower it took to send you away,' he said. 'But think of the consequences, Tansy. You're an undergraduate. I'm a Dean of Faculty and, although you're technically not one of my students, you did work with me as a research assistant and that compromises both of us. And the age difference is enormous.'

'I don't see the age difference as a problem. I don't know why you're so hung up on it. Sitting there with you and Álvaro, who is five years my senior, I didn't see any difference between the two of you. And I won't always be a student.'

'I'm not hung up on it and I know you won't always be a student, but you are now and everything about a relationship between us goes against the code of ethics in the university. No one wins in these situations. Trust me. I know. So it's best that we stop it now before we hurt each other.'

'I can wait,' she said, feeling she was losing him already, the intimacy they enjoyed fading away.

'And I won't ask you to. As I told you before, these years are your time to grow and try new things. Don't waste them on me, Tansy.'

Standing there holding his hands, her head told her that everything he was saying was right and common sense. Her heart was trying frantically to find a counter-argument or solution. She wanted him with every fibre of her being. She wanted him so badly it hurt.

'I don't want to cut you out of my life, Tansy, but it's for the best, for you and for your future. Find someone your own age and be happy. I won't keep in touch after this, but I just want you to remember that I'm here if you ever really need me. Now I have to go.'

'Sean, will you do one thing for me?' she asked, her tears glistening in the light from the street lamps. He nodded.

'Kiss me.'

'Are you sure?'

'Very,' she replied.

He looked deeply into her eyes for a few seconds and her heart revved into overdrive as he brought his lips to hers, tenderly. She felt his breath on her face. Currents of passion and desire like she had never experienced before raced through her. He kissed her gently at first, both savouring the sensations before they kissed more deeply. She tightened her arms around him and they clung to each other with a kind of desperation, their tongues exploring, their hands discovering. After some time, breathless, they separated, their gazes locked. They kissed again and again. When he finally released her, he put a finger to her lips and said, 'Goodbye, Tansy. Please don't say anything. Just remember these stolen moments. I know I will, forever.'

He turned and walked away. She willed him to look back, but he didn't. She didn't want to go into the house because she knew Rosa would still be up, so she went quietly around the side into the garden, sat down on the seat beneath the pergola and cried.

She didn't know how long she sat there, but it was long enough for her to get cold and start shivering. She stood up, went to the front door and let herself in. As if on cue, Rosa appeared. She took one look at her and said, 'Into bed with you, *querida*, and I'll get you a hot drink.' She asked no questions and passed no judgements, but she sat on the side of the bed until Tansy fell asleep.

Tansy woke at eight the next morning, the time Sean's plane was taking off from Madrid airport – and out of her life. She felt bereaved. Bereaved of a lover who had only consumed a few days of her life, but whose presence, however brief, had changed her utterly. And with the same strange certainty she knew he would always colour it. She also knew that she loved him with all her heart and would always regret never having told him so.

She sat down at her laptop and tried to write to Phyllis, her go-to in any sticky situation, but she didn't know where to begin. She didn't want to share her most intimate thoughts with anyone. They were too brittle and so was she.

A series of pings sounded on her laptop. Sean had sent through the photos he had taken. There were a few of her in Mags's black and white dress, shaking hands with the King and Queen. Some the waiter had taken of the two of them together in the cloistered bar, and others in the Retiro Gardens. She had to admit she looked radiant in them all. That wasn't how she saw herself now. She felt empty and drained of vitality and lustre.

She felt her eyes fill up again as she looked through them. Proof, if ever she needed it, that she hadn't imagined those few magical days.

She switched off the computer, lay down on her bed and cried some more.

◆

Phyllis noted the change of tone in her friend's emails after the professor's visit. They were not as frequent nor as informative as before. She kept her thoughts to herself and hoped nothing had happened to sour Tansy's Spanish adventure. She never quite trusted Sean, but if she said that to Mags and Gina, they'd have shot her down instantly, telling her that her imagination was running away with her common sense again.

But something was not right. She just sensed it. She became even more suspicious when the only photos they received were of Tansy shaking hands with the royals, wearing Mags's dress. Sean and Álvaro were missing and, knowing Tansy as she did, she was quite sure that she'd have asked someone to have snapped her with one or the other, maybe even with the two of them together. So where were they and why did she not send them?

There were so many things she wanted to ask her friend, and regretted that they had all got into the habit of cc'ing each other and sharing all their news. This left no space for private communications without unbalancing the equilibrium between the flatmates.

She couldn't help wondering, though, if Tansy had fallen for Álvaro. She sent several pics of him, some of her in his father's fabulous sports cars. He was very easy on the eye and they seemed to spend a lot of time together, and he had taken her home. The fact that he was about to become engaged to someone else would certainly be a massive complication.

It was with all these unanswered questions whirling around in her head that she'd allowed herself to be persuaded to go to Spain for the summer and see for herself what was going on.

She and Tansy had both secured English-language teaching posts outside Málaga.

She had learned that the 'fanciable guy' who had dined quite often in the restaurant with his parents and siblings was called Jack. She was going to miss seeing him and wondered what he had planned for the summer.

Chapter Twenty

'Phyllis is not arriving until next week?' her mother echoed. 'And you'll be there on your own until then?'

'I don't mind that – there's plenty to explore.'

'Is it safe?'

'Mam, it's not darkest Africa. Of course it's safe. Málaga's a bustling city and we're practically on the beach. The school found us a small apartment, within walking distance. It has only one bedroom but has two single beds. And as I told Phyllis, if you stand on the balcony and crane your neck to the right, you can see the Mediterranean, but only when there is nothing parked at the kerb in between.' She laughed. 'It does have air conditioning, though, and that makes up for the lack of space.'

That didn't seem to make any impression, but then *she* hadn't realised the value of this commodity until the temperatures began soaring in Alcalá. She'd never appreciated either how valuable living near water could be. Here they'd be able to go swimming in the sea whenever they felt like it.

'Could you not have come home for a short stay first?'

'That wasn't possible. The new courses start next Monday,' she said patiently, 'and we have to do some training first.'

'I suppose,' Peggy said in that resigned voice that conveyed much more than the words that were uttered.

'I'm looking forward to it. Would you and Dad never think of taking a holiday here?'

'You know your father doesn't like the idea of flying. He wouldn't go that far away and leave his animals in anyone else's care.'

'Maybe you'd come with Mary McLaughlin? She's been away before. You'd love it.'

'I'm not sure I would. I'm not one for foreign food and all that. I didn't like it when I was in Lourdes. That unsalted butter was tasteless. But you enjoy it, and give my love to Phyllis, when she gets there.'

She wished her mother wasn't so unadventurous. If only she'd try something different, break out from the narrow confines of farm life. Maybe if she did, she'd understand Tansy's need to fly, instead of trying to keep her wings clipped. Had she always been like that – uncurious and resigned? Would she die having been abroad only once? It was thoughts like these that made Tansy more determined than ever to make the most of every opportunity. There were so many places she wanted to go. 'Morocco, Mauritius and Malta' from the childhood nursery rhyme were just a few of them.

She didn't tell her mother that their flat was above a fast-food restaurant and already everything she owned reeked of frying fat. It was also extremely noisy. There were two bars on opposite street corners and they never seemed to close. The bins from these were collected just after five and she'd woken to the sound of bottles crashing into the trucks the last few mornings.

Sean had kept his word. She hadn't heard from him since his

last night; nothing at all but those message-less photos. And she hadn't tried to get in touch with him. He'd made it quite clear where he stood. He'd left a huge void in her life and she found it hard to reconcile the depth of her loss with the brevity of their relationship, if she could even call it that. She missed him every moment and, despite understanding his rationale, it hurt. It really hurt.

Tansy spotted Phyllis first, pulling an enormous suitcase and a carrier bag. She ran to greet her.

'Look at you, Tans, all brown and healthy-looking. You look fantastic.'

'*Bienvenida*, Phyllis. You don't know how happy I am to see you.'

'God, it's hot. I can't wait to get out of these clothes.'

'It'll get hotter, but you'll get used to it.'

'When can I take my first dip in the Med?'

'Once we've got rid of the luggage. Then we'll go for a walk along the promenade and I'll show you around. You can unpack later.'

'I'm so excited to be here. I just hope I'm up to the job.'

'Have you got a sun hat?'

'I've got two. Mags had them and she sent one over for you, as well as a bikini, a wrap and two sundresses.'

'So, she's still spending money as though there's no tomorrow?'

'Yes, and this is a chance for her to clear out her stuff to make room for more.'

Then, later, as they had dinner in a little café with a panoramic view of the beach and the open sea, Tansy asked, 'How's Mags's romance going?'

'Really well. Trevor's sound and they suit each other. But I wonder about you. Did something happen between you and Sean? Your mails have been very guarded, but I sense all is not well and I can't figure out if it's because of him or Álvaro or something else completely.'

'Still the sleuth,' Tansy replied. 'It's Sean, and I will tell you, but not right now.'

'He didn't try anything on with you, did he?'

'Of course not, Phyllis. That imagination of yours will land you in trouble someday.'

'I don't know why you're so defensive. It happens.'

'Well, it didn't!' she said emphatically.

'I'm just sayin', it must happen.'

Tansy didn't reply. When it got cooler, they walked around and she showed her friend the local haunts she had discovered in the previous few days. They stopped for a drink on the corner of their street.

'I don't believe it,' Phyllis said, rushing up to the bar to say hello to a tall redheaded man. 'What are you doing here? Tansy, come and meet the only other person I know in Spain – this is Jack.'

She later explained he was the fanciable guy from the restaurant. 'I mean, what are the chances? Of all the gin joints in the world he's working in the one at the corner of my street!'

◆

'I never thought I'd enjoy this summer so much,' Phyllis told Tansy a few weeks later.

'Thank you for making it happen. The only problem is that it's going by so quickly.' They'd been sitting on the beach with a crowd of other Irish students. Most were in celebratory mood over their exam results. Not all were jubilant, though, and needed to drown out all thoughts of failure, repeats and the prospects of facing disappointed parents.

Tansy, too, was enjoying the new faces, the classes and socialising, the sightseeing, the sunbathing and the early-morning runs along the promenade. They had both received the results they had hoped for that afternoon and had celebrated with gusto. They'd had a lot of wine at dinner and after that, they'd sat on the beach discussing their plans and ambitions. When they got back to the apartment, the air conditioning was on the blink again and the heat was stifling.

Sleep was impossible and Tansy was aware of her friend tossing and turning, sighing and moaning. Eventually she heard her sit up and declare, 'I've had enough of this. I feel like going down and sleeping on the beach.'

Tansy smiled, agreeing with her. 'I think that's a great idea. Where's the mozzie lotion?' She was up and out of her bed in a flash. Laughing at the ridiculousness of their plan, they smothered themselves in the foul-smelling unction and made their way to the corner, where a few stragglers still remained outside the bars, too tired to go home and too drunk to stay awake. Giggling like schoolgirls, they crossed the road and the promenade and stepped onto the sand. They took two sun loungers from the stacks and carried them right down to the edge so that they could sit with the water lapping at their feet.

'I'm never going back to that stuffy flat,' Phyllis said.

'I don't ever want to go back to Dublin.'

'What are you talking about?'

'I don't ever want to go back to Dublin. I just want to run and keep running. Morocco, Mauritius and Malta. Oh, I don't know where,' Tansy said emphatically. 'Anywhere.'

'What's got in to you? You love college.'

'I do. I did. Oh, I don't know. Don't mind me. It's the wine talking.'

'Has this anything to do with your professor?'

'Don't call him that. Please don't ever call him that. He's not mine and he never will be.' She burst into tears.

'I knew something had happened. After he was over here, you never mentioned him in your mails. I just knew it. What did he do? Did you have a falling-out and, if so, over what?'

'No, we didn't. It's much worse than that, and before I tell you, there's no way to sort it out, so don't even entertain that thought for a moment. No platitudes, please. Promise me.'

'Tans, whatever it is, it can't be that bad.'

'Promise me, please, otherwise I can't tell you.'

'OK, I give you my word.'

Tansy unburdened her soul to her friend, who agreed that they had done the right thing.

'A relationship would have been an impossibility.'

'I know that, but it doesn't make the pain go away.'

'It's good to get it out in the open, though, rather than keeping it bottled up inside.'

'I told Álvaro. He said he'd guessed there was something there from the way I was so excited at the prospect of Sean's visit. That was even before I was sure. He said the night we all had dinner together he'd been aware of the sexual tension between us.'

'I'm glad you've had someone to confide in.'

'He's such a dote. You have to meet him sometime. Can't you

see why I couldn't write that down anywhere? I didn't want Mags to know because of Sean and Ernest's friendship and all that. I hadn't realised I was so transparent. Rosa also hinted that she thought from the way she'd seen Sean look at me, he had feelings for me. I never admitted anything to her. I just laughed it off. Somehow, I felt she might have been more judgemental because of his age and his position. Why does it have to sound so sleazy? It just felt so wonderful and right and he was the one who acted with propriety. I'd have done anything and there was nothing remotely sleazy about it.'

'Of course there wasn't, but could you just imagine what his colleagues would say?'

'The truth is he opened up to me about all sorts of things, but please don't repeat any of this. I'd hate him to think I was idly talking about his personal life behind his back. Your impression of him is so far off the mark, I had to set you straight.'

'The age gap is enormous. Just picture what your parents would have to say if you brought him home as your boyfriend.'

'I could handle them. I think.' Her voice broke again. 'Well, maybe initially it would have been difficult, but I could have made them understand eventually. I know I could.'

Phyllis moved over to give her a hug. She sat down at the end of Tansy's sun lounger. It tipped up under the weight of the two of them and they ended up in the water. They stayed there for a few seconds and started laughing their heads off.

Some late-night revellers shouted at them to come and join their party.

'No, thanks. We're off men for life,' Phyllis shouted back as they helped each other get to their feet.

'We'd better go and get out of these clothes.' Arm-in-arm

they walked to the flat, dripping wet and still laughing. The bars were deserted, and the air conditioning had come on again in their absence.

'Thank God for that. Things will seem better in the morning, Tans. You got great exam results. We'll be going into our final year when we go back, and you never know who we'll meet next term.'

'Always the optimist,' Tansy agreed, but she knew things wouldn't be any better and she didn't want to meet anyone else, ever. She felt certain that she had already met the one. She wanted to preserve the time they had shared in Alcalá in a capsule forever, in glorious Technicolor. Her private memory, to relive over and over again. Would it ever diminish in intensity and would it eventually be like Picasso's monochrome, telling its story in black and white and tones of grey on the canvas of her life?

Whatever happened, the prospect of seeing Sean again on campus excited and bothered her at the same time. How would she react to him and how would he react to her? Would there be an awkwardness, or would they be normal and natural with each other? Would her feelings and desires go away?

Chapter Twenty-one

Phyllis thought she was in love, the only problem was she wasn't quite sure which of her two favourite officers in her current batch of UN students was *the one*. As the wine took effect, the rose-coloured lenses through which she was viewing the world deepened, and she decided that she loved both of them.

'You know you could get dismissed for going out with one of these guys. It's against protocol,' said Jack, the redhead from Dublin, who had aced his exams, with firsts everywhere, and who was spending a lot of his free time with them.

'No, it isn't,' said Phyllis. 'Technically they finished at the language school this afternoon, so they are no longer my students. Besides, I'll have a new batch on Monday.'

'And these guys will be back at their bases, to their wives and girlfriends.'

'You're such a spoilsport, Jack, or Ginger or whatever you want to call yourself.'

'I'm a realist and I think it's time to walk you home.'

'Why can't you have dark hair and velvety eyes like the Spaniards?'

'Then you couldn't call me Ginger, could you?' He grinned.

'Anyway, look around you. They're two a penny. I'm quite a rarity, you know. Only two per cent of the world has red hair and only seventeen per cent has blue eyes. As for my freckles …'

'Enough, enough.' She laughed, linking his arm.

Tansy was watching as he led her across the sand. She decided to stay on the beach a little longer. She liked Jack. He was one of the good guys, fun and dependable. She thought he and Phyllis would be good together. She kicked off her sandals and walked into the sea. She stood as the tepid water gently licked her ankles. She loved that feeling. The moon laid a silvery pathway across the calm surface, a pathway to all sorts of possibilities, but she had only one thought in her mind and that was the text she'd received the previous morning, the text she hadn't told Phyllis about.

It had simply read: *'Great results, Tansy. Well done. Delighted for you. No need to reply. Sean.'*

Why had he done that? She was so confused. Did she wish he hadn't? But he had and it wasn't enough. She wanted so much more. She wanted to think they might have stolen kisses in his booklined office when everyone had gone home. She wanted to think of what might happen after that.

She had just been getting used to the idea that he was off limits in every sense and now he'd popped back into her consciousness and her life. He'd have had to go delving to find her results before she'd known them. In doing so, he'd opened up a deep wound that had scarcely begun to scab over. And he'd firmly pulled the shutters down behind him, again.

No need to reply.

She didn't know whether she was more sad than angry, but she did know that she was more confused than ever.

When she got back, she banged the door and made some noise before entering their cramped apartment in case Jack had come in with Phyllis, but she was alone, stretched out across the two beds in a deep sleep.

'It's just as well we have no classes tomorrow,' Tansy said out loud as she pushed her friend over to her own bed. She lay down and replayed her memories one more time. What would Sean do if she chucked in her studies to be with him? She knew how she'd feel, but she wasn't sure about him. Would he take her in his arms and celebrate, or would he run a mile?

Was she desirable because she was unobtainable? She was more determined than ever to get a good degree and not let her independence or happiness depend on any man or woman, but on herself. She wasn't going to be let down again. First Ross and then Sean. Perhaps she was just too gullible or trusting, or trusting *and* gullible. Or stupid and gullible. Or ... eventually she fell asleep.

Time seemed to speed up after that and everything was measured in the number of weeks until they'd be back in college. They packed up reluctantly, with promises of jobs again in the language school the following year, and they headed back to student life.

Before she left to catch the bus to Dunmoy to see her parents, Tansy warned Phyllis, 'Don't take all my drawer space while I'm gone.'

'I won't.' She laughed. 'And that's not because I don't want to – it's because Gina's already claimed all the deeper ones.'

'It's great to be back.' Tansy laughed. It seems a very long time since January and I missed the squabbling.'

Chapter Twenty-two

The walk across the courtyard was interrupted by groups of friends all wanting to catch up on each other's summer exploits. Phyllis spotted a redhead among the students – Jack. He saw them at the same time and cut across to talk to them.

'Let's catch up for a drink later,' he suggested. She readily agreed.

'I'm missing the beach already,' she said. 'This is Mags.'

'I heard all about you from these two.'

Tansy scanned the expanse, hoping, yet apprehensive, that she might catch a glimpse of Sean without having to be too obvious about it.

'Tansy. Earth calling Tansy. Come in, Tansy. What planet are you on? Jack wants us to join him later for a drink,' Phyllis said.

'Oh, great. Lovely. Right,' she agreed, dragging her attention back. He headed over to his friends and Mags said, 'I don't know if there's history there, but you were positively rude to that poor chap, whoever he is.'

'Was I? I didn't mean to be. He's cool. He was in Spain with us. Anyway, I doubt if I'd be missed – he's keen on Phyllis.'

'No, he's not,' Phyllis argued. 'He's keen on Tansy, but she hasn't given him a look-in. You saw just now how she dismisses his presence.'

'I do not. I didn't intend to be rude. I'll apologise later. My mind was elsewhere. I was just thinking about popping in to see the Prof and say hello.'

'He's not there. He's already gone.'

'Gone. What do you mean, Mags?' Tansy thought she had heard her incorrectly, yet she knew she hadn't.

'Trevor's old man and your professor have headed off somewhere for a year.'

'Ernest and Sean?'

'Oh, I'd forgotten you'd met him. Yeah, Sean's taking a sabbatical. They're working on some research project abroad together.'

Tansy made no comment. She didn't trust herself to talk. She felt betrayed. Why hadn't he told her? Why should he have?

'Didn't you know?' Phyllis asked a little later.

'No,' was all she said, and Phyllis squeezed her arm.

Earlier, when they had entered the picturesque courtyard, the sun bathing the surrounding historic buildings with a golden light, she had been filled with the anticipation of a meeting, chance or contrived, with Sean. She had been excited at the thought. Now it felt as though he and her dreams had evaporated. The magic of the setting had evaporated too. There she was surrounded by old, grey buildings.

You're delusional, woman. Accept it. You never meant anything to him. You were just another star-struck student with fantasies. Of course, he was flattered by such attention. And now he's gone without a backwards glance. Get over yourself and move on. It's a new semester.

But try as she might, she knew it wasn't going to be that easy to get over her professor.

◆

In later life, when she thought of these years, they had condensed into chunks of memory and seemed to follow a pattern, although at the time they had been crazy and humdrum in equal measure. In hindsight their time comprised mainly laughter and lectures, assignments, drinks, late nights, restaurant shifts, swapping clothes and tales of romances that were on and off, pizza parties, but above all they were about friendships, however ill-matched, random or enduring.

It turned out that what her friend had said was true. Jack wasn't interested in Phyllis romantically. They were mates and, as the term progressed, he spent more and more time in their flat. He was sharing with other students in Rathmines too. Tansy always enjoyed his company and he took to calling when Phyllis was working. They'd often still be sitting there talking when she returned from her shift.

'If talking would solve anything, then you two must have resolved the problems of the world by now,' she said to Tansy one night.

'I like the way he sees things,' she replied.

'Obviously,' Phyllis answered.

Tansy laughed at her. 'Don't go getting ideas. I just said I like the way he sees the world.'

'And I just said obviously!'

'I know. Now I'm off to bed. Goodnight!'

◆

'What's the story with Tansy?' Jack asked Phyllis one Friday night. A bout of laryngitis had seen Gina step in for her with the others at the restaurant. Jack had called with lozenges, lemons, honey and grapes.

'What do you mean?' Phyllis said in a croaky voice.

'She seems to have a fence around her. I've been wanting to ask her out for a while. I really like her, and I think she likes me, but she seems to close down whenever I get anywhere near asking her and I retreat.'

'You retreat? Well, that's a novelty,' she said.

'I know. I can't believe I'm even admitting that. I've never been like this with anyone else. Is it me or is it her? Should I just back off?'

'This is awkward, Jack. I can't tell you without breaking her confidence. Maybe she just needs time.'

'Am I right in thinking that there's no one significant in her life? I thought when we were in Spain that she might have had someone back here. Was I wrong?'

'I can't answer that, but all I can say is you're not a million miles off course.'

'I figured as much. It's obvious she's been hurt.'

'My lips are sealed. Why not ask her out anyway? All she can do is say no. That doesn't have to change anything, does it?'

'Thanks, Phyllis, I will. And you're wrong. It could change a lot. If she says yes, I'd be the happiest guy in the world.'

Phyllis laughed. 'You have got it bad. What are you waiting for? You have my seal of approval – whether you want it or not. Any guy who looks after me like this is way up there in my book

– and if she says yes, then she can answer all your questions for you and that'll let me off the hook.'

'Thanks, Phyllis, I will.'

◆

'Do you think it'll feel weird, being friends and all that, going on a dinner date?' Tansy asked Phyllis.

'There's only one way to find out, Tans, and you look great. Where's he taking you?'

'I never asked.'

Phyllis said, 'Jack is one of the good guys.'

'I know that.'

'Seriously, he's the genuine article, kind, funny, caring and ambitious too. A rare breed, in my vast experience.'

'And in my limited one! There's the bell. Don't wait up for me!'

'I won't!'

◆

'I thought we'd go Spanish and see how it measures up. Have you been here before?' Jack said, stopping outside the same restaurant that Sean had taken her the night she had finished up working as his research assistant.

'I have. Just once.' She was about to tell him but had promised herself she would not mention Sean's name ever again. 'And the food was great. I love *tapas*.'

After they'd ordered, they chatted about college and their plans.

'You know I love travelling,' he said, 'and I've always seen myself doing the gap year thing, Australia's definitely on the cards. A few of my friends took a year off before starting college to do it and, if I'm honest, I've always envied them, although I think I'd get more out of it now that I'm a tad more mature.'

'Are you?' she asked, and he laughed.

'I hope so. What about you? Can you see yourself going back to country life?'

'Now that I'm a tad more mature myself, I don't ever see that as being an option.'

'I don't want to cross any lines with you, Tansy, but you're something of a mystery woman to me. I want to be open with you, and I do understand it might take a while for us to reach that stage of intimacy, where we can share our pasts and possibly our futures. I suppose what I'm trying to say is that I want more than just being your good mate. And I wonder if I'm in there with a chance.'

She smiled at him, not put off a bit by that prospect, and said truthfully, 'I think you might be. Just don't rush me, Jack. I need a bit more time.'

He reached across the table and took her hand in his, raised it to his lips and kissed it. Still holding it, he said, 'Take all the time you need, Tansy. I'm not going anywhere.'

And she knew he meant it.

Chapter Twenty-three

It was impossible to avoid Christmas while walking down Grafton Street. The shops were transformed into glittering grottos of seasonal clothes and ridiculous gift ideas with ever more ridiculous price tags.

When did the fashion police decide that every girl and woman should have a red dress for the season? Red is definitely not my colour. Tansy was contemplating such imponderables when the heavens opened and she was deluged by cold, biting rain. She was fighting with her fold-up umbrella, the one Phyllis had borrowed and returned with a twisted spoke that she had neglected to mention. It refused to open. She was still tugging at it when she walked smack into a tall man who was walking in the opposite direction, and the broken spoke shot out and caught on his jacket. She hardly looked up as she offered effusive apologies. A familiar voice said, 'Tansy, are you trying to spear me?' It was Sean.

'I'm sorry – this wouldn't open …'

'I can see that. Here, take mine. I have a hood I can use.'

Even through her gloves she felt the warmth of his fingers as he relieved her of the offending weapon. In the intimacy of his shared umbrella, the Christmas crowds disappeared, the din stopped, their space was ringed off from the world by falling raindrops. She wanted to reach up and touch his face, smell his aftershave, feel his lips on hers. She wanted to ask why he hadn't told her he was going away. Instead she said, 'You're home – and looking very healthy and tanned.'

He smiled and held her gaze. She remembered their 'stolen moment' and felt her colour rise. There was an awkward pause.

'Thank you. How are you getting on? Are your studies going well?'

How did he do that? Change their relationship by his tone? From friends with feelings for each other to relegating her to student status and he to professor again.

'Yes, great, thanks. I'm looking at options for next year. How is your project going?'

'It's one of those slow-burners, but it's progressing. It's challenging having something personal to work on and also to take a break from students for a while. I think both they and I will benefit from this time apart.'

She wanted to suggest going to have a coffee, to reminisce about Alcalá de Henares, talk about art, the weather, anything, but she didn't. He seemed to read this hesitation as running out of small talk. He glanced at his watch and said, 'I must dash. I'm meeting someone, but it's nice to see you looking so well. Watch how you go with that brolly.'

◆

'I felt such an idiot. I just stood there like a tongue-tied teenager,' she told Phyllis later. 'He took off into the crowd and I watched him discard the broken umbrella in a bin as he passed by it. He just tossed it away and I felt he'd done exactly the same with me. I keep wondering who he was going to meet.'

'Don't give him another thought. He's getting on with his life and you're getting on with yours.'

'I sure am.' She smiled. 'And I'll miss you over the holidays.'

◆

'Your mother's been baking and getting the house ready for weeks,' her father told her when he met her off the bus in Ballinasloe. 'You'd think we were expecting the Queen of Sheba to visit! Your mam misses you a lot, you know.'

'And I miss you both too, and Mam's cooking,' she said, noticing as they swung into the farmyard that there was no Christmas tree in the window. She asked her dad why and he replied, 'It's there all right. Your mam didn't want to decorate it until you got here, so that you could do it together, like you always did.'

She felt ten again and once she walked through the door, it was as though she had never left. There was something reassuring about the way nothing ever seemed to have been moved since her last visit. The only major difference now was that the photo of her with the King and Queen of Spain was framed and prominently displayed on the dresser. Tansy knew that her mother had chosen the large frame to give it even more visibility.

Her mother's bombardment of questions always began with, 'How long will you be staying for this time?'

'You have me for a week.' Tansy laughed.

'I have loads of things for us to do.' And she had.

When the phone rang early on Christmas Day, her mother thought someone had died. 'I mean, who'd ring anyone at this hour on a Christmas morning, before the turkey's even in the oven?'

They heard her father say, 'Yes, Mary, I'll get her for you now,' and call, 'Peggy, it's for you.'

'She's probably been to Mass again this morning and got a fresh bit of earth-shattering gossip to impart, something that can't wait until dinner time.' He laughed. 'I'm off out to check the animals. Do you want to come along, Tansy?'

'I'd better stay to help, although, as far as I can see, everything is already prepped.'

Her mother was acting most peculiarly and didn't expand when Tansy asked who had died. 'Oh, no one.'

Later, when Mary arrived, with the customary bottles of Paddy and Baileys for her parents and a tin of fancy foreign biscuits and a woolly scarf for her, Tansy heard her whisper to Peggy, 'Did you tell her?'

'I did not. It's Christmas Day, Mary. I'm not going to ruin it for her.'

Tansy's curiosity got the better of her as they made their way through mountainous portions of turkey and ham, sausage-meat stuffing and a selection of roasted vegetables. By the time the plum pudding and brandy butter were served, she couldn't hold it in any longer.

'What did you not want me to find out? I'm a big girl now, you know.'

Anguished glances passed between the two women and Mary's sigh seemed to indicate, 'She's your daughter, it's up to you.'

'It's nothing to concern yourself with.'

'That's not what it sounded like. I heard you two whispering before and the way you stopped when I came in was a real giveaway.'

'Go on, Peggy, you might as well tell her. She'll hear it once she goes out anyway.'

Even her dad, who normally had no time for gossip, looked curious now, and he turned to look at his wife and asked, 'What is it? Is it bad news?'

Peggy hesitated, as though mustering her words. 'I'm not sure. Tansy, Ross Doyle is home from Dubai for Christmas.'

Tansy burst out laughing. 'And that's what all the cloak and dagger stuff is about?'

'It's not just that. He's brought a girl home with him,' Peggy said. 'His fiancee!'

Mary joined in the telling then. 'I hear she's in the family way. Now I'm not one hundred per cent sure if that's true, so don't quote me on it.'

'It must be hard to hear this,' her mam said and Tansy realised it didn't mean anything at all to her. Sean had eclipsed and obliterated Ross Doyle from her consciousness and her world. And Jack was quietly and steadily exorcising her crush on Sean. She became aware that they were all looking at her, awaiting her reaction to these unexpected revelations.

'Isn't "in the family way" a very outdated way to describe being pregnant? It sounds almost biblical, like she's with child. Doesn't it?' Tansy asked.

'She's a foreigner too,' Mary said, determined not to have her scoop interrupted. It must be hard on you, but I thought it best to let you know in case you bump into them, so you don't put your foot in it.'

'Bump being the right word for it,' Tansy quipped.

'Mary, why should she worry about that? She's done nothing to be ashamed of. If anything, it's he who should be avoiding Tansy,' her father said.

'All the same … to see someone dump you and take up with someone else so quickly, I don't know …' She paused for effect. 'And now an engagement and a baby. That must hurt.'

'Honestly, it's not a big deal. What Ross Doyle and I had was puppy love. We were just kids then.'

Mary nodded at Tansy's parents. 'I'm not sure about the new woman. I mean, time will tell. Marry in haste and repent at leisure. Isn't that what they say? Time will tell.'

'You're great value altogether, Mary,' Pat said, but there was no distracting her when she was on a roll.

'Tell me, Tansy. Has someone else caught your eye up in Dublin?'

'As if I'd answer that! I'm taking my time picking the right one this time.'

Her dad lifted his glass and smiled over it at her. Later he told her, 'There was no stopping that old witch, was there? She had her scoop and nothing was going to get in the way of her telling it. I don't know how your mother puts up with her.'

'Mary's lonely, really. That's all she has in her life.'

The week crawled by, Tansy feeling more trapped and stifled with each passing day in these familiar surroundings. She didn't meet Ross Doyle or his 'foreign woman'. And she missed Jack much more than she thought she would. He had respected her wishes and was taking things at her pace, but she was getting seriously attached to him the more time they spent together. She didn't admit to her parents that she couldn't wait to get back to Dublin, to the flat in Rathmines and to Jack.

Chapter Twenty-four

'Country life is no longer for me. It's too parochial, almost claustrophobic.'

'I'd hate that,' said Phyllis, inspecting the goodies Peggy had sent back with her daughter. 'I'd find it suffocating, everyone watching your every move.'

'Tell me about it. I feel guilty even saying it, but I couldn't wait to get back. I know my folks really enjoy my visits, but a week is too long.'

'Well, you're here now and we can look forward to tonight,' Gina said.

'What's tonight?'

'Tansy, are you for real?' Phyllis asked.

'I know it's New Year's Eve, and it's my first one away from home. So what's happening tonight in Dublin?'

'The party,' said Gina.

'What party?'

'Did no one tell her?' asked Gina.

'Obviously not,' said Mags. 'We're all invited to Trevor's for a party. His parents always had a big bash and Ernest has continued the tradition. Jack is invited too. It should be a bit of craic.'

'Will it be a very swanky affair?' Tansy asked.

'Yep, I suppose "swanky" sums it up. It's not exactly casual – or formal either. There'll be a lot of Ernest's colleagues from college and the world of academia so I'd say cocktail wear.'

'Jaysus, will you listen to that one?' Phyllis laughed. 'Cocktail wear. It's far from cocktail wear we were reared. If we'd seen that on an invitation, we'd have thought you had to wear feathers from a cock's tail!'

Gina said, 'That's coming from the one who thought RSVP stood for the Royal Society of Vincent de Paul.'

'I knew I shouldn't have told you that. That was years ago when I was in primary school, before we started learning French. I know it was the wrong answer, but I'm still quite proud of it. They should have given me marks for creativity instead of a red X.'

'We plundered Mags's wardrobe so we're going to be the best-dressed students ever to grace that Dublin 4 house. Come on. Let's get you sorted.'

'Help yourself,' said Mags. 'I'm off to Trevor's now.'

'Do you think Sean will be there?' Tansy asked Phyllis after they had kitted her out in a feminine wraparound dress in shades of aquamarine and eau de nil. It clung in all the right places.

'I'd say the chances are high, but so what? Let him think what happened was as casual for you as it was for him. You'll have Jack by your side as moral support, and when Sean sees you in that dress, he'll realise what he let slip away.'

'I still can't understand why he never told me he was taking a sabbatical.'

'Cowardice! Now get out of that dress and keep it fresh for

tonight. I'm making coffee and having some of your mother's cake.'

'What's keeping you?' Phyllis asked a while later, coming back into their bedroom. She found Tansy looking through some printouts of pics. 'What are they?'

'Just some photos of my time in Alcalá,' she replied.

'Let me see.' She flopped down on the bed and looked through them with her. 'I've never seen half of these,' she said, picking up the one of Sean with his arm draped across the back of Tansy's chair in the fern-filled bar in the *parador*, and the one of the two of them in the Retiro Gardens, where the gardener had swept the cherry blossom petals into little pink piles along the path.

'I don't know why you keep those if they upset you so much,' she told her friend.

'Maybe I'm not ready to get rid of them yet,' Tansy replied.

◆

'Very sexy,' Jack said when he took her in his arms. 'God, I missed you. It seems like you've been gone forever. You look really stunning.'

'Thank you,' she said as he came over to kiss her. 'I missed you too – very much. And you look very – very sophisticated altogether. Nice jacket and tie.'

'You all look fabulous,' he said, giving the other flatmates a closer inspection.

'You scrubbed up well too, Ginger,' Phyllis told him.

'I had to, to escort a bevy of beauties like you,' he said as he held the door open for them.

'This is what Rathmines must have looked like before it

became flatland,' Tansy exclaimed when she saw the house in
which Trevor had grown up. 'Imagine our road without all the
doorbells, the rusty bicycles chained to the remnants of railings,
the ugly post-boxes, the makeshift partitions and the curtains
hanging off poles. Ours looks like a tenement from the outside.
This is the way these houses should look – beautiful and elegant.'

'It looks like the guests fall into the same category,' Gina
said, 'and Mags assures me some of Trevor's eligible cousins are
expected.'

Ernest welcomed them as old friends. Waiters mingled with
trays of champagne.

'None of your Aldi Prosecco here – this is the real thing,'
Phyllis whispered as she tasted the golden liquid and took a
second gulp. 'Just sayin', I could get used to this.'

'Go easy on that stuff or you'll suffer tomorrow,' said Jack.

'Tomorrow's a whole year away.' She laughed.

Trevor made sure they circulated. There was no sign of Sean
and Tansy dismissed him from her thoughts. It was going to
be a good evening. She'd decided it was going to be the one on
which she told Jack she was ready to take the next step in their
relationship.

A four-piece band played at one end of the drawing room to
the right. A man in a mustard-yellow suit with a crimson cravat
asked Phyllis to dance. She downed her champagne and put the
empty glass on a side table.

'Would you consider throwing a few shapes with me?' said
Jack, and Tansy laughed. His gangly height didn't lend itself to
gracefulness on the dance floor, but she didn't care about that.
She was delighted to be here with him. She became aware of
some late arrivals making an entrance. She did a double take

when she saw Linda, the research assistant. Gone were the pink hair and loose-fitting garments she usually favoured. Instead she sported a black bob with a fringe, a figure-hugging black sheath dress and several long ropes of pearls hanging around her neck. She waved at Tansy and when the music stopped, she went over. Trevor had reached her first.

'Is this a vision or Linda which I see before me?' he asked, giving her a hug.

'I'm trying the demure seductress look to see if it will impress Sean, seeing that nothing else worked.'

'You might have wasted your time,' said Tansy. 'He's not here.'

'Yes, he is, he arrived just after me.'

Tansy felt a moment of panic and resisted the urge to scan the room. When she did, she saw a very colourful headdress peeping over several of the heads. It was Lewa, the Nigerian professor she had met the night of Sean's lecture in Dublin Castle. She waved over at them.

'Jack, I want you to meet this woman,' Tansy said, taking his hand and negotiating her way towards her. It was then she saw Sean following close behind.

'How lovely to see you again. I was just asking Sean about you. I have often thought about that night we met and wished we had had longer to get to know each other.' She stood aside to make space for him to join in. Sean stood there watching Tansy, his gaze a challenge, and she felt herself colouring.

'You haven't met Jack before, have you?' Tansy said, after introducing him to Lewa. Sean extended his hand in greeting and said, 'I don't think I've had the pleasure. Did you two meet on campus?'

'No, Tansy and I met in Spain this summer.'

'Spain. I'm going there next week, for my first visit,' Lewa told them, looking at Sean.

For an insane moment Tansy imagined him bringing Lewa to see the things he'd shown her. The Picassos and Goya's clothed and unclothed maidens. She felt a stabbing in her chest and willed herself to avoid his gaze. She turned to Jack and began explaining Sean's project to him. He seemed captivated by it too and while Sean and he went on discussing it, Lewa and Mags chatted like old friends. Tansy needed an escape route. She spotted Phyllis at the other side of the room. She mouthed 'Help' and Phyllis emptied her glass, put it on a passing waiter's tray, took a fresh one and made a beeline over to their group.

'Well, if it isn't Professor Love 'Em and Leave 'Em in person. You disappeared off the face of the earth very suddenly, without a word to anyone, didn't you?' she said, addressing herself directly to Sean. He looked shocked and turned to look at Tansy. She was not only shocked, but mortified, embarrassed and furious at her friend's outburst.

He didn't answer, or make any attempt to engage with Phyllis, but turned to Lewa and said, 'Ah, there's Ernest now.' He steered her pointedly away from their group.

'Well, that put him in his box. What did I miss?' Phyllis asked.

'Let's start with a bit of good manners and minding your own business,' Tansy said. 'I'm leaving now, Jack. You can stay if you want to, but I'm not in a party mood any more. Maybe you'd like to drink my champagne too.' She handed her glass to Phyllis and turned away.

'I'm sorry, Tans. It was just when I saw him there looking all smug … and I know –'

'You've said enough. Don't make it any worse.'

'I didn't mean … Ginger —'

'I don't care what you meant. Just stay away from me … and stop calling him Ginger! His name is Jack!'

Jack followed her out of the room. He didn't question her but went to fetch their coats. 'You stay in here in the heat and I'll see if I can flag a taxi.'

'You'll be lucky, sir, the night that's in it,' said one of the catering staff who was manning the entrance. 'And all the ones we've tried to hail are already occupied.'

She didn't care. She just wanted to get out of the house. For a second, she thought she should seek Sean out and apologise for her friend's outburst, but she dismissed the idea just as quickly. It would probably make things even worse, if that were possible.

'We can start walking; we might be lucky.'

'I'm not sure what happened in there,' Jack said as they walked. 'Did I miss something?'

'It's nothing. I'm sorry to cut the night short, but I had to get as far as possible from both of them. And if you don't mind, I don't want to talk about it.'

'Did that professor try something on with you at some stage?'

'Of course not, but Phyllis overstepped the mark tonight. Big time. Now, can we change the subject?'

They walked on in silence for a bit before he asked, 'Are you making any resolutions?'

'Yes, never to trust Phyllis again!'

'That sounds serious.' She gave him a look. 'OK, I'll shut up now!'

She laughed. 'I'm sorry. I'm really upset by what happened

back there. I shouldn't be taking it out on you.' She took his hand and kissed him. As though on cue, bells starting ringing across Dublin, car horns sounded and multicoloured fireworks burst and showered down over the partying city.

Happy to see the old year end, she turned and said, 'Happy New Year, Jack, and to whatever it may bring.' He smiled back at her.

'Is it too soon to tell you I love you, Tansy Nugent?'

'No,' she said. 'It's not.' And they kissed again. 'And I think I've fallen a bit in love with you too.'

'That's one way to end a year. But you're shivering and you're all dressed up. Would you like to go somewhere else? Clubbing? We've had nothing to eat either.'

'And I believe the food was going to be great. Mags said their caterers were the ones her folks always use and they're supposed to be fabulous.'

'Oh, to be wealthy!' Jack laughed. 'And just have to think about which caterers to use.'

'It's a different world, and yes, I'm frozen. This dress is not exactly meant to be worn without thermal underwear or in Irish winters. I've a better idea, Jack. Let's forget about clubbing. There's no one at home. Let's go back and enjoy having it to ourselves.'

'Are you suggesting what I'm thinking?'

'That depends on what you're thinking, doesn't it?' she teased. 'And as regards food, there's loads of my mother's Christmas cake and mince pies.'

'I like the sound of that – all of it.'

Dull explosive thuds burst out occasionally as the last of the fireworks lit up the sky. 'Happy New Year, Tansy.' He took his scarf off and wrapped it around her neck. He tucked her hand in his and they started walking briskly towards Rathmines.

That night she gave herself wholly to Jack, drowning out all thoughts of Sean.

And it felt so right.

Chapter Twenty-five

Tansy felt completely betrayed by Phyllis. She'd never forget the look Sean gave her after that unexpected and uncalled for outburst. The nerve of her to approach him like that and to say what she did. It wasn't her place or her business to pass judgement or comment. What had happened between them had nothing to do with anyone else. Tansy wished she had never told Phyllis any of it.

Whatever they had felt for each other was very real, and very private. With her tirade, Phyllis had somehow diminished and trivialised it.

Relationships in the flat didn't improve as the new year settled down. Even Jack tried to act as peacemaker and the other flatmates did everything they could to re-establish the order of things, but nothing had any effect. Tansy just stopped communicating with Phyllis, except when absolutely necessary. The impasse lasted almost two months and it was only when they were applying for teaching placements that the two of them actually began talking civilly to each other again. That was when Phyllis made yet another effort to clear the air.

'I know you're still mad with me, and I admit I deserve it, but we can't go on like this. What happens if we get places in the same school? Or we are called for interviews together? How do you think it will look if we're not on speaking terms? It'll scupper both our chances of succeeding. Besides, Tansy, I miss our friendship, don't you? I'd do anything to go back to the way it was.'

'Of course I miss it, Phyllis, but I'm not the one who broke it. You really let me down. You were totally out of line and Sean probably thinks I didn't just talk to you about his personal life and what happened in Alcalá, but that I blabbed about him to anyone who'd listen.'

'I didn't mean to.'

'Maybe not, but you did.'

'I was upset that day when I found you looking at those photographs before we went out, and hearing you say you still thought he should have told you he wasn't going to be in college in the autumn.'

'So I did and I still do, but I also still think it isn't yours or anyone else's business. If we're going to be friends again, that subject is off limits – permanently. Understood?'

'Understood.'

'Permanently.'

'Permanently, and I'll shout you a pizza and garlic bread to prove I'm serious.'

Tansy laughed. 'Oh Phyllis, that's your answer to every problem. Give me a hug instead.' That was when Mags walked in.

'Do I take it that the war is over?' She joined in the hug. 'Detente at last. How did this come about?'

'I felt like some pizza,' said Tansy, and Phyllis made a swipe at her.

'Thanks be to Jaysus. It's just like old times,' their friend muttered. 'Gina's stopped to get milk, but you can count us in on the pizzas too, to make up to us for being collateral damage since the conflict erupted.'

'Well, you can forget the milk – I want some wine,' said Tansy

Phyllis kept her word and didn't mention Sean's name again.

Chapter Twenty-six

All through their exams Gina moaned, 'Isn't this bloody typical – it rains for weeks and once the finals start, the sun comes out.'

'Let up, will you? I've more on my mind than the weather. I can't remember anything.'

'It'll all come back once you see the questions, Phyllis. You've been cramming for weeks – all the answers are in there – you just have to find them. Keep telling yourself that and, remember, once they're all over, we'll be off to Spain.'

Exactly a fortnight later, with their finals behind them, Tansy, Phyllis, Jack and Gina found themselves amid a throng of other students at Dublin Airport, waiting to board the plane for Málaga.

Phyllis said, 'It's hard to believe it's a year since I did this, and I'm even more excited this time. I almost feel carefree.'

'And so you should, but remember, no talk of exams or studies until we get our results. Although I hope it isn't, this could be the last time we'll be able to go away like this together, so let's make the most of it,' Tansy said.

'You won't find any objections from me. I've forgotten them already,' Gina said.

And Tansy added, 'But I still think we should have tried harder to persuade Mags to come with us.'

'If Jack was the one working towards his master's, you'd have made the same choice.'

'I'd forgotten how hot it gets,' Phyllis said as the heat hit them once the aircraft doors were opened.

'I hope these lodgings are better than last year. I swear some of my clothes still smell of cooking fat from the chipper below us,' said Tansy.

'Don't remind me. Then I was so excited to be abroad, I didn't care what the digs were like. Let's say I'm a bit more discerning now,' said Phyllis.

'I don't care. I just want to dump our stuff and go for a swim in the Med,' said Gina. 'We've only got two days to get a tan before we start work.' The others laughed at her.

'It'll be a nice change for you, from sitting on the fire escape trying to catch any rays that were going,' Tansy said.

◆

Sorry for the one-liners up to now. It's been hectic, but we're settled in and know where everything is and how everything works.

Our condo is actually big – nice bright rooms, and enough windows that a welcome breeze from the sea blows right through and keeps us comfortable. There's tons of storage space and we're just a stroll away from the sea.

Jack and his mates are living only two streets away. We've established a kind of routine – whether we stick to it is another matter, but that's the intention – early morning runs along the beach before the sun begins scorching it. Jack prefers to run on the prom. If we don't manage that, we'll go in the evenings, when it cools down a little.

It was nice meeting some of the people at work whom we knew last time. We take our lunches up on the roof under gigantic parasols (they didn't have these last year) and we usually go swimming once our classes are over. Sometimes we cook for the lads or they cook for us. We intend eating out at weekends. Food is very cheap and delicious.

I hate telling you that we're having fun, and we are, but we miss you.

Love from us all, to you and Trevor.

xxx

◆

Álvaro came down to stay with them twice during the summer and, as Tansy had predicted, he was a hit. He told them the date for his and Elena's wedding had been set for the following New Year's Eve.

'I expect you two to be there – and I won't accept any refusals,' he told Tansy and Jack.

Later she said to Jack, 'In a way, I envy them knowing where their lives are headed. I wish I knew where mine was.'

'I don't,' said Jack, looking at her. 'I like the uncertainty of not knowing what's going to happen next, or where the journey might take us. The anticipation – that's what keeps it exciting.'

'So much of that depends on our results,' she replied.

'We'll know soon enough. If we flunk, it's not the end of the world.'

'That's enough. Have you pair forgotten the moratorium on that kind of talk?' Phyllis said, and they stopped speculating.

Finally, the wait was over. Mags phoned them to give them the results. 'Congratulations You did it. We all did it. Can you believe?'

'We actually did it. There'll be no repeats and we can all look forward to our new schools for the H Dip year.'

One by one they grabbed the phone to congratulate Mags. There were excited phone calls home as the news sank in. They went to a little restaurant for a celebratory barbecue and they ended up on the beach. Some of the guys were kicking a ball about on the cool sand.

'That pair are getting on very well,' Phyllis said to Tansy, nodding in the direction of Gina and one of the teachers from the language school, a Spaniard called Gonzalo. They were wrapped around each other on a sun lounger.

'Good. Now all we have to do is get you sorted,' Tansy said as they set off in the direction of the little harbour, a walk they frequently did in the late evening. 'It was the night we got our results last summer that I told you about Sean. Remember?'

'Good God, Tansy, that's the first time you've mentioned him in aeons.'

'I'm sorry I was such a pain. I can see that. Common sense eventually prevailed and I can now acknowledge that the whole thing was madness. It was a classical student's fantasy. You know I had inwardly scoffed at Linda and her efforts to try to grab Sean's attention when I was working for him. I laughed at her flamboyant dress and at her often-outrageous and challenging declarations to him. She tried so hard to get him to notice her. Despite her efforts, he never regarded her as anything other than a scatty research assistant. Why did I think I would be any different? I'd have had as much chance snaring Harry Styles.'

'You'd have had to fight me for him.' Phyllis laughed. 'When you think about it, though, it's got to be a huge ego boost for lecturers to have their own groupies. They must have students throwing themselves at them all the time. Not that I'm suggesting you did that, but you know what I mean.'

'I do, and he probably spared me from making a fool of myself.'

'Probably, and you wouldn't be the first that happened to, and you can be sure there'll be plenty more after you.'

'In a roundabout way he helped me forget about Ross. And I now realise that Jack has probably helped me forget Sean.'

'You're really into each other, aren't you?'

'Very much so. I love him for being so reliable, fun to be with, spontaneous and really thoughtful.'

'He certainly only has eyes for you.' Then she asked, 'Is Sean due back to campus next year?'

'I haven't a clue. Not being with Trevor and Mags, I miss out on the gossip and, after your *faux pas* at the party, surprisingly it's not a topic that comes up very often!'

'*Argh!*' uttered Phyllis. 'I'll never live that down.'

They'd reached the little pier where the pleasure boats were tied up. On one side, rows of yachts were moored, some with party lights and party people on their decks, making the most of the balmy night. Snatches of conversations, laughter, music, waves washing against bows and the tinny clanging of metal against rigging provided the soundtrack. Further out at sea, lights from some fishing boats bobbed up and down while a large cruise liner dwarfed them as it headed towards the horizon.

'Do you ever wonder where we'll be this time next year?' Phyllis asked.

'If Jack has his way, we'll be heading off Down Under, buying an old van and touring around.'

'You lucky things. I can see you diving at the Great Barrier Reef, seeing the sun rise over Uluru, walking over Sydney Harbour Bridge, cuddling wombats and kangaroos.'

'You would.' Tansy laughed. 'I'd actually prefer to get a bit of teaching experience first, but he has his heart set on it.'

'I can't think that far ahead. All I can focus on is going into a school this September. It's scary, suddenly having to be grown-up and serious, and having to stand before a class of teenagers as the responsible adult.'

'You *are* grown-up and responsible, Phyllis – well, most of the time.' She laughed. 'And you don't have a country accent like me for them to mock.'

'Tans, teenagers don't need a reason to give teachers a hard time. It's their mission in life. Don't you remember?' They laughed.

Chapter Twenty-seven

A few months later, the friends were comparing notes. It was half-term and they were having a night out in the local. Gina was the only one who was missing, having offered to do a shift at the restaurant for one of the other girls so that she could go to a cousin's twenty-first birthday party.

'The next person who tells me that teachers have "a jammy job with all those holidays" is putting himself or herself at serious risk,' Phyllis moaned. 'It's bloody hard work, and this getting up at six-thirty is killing me. It's like the middle of the night.'

'I never realised this was going to be such an intense year,' Mags said.

'It's not as though we hadn't been warned,' Tansy said. 'I am enjoying it, though. Not the constant scrutiny bit, but when someone answers something properly and you know they've been listening. I get a great buzz from that.'

'I don't know why you're complaining. You're at least within walking distance of your place. I spend half my day travelling – two buses to get there and two back for lectures. And I meet half the kids in my classes on the second one, talking about me and making comments they want me to hear and that I daren't pretend I have.' Mags laughed.

'Well, it was your choice to go back to your old school,' said Phyllis.

'I know that and it helps that I know a lot of the staff and they are really supportive, but it's harder than I thought. I'm sure the kids have seen me shaking when classes begin.'

'We're all like that,' she said to Mags.

'Just remember, even the ogres who taught us when we were their age had to start somewhere too,' Jack said.

'Gina was saying how the kids at her place are all dropped off to school. And several of the sixth years and three of the *fifth* years drive themselves in every day. She said the whole topic of conversation in the staff room the other day was how this should be handled. Should there be designated student parking? Designated student parking! Apparently, their Toyotas are newer than those in the staff car park,' said Phyllis. 'Spoiled brats.'

'I had a mini when I was in sixth year,' Mags volunteered.

'See what I mean? Spoiled brats!' Phyllis said and they laughed.

'Not the right attitude at all, Miss. Those little brats are somebody's precious darlings,' Jack said, 'and their education is costing their parents an arm and a leg.'

Phyllis said, 'Our kids aren't like your privileged ones. They don't give a damn about things like academic or sporting achievement – in fact, most of them would be hard-pressed to describe what they even meant. The truancy rate is one of the highest in the country. Having a baby by the age of sixteen, like their mothers did, is up there on their priority list. We're talking here about one of the first schools in the city to provide a crèche for its pupils so that they didn't have to drop out during, or after, their pregnancy.'

'That's so sad,' Tansy said. 'They haven't a hope of breaking the pattern. It's all they know.'

'What job satisfaction can you expect to get from that?'

'Maybe more than you think, Mags, especially if you could influence even a couple of them every year to escape the cycle they are caught up in. Wouldn't that make it all worthwhile?' Jack asked.

'Maybe you could be the one to do it. A modern Miss Jean Brodie.' Mags laughed. 'God forbid! Just look at us, will you? We've a whole week off and what are we talking about? Work! Let's forget about saving the world for now and enjoy ourselves.'

Later, back in the flat, Phyllis settled down to check her mails in the hotspot for reception. Rags jumped on her lap. He was an uninvited addition to the flat – a tabby kitten who ran in after them whenever the hall door was opened. He'd race up the flights of stairs, rub against their legs and purr as loud as a steam train. Tansy named him Rags and he was now a fixture in their lives. As he became more used to them all, he spent more time indoors, choosing whatever vacant knees were available for his naps and strokes.

'God, Phyllis, can you not take a hint,' Mags said, looking at Tansy and Jack. 'Can't you see the lovebirds want to be alone.'

'Oh. Stupid of me. Of course. I'm not thinking straight. Sorry.'

'At last,' Jack sighed when they'd finally gone to bed. 'I thought they'd never leave us alone! Come over here to me.' They snuggled up on the squashy sofa. Tansy loved moments like this. He began running his hand gently up and down her arm. Her body responded to his touch as always. He lifted a strand of hair that had fallen down over one eye and tucked it back behind her ear, kissing her forehead where it had been.

'It's awkward, isn't it, trying to find time to be together like this?'

'We've managed somehow.' She laughed.

'I'm fed up with having to tiptoe around their shifts, and with waiting until they've all gone to bed so we can have some alone time, and even at that, they could walk in on us any minute. And it's no better at my place and that's not going to change any time soon. My mother's ban on bed mates until the twins are older is written in stone.'

'You can't blame her for that.'

'I don't. I actually agree with her, but it's a great inconvenience to my personal life! So, what do you think about sharing?'

'Jack, I'd love to. Really I would, but I'm not sure how the girls would feel. We split the rent and expenses four ways, and me dropping out would put an extra burden on them. It just wouldn't be fair.'

'But it might convince you that Australia is a good idea. You know what they say, if you want to know me, come live with me.'

'That goes both ways, Jack. What happens if it doesn't work out?'

'And what happens if it does?'

'You tell me.'

'Then we can head off once we graduate. Enjoy our gap year and do some exploring. You're always saying you want to travel, Tansy. It doesn't have to stop at Australia either. It's the perfect time for us in so many ways. We'll be qualified and carefree, with no responsibilities, maybe for the only time in our lives.'

She didn't answer immediately and he asked, 'What are you thinking? Your silence is unsettling me.'

'You make it sound very appealing.'

'That's because it is.'

'Much as I'd like to live with you, I'll stay till we finish college. It's the wrong time to change everything.'

'I suppose you're right,' he said, nuzzling her neck. She surrendered to him and they had sex as quietly as they could, knowing that if the other two were awake, they'd hear everything.

'I just want to curl up beside you in bed and make love to you again. Properly, skin on skin, no holds barred,' he said, pulling her closer and kissing her gently on the forehead.

'Well, you can't. Go home!'

'And speaking of which – when are you going to reveal me to your folks? Isn't it time you did?'

'Yes it is. They're dying to meet you Come down at Christmas.'

Chapter Twenty-eight

'Ever since you let it be known that you were bringing a fellow home to meet us, your mother's been in a tailspin. She's been making preparations for weeks,' Tansy's father told her after meeting her from the bus in Ballinasloe.

'That's what I'm afraid of. She probably has us married in her mind.'

'You know your mother; subtlety is not her strong point and when she and that Mary McLaughlin one get together, they're dangerous. They have no filters. Don't let her push you into anything you're not ready for.'

'Oh Dad, there'll be nothing like that. I'm really into Jack and I know you'll love him when he gets here in a few days, but there are things I want to do before I'd ever consider settling down.'

'And rightly so.'

Peggy was waiting by the open door when Tansy got out of the car.

'I don't know what you have in that bag of yours – it's a ton weight,' her father said as the women hugged each other.

'Just some of the loot I got from my pupils. I have enough

chocolates, candles and body lotions to keep me going for years, so I thought I'd bring some home with me.' Noticing the forlorn specimen standing in the corner, she said, 'I see you haven't done the tree yet.' And her mother replied, 'I thought we could do it together, like we always do.'

'Great,' she answered and wondered how her mother always managed to make her feel guilty for having been away from home. On the surface it was a harmless remark, but she felt herself being pulled back in like a fly who had just flown into an innocent-looking web.

'It just wouldn't feel right doing it without you. How long are you staying for?'

'I'm scarcely in the door and you're counting the days until I'm gone,' she teased.

'That's not what I meant at all.'

'Jack'll be down on St Stephen's Day and we'll leave on the twenty-ninth. Initially, we'd planned to spend a few nights in Madrid before Álvaro's wedding, but once Pedro and Rosa heard I was coming over, they scuppered those plans. They've insisted we stay with them, as their guests.'

'That's kind.'

'It is, because it'll save us a fortune.'

'They seem like really genuine people.'

'They're the nicest people in the world. I was so lucky to get them as my Spanish family.'

'So, this Jack – tell me all about him. Have you met his family already?' her mother asked.

'I have, but that's not a big deal.'

'Not a big deal? Of course it's a big deal. Believe you me, men don't just bring anyone home to meet their mother. Has he brothers and sisters? What do his parents do? Are they teachers too?'

'Just his mother. His dad's a civil servant. And you, Mam, you're beginning to sound like Mary McLaughlin.'

'You can't blame me for being curious. I'm interested. It's the first boy you've brought home since Ross.'

'I hardly brought Ross home, as you put it. He lived a few miles away and you already knew his folks.'

'I can't wait until I meet Jack. I hope I like him.'

'I know you will – everybody does. He has an older brother and there are twin girls of twelve. Is that all or is there anything else?'

Peggy laughed. 'Oh, there are loads more things I want to know, but so long as he's kind to you, that's all that matters. I'd like to see you marry into a big family and have lots of in-laws. It can be lonely being an only child, even though you're grown-up.'

'Promise me you won't interrogate him, Mam.'

'I'll be very discreet. I promise.'

Her father raised his eyes to heaven and grinned over at Tansy.

She got through the next few days, catching up and using the four customers in Mary McLaughlin's shop as an excuse just to wave at her and leave. She suspected she'd be subjected to another cross-examination by her over Christmas dinner. And she was. Predictably she arrived, straight from the last Mass, with the latest gossip and her customary bottles of Paddy and Baileys for her folks and some fancy Butlers chocolates for Tansy and her 'young man'.

Ross Doyle and his 'foreign girl' were never mentioned. Tansy didn't enquire if the baby they were expecting had arrived safely, or if it was a boy or a girl. That was another world and she was a different person then. She tried to imagine what her life would be like if she had stayed and eventually married him. Perhaps it would have been enough had she not gone away to university. But she had, and she immediately turned her thoughts to other things.

Her father hadn't been joking when he said Peggy had been fussing for weeks in anticipation of Jack's visit. She had rearranged the furniture in the spare room, and the bed had a new duvet. The bedside lamps were new too.

Tansy told Phyllis later on the phone, 'When Mam brought me in to show them to me, I got the distinct impression she was telling that there'd be no funny business in her house. That was Jack's bedroom and Jack's alone! In a way I felt relieved. At least there was some indication of what they were thinking.'

'I don't think I'd be able to have sex within earshot of my parents.'

'Me neither. I wonder if Rosa and Pedro will do the same thing when he comes over for the wedding. I think I'd feel just as intimidated doing it in their house.'

'Your mam probably wants to check him out first, to see if he's suitable.'

'You've no idea how near the mark you are. That's exactly what she's doing. I'm afraid she'll frighten him off altogether. I hope he doesn't get fed up with all these shenanigans.'

'Don't worry, he'll pass with flying colours and he's far too smitten to be put off by a protective mother.'

'We'll see.' She laughed. 'I'd better make myself presentable before he arrives.'

Chapter Twenty-nine

Jack said all the right things to create favourable first impressions and Peggy fell for his charm. After dinner, they heard her on the phone in the hall, telling Mary McLaughlin all about this first encounter.

'They've been doing this nightly phone call thing for years. No one and nothing escapes them. It started when they both took up bridge. Even though the phones are mobile now, she always goes out to the hall to chat,' her dad told Jack before going out to do his nightly check on the animals.

Tansy put her finger to her lips to silence Jack as she opened the door a little wider to eavesdrop. They listened and heard Peggy say, 'What a nice young man he is, very presentable too. He has red hair, but then so did my grandmother. And he's a teacher too ... like his mother. No, I think his father does something high up in the civil service.' Jack and Tansy looked at each other as if to say 'Where did she get that from?'

When they heard her saying, 'Approve, Mary? Of course I approve', Tansy eased the door over and they fell back on the couch laughing.

'I did warn you.'

'Does that mean I've passed muster?'

'From those comments, I think you probably have.'

Over the next few days, they went for long walks and drove to the sea, where the wild Atlantic Ocean was doing its best to redefine the coastline, its greedy foam gnawing at the fringes. Back home again, Peggy fussed over them and stuffed them with goodies. While going into each other's bedrooms was clearly not an option, her parents did retire before them to give them time alone. Tansy texted Phyllis to tell her it couldn't have gone any better.

They had to leave at half-six in the morning to drive back to Dublin, return the car to Jack's brother and get to the airport for their early-afternoon flight. Tansy's parents were up to make sure they had breakfast and to wave them off.

'Take lots of photographs and make sure you hang your dress up as soon as you arrive to let the creases fall out, and don't forget the cake,' Peggy gushed through the open car window. Her breath condensed as it hit the frosty air.

'Drive safely,' they heard her shout as they pulled out of the drive, giving a final wave before turning onto the road.

'My mother never lets me leave empty-handed. If I'd been going back to Rathmines, that fruit cake would have been for the girls. Instead, she earmarked it for Spain. She never thinks about things like baggage allowances or space restrictions.'

In Dublin, Jack's brother insisted on driving them to the airport. They queued at check-in and for security checking. They queued again in the bookshop and for lunch and took their seats while they waited for their flight to show up with a departure gate number. The knock-on effect of early-morning delays due to fog was still disrupting some schedules.

'I love travelling, but all this hanging around drives me nuts,' Jack said. 'I used to tell my folks that when I'm wealthy, I'll only go first class.'

'On a teacher's salary? You'll be waiting! This is only my third time going abroad so I'm not as jaded as you are by it. I still find it a bit of a novelty.'

She sat there observing the moving tableau in front of her.

The airport was hopping, bustling amid the chaos of young people heading back to jobs and lives overseas. No matter where she looked, she found someone or something about which to be curious. Winter sports enthusiasts already half dressed for the slopes in padded salopettes and jackets; groups of golfers tagging oversized baggage and checking in other paraphernalia; parents with kids whose routines had been disrupted; and tearful relatives bidding fond and reluctant farewells to their offspring and friends. There were accents of all kinds and sporadic announcements that no one could either hear or decipher. The playlist of scratchy mood music still included Christmas songs and when 'Driving Home for Christmas' began, Jack said, 'They ought to be banned once Christmas Day has arrived. They sound so redundant once it's all over.'

'Except for "The Twelve Days of Christmas". My cousin and I used to try to sing it backwards when we were on our summer holidays in Bundoran or Salthill. Usually when it rained, which it seemed to do a lot. We'd sit on the top bunk in our rented cottage, with our legs dangling, and we'd sing our lungs out. It was great fun. Every time we got it wrong, we'd start all over again.'

'Oh Lord, what have I got myself into? Tell me you don't do it at weddings, do you?'

'Not so far,' she said and grinned, 'but then I've never been to one before. You never know what might happen!'

'You've never been to a wedding before? Tansy Nugent, that's one of the things I love about you. You constantly surprise me.'

◆

Both Pedro and Rosa were waiting for them when they alighted from the bus in Alcalá de Henares. They seemed genuinely delighted to see Tansy again and to meet Jack.

After they arrived at the house, Rosa announced, 'I love your red hair and those freckles, or am I allowed say things like that any more? I hope it's not considered racist or anything.'

'Of course not.' He laughed. 'I'll always accept flattery. I don't get it very often.'

'Pay no attention to him. He's just looking for compliments,' Tansy said. 'It's so great to be back. It's all so familiar that I feel I've come home again!'

'It is your home, your Spanish one, and you know you'll always be welcome here.'

'That's some nativity tableau,' said Jack, studying the detail in the miniature scene spread out across the top of a long console table.

'This one has been in my family since my grandmother's time. She and my grandfather made most of the buildings and the barns, some of the figurines too. Where have my manners gone? I haven't shown you to your rooms yet. Pedro, take one of those bags, will you?' Tansy caught Jack's eye over Rosa's shoulder and he mouthed 'Rooms' at her, then winked. She had to try hard not to laugh. That answered the question they'd never have asked.

'We'll leave you to unpack your things. Come down when you're ready and we'll eat.'

A few minutes later, Jack came into Tansy's room, grabbed her and kissed her. 'It looks like we'll have to be creative if we're to find a way to spend time together,' he said, his breath hot against her ear.

Little flickers of desire ignited within her and she felt herself wanting more. She kissed him back. She didn't want one of Rosa's tempting dinners, or to listen to her chat. She wanted to lie beside Jack and for them to make love until they were breathless and their skin glistened with sweat, until they had satisfied each other to the point of exhaustion. She wanted to stay like that until —

She thought she heard a door open downstairs. She pushed him away and said loudly, 'Jack, will you bring that down to Rosa? Tell her I'll be down in a minute.' She took the tin with Peggy's cake and handed it to him.

'I love you,' he whispered.

'Me too,' she said.

Over dinner, the Spaniards filled her in on their news and, apropos of nothing, Pedro said, 'Did Rosa tell you I met Professor Sean in the square one day?'

Tansy had not been expecting to hear that. 'Sean?' was all she said.

'Yes, Sean. I'm surprised he didn't mention it to you. You were all he talked about, and his Spanish Civil War research project of course.'

'Our paths don't cross any more, since he took this sabbatical. It would be impossible for him to keep in touch with all his students.' She felt Rosa watching her and knew she had always suspected something had happened between them when he had visited. She had never questioned her and Tansy had never volunteered anything. The last thing she wanted to think about now was that disastrous party the previous New Year's Eve.

'Have you any suggestions as to where we should go tomorrow?' Jack asked. 'We're hoping to catch up with Álvaro at some stage. He's insisting we at least have a coffee with him before the wedding, although he must be up to his eyes.'

'You could take the train into Madrid, or you could just explore our town, which I'm sure Tansy has told you has some pretty interesting places to see,' Pedro said. 'She tells us history is one of your subjects – well, you'll find that there's plenty of that around here to keep you happy.'

'She's been telling me about the storks' nests and their bill-clattering. I believe the university campus and the stick man statue are on the agenda too.'

'Sounds like she knows what's she doing,' Pedro said as Tansy stifled a yawn. 'You must be exhausted after your journey. Go to bed now and don't overdo it tomorrow. You don't want to be too tired to enjoy the wedding.'

Rosa said, 'From what I hear, it's going to be a very classy affair. That family has so many businesses and personal interests, there'll be all sorts of well-known tycoons from industry and, I suspect, from the nobility and – oh, what is that expression they use – the upper crust. That's it – it'll be an upper-crust wedding.'

'I'm looking forward to it. I just hope it won't be too stuffy,' Tansy said, yawning again.

'Spanish weddings are never stuffy,' Rosa said.

'It'll be strange going to an evening one.'

'And you can expect it to go on all night.'

Tansy laughed and, seeing Rosa's expression, realised that she wasn't joking. 'Really? All night?'

'Probably until four or five, finishing up with *churros* and melted chocolate before you leave.'

Tansy stifled another yawn. 'It sounds great, but I'm wrecked. The early-morning start is catching up on me. Forgive me, but I have to head off to bed.'

Chapter Thirty

They had arranged to meet Álvaro at La Casa de Abuela (Grandmother's House), the coffee shop that had been their usual haunt. He was already there and jumped up from the table when he spotted them coming in.

'It's so great to see you. This is just like the old times. Elena sends you both her love and apologies for not being able to join us.'

'I'd never have expected her to be free the day before her wedding. She must be up to her eyes,' Tansy replied.

'You've no idea! I'm really glad that you're both here and to get a few minutes to myself. And if I'm really truthful, just to talk about something other than the preparations. You know Spanish mamas plan for this day from the time the child is born and, because Elena's mother is dead, mine has stepped into that role, with gusto, I might add. And although she won't take a bit of notice of anything I might say, she still insists on consulting me and asking my opinion about every single thing.'

'That could be my mother you're describing.' Jack laughed.

'Or mine,' said Tansy. 'I often think mothers talk in a soliloquy that's almost Joycean. Everything is given the same value. It doesn't matter if it's a birth, death, Mrs Murphy's new car or someone's marriage breakup. Nor does it really matter if we answer or not, just so long as they can impart the gossip. All we have to do is make noises in the right places.'

'They may be on to something there,' Jack said. 'If we developed that technique a little, maybe we could adapt it in some way for standing up in front of a class, especially when some little smart-arse asks us a question that he's found on Google and that he knows will confound us while it impresses his mates.'

'Happily, I don't have that problem. I only have my father and grandfather to keep happy, and my mama and *abuela* too. Of course, I'll shortly be adding a wife to that list.' He grinned.

'So, no pressure, then?' Jack replied.

'Not too much so far. Actually, I'm quite surprised at how they treat me. I always knew the old grandfather would have my back; I wasn't too sure about my father, though. I thought I'd be very much the "new boy", but it's not like that at all. He's involving me much more than I'd imagined. I am shadowing him for the time being. He said that's how his father taught him the ropes.'

'I think that's a sign of wisdom, and a vote of confidence in you,' said Tansy. 'If he was to treat you as though you knew nothing, it might make it hard for the workers to take you seriously down the line.'

'I hadn't thought of it like that.'

'You seem to be enjoying it, though,' Jack commented.

'Hugely.'

'And are you happy about your wedding?' Tansy asked. 'No doubts?'

'Definitely and none whatsoever. Elena's a very special woman, Tansy, and I'm lucky to be marrying my best friend.' This was said with such simplicity that she knew he meant it.

They chatted some more and when the out-of-tune church bells tolled the hour, he excused himself. 'I hate to have to run but if I don't, my mother will send out a search party for me. You're clear about the arrangements for tomorrow? You're sure you don't need transport?'

'Rosa would throw us out if we didn't let her drive us. She's dying to get a glimpse of your home.'

'Well, tell her from me that she must come with you for a visit the next time you're here. I really appreciate you coming over. There's going to be quite a throng, but so many people will only have been invited because of our families' associations. You are here, Tansy, because you are my friend and that includes you, Jack. Now I really do have to go. Meanwhile, enjoy your sightseeing.'

'Don't worry about us. We'll not get lost!'

They watched him disappear across the Plaza de Cervantes before Tansy set about showing Jack around some of the places she knew he'd enjoy.

'Let's start with the university,' she said, leading him in the opposite direction, pointing out the white storks' nests on the spires and rooftops.

'I'd no idea before that they lived in towns.'

'I was exactly the same the first time I saw them too. Wait till you hear the racket they make.' She led him through the old entrance to the tiered courtyard, on into the chapel and the rooms used for the King and Queen's visit.

'I recognise some of these from the photos you have. You weren't exaggerating when you described this campus. It's astonishing. I'm ashamed to say I had never even heard of the place before I met you.'

'Neither had I before I came here.'

'It just wraps you up in its history. I'll have to come back again. Correction, *we'll* have to come back again.'

'That sounds like a plan and if you don't slurp your soup or flirt with Álvaro's granny tomorrow, perhaps he and Elena will invite us over sometime. I think she may have had a bad impression of me initially, when she heard about me being invited to Easter lunch at Alvaro's, but that's changed now. Once she realised that I was not out to steal her boyfriend, she warmed to me.'

'How could she not? Everyone warms to you, and I'll do my best not to let you down.' He laughed. 'They're not going to live with his parents at the villa, are they?'

'No, but on the grounds. There are several estate houses there.'

'Lucky sods.'

'Have you seen enough? I'm starving and cold and keep thinking of that meal Rosa promised us.'

They could smell it at once when they opened the door. As good as her word, Rosa produced dish after dish of appetising food, Pedro kept the wine topped up and Tansy and Jack did justice to it all.

◆

They were all still at the breakfast table the following morning when Peggy phoned. Despite only being able to hear one side of the conversation, it wasn't difficult to fill in the blanks from Tansy's barrage of answers.

'No, Mam, Rosa isn't coming, but she's as excited about the wedding as I am.

'Yes. I'll make notes of every little detail – the flowers, the food, the dresses, the hats. Yes. Everything. I promise.

'By the time you tell it all to Mary McLaughlin, you'll both feel you'd been there with us!

'... Yes, yes ... Oh, and remember, don't ring me in the morning because the wedding will go on till dawn and I'm sure I won't surface until the afternoon.

'... Yes, dawn – that's how they do things here. It doesn't start till seven ... Goodbye Mam!' She laughed as she turned to them with a resigned expression on her face as she replaced the receiver.

'You know, it's at times like these that I wish I had a load of siblings. That way she'd be too busy with us all to want to know every detail about my life.'

'And if this is typical female behaviour, if I ever marry I'm definitely going to elope,' Jack said to Pedro.

'I wouldn't hold out much hope of that happening,' he answered. 'They may be called the fairer sex, but when you try to deny them their big day, just watch the claws come out. And I know what I'm talking about.'

Rosa laughed at him and Tansy knew there was a story there.

As they were heading out to do a bit more sightseeing that morning, Rosa reminded Tansy for the umpteenth time that she had the afternoon blocked out for pampering and preparations.

She had insisted that she'd drive them to the wedding in the hope that she might catch a glimpse of someone or anyone important arriving, so she was getting her hair done too, just in case …

◆

'I'll be the envy of everyone there tonight,' Jack said when he saw Tansy coming down the stairs before they left. 'You look absolutely gorgeous.'

'Thank you, kind sir.' She curtsied to him, the two long feathers in her hat quivering and the black and white voile ensemble caressing her as she moved. 'And I feel it in this dress. I know Mags drives me mad at times, but there are advantages to having a shopaholic flatmate. You look very good all spruced up. I haven't seen you in a proper suit before. It's quite a change from the uber-casual student look you usually sport.'

'I work very hard to achieve that sartorially casual look – understated, often mismatched, scruffy sometimes, I'll admit, but never shabby!'

'You've got it in one, that's a perfect description.'

'However, I have made a real effort for this and I'm glad you approve. I can't let you down. Isn't that right, Rosa?' he asked.

'A woman's best accessory is a well-dressed man!'

'See, I knew it would be worth it.' Jack laughed.

Rosa got her phone. 'I must take a photo for you to look back on in years to come.'

'For when you're as old as us, she means,' Pedro said and he cautioned Jack, 'and keep your eyes on your young lady – we Spanish men get carried away very easily in the company of a beautiful woman, and she is certainly that. I only went to the shops to buy coffee when I saw Rosa for the first time and look what happened.'

Rosa laughed. 'That's true. I had just started a student job that week and in he walked – into the café and into my life. Now we'd better get a move on. We don't want to be late.'

At the car she fussed some more over Tansy, telling Jack not to sit too closely in case he sat on her skirt and it might crease.

'You're beginning to sound just like my mother,' Tansy said.

To which Rosa replied, 'And you're like a daughter, not listening to me.'

'I'll behave, I promise,' Jack said, taking Tansy's hand.

Happy with the arrangements, Rosa got into the front of the car and took off like an ant leading a colony, chattering all the way as they headed out of town into the countryside.

Chapter Thirty-one

'This is like something from a movie set,' Tansy said as they identified themselves to the security men at the gates before they were allowed to proceed. Rosa drove slowly up the long driveway, which was illuminated with flaming torches.

'It's like a fairy tale,' she added, to no one in particular, 'and so romantic.'

'This is not a villa. It's a castle!' Rosa exclaimed when it came into view, lights shining from every window. The pillared porch was festooned with flowers and garlands of greenery and countless candles in clear glass lanterns. Although it was a chilly night, Rosa let the windows down to savour the atmosphere and hear the sound of strings as they rose over the hubbub of conversation.

'I can't imagine what the inside must look like,' Tansy said. 'And I can't imagine what the florist's bill will be like either, although I don't suppose those things matter when you're this rich.'

They had to wait in a short queue as limo doors opened and the glitterati disgorged themselves from their shining chariots. A few handed over keys and these vehicles were driven away to designated parking areas. Others, like Rosa, dropped off their passengers and drove reluctantly away.

Before she closed the windows and engaged the gear, she said, 'I feel like the only kid in the class who hasn't been invited to someone's birthday party.' Tansy and Jack laughed at her.

None of the family was to be seen anywhere. Footmen and maids took coats and wraps and sent the guests in different directions – 'chapel or ballroom'. They were appointed to the former line, but before moving on, Tansy was directed to a side table, which was laid out with dozens of corsages of intertwined orange blossom and peach-coloured roses. One of the young girls beside these smiled at her and asked, '¿Casada o soltera?'

'Soltera,' she replied. 'Single.' The girl picked one of the corsages and pinned it upside-down on her dress. Tansy noticed those who answered 'Married' had theirs pinned on the right way up. Before she could ask why, they were ushered on again.

She hadn't been in this part of the villa when she'd lunched there the previous Easter and she whispered to Jack, 'I was assuming it'd be a little chapel, more of an oratory, I suppose, not something as vast or lavish as this. It's like something I'd expect to see in the Vatican. Just look at all that gold and those frescoes.'

He nodded as his eyes travelled over the paintings that covered the walls and ceilings. 'So, this is how the other half lives.'

A gloved attendant escorted them to their seats, way more than halfway up the aisle and Jack whispered, nodding towards a side altar, 'Do you think they decked out the Madonna of Something or Other over there in that hideous garb for the occasion?'

She whispered back, 'I should imagine they did. And that "hideous garb", as you describe it, is probably priceless and embroidered in real gold threads.'

'But it's awful. You can't pretend to like it, can you?'

'No, I hate it. It's garish and ostentatious.' She grinned at him. 'I presume all those shields and coats of amour represent some part of the family history. Probably for glorious and heroic feats carried out by different ancestors. This castle and the estates were probably acquired after helping win battles or gifted for loyal service. It makes my Dunmoy roots seem very trivial. There are no flags or standards to us Nugents in our local church.'

'Nor for us.' Jack laughed. 'There's not a nobleman or a hero anywhere. There's no money either.'

'Ditto,' she replied, 'but I'm delighted to be here. It'll probably be the only time I'll ever get the chance to enjoy something like this.'

'That's one of the things I love about you. You're such a romantic, Tansy, and you take pleasure in everything in life. Don't ever change.'

She squeezed his hand and she left it in his.

She sat back to savour the ambience. Delicate scents from enormous floral arrangements scented the air, while wafts of expensive perfume followed some beautifully attired women as they took their seats. The chapel was filling up rapidly and somewhere out of sight an organist was showing off their repertoire.

Jack's touch made her feel safe and cherished and she found herself wondering what it would be like to be waiting for her own wedding service to begin. Would it feel right? Would the certainty of forever afterwards be there? Would it be with Jack?

She loved him, but was that love enough to make a lifetime commitment? She didn't know if she could ever be that sure about anyone. Yet here was her friend about to pledge his future in an arranged marriage that both were determined to make work. She knew in her heart that if it had been Sean sitting next to her, she would feel differently.

She had put him out of her mind every time he popped into it, but since coming back to Alcalá de Henares that had been quite often. She found herself reliving the kiss, his declaration, their stolen moment of bliss. She had to make an effort not to remember it when she and Jack snatched any moments of intimacy together.

He was still holding her hand, stroking the back of it with his thumb, when the music stopped and the chattering died down. Gradually everyone stood up and the organ began again, this time with serious intent.

'You're day-dreaming again,' Jack said as they rose to their feet.

She smiled at him. 'I was.'

Álvaro was escorted up the aisle by his mother, both focusing on the altar ahead and not looking at anyone. She remained by his side while they waited for the bride to arrive. A few minutes later, Elena made her entrance. She was on her father's arm. There were no groomsmen or bridesmaids, just the two of them. A traditional wedding *mantilla* trailed several metres behind her gown.

'Ethereal' was the word Tansy would use to describe her later. 'Her dress was seductive, yet modest too, and so very elegant. It sounds clichéd, I know, but she was radiant.'

After the rings were exchanged, one of the three celebrants

blessed a little casket that the groom had handed him. He gave it back and Álvaro then presented it to Elena.

'What's all that about?' asked Jack.

'I haven't a clue,' she replied. 'Something called *arras*, but it's not a word I've ever heard before.'

Her father remained by Elena's side throughout the ceremony. At the conclusion, the organ reached a crescendo and the newlyweds processed slowly down the aisle, smiling and nodding in recognition as they spotted certain faces in the congregation. Row by row the guests left their seats and followed them into the vestibule and down a wide hallway to the ballroom.

'No wonder they separated us. They'd never have fitted everyone in the chapel,' said Jack as they waited in line to be received by the bride and groom, her father and Álvaro's parents.

'They must have had screens in here for the overflow to watch the ceremony on,' Tansy replied. 'I think we were in with the VIPs.'

'And rightly so,' he replied, giving her a hug.

Their welcome couldn't have been warmer and, after they offered their congratulations, they were tactfully moved along. Tansy scanned the room and spotted Álvaro's grandmother. She towed Jack over to meet her. She thought she recognised Professor Cortez. Tansy had always suspected she had been Sean's contact for her Erasmus placement. A tall man with a Dalí-esque moustache and a flamboyant cravat seemed to be shepherding her off in another direction and she vanished in the crowd. Tansy would make a point of finding her later to say hello.

Waiters circulated with trays of drinks and nibbles. An

ensemble played background music and two of her classmates
came up to her. 'Tansy!' Jack watched as they embraced and
kissed her on both cheeks, and told her how lovely she looked
before she could introduce him.

'Álvaro told us to look out for you. You can sit anywhere
you like, but we've managed to get a table for all of us. Come
and join us. You'll know most of the people there.' The smaller
of the two negotiated his way through the guests like Moses
parting the waves and they followed him to the other side of
the ballroom, where she met up with several more of her former
fellow students.

'I can't believe it's just two years since I met you lot. You all
look seriously grown up and much more mature.' She laughed.

'So do you. What have you been doing since?'

She filled them in on her teaching placement and asked about
them.

'It's so lovely being back here among you all,' she said,
relishing the camaraderie of her college friends as the drink
flowed and the food was delivered in a continuous stream. 'I'm
thoroughly enjoying myself.'

Jack seemed to be too. He was deep in conversation with the
guy on his other side, the taller of the two who had first met
them.

'I'm presuming that, like us, you actually managed to get
your degree,' the smaller one said to her.

She explained about the H Dip year and Jack joined in. A
perfectly choreographed fleet of waiters and waitresses fanned
out around the ballroom, placing little dishes in front of every
guest. Each contained the same number of grapes. Jack reached
for one and a woman at the table cried, 'No! You mustn't eat

them yet.' Noticing his bemused expression, she offered an explanation.

'They're not to be eaten until the final countdown of the old year. They're good luck grapes. If you manage to eat all twelve of them in that time, tradition says that the next year should be filled with good luck and prosperity.'

'I'm up for both.' He laughed.

'And so are we,' said Álvaro. He and his bride were doing their rounds of the tables and had just reached theirs. A bell rang and people went back to their tables for the countdown and good luck grapes. They toasted, kissed, hugged and shouted new year greetings at each other. The noise level increased a hundredfold.

Elena led her new groom onto the dance floor and everyone stood around watching them circle it once before they joined them.

'This is so far removed from what I had expected,' Tansy told Jack. 'Far from being a sedate affair, it's quite mad and raucous.'

'And if I'm totally honest, I was dreading it. I thought I'd be bored out of my boots.'

'And you're not?' she teased.

'And I'm definitely not!' He looked into her eyes. The music was slow and Jack took her in his arms and kissed her. He held her closer and she closed her eyes, drifting along in a happy place. 'It's been a wonderful evening.'

'Mmm, and it's not over yet.' She could feel his warm breath on her neck and held him closer.

He said, 'Do you remember this night last year? That was when we had the place in Rathmines to ourselves for the first time and it was also when I told you I loved you for the first time.'

'Of course I remember. It was when Phyllis and I had our falling-out too.' She pulled away, recalling that time. The music stopped and she spotted the Dalí-esque moustachioed man close by with Professor Cortez.

'I have to go over and say hello.' They made their way through the dancers and, as they were talking, the music started again.

'Ah, the sardana. Come and join us,' Professor Cortez said. 'It's easy and it's a tradition at festivities.' Her partner steered them with sinuous gyrations into the swaying crowd. He wagged his finger at them as Jack took Tansy in his arms. 'It's not that sort of dance.' He laughed, opening a wide circle. There they all held hands up high and danced steps that were neither ballet nor folk but fell somewhere in between and were completely unfamiliar. They kept going the wrong way, to the amusement of the others in their group.

Tansy's corsage got caught in Jack's sleeve as she twirled under his arm and it fell to the floor. This seemed to cause an exaggerated reaction from their circle. Professor Cortez picked it up and, as she was pinning it back, upside-down, on Tansy's dress, she asked, 'Don't you know the significance of that?' Tansy said she didn't. 'If you lose your corsage during the wedding, it means you'll be the next one to marry.'

'Well, that will be a surprise to everyone, not least of all me,' she joked, 'as I'm not planning to do that for a long time.'

After that, the beat changed and they danced for what seemed like hours, together, with their friends, with the bride and groom and then together again.

The musicians had already changed twice during the celebrations and it was clear that in all the preparations everything had been considered, right down to the diverse musical tastes of such a huge group of people. Splinter groups chatted in the smaller reception rooms and in the huge vestibule. Others stood on the balcony overlooking this.

Tansy was coming back from the bathroom with one of her friends. She spotted Jack immediately below, his one hundred and ninety-two centimetres dwarfing whoever he was talking to; his red hair standing out like a beacon among the predominantly dark-headed people around him.

'Isn't this some party?' she said to her friend as they watched the guests move about.

'The best. I suppose every wedding we ever go to will be compared with this. You and your boyfriend – he seems really nice – is it a serious relationship? Will you be the next ones to marry?'

'Good God, no! I mean it is serious, and yes, we probably could end up getting married, but not for a long time yet. Our families are not like Elena's and Álvaro's. We'd have to save up first, although Jack says he'd rather elope. He says he couldn't cope with all this palaver.'

'Men! They just don't get it, do they?' Laughing, they came down the sweeping staircase together. More food was being served in the ballroom as she and Jack made their way back inside.

'Are you enjoying yourself?' he asked.

'Absolutely.'

'I've never been as happy. I do love you, Tansy Nugent, and I don't ever want to lose you. Promise me you'll always be by my side. I couldn't bear the thought of ever losing you and I feel with you there, I can do anything.'

'That's quite a speech,' she said.

'I hope you feel the same way about me.'

'Do you know what, Jack? I do. You make me very happy too.' They shared a few moments, kissing, tongues exploring. She felt her heart quicken and her desire rising. The tempo changed again and then Jack said, 'I met that professor friend of yours while you were upstairs. We had an interesting chat.'

'I'd hardly describe Professor Cortez as a friend, although she was particularly pleasant earlier on and she seemed genuinely interested in how I was getting on.'

'No, not that one, although I think he's staying with her. It was the fellow from Dublin. The one Phyllis tore into last New Year's Eve.'

'Sean? Sean Pollard? Here?'

'The very one. He's working on some project in conjunction with the university here in Alcalá, and Álvaro's father, or his foundation, is bankrolling a huge portion of it, although you probably knew all that.'

Tansy felt like a child whose balloon had burst.

'He said to drop by his table and say hello. Do you want to do that now?'

'No, let's not bother. I haven't seen him since last year and I don't really have anything to say to him now.' Jack took her in his arms again and she leaned closer, but somehow the magic of the night had evaporated.

No matter how hard she tried to eradicate Sean from her mind, the very fact that they were both here, sharing the same space, threw her off-kilter. It had taken her a year and a half of heartache to reach the point she was now at and she had no intention of going back. She had to stay out of his way. She closed her eyes and tried to concentrate on the rhythm of the Spanish guitars and the closeness of Jack.

The crowd was beginning to thin out somewhat and he muttered, 'What's the drill? We don't have to stay till the very end, do we?'

'Of course not. I've had enough. It's after four and that's way past my bedtime.'

'Let's hope Rosa and Pedro are asleep when we get back and we can be together.'

'That's not going to happen,' she answered, almost too quickly. Then she added, 'It just wouldn't feel right, not under their roof.' She knew Jack was hurt, but she was hurting too. She'd just spied Sean in the distance looking very cosy with a friend of Elena's.

In the taxi going home, she put her head on Jack's shoulder and pretended to be asleep.

She wanted at once to remember and to forget. Not for the first time she asked herself what was the mysterious power Sean Pollard had over her?

Every time he came into her life, it spun off its axis.

Chapter Thirty-two

The wedding faded into memory. Once they had returned to Ireland and back to their respective placements, Jack threw himself into some serious forward planning for their grand adventure. Phyllis dubbed him 'the Spreadsheet King', as every time he visited, and that was several nights each week, he had pulled up charts for journeys, distances, timetables, alternative destinations, special deals, budgets, visa requirements and deadlines.

'Does he ever talk of anything else?' she asked Tansy, who just laughed and said, 'Sometimes! It can be a bit much, I admit, but it's his dream and I respect that.'

'Doesn't it excite you?'

'Of course it does, but I have to concentrate on my exams or I won't be going anywhere.'

'When did you all become so ... so responsible?' Phyllis asked.

'The realisation that in less than three months we'll have finished college is enough of a sobering thought to have that effect,' said Gina. 'That, coupled with the fact that then we're on our own – to make our way in the big, bad world – did the rest.'

'We'll be fine. We've done the work. Are you still considering a master's?' Phyllis asked Mags.

'I think so. Trevor has another year to do on his and we're kinda in that frame of mind.'

'He'll end up being a prof like his old man. I'm not sure I could face any more study after this, not immediately anyway. What about you, Tans?'

'I'm undecided at this point, but who knows, after a year away I might feel differently.'

'It looks like you all have the future mapped out,' Phyllis said.

'I'm not sure if that's ever possible,' Tansy said.

◆

Tansy's plans were disrupted, not by anything shocking, but by the delivery of an innocuous white envelope, which she found on the threadbare hall carpet, along with a bill and some junk mail.

It was addressed to her. She slit the envelope with a kitchen knife and pulled out the card. It was from Sean's publishers – an invitation to the launch of the book she had worked on for him: *Anthropology – it's not just Another Ology*. She'd flippantly suggested that title and he hadn't made a comment. It had obviously registered. Mixed emotions flooded through her. That glimpse of him at the wedding had been fleeting and unexpected and was proving much harder to erase than she would have wished. Now it was this stiff little white card that was making her ask the questions that she was trying not to answer.

She slid it back into the envelope and, in doing so, saw that it had something written on the back. It simply said, 'Please come,' and was signed with an 'S'.

She immediately decided she would be busy that Tuesday

night. She'd send a card of congratulations instead. She didn't mention it to the others, or to Jack. She bought a card, agonised as to what to write on it, opted for a few very formal and uninspired words of congratulations, sealed it, carried it around in her bag for a few days and didn't send it.

Then Trevor asked her if she would be bringing Jack along to the launch. Of course, Trevor would know all about it. How could she have not figured that out?

'I thought we could go for a few pints afterwards. We've all been so busy it seems ages since we had any fun.'

'You're right, we haven't. Anyway, I wasn't going to bother going, so I didn't mention it to Jack. Tuesdays are his training nights and he never misses those, especially now that he's working on his Bondi body,' she said, and she could feel Phyllis watching her. 'I'm sure I'll not be missed.'

'If you change your mind, Tansy, Mags and I will be there. The old man's coming home from Spain for it too.'

'I've not been invited,' said Phyllis.

'Are you surprised?' said Tansy.

'Lighten up, Tans, I was only joking. I could always sneak in and report back to you.'

'Now you are beginning to annoy me, Phyllis. Can you see why I didn't tell you?'

'At the risk of pushing you over the edge altogether, I think you should go.'

'And at the risk of doing the same to you, I think you should not be so concerned with my business! I can make up my own mind.'

By the time the date arrived, Mags had persuaded Tansy to go with them. Trying the perennial excuse of having 'nothing to wear' had failed. Mags had simply opened her wardrobe and gone 'frock fishing' and produced a sophisticated little number in cerise silk.

'That really suits you – you can keep it, if you like it. It's only been worn once, to the races. My mother chose it, so I felt I had to wear it, but it's not really me.'

'It's beautiful, Mags.' It fitted her perfectly and she had to admit she looked good in it. 'But I can't keep taking your things like this.'

'I'd have no problem,' said Phyllis, walking in on the dress rehearsal. 'That'll dazzle him.'

'Jack won't be there,' Tansy answered.

'I wasn't talking about him,' Phyllis said as she left the room.

◆

The library was buzzing with invited guests, some familiar faces from the media world as well as other personalities and academics. Trevor was already acquainted with several of them and made the introductions. Tansy couldn't see Sean anywhere. There were several tables dotted about, manned by assistants and stacked high with pristine piles of books – *Anthropology – it's not just Another Ology – Sean Pollard* clearly visible along their spine. People were queueing up to buy it and everyone seemed to be carrying at least one copy.

She got her first glimpse of Sean as a hush descended and he mounted the podium. She felt her heart quicken as he spoke, his familiar voice telling the guests how and why he had decided to write this 'accessible tome'. She felt she was the only person in the room and he was talking to her alone. She was back dining with him in Spain, sharing his car and his confidences.

She was back in Rosa's porch sharing that unforgettable 'stolen moment' where they clung to each other, wanting to give and take so much more from each other. She became aware of Mags and Trevor turning towards her, then people around her began looking. Good God. She hadn't said anything out loud, had she?

But they were smiling and clapping, and Sean began speaking again.

'As I was saying, it was due to the diligence of this young research student, Tansy Nugent, that a major *faux pas*, which I had missed, was spotted and a charlatan professor exposed and deposed.' The crowd clapped again.

'Thank you, Miss Nugent for that, and for saving my reputation and for the rest of your valued and valuable contribution. Thank you all again for coming along tonight, and please enjoy the rest of the evening.' The applause was more sustained and louder this time.

Had she imagined all that?

She knew she hadn't because people started coming over to her, offering their congratulations.

'You're a dark horse. You never told us anything about that,' Mags said.

'I had no idea that was going to happen.'

'A likely story. And to think you weren't even going to come tonight.'

'Honestly, Mags, I didn't think it was a big deal when it happened. I just figured that's what I was there to do. And, to be perfectly truthful, I'd forgotten all about it.' She laughed.

'Obviously Sean didn't. He was quite uncharacteristically effusive in his praise,' Trevor remarked. 'He'll probably want you on his team again when he's back in Dublin.'

It was only a matter of minutes before he found her. She extended her hand formally and he held on to it as she offered her congratulations.

'Well done, Prof. You must be delighted with the final product. It looks great. Another one for the bookshelf.'

'I signed this copy for you. You might find a space for it on yours,' he said. 'A few of us are going across the road to the hotel for a drink. Please join us. Ernest is already over there holding some tables in the bar.'

'I haven't seen Ernest for a while. How is he?' she asked.

Sean replied, 'Come on over and you can ask him yourself.'

Fifteen minutes later she found herself being invited to sit beside Ernest.

'The old legs aren't as efficient as they used to be,' he said, patting the bench. She was just seated when Sean arrived and plonked himself on her other side. She was trapped, sandwiched between him and Ernest, an assortment of beverages on the table before them.

'That's my duty over for the night. I've done with talking and making polite conversation. How have you been? You're looking extraordinarily well.'

'So are you,' she said before turning to ask Ernest, 'How are you enjoying working in Spain? Is it going well?' She tried to ignore the heat she could feel from Sean's arm and leg. It seemed to sear through the silk dress.

'It's going exceptionally well. Having a foundation with loads of money backing a project like this makes a huge difference. It's rare to have one with personal and historic connections too. I keep telling Sean that's what we need in Ireland. The money is here, but it needs to be harvested. It's not intellectuals we lack, but altruists. I believe you are friends with Álvaro Junior, of the Lopez-Cabellos. They head the foundation.'

'That's right. My boyfriend and I were at his wedding—'

'Ah yes, the wedding,' Sean butted in. 'That was some pageant. Did you enjoy it?'

'We had a marvellous time,' she said, smiling up at Trevor who had just approached to introduce someone to his father. She felt Sean's hand on her arm as he turned towards her.

'And you managed to avoid me all evening,' he said quietly.

'I didn't know you were going to be there, or indeed that you were …' She stammered and felt her checks reddening.

'And I didn't know if you'd be here tonight.'

'Neither did I,' she answered.

'Nothing has changed, has it?' he whispered, and she looked down. She didn't trust herself to answer. She couldn't. Nothing had changed. Nothing would ever change, as far as her feelings for him were concerned.

'Let's get out of here,' he suggested.

'We can't. People will notice.'

'Let them. We've got to talk.'

She kept her eyes down. 'I can't do this, Sean. I'm going to go home.'

'And you think that will make "this", whatever "this" is, go away?'

'Be quiet. Someone will hear you.'

'Do I care?'

She knew he didn't. But she did. There was Jack to consider.

'Let's just walk out together. We could be going outside for a cigarette.'

'We don't smoke.'

'Does anybody know that? Does anybody care?'

She laughed. 'I don't suppose they do.'

'Come on, then,' he said, standing up. He led her out of the bar and towards the lifts.

'Where are we going?'

'To my room. I'm staying in the hotel. I've let my place out to some academics for the summer. Come on. We have to talk.'

Neither said anything as another pair got into the lift just as the doors were closing. They just smiled at each other and waited as it stopped at each floor. He led her down the plush corridor, swiped his key and stood aside to let her enter in front of him. She turned to tell him she shouldn't be there. It was a mistake, a moment's madness, but he reached out and took her in his arms and kissed her, gently, teasingly, before stepping back.

'You were going to say … ?'

'Sean, this is madness. I can't do it. I'm with Jack now. We're going off to Australia together in a few weeks. I shouldn't be here.'

He leaned forward and kissed her again, slowly at first, then more demandingly. In spite of her protests, she felt herself responding, her arms going up around his neck as she drew him towards her, leaning her body closer to his. Still holding her, he grinned and muttered, 'What was that you were saying?'

'I shouldn't be here. What would Jack think if he knew I was? How would I feel if the situation was reversed and he went to someone's bedroom, someone he had had feelings for before I came along?'

'I don't know. How would you feel?' he asked, kissing her again and leading her to the bed. 'How do you feel? Is it fairer to be with him out of duty and to pretend everything is perfect when you know you feel like this about me?' He ran his hand up and down her arm.

'I don't know. I'm so confused. I've got to go.'

'I understand, but let me tell you something, Tansy. I've never stopped thinking about you. From that first day when I gave you a lift to the west. I've had dalliances with other women since then, mainly to prove to myself that it, you, us, meant nothing, but I couldn't fool myself. You got under my skin, Tansy Nugent, like a sting that can't be soothed. When I saw you there tonight in the library, I could hardly get my words out. I was so happy. I had told myself that if you turned up, it would prove that you must still feel something for me and if that was the case, I wouldn't let you escape again. Say something. Put me out of my agony. Do you? Do you still have feelings for me?'

'I won't deny that I do. But I'm not going to throw away my relationship with Jack because of a few kisses. You have your life, Sean, and I have mine. They might cross occasionally, but we both know that you'll board a plane in a few days and disappear without a word again, and that you'll move on to the next student or graduate who falls under your spell.'

He tried to interrupt. 'It —'

'That's all that I was, a gauche country kid let loose in the big smoke. I was a sitting target, naïve and impressionable. You are a man of the world, travelled, erudite, a suave university professor and you noticed me and treated me like a woman. What's not captivating about that? It's an ageless story and I fell, oh so willingly, into the trap. But, Sean, I've changed in those two years. I've grown up and can now see it for what it was. I'll admit I was hurt, very hurt.' Her voice broke as she remembered. She swallowed hard and continued.

'I was devastated when you were missing the next term without a word. I felt humiliated too that I seemed to be the only one who hadn't an inkling of your plans. All summer I had been looking forward to seeing you and I had accepted that no matter how I felt, it could never be more than as friends. But that's in the past. I'm over you now, and assuming I've got my H Dip, I'm off to see the world and build my own memories and you'll not be in those. You'll always be there among my college ones, though. I can't deny that.'

'I'm sorry you were hurt, Tansy, that I hurt you, but I had no alternative. I wanted you so badly. You've no idea how hard it was for me. I wanted to tell you how I felt in Alcalá, to take you to my hotel and make love to you. That's why I insisted you invited Álvaro to dinner with us that last night. You must see how impossible the situation was. I couldn't trust myself to stay away from you had I been seeing you in college every other day. It would have cost me my job, had the ethics committee been informed, and you wouldn't have been looked on too favourably either.'

'You didn't give me the chance to find out, did you?' He was still holding her hands, stroking the backs of them with his thumbs, a simple action that was causing seismic reactions within her.

'I knew I had to get away and when it became obvious that the Spanish Civil War project might be a viable one, it seemed like the perfect solution.'

'For you, maybe.'

'For us both, believe me. If you can honestly say you don't care for me, I'll let you walk out the door, but after the way you kissed me just now, I refuse to believe that. If you feel the way

I do, then I'll never let you go again.' He pulled her towards him and they kissed with a fervour that released all the pent-up emotions they had contained since their stolen moment on Rosa's porch. He lay her gently back on the bed and began caressing her. She surrendered and as his hand grazed her nipple, she pushed him away and sat up.

'Why did you have to do that? You've ruined everything.' She started to cry. He took her in his arms and began to rock her backwards and forwards, pushing her hair out of her eyes.

'How can I face Jack? He doesn't deserve this. How can I go away with him now?'

'Don't. Stay with me, Tansy. Marry me, Tansy. We'd make a great team.'

'Have you lost your reason, Sean?' she asked. 'Marry you? How much have you had to drink?'

'Just enough to give me the courage to ask you that. I've thought of nothing else since our few days in Alcalá. I mean it, Tansy. I know how I feel and I've been going crazy not being able to tell you. Say something, please.'

'I'm in shock. I don't know what to say. I don't know anything any more.'

'Stay with me tonight, Tansy, and let me show you how I love you and how much I want you.'

'I can't. I won't do that to Jack.'

'Admit it, you want to. You can't lie to yourself, or to Jack.'

'I know. Oh God, why did I have to go to your blasted launch?'

'Tansy, I won't force you into anything you don't want, but I'm going back to Spain in three days – come back with me and we can get to know each other properly.'

'You expect me to make a decision that will affect my whole

life just like that? It's too big to rush into. I need time to think, Sean. It's like my head's going to explode.'

'That's not a no, though, is it? Is there any way I can persuade you?' He kissed her again. She felt herself drowning in a whirlpool of desire.

'No. I mean, yes. It's got to be a no. I have to go.'

'I'll ask you one thing. While you're thinking about it just remember how this feels,' he said, taking her face in his hands and looking into her soul, before kissing her again, his tongue igniting waves in her very core.

'I should never have agreed to come to your room.' She stood up and straightened her clothing. 'What are you doing in a hotel anyway? Why aren't you staying with your mother? Is she well?'

'Very, thank you for asking, but I couldn't have brought you back there and my publishers put me up here.'

'So, you were planning a seduction? With me, or with whoever was available?' she said, feeling let down.

'That's not fair.'

She made for the door. There's nothing fair about what I've just done, she thought. 'Thank you for your generous words at the launch. I was very touched by them.'

'But obviously not enough. And for the record, you're wrong about my intentions, Tansy, very wrong. I want you for my wife, no one else. You're the only reason I agreed to this launch. It was the only way I could think of coming into contact with you. When you've finished your H Dip, we can be open about our relationship. I'm asking for a chance here.'

'I didn't know we had one,' she stammered.

'Yes, you did. Your eyes told me a long time ago and just now so did your whole body, the way you responded to me. I won't try to force you, but you know where I am if you change your mind.' He remained sitting on the end of the bed.

'Goodnight,' she said.

She fled to the lift, feeling conspicuous and foolish. What sort of a mess had she created for herself? If he'd realised how close she was to succumbing to his touch, his smell, his proximity, she knew he'd never have stopped trying. Now she had to face Jack and pretend this evening had never happened. She loved Jack and he deserved better from her. She had to get as far away from Sean Pollard as possible before he wrecked her life.

She checked the bar and when there was no sign of Trevor and Mags, she was relieved. She needed time on her own to process the events of the evening. She decided to walk home to Rathmines. It was still bright and the evening warm and it would give her time to compose herself before coming face to face with Jack. He always came over on Tuesdays, after his training sessions.

Everywhere she looked there seemed to be couples – happy, smiling, laughing couples, holding hands, embracing, sharing intimacies. Could she have that with Sean? What did she really know about him? Would she have been a pleasant interlude for his brief visit to Dublin, maybe even someone who'd be waiting for him on his next flit in and out, between the ones he probably had in Spain or wherever else he visited? Were there other gullible women fulfilling the same role? She might be a country girl, unschooled in the cosmopolitan ways of the world, but she wasn't going to take a chance on being duped by a smooth-talking, practised older man. She wasn't that naïve.

What if she had stayed? What if she'd called his bluff and taken his proposal seriously? What would he have said or done?

Would he still head off to Spain in three days and forget all about her? Or did he mean all those things he had said and that his body had confirmed?

Instead of clarifying matters, she was more confused than ever by the time she reached the flat. She didn't stop to stroke Rags, who was stretched proprietorially out on the window ledge enjoying the stored heat from the granite sill. He looked askance at her neglect. Even the cat knows I'm guilty, she thought as she let herself in and heard the sound of Trevor and Jack's laughter coming from the kitchen.

'Good God, you look stunning, Tans,' Jack said. 'That dress is a knockout.' He came towards her to give her a kiss. She pushed him away. 'No. Don't. It's Mags's and I don't want to mess it up. You're all sweaty from training.'

'And Gina has used what was left of the hot water, so I'd think you're out of luck tonight, Jack.'

'Phyllis! That's none of your business.'

'Just sayin' it as I see it!'

'Tansy's right, Phyllis,' said Trevor. 'It's not.'

Did he know as well? Had he and Mags noticed her leave the bar with Sean?

'Anyone for tea? I'm going to make a pot,' she said.

'OK. I can take a hint. I'll have a mug and take myself off. I'll come back again tomorrow, all shiny and clean and we can celebrate,' said Jack, and she breathed a huge sigh of relief. 'The guys showed me how you saved your professor's reputation. That's pretty impressive.'

'It's nothing really, but I might go home to Dunmoy tomorrow and spend a few quality days with the folks on my own. It'll be a chance for some revision. I haven't been down for a while and they're still miffed that I'm abandoning them and heading off to the other side of the world.'

'It's not forever,' he said.

'A year is nothing,' said Mags. 'It'll fly by. We've spent four together and it doesn't seem like that at all.'

It might fly by, but right now that wasn't what was concerning Tansy. She had to get away from Jack. She couldn't look him in the eye.

'By the way, Tansy,' Mags said, 'you left your signed book on the table when you left. I ran after you, but the lift doors were just closing, so I took it home for you.'

'Thanks, you were gone when I went back. I'd hoped you had it,' she said as casually as she could. Was Mags trying to tell her she knew something?

She had to get away. Sean was only going to be in Dublin for a few days and heading to Dunmoy would eliminate any chance of her bumping into him. Out of sight, out of mind, she told herself as she got ready for bed.

But fleeing from this whirlwind of emotions was not going to be a simple matter.

Chapter Thirty-three

Erasing the previous night was proving more difficult than she'd imagined. Sean Pollard might have been out of sight, but he certainly was not out of her mind. She replayed every bit of the evening, over and over again. Had Sean's feelings been there all along? He'd actually proposed to her, or could it have just been a throwaway remark? Had he really meant it? Was it a chat-up line that had worked on others over the years? What did she really know about him? Was she just one of many other naïve women to have fallen for his charms and, if so, had he expected her to as well? She kept coming back to the same thought. What if she'd acquiesced – would he have had his way with her and then disappeared, as she had predicted?

What if he was being sincere? He had proven he was honourable – hadn't he stepped back so as not to damage her reputation?

He'd never seemed to be hiding anything from her and he had been so openly frank when she had confronted him in the car in Spain. He hadn't been under any obligation to confide in her or reveal those personal details of his life to her, so why had she been so vehement in her rejection of his declarations of love?

Could she honestly deny how she felt when he took her in his arms, when she heard his voice, when he looked at her the way he did? When he touched her?

Several times during the night she stopped herself comparing Jack and Sean. That was unfair. Jack had done nothing to merit that. She was now an intrinsic part of his dreams and his plans for a faithful, long-term partnership. Or she had been until a few hours ago. But now she doubted that. She doubted everything.

Had she just thrown away her chance of happiness with either or both of them? Had it even been a possibility that Sean and she might have had a future together? She'd never know now, but she knew that she might spend the rest of her life regretting not finding out.

As the night gave way to the first early streaks of dawn, she'd made up her mind about one thing. She had to tell Jack what had happened. She couldn't start a new life with him with this guilty secret hanging over her. She wasn't looking forward to doing it, but do it she must.

She'd tell him when she got back from Dunmoy on Friday.

◆

The smell of frying bacon always woke Tansy and the possibility that Gina was making pancakes to go with it enticed her from under her duvet.

'God, you look ropey. Did you have a lot to drink last night? You were all in bed when I got back from the restaurant.'

'Not at all. I just didn't sleep very well,' Tansy said.

'You'll feel better after a Gina special,' she said, putting a plate in front of her and dousing the contents with maple syrup. 'Tell me how the launch went.'

At that moment their doorbell rang aggressively and repeatedly.

'Have a bit of patience,' Gina shouted. 'Are you expecting anyone, Tansy?'

'Definitely not!' she replied as she wrapped her dressing gown more tightly around her and headed down the stairs.

'These are for Miss Tansy Nugent,' a delivery man said, handing over an enormous bouquet of flowers. 'Is that you? I'd say this lot cost a pretty penny.'

Tansy signed for them and returned to the kitchen.

'Wow. That's some bunch of flowers,' Gina said. 'I'm presuming they're for you. You must have impressed someone last night.'

Before she could mask her reaction, Mags and Phyllis appeared.

'Who was making that bloody racket? Oh my God – did we inherit a flower shop?' asked Phyllis. 'I haven't seen so many blooms since our GP's funeral. Who are they from? There must be a card.' She made straight for the bouquet to investigate.

Tansy ignored Phyllis's reaction, too taken up with her own. She hoped the card would not be too incriminating because there was no way she'd get out of reading it aloud.

They had to be from Sean, Tansy reasoned. Jack only did flowers for birthdays and usually ones from the supermarket in keeping with his financial status, and these were definitely not in either league. There were lilies and gerberas, roses and chrysanthemums. She was sure whatever they had cost would have kept them all for a week. She pushed the blooms gently apart, looking for a tell-tale envelope. She was relieved when she couldn't find one.

'You've obviously got a secret admirer,' Phyllis continued. 'How intriguing. I wonder if we can guess ...'

Mags stopped the interrogation. 'They're beautiful, but what are we going to put them all in? We haven't enough vases and the ones we have are not tall enough. You could bring some home with you to your mam.'

'You're a genius, Mags. I'll do that.'

'Have you any idea who they're from?' Phyllis urged.

'Not a clue,' she lied. 'Not the faintest clue.'

At the bus station later that day, she had to do a balancing act with the flowers, her purse and her rucksack. A young mother with two small children, one of whom refused to sit still, slid up to make space for her on a bench and she accepted gratefully.

'What beautiful little girls,' she remarked as the smaller one put out a chubby little hand to touch the petals of a pale pink gerbera. Her mother tried to stop her, but Tansy said, 'It's OK. She's not doing any harm. And they are perfection, aren't they?' She suddenly remembered fingering velvety gerbera petals while dining with Sean in the *parador* in Alcalá de Henares. He had told her Egyptians called them happiness flowers. That was why there was no little envelope attached. The gerbera was his signature. He had sent her a message only she would understand.

The little one put her fingers back again, looking solemnly at Tansy with big blue eyes as though reading her thoughts, and still holding Tansy's gaze, she began stroking the petals almost reverently.

'She's a very curious child, interested in everything, not like her sister, who just has to keep on the move all the time. Chalk and cheese, they are,' the woman said.

'They must keep you busy.'

'You can say that again. Never a minute to myself, but I'm from a big family, all boys except me, so I'm used to it. Have you any?'

'No, but I look forward to the day. I've no brothers or sisters either. I'd like to see myself with four. Wouldn't it be great if you were able to order them, two of each?'

'And have them delivered like a takeaway. That would be the way to go. Despite all the advances in technology, no one has found a shortcut for having kids, have they?' the woman said, and they laughed. 'Here's my bus. It was nice talking to you.'

'And to you too,' Tansy said and, on impulse, she handed her the flowers. The woman tried to resist, but Tansy insisted. She watched her shepherd her little ones ahead of her as she boarded her bus and waved back at her. There were tears glinting in the young woman's eyes. At least they had made somebody happy, Tansy thought as her bus pulled into the concourse.

Why had he sent them? Perhaps he had really meant what he said. Was she reading more into the inclusion of the gerberas? Maybe they were just in season. Or maybe not. Or was that just wishful thinking on her behalf?

The bus followed its route westwards across the country. She stared out at the landscape along the way, as it changed from the manicured fields and large sprawls to the smaller, more rugged, sheep-dotted ones, whose borders were forever delineated by dry-stone walls. She rang home to tell her mam she was on her way and as soon as she heard her voice, she felt the familiar claustrophobia descending like an ominous cloud. She had thought a bit of mothering would soothe some of her anxiety. Instead she knew she was heading straight into a wave of smothering and that was not what she needed right now.

'Where are you, love? You sound like you're on a bus.'

'I am, Mam. I'm just going to meet some people. I can't hear very well. The line is very bad. I'll ring you later,' she lied and hung up. She got off at the next stop, went and had a coffee, and then some lunch while she waited for the next bus back to Dublin. She'd have to think up some excuse for her flatmates. She wasn't ready to share the circumstances with them. She phoned Phyllis and instructed her under no circumstances was she, or any of the others, to tell her mother if she rang that she was on her way home.

'Why? Where are you? Are you OK?' Phyllis asked.

'Yes, I'm fine, really. I've changed my mind. I'm on my way back to Dublin.'

'Tans, tell me what's going on? You have me worried.'

'I will, but not now. Just do what I ask, please. It's important and there's no need to worry.'

With that out of the way, she still had to confront Jack. She took up her phone several times to call him and chickened out each time.

'Do it, girl, do it and get it over with,' she told herself and stopped short yet again, opting for a text instead.

'Jack – a change of plan. Are you free? I need to see you, somewhere away from the flat. I'll be in town in less than an hour.'

'Mystery and intrigue – I thought you were heading west. I'll have to put my other woman off … very inconvenient!!! I'll be in town too. Meet me in Stephen's Green at 3.30. Luvya xxx.'

She replied with a simple 'x', knowing she was about to break his heart.

◆

She reached the little bridge that straddled the narrowest part of the two lakes and led to the formal gardens in the Green. It was hard to imagine that people used to graze their sheep here a few centuries earlier. The Victorian flowerbeds sang with early-summer colour and people of all ages took advantage of this oasis in the bustling capital.

The rangers turned a blind eye to those ignoring 'Keep off the grass' notices. Scorchers like today were all too rare in Irish summers and little knots of people sat everywhere, making the most of the good weather. Children threw bread to the ducks, who quacked and squawked as they fought off the cheeky seagulls in an effort to win it first. Ignoring the feathered chaos around them, a bevy of swans glided serenely along, haughtily tolerating those who shared their domain.

Jack's 'Hi, gorgeous' announced his arrival. He was holding two ice-cream cones. 'I was hoping you'd be here, or I'd have had to bin one of these as they're already melting.'

She took the one he held out to her and, smiling at him, she rescued the drips before saying, 'You think of everything, don't you?'

'I aim to please. Let's find somewhere to sit. There are some people leaving over there. Let's grab that spot.' Once they were settled, he said, 'Now talk to me. Why the change of plan?'

'I have to tell you something and I know you're not going to like it.'

'You're not sick, are you?'

'No, nothing like that.'

'You've changed your mind about Australia.'

'No, not that either.'

'Whew – that's a relief. Since I got your text, I was convinced that was what you wanted to tell me. So, what is it? It's not something bad, is it?'

'No, yes, no, but I think you should know … I kissed someone last night.'

'You what?' She could see the incredulity in his eyes. 'So that's why you were so off when you came in, keeping me at arm's length. Who was it?'

'You don't need to know that,' she said quietly.

'Was it at that book launch?'

'No, afterwards. In the Westin. The hotel. In someone's room.'

'Might I ask what in hell's name you were doing in someone's room in that hotel? Did you go up to see his etchings? Did you sleep together?'

'There's no need for sarcasm. I'm trying to be honest here.'

'Is that what you call it? I wouldn't have put cheating in that category. I thought you loved me. Who was it? Did you just meet last night? Is it someone I know?'

'I didn't mean to cheat and I didn't sleep with him. I'm sorry, Jack.'

'Sorry it happened, or sorry that you didn't walk away?'

'I did walk away …'

'After you walked to his room with him, Tansy. What do you expect of me now?'

'That you'll hear me out and let me explain. I didn't have to tell you and maybe you'd never have found out, but I couldn't live with myself knowing that was there between us. I wanted to get it out in the open and move on.'

'Move on. And am I now supposed to pretend this never happened? If that's what you're expecting, then you're wrong. I can't. I'd never have put you down as that sort of woman. I could never trust you now. What's to say the next guy who chats you up won't have more success with you?'

'That's not fair. Have I ever given you reason to think like that?'

'Not until now. And *not fair*? I'll tell you what's not fair. Jesus Christ! Cheating is not fair! I feel disgusted and let down. How could you go off with someone you just met like that? And yes, you've just given me reason never to trust you again! Ever!'

'You don't understand. It wasn't someone I'd just met. It was someone I've known for a few years.'

'And that changes what? Had you kissed before? Tell me that. Was there something between you before last night?'

'There was.'

'Tell me it's not that middle-aged professor.'

She didn't answer.

He went to stand up but she restrained him. 'Jack, listen, please. There was one other occasion, before I knew you. There were insurmountable obstacles in our way. We both knew nothing could come of it and we agreed not to take it any further. And we didn't.'

'Was he cheating on someone too? A wife perhaps?'

'That's not worthy of you, Jack, and no he wasn't. Circumstances got in the way.'

'Are those "circumstances", as you call them, still there?'

'Actually, no, they're not.'

'So, I conveniently filled a gap, did I?'

'No. That's not the way it was … is. I never meant it to happen. I stayed out of his way ever since I met you.'

'But you obviously still have feelings for him if you had to go to such lengths to keep him at bay. And to keep him a secret from me. And then you fall into his arms when you meet up again. How do you think that makes me feel, Tansy?'

'You make it sound – so calculated.'

'I don't make it sound like anything. I'm calling it as it is. You cheated. No one made you do that. We're through, Tansy. You're not who I thought you were.'

'I didn't mean to hurt you, Jack.'

'Well, you did. Don't try contacting me because I won't change my mind.'

He stood up and this time she didn't try to stop him. She knew he meant what he said. She watched him stride across the grass, out onto the path and up to the bridge. It was over between them and she had ruined what they had had. In doing so, she had destroyed his trust too and she'd never forgive herself for that. She loved Jack. He was kind and caring and he never tried to hide the fact that she was the centre of his world.

She really loved him, just not enough, it seemed. This realisation added to her distress.

She now had to face her flatmates and tell them what had happened, and she wasn't looking forward to that.

Chapter Thirty-four

'You've broken up! You can't be serious,' was Phyllis's reaction.

'I did the unforgiveable. I was with someone last night and we kissed. I told Jack this afternoon.' She broke down and cried. 'Why does life have to be so difficult? You should have seen his face. He was devastated. He wants nothing more to do with me.'

'He's probably just shocked. I bet it'll blow over,' was Gina's uncharacteristically optimistic pronouncement. 'Let him cool down for a bit, give him time to miss you and he'll be back. Just wait and see.'

'He won't. I assure you. I've broken his trust.'

Tansy looked at Mags, who said nothing at first. When she did speak, she said, 'He'd probably never have found out.'

Tansy knew that she'd put two and two together. 'Maybe not, but I would always have known, Mags, and the guilt would have eaten me up. I had to tell him.'

'So that's what the flowers were about? Where are they, by the way?' Phyllis enquired, looking around the room.

'I gave them to a woman I met at the bus station.'

'A bit of joined-up talking here, please. Everything seemed all right last night. You're going home, then you're not. You give your flowers to a stranger – I assume before you met Jack – and then you arrive back and drop this bomb. Is anyone else as confused as me? Please start at the beginning.'

'That wasn't why I gave the flowers away. Look, if you don't mind, I'd rather not go into any more detail right now. Can you just give me a bit of space? I didn't sleep very well and I'm wrecked.'

A while later Phyllis brought her a cup of tea.

'You needn't talk if you don't want to, but I'm here if you do.'

Tansy started to cry again. Her friend took her mug and put it on the bedside table. She sat up on the bed beside her and hugged her. 'I'm sure Jack will come around. He's mad about you.'

'I don't think he will. You should have seen his face and the hurt in his eyes. It was awful.'

'I'm assuming Sean features somewhere in this equation, or is that just my suspicious mind going into overdrive?'

'No, it's not.'

'That man is bad news. He's far too old for you and he somehow always manages to mess with your head. Don't let him destroy everything for you. You and Jack have made all those plans together.'

'It's too late for that.'

'Tell me you don't still have feelings for him?'

'I can't do that. They never went away. I was fooling myself thinking they had. When he suggested we leave the party last night to discuss things, I couldn't refuse, try as I might. His publishers put him up in the Westin and we ended up in his room.'

'What were you thinking? You should have run a mile.'

'I could have, Phyllis, but can't you see? I didn't want to.'

'Oh Tans. Did you sleep with him?'

'No, I didn't. Not because I didn't want to, but because I couldn't do that to Jack.'

'And he let you go, just like that?'

'Jack?'

'No, Sean.'

'He did – after he asked me to marry him, yes.'

'Holy shit – he did what? That's some seduction line. What did you say to him?'

'I told him I was completely confused and that I was going home.'

'And … ?'

'And he stayed sitting there on the bed, watching me leave. He told me I knew where to find him if I wanted to and that he'd be in Dublin for another few days. I left and walked home.'

'What are you going to do?'

'About what?' Tansy asked.

'About it all, or any of it. Do you want to fix things with Jack? If not, there's nothing to stop you going to Australia with the gang, not as a couple as planned but just as a group of friends.'

'I'm not sure that would ever work. I do love him, you know, and I'll always regret hurting him.'

'You're talking as though there is no way back, or even as though you don't want there to be one.'

'I can't see one and I can't help wondering what would happen if I said yes to Sean. He asked me to go to Spain with him. We could get to know each other openly. There's no obstacle to that now. Do you think if I don't try to find out, I'll spend the rest of my life regretting not giving it a try?'

'If you do that, you'll be scuppering any hope of a reconciliation with Jack, Tansy.'

'But I can't entertain the thought of that happening now that I know how Sean feels about me, and knowing how I feel about him. It's such a mess, Phyllis. What am I going to do?'

'From where I'm looking at this, it seems to me that you've already made up your mind. What I think doesn't enter into it. I never thought I'd say this and, as you know, I'm not his biggest fan, but if you like the guy that much, then go for it and see where it takes you both. And if he hurts you, tell him he'll have me to contend with.'

'Thanks, Phyllis, I needed to hear you say that. Not the last bit, though. I think he already knows that.' She smiled.

'You realise the others don't know anything about your "history" with your professor, or that it was him you were with last night? Are you going to tell them, or do you want me to?'

'I think Mags and Trevor have twigged. I think they noticed us going off together. None of them need to know the rest, though. Not yet. Now leave me alone until I try to figure out what to do.'

A while later she sent Sean a text. She regretted it and sweated while the minutes ticked by. The reply simply stated a time and a place. She did the best she could to disguise her puffy eyes and no one asked where she was going.

Once she saw him sitting at a table for two in the corner of the little Italian restaurant he'd suggested, any doubts she'd had vanished. She knew she'd follow him anywhere. She never wanted to spend another moment away from him.

'What made you change your mind?' he asked.

'I had to be sure I hadn't misunderstood you last night.'

'You didn't. I was afraid I'd lost you forever.' He took her hand across the table. The warmth sent pulses of electricity through her body.

'I meant everything I said, Tansy. I want you for my wife. I love you and have done since the first day when you tried to hoodwink me with the cock and bull story about having worked in Peru.'

'That wasn't me. It was Phyllis who did that.'

'Ah, Phyllis,' he said. 'My biggest fan! Does she know?'

'Yes. It was actually she who told me I should come and talk to you.'

'Perhaps she has more sense than I credited her with.'

'She's a wonderful and loyal friend.'

'What about the boyfriend and your plans for Australia?'

'I told him what happened between us last night, and he wants nothing more to do with me, ever. I feel very bad about him. I never saw this happening. Neither did he. I never meant to hurt him.'

'I know that. But you have to be true to yourself too. Tansy, I'm well aware of the considerable age difference between us. Is that a problem for you? I've another year to finish this Spanish Civil War project, then I'll be back in the university here, resuming my tenure. Will you come to Spain with me in the meantime? You could teach English, or help me.'

'We've so much to talk about.'

'Let's skip dessert and go back to my room and begin, but be warned, I won't let you leave so easily this time.'

She smiled at him. 'Maybe I'll not be in such a hurry either.'

He kissed her as they left the restaurant. By the time they reached his room, their desire had ignited to such an extent that there was only one way to quench it.

He made love to her with an expertise and a tenderness she had not experienced before.

Afterwards, as they lay entwined together, in the afterglow, he asked, 'How will your folks take the news?'

'With disbelief, I imagine. The age thing will definitely be an issue for them, but I've no doubt that you'll win them over too. When they had me, Mam was well into her thirties, and that was considered old then – they'd been married for fourteen years. I was a bit of a surprise.'

'I'd say you were.' He laughed. 'I have to go back to the university in Alcalá on Friday for meetings about further funding for the research, but I can come back over at the end of next week and perhaps we could go down together and tell them, if that's what you'd like.'

'I'm not sure I can keep it a secret for that long.' She laughed. 'I want everyone to know. What about your mother? You could bring me to meet her tomorrow.'

'Tomorrow?'

'Yes, tomorrow. I mean, today. It's broad daylight already. Don't you want to tell her that you're finally going to get married and that I'm the lucky lady? How do you think she'll take that news?'

'With disbelief and disapproval.' He laughed. 'As she always does to anything I do.'

'She can't be that bad.'

'Since she started having those mini-strokes, she's become a bit unpredictable in some ways. I can understand how frustrating it must be – to have been the one sorting out other people's lives for decades, and now to be the one needing sorting.'

'Maybe this will give her a lift. The prospect of a new

grandchild or grandchildren to carry on the Pollard name might change all that.'

'Let's not make that our opening line.' She sensed he was uncomfortable as he told her, 'Actually, I'd steer clear of that topic. Even though it's a lifetime ago, she never got over losing her only grandchild, little Ivan, despite not approving of his mother or of our shotgun wedding and subsequent annulment.'

'Got it. But you make her sound like the mother from hell.'

'I wouldn't go quite that far. She's kind and opinionated and, well, she's my mother!'

'Kind and opinionated? An apple falling far from the tree?' She laughed.

'You can make up your own mind when you meet her.'

'I have to get back to the flat and make myself look respectable. It's been a crazy, wonderful, unforgettable and highly emotional day and night. I can't believe this has all happened or that I've agreed to be your wife.'

'Nor can I.'

'And I can't wait to see what my flatmates say.'

•

As Tansy had expected, they were all still in bed when she arrived home. She made as much noise as possible and started frying bacon. That always got everyone up. As she put it on plates, she said, 'I have some news. A lot has happened since yesterday and ...'

'You're back with Jack,' said Gina.

'No, but you might like to sit down for this one, Gina. I'm getting married. Sean Pollard proposed and I've accepted.'

'Sean – your professor Sean? You can't be serious. He's years older than you. Do you even like him?' Gina said.

'Of course I do. I love him. And you could pretend to be happy for me.'

Gina looked accusingly at Phyllis and Mags. 'Why have you two said nothing? Don't tell me you both knew. Why am I only finding out now? Whose idea was it to keep me in the dark?'

'It wasn't anybody's idea,' Tansy said. 'We had a situation when I was working for him.'

'You mean it's been going on all this time? All the time you've been with Jack?'

'No, nothing like that. Something happened between us and we knew we were attracted to each other, but we knew it couldn't work then, and he walked away from the situation. Meeting up again the other night, we both knew that we still felt the same way. I told Jack about it and that's why we parted. He's gutted. I'm not proud of that, but there's no big conspiracy behind it. It was all very quick and definitely unpremeditated. Then Sean proposed and I've accepted.'

Mags said, 'I suspected something was going on when I saw the pair of you getting into the lift in the hotel the other evening, but I couldn't be sure. Trevor told me I was imagining things.'

'And because I'm nosey I knew something had happened in Spain,' said Phyllis. 'I prised it out of Tansy and she asked me to say nothing, but I broke her confidence at the New Year's Eve party eighteen months ago in Trevor's house and that's what our big falling-out was over. I was furious at how he'd just vanished from the campus without letting her know.'

'I always had my suspicions about that,' Gina said.

'No one meant to keep you in the dark. I hadn't a clue that things would turn out like this, or move so fast either. We're going ring shopping this morning and this afternoon I'm going to meet the mother-in-law!'

'Are you nervous?'

'Terrified!' She laughed.

'Is he coming back to the university this autumn, or will you be heading off somewhere exciting with him?' Mags asked.

'I don't know yet. Up to now, all I'd thought about was Australia. Sean doesn't see any point in waiting. He wants us to marry as soon as possible.'

'Have you told your folks yet?' asked Phyllis.

'Not yet. I'm going to call them now and fill them in. I suppose I can expect to be castigated for hurting Jack. Mam really likes him. Mind you, she liked Sean when she met him, albeit very briefly. She'll probably go into a flap at the idea of a wedding.'

◆

Tansy wasn't wrong about her mother's reaction. Her announcement was met with a bombardment of questions.

'Are you telling me you're going to marry your professor? The one who brought you down to Ballinasloe the time of Gappy Jim's funeral?'

'That's right, Mam, and he's not my professor, although,' she said, laughing, 'he probably is now that I think about it.'

'Isn't it all a bit sudden?' was the next question and Tansy knew that was loaded with the unasked one – was she pregnant? 'Poor Jack. How did he take this news?'

'It's complicated. He doesn't know about the engagement yet.'

'Tell me you weren't double-crossing him. I would hate to see any daughter of my mine treat someone like that.'

'No, Mam, I wasn't. He's not happy, though, and I do understand, but I couldn't keep going out with him knowing the way I feel about Sean and how he feels about me.'

'He's a lot older than you. Will he want to start a family, at his age?'

'Mam, you say that as if he were Methuselah. Lots of men don't get married nowadays until they're in their fifties, and he's a good bit off that. George Clooney was fifty-three when he tied the knot and then they had twins.'

'I suppose you're right. Don't mind me. Your father and I got married in our early twenties. I can't wait to tell him when he gets in from the fields. As usual, he's left his phone in the porch, although what good it would be to him there if he had an accident, I don't know. And Mary McLaughlin. She'll want all the details. What sort of ring are you going to get?'

'I haven't an idea, Mam, but I'll know when I see it. We'll come down very soon, maybe this weekend, and you can get to know Sean a little better.'

'That would be a good thing. I was very fond of Jack, though …'

'I know you were, Mam, and I know you'll feel the same about Sean.'

'We'll see,' she replied, and Tansy could feel the reservation in that comment.

Chapter Thirty-five

Tansy felt there were eyes on her as they approached the house and climbed the steps to the hall door. While Sean fumbled with the large bunch of keys, Tansy had yet another look at the diamond glinting on her left hand. He guided her into the hall, past a carved mahogany console table with an enormous display of peony roses. Whoever had arranged these had done so with precision. He opened the door to the right and entered first. It was a comfortable and welcoming space, but it smacked of being the home of someone who liked to be in control of everything and everyone in her sphere. His mother didn't stand to greet them as they came in but stayed sitting on one side of the bay window, positioned so that she could keep an eye on proceedings in both vistas, inside and out.

Sean went across the room and kissed the older woman on the head. 'Mum, this is Tansy – about whom I told you – and Tansy, this is my mum, Celia.'

'I'm delighted to meet you,' Tansy said. 'Sean has told me so much about you.'

'I'm afraid I can't say the same. He keeps his private life to himself and he hasn't introduced me to many of his students,' came the loaded reply.

'Tansy's not a student, Mum. I've asked her to marry me, and she's accepted. I bet you didn't see that coming, did you?'

'I wondered what you were up to when you rang and insisted on calling this afternoon.'

'And now the wondering is over. I'm sure the two of you will get on really well,' he said, looking from one to the other with uncustomary unease. Tansy wasn't too sure about that at all. Despite her nervousness at such formality, she made an effort, smiled and reached out to Celia. If she had been hoping for a hug or something more than a cursory handshake, she was disappointed.

'I'm sure you were sorry to miss Sean's launch. It was a lovely evening. I hope you're feeling a little better.'

'Life sometimes gets in the way. Do sit down,' the older woman commanded, indicating the chair she should occupy. As Tansy made towards it, she knew she was being scrutinised from head to toe and all the way back up again.

She listened to the stilted exchange between mother and son. How was she? How was he? Were her new tablets agreeing with her? Where was he off to next? Spain again. For how long?

'Just ten months left on the project, if it all goes according to plan, but I'll be back regularly. You won't even notice I'm not around, and Tansy can pop in and visit you from time to time, when she's here. It'll be a good way for you two ladies to get to know each other.'

Thanks for that, she thought. That would be a great chance for Celia to come between them. *He's told me what a snob you are, how*

you've interfered in all his relationships in the past, how no one is good
enough for your precious boy wonder.

'Will she be going with you?'

'Mum, her name's Tansy. Perdita's, where I lodge now, is not
really suitable, so there are a few practicalities to be figured out
first.'

Celia responded to that with a quiet, 'I see.' After a pause she
added, 'Maisie left the tray in the kitchen, Sean. Perhaps you'd
be good enough to make the tea for us, while I get to know
your ...' she hesitated for a millisecond and continued, '... your
young fiancée.'

He smiled and raised an eyebrow at Tansy as he left the room.
She interpreted that as a time-for-the-interrogation look.

'I believe you met my son in university when ...'

'Yes, that's right. I did some summer work on one of his
papers – the ones he's just had published. It was a fascinating
topic and I learned so much from it.'

Celia raised her hand to stop Tansy. It was clear that she wasn't
interested in whatever Tansy was going to say. It was obvious to
Tansy that Celia had an agenda to work through and quizzing
her was her preferred modus operandi. This woman is not going
to intimidate me, Tansy decided. I'll question her instead.

'I often wonder, did Sean get his interest in anthropology
from you or from his father?'

The older woman couldn't ignore the question, although she
seemed surprised at being asked.

'I don't think from either of us, really. He was a late baby.
We'd given up any hope of starting a family when he surprised
us. Of course, he was our only one and was always inclined to
be bookish. He spent a lot of time with adults and, as his father

and I had very busy lives, professionally and socially, he was exposed to a wide range of interests.'

Tansy interjected again. 'I know what that's like. I was a late baby too. I don't have any brothers or sisters either, and I was with grown-ups more than my friends were.'

She may as well not have said anything because Celia was on a mission. 'He's the last in the Pollard line,' she said with a finality that suggested she wasn't expecting him to provide an heir or a spare. 'His father would have loved to have seen him with another son of his own.'

'But he's still a young man,' Tansy ventured, wondering was she testing her to see if she knew about the baby he had lost. It was strange that the only taboo subject was the one Celia had chosen to discuss.

'That's as may well be, but I won't go on forever so he'd better hurry up if he wants to do anything about it. You do want a family, I assume?'

Tansy was saved from answering that as the door was pushed open quietly behind her and Sean came in with a tea tray. She offered to help but was shooed back to her seat. She watched the birdlike woman serve with economic moves, pouring the tea through a silver strainer and replacing this on its own little receptacle. Tansy declined the sugar and out of politeness accepted one of her least favourite sandwiches, cucumber and cress. There were fingers of fruit cake and Madeira too. They ate and drank in silence while Sean went out to get some boiling water. There was a whisper as some petals glided down from a large peony in another beautiful display on a side table, scattering brush strokes of pink and blush on the highly polished surface.

Before Celia could move to rectify this lack of symmetry, Tansy said, 'How pretty they look, so dainty and delicate. I always think they should have an exotic perfume, but they seldom do. They smell more like a woodland.'

Words weren't necessary – Celia's expression said more. She looked at her as though astonished that a young person would have any such knowledge about flowers.

'My mother has them growing out the back,' she told her as Sean returned.

'*Out the back?*'

'Yes, in the yard. My father is of the opinion that farmland should be used for crops and stock, but my mother sees no conflict in adding beauty and colour anywhere she can. Consequently, she has nasturtiums all around the hen runs. Clematis clamours over the old barn wall, and there's a big bed of giant and dwarf agapanthus outside the front door. They're my favourites. They're so elegant and feminine. She has lemon geraniums in the back porch too – they're great for keeping the flies away.'

'Who'd have thought?' Celia mused, but neither of them asked her – who'd have thought what?

It was to be another hour before they left. In the safety of the car Sean took her hand. 'That wasn't too bad, was it?'

'Let's just say I'm glad it's over. I suppose it could have been a lot worse.'

'She liked you. I could tell. Normally she doesn't say much.'

'I didn't give her much choice. You were ages making the tea. I thought you'd never come back. What took you so long?'

'I was outside the door enjoying the exchange. I don't think she knows what to make of you!'

'Can I take it that I'm deemed to be suitable wife material for Professor Sean Pollard, son of the late cardiology wizard G.K. Pollard and his wife paediatrician Celia, or am I too gauche, too country, too young and too unsophisticated to fill the role?'

'Probably all of the above, but we have time to work on you,' he teased. They drew up to the traffic lights. He leaned over and kissed her on the cheek. 'Don't change. You're perfect.'

'You're biased.'

'You're still perfect and I love you.'

'I love you too! And the lights have gone green, Professor.'

'I'm glad I've already met your folks, however briefly. At least I don't have to go through all that with them.'

She laughed and said, 'That's what you think. You weren't potential son-in-law material then, and we still have to introduce them to your mother! That could be very interesting.'

'That's one word for it.'

'And you have to meet Mary McLaughlin, my mother's best friend and gossip queen. She'll want to know your seed, breed and generation!'

'I'll consider that I've been suitably warned.'

They drove in silence for a few minutes before he said, 'I hate the thought of leaving you. Why don't you come over next week for a few days?'

'You know I can't. I've got to finish my term and the guys in the restaurant have been very good to me giving me extra shifts so that I could save for my big trip. I can't let all of them down.'

'You won't need those shifts now.'

'And be a kept woman? No, thank you.'

'What about the following week? You could come back over with me then.'

'Let me think about it. I could visit the Torres and the newlyweds too.' Suddenly she remembered the incident at the wedding when her corsage fell off and everyone told her she'd be the next to marry. She'd laughed off the suggestion. How wrong she'd been.

'I'll book us into the *parador* where we had our first dinner together and we can do all the things we wanted to do that night. I'm not sure you'll have the time or the energy for much else.' He grinned.

'I can't believe this is really happening.'

'Neither can I.'

She went back to his hotel and this time spent the whole delicious and passion-filled night with him.

Chapter Thirty-six

A few weeks later, she found herself back in the familiar environs of Alcalá de Henares. So much had happened in the seven months since she had been there with Jack for Álvaro's wedding. She still got a pang of guilt and remorse whenever she thought about Jack, which she did quite frequently. She was tempted to phone and enquire how he was doing but held back. Would that be too cruel? Would it be better to allow him to get on with his life and forget all about her? She really hoped he was not hurting too much.

She had loved him – she still did if she was being honest – but comparing those feelings with her all-consuming passion for Sean, she could see such emotions were poles apart.

'What makes what you have with Sean special?' Phyllis asked her. 'I'm just curious how you can be so sure you're making the right choices.'

'If I had to describe it, what I had with Jack was a warm, comfortable relationship, like being in a cocoon or wrapped in a cosy, snug blanket. I knew I'd always be safe there. Being with Sean, there's an element of the unknown and of excitement. He's a man of the world. He's done so much. He speaks several languages, is sophisticated and cultured and has been places I've only seen on a map.'

'How do you know Jack won't be all those things when he's Sean's age?'

She smiled and added, 'I don't and I can't wait that long to find out. I just know I admire the way Sean's at ease anywhere. I love his velvety speaking voice. It sounds authoritative without ever needing to change decibel.'

'Enough, enough. I'm beginning to regret asking!'

'You'll know when it happens.'

'If it ever happens.'

'It will, Phyllis.'

'All I can say is, he's one lucky man to have reeled you in.'

'No, I'm the lucky one, to have snared him!'

◆

On hearing the news, Rosa expressed amazement and Pedro opened a bottle of his best Rioja to toast their future. Álvaro's reaction seemed guarded although Elena insisted on hosting a dinner party for them in their new home, a villa on the family estate. Tansy was delighted at the warm welcome Elena gave her although she sensed it was somewhat cooler towards Sean, or was she imagining that? They had both really liked Jack. They had invited six other guests, some friends of Elena, others Tansy knew from the university. All had been at their wedding.

Álvaro took her to one side and said, 'I was very surprised at the news of your engagement. I thought it would have been you and Jack. You seemed to have your future plans all mapped out when you were here last.'

'I fell in love with Sean.'

'I had no idea you two were romantically entwined. Do you know each other well?'

She laughed. 'Romantically entwined. That sounds delightfully olde-worlde-ish, like something from one of the Brontë sisters.'

'Perhaps,' he said, 'but seriously, are you sure? I did think he was attracted to you the night we had dinner when he visited, and as you never mentioned him again, I forgot about it. We got to know him through the foundation and Professor Cortez. But, Tansy, getting engaged is one thing. Marriage is quite a different matter. You're not rushing into things, are you? Sean has seen a lot more of life than you. Are you sure he'll make you happy?'

'Absolutely. And didn't I drop my corsage at your wedding – so you can take part of the blame,' she joked. He didn't smile. 'Listen to yourself, Álvaro – you're one to be dishing out premarital advice! I seem to remember having similar conversations with you, and did you listen to me? No.'

'No, I didn't, and I wouldn't change a thing, but Elena and I have known each other all our lives. You can't say the same thing for you and Sean.'

'You don't sound as though you approve.'

'I'm not sure I do. Do you really know him well enough to marry him? Do you know all about his past, if he has one?'

'Obviously I don't know everything yet, but I'm enjoying finding out.'

'Don't let him make you rush into anything you'll regret. You're very dear to me, Tansy, and I want you to be happy too. I'd say the same to you if you were my sister.'

'You're being overcautious. Ask me this time next year, Álvaro, and I'll remind you of this conversation,' she replied.

'I will,' he promised and kissed her on the cheek. 'I'm just giving Tansy some premarital advice,' he told Elena, who had come over to join them.

'And I'm not listening.' The women exchanged smiles. 'What a beautiful home you have,' she told Elena.

'Thank you,' she said, and showed Tansy around. 'The others have already seen it. It was rather dark and gloomy when we started doing it up, depressing really, full of sombre antiques. I moved some of them into the *bodega* – that's Álvaro's domain, and somehow they seem to work better out there. But I wanted to make it brighter and younger somehow, if you know what I mean.'

'I do,' she answered. 'You've certainly succeeded in putting your stamp on it. It's elegant and modern, yet really welcoming. I love it.'

At the table she complimented Elena again and she replied, 'It's exciting having a house of your own to play with. Do you know where you'll be living when you two are married?'

'We're still a bit at sea,' said Sean. 'I have an apartment in Dublin, which we'll use when we're there for the time being. Meanwhile, my work will keep me here until next summer, but Tansy will be joining me as soon as I find more suitable accommodation. Where I am now isn't an option.'

'No, it isn't,' Tansy said. 'We were there today. It's a lovely old house, though, but we'd have to share the kitchen with the owner and her child.'

'You brought her to meet Perdita and Juan?' Elena said to Sean, seeming surprised.

'Not specifically. I needed to collect some things and they came back while we were there.'

'How did that go?' Álvaro asked Tansy.

'It was difficult enough. The woman speaks Galician, which I don't understand, and she has little or no English, so communication wasn't that easy. She seemed really upset when Sean told her that he would be leaving, but he paid her to keep his room for the time being and we can always stay there if we haven't found anything more suitable in the meantime.'

'We'll ask around for you, won't we, Álvaro?' Elena looked at her husband as if seeking an endorsement. 'Starting married life there wouldn't be a great idea. You need somewhere that you can be together without a noisy little boy under your feet.'

'I suppose you're right,' said Tansy. 'He a beautiful child, with those big blue eyes.'

'Yes, but he's severely autistic and has dreadful tantrums sometimes, for hours at a time, and yet he can be angelic at other times.'

'Is there a husband?' one of the other guests asked.

'There was. He left when the child was born. I presume he couldn't take the responsibility,' said Elena.

'He came from a decent family too. His father works on the estate,' Álvaro said. 'Perdita helps us out occasionally, and more frequently at my parents' place, when she can get someone to mind Juan. It's usually a younger cousin. He doesn't take to strangers and it gives her a well-earned break and a little bit of extra money.'

'I'm impressed by the way you care about your workers' welfare,' said Tansy. 'Aren't you, Sean?' He nodded.

'That's the way these estates function,' Álvaro said. 'We try to be there for each other, and she's had a raw deal. We're all cogs in the same wheel, and we all depend on each other to keep everything turning smoothly.'

Elena changed the subject, saying, 'I hear you've been selected as a guest lecturer at the university in Alcalá de Henares. That's a prestigious appointment.'

The others all congratulated Sean, and Tansy smiled with pride.

◆

With the approaching nuptials in the planning, Tansy kept her shifts at the restaurant. Sean wanted to get married as soon as possible and, at his urging, they set a date towards the end of November, the only time that term that he could schedule leave for a honeymoon.

Her flatmates started their 'proper careers', as Phyllis called this phase.

Gina was the first to flee the nest. She left for Málaga to see if the long-distance relationship she'd been having with Gonzalo since the previous summer had any future. Eight years older than her, he had big plans to open his own language school, where kids whose parents couldn't afford to send them to Ireland or the UK for weeks at a time could hone their linguistic skills.

Mags secured a job in her own old school. She told them that it was only as a maternity-leave substitute, but she had been assured that there were definite prospects down the line.

Phyllis had made such an impression during her H Dip year that she was welcomed back to the school where she had done her rotation.

'I know it will be hard, but I'll make a difference there if it kills me,' she told them, and they didn't doubt that she would. Tansy made several trips back and forth to Spain with Sean. She told anyone who'd listen how they'd met, stepped away from each other and then found each other and love again.

Sean found a rental cottage about ten miles outside Alcalá de Henares and over one weekend they moved his stuff in several trips. It was mostly books and papers, hectares of papers.

'I'm going to need a PA in the new year, to put all this in order for me. Would you be interested? I know you've taken on teaching commitments, but you could probably work around those. The foundation has given me a generous allowance to cover the salary and expenses. What do you think?'

'It would depend on the fringe benefits,' she teased.

'They can be negotiated!' he replied, kissing her. They ended up having sex among the boxes of files.

The flatmates graduated and planned for Trevor to move in when Tansy moved out. On graduation day, she saw Jack. He spotted her at the same moment and graciously came across the rain-sodden quadrangle to congratulate her, although he went out of his way to avoid Sean.

'I heard about your engagement. I can't say I approve, but I really wish you every happiness, Tansy,' he told her. 'And remember, if you ever need me, you can get in touch.'

'Thank you, Jack. I appreciate it.' She resisted the urge to straighten his mortarboard. 'I'm sorry about how things ended. I never saw things panning out like this.'

'Let's leave it in the past,' he said. 'New beginnings and all that. Take care of yourself.'

Before she could wish him well on his travels, some of Sean's colleagues and students came to congratulate him on his engagement. Her parents were in awe of how well he seemed to be regarded by everyone.

Her mother told her, 'It was a great idea to use this occasion to meet Sean's mother. It took some of the pressure off, having a distraction. I'd have been having a heart attack if he'd suggested bringing her to the farm to meet us.'

'I quite like her, really. She had a very busy life, and I think she's lonely but won't admit it. Anyway, you'll have the chance to get to know each other better at dinner.'

'I wish we weren't staying, though; I don't like leaving the animals overnight.'

'I know, Dad, but your daughter's graduation is surely a big enough occasion to warrant it and it's not as though you had several of us. There's only little old me,' Tansy said.

'I agree and we're very proud of you,' Peggy said, 'and you won't hear any objections from me, especially when my future son-in-law is putting us up in such a posh hotel.'

The following morning Tansy told Phyllis, 'They were all getting on fine when Sean dropped the bombshell about having our wedding ceremony in a registry office, in Dublin. We'd never discussed any of that. My folks are not overly religious, but I know they'd always seen me getting married in our local church.'

'How did his mother react?'

'I couldn't read her face. It's inscrutable at the best of times – probably from years of seeing patients and having to hide any emotions. I still find it hard to call her Celia. It seems too familiar somehow, but I actually thought Sean was very clever in the way he handled it, telling them all in a restaurant, where no one would react adversely.'

'Are you happy about the decision?'

'I don't mind, really. I'd just be happy to elope tomorrow and avoid all the fuss.'

'And do us all out of a big day? Never!'

That wasn't the end of it, though. These plans caused friction with Tansy's parents and were brought up on each phone call. But when Sean's mother became unwell again, Tansy gave in to the innuendos and suggestions that Celia would probably have a better chance of seeing her son make his vows if the venue was nearer to her home.

'When it was put like that, Mam, I didn't have much choice.'

'I suppose you didn't,' her mother replied, followed by a huge sigh of resignation.

'It would be unthinkable for her to miss it.'

'I would like to have been able to invite a few more people. Your father and I have been to so many weddings.'

'I know, but it's what Sean and I want. Just close friends and family and you won't find much smaller than both of ours.'

'But you haven't invited your cousin from Galway.'

'I haven't seen him for years.'

'That doesn't matter. He's still family.'

'The number is capped. I have an idea, though: if you really want him there, maybe we could un-invite Mary McLaughlin and let him substitute,' she suggested, knowing that it would close the discussion.

Chapter Thirty-seven

'I can only take off ten days max in a block for our honeymoon, but you can choose where we'll go.'

'Really?'

'Really.'

'Wow, this is overwhelming. I can't think. Morocco, Mauritius, Malta, Rome, Paris, Vienna, Copenhagen, Budapest, New York, Buenos Aires. I don't know, Sean, I'm like the proverbial kid in a sweet shop, befuddled by the choices. Why don't you decide?'

'No, Tansy. It's your choice. Name your top ten, I'll write them down and we'll go to whichever one you draw out.' He tore paper into strips.

She closed her eyes and picked one out. 'This reminds me of making a wish after blowing out my birthday candles.' She handed it to him.

He read it and announced, 'And the winner is … drum roll … Vienna!'

'Oh Sean. I've always wanted to go to Vienna. Mam and I watch the New Year's Day concert from there every year. This is so exciting.'

'It is a wonderful city and it will be all the more wonderful with you by my side, as my wife.'

'I can't wait!'

'It's not long now. Let's go online and start planning it. Has madam any special requests?'

'Can we go to an opera? I've never been to one, or a Strauss concert?'

'Of course, your wish is my command. We'll do a horse-drawn carriage ride and I'll take you for hot chocolate and some *Sachertorte* – their famous cake. We'll go to the Belvedere Palace and I'll show you Klimt's masterpiece, *The Kiss*. We can't honeymoon there and not see *The Kiss*.'

'I'll be so cultured when I get back that I won't know myself.'

'I want it to be memorable.'

'It will be. I do love you, Professor Pollard.'

'And I love you too, Miss Nugent.'

◆

'The old witch has hijacked the day,' Phyllis told Mags and Gina, who had flown home for the weekend, after they had packed Sean's car with more of Tansy's belongings and waved them off.

'Do you not agree that once she played the sick card, she had a miraculous recovery? I'm not saying that was intentional but, well, I'm just sayin'! She seemed to have gone into overdrive and got her way about the reception too. I bet she had that in mind all along.'

'I think you're being very hard on her,' Mags said. 'It actually makes good sense. The house is one of those gi-normous period ones and it is her son's wedding too.'

'I don't deny that, but there are limits. It's also the bride's day,' said Phyllis.

'I haven't heard her complaining and Tansy's no shrinking violet about voicing her opinions,' Gina argued.

'Do you think she would have wanted a – and I quote – "a small but classy affair"? That's Celia Pollard shorthand for no big puffy ballgowns, or bride or bridesmaids wearing anything too revealing or inappropriate.'

'I believe she suggested that two bridesmaids would be enough, but Tansy stood her ground on that and insisted we're all in this together,' said Mags.

'Her florist, if you don't mind, *her* florist is doing the flowers for the house, the bridal bouquets and buttonholes. Oh, and for the tent. And guess who's doing the food – *her* caterers.'

'You'd better not let her hear you calling it a tent, or you'll miss seeing the crystal chandeliers.'

'I'm just sorry Gonzalo is missing this,' said Gina. 'And I'm amazed at the way Tansy is keeping her cool. I thought it was just coming across like that in her mails. I've never seen her as happy.'

'That's love for you. She was never the sort of girl who spent time dreaming about a society wedding, though.'

'There's no denying that she seems to be really happy and in love,' Gina said.

'She makes Trevor and me look like a staid old married couple.'

'Oh Mags, you pair are perfectly suited,' Phyllis said.

After a bit Gina said, 'I just hope she doesn't lose herself along the way, giving in to everything Sean wants.'

'Tansy is a woman who knows her own mind. Remember, she's lived in Spain and has other friends in that part of the world; she'll integrate in no time. We might even get over to visit while they're still there.'

'Now there's a thought!' said Mags.

'Enough chatter. We'd better get this place tidy before the dresses arrive, or we'll have no place to put them. It's already beginning to feel empty and she hasn't left yet,' Mags said.

'It's the end of an era,' said Phyllis. 'Let's hope the beginning of a great one for us all and for Tans and Sean.'

Chapter Thirty-eight

Sean's mother had thought of everything. Once the brief civil ceremony was over, the party headed back to the red-brick period house where Sean had grown up. It was in leafy suburban Dublin, although the trees were mostly denuded. The house and the marquee were decorated with elegant arrangements of white flowers and winter greenery. The large arrangements in the hallway: the snowy gerberas, had been specially chosen by Tansy. The guests were shown into the drawing room. Folding doors opened onto another spacious reception room, allowing everyone to circulate with ease. Champagne was served in tall flutes with a fresh raspberry at the bottom of each one.

'I think our Tansy has fallen on her feet. She could be living in this mansion someday,' Gina said to the others when they were upstairs in a room that had been allocated for the bridal party only.

'I heard that, Gina, you mercenary minx,' the bride said, coming in behind them, smiling. 'And it's possible I will someday, but that's not what attracted me to Sean. I'd have married him if he'd lived in a yurt.'

'She knows that,' said Phyllis. 'You look radiant, and

downstairs there's a whole bunch of people waiting to greet the newlyweds, so get down there and knock them out.'

The guests had lined up along the archway that led from the house into the marquee, which Phyllis had to admit bore very little resemblance to a tent of any sort. On seeing it, Peggy whispered to Mary McLaughlin, 'It's beautiful. It's not at all what I was expecting. I think it's those pale pink draperies – they soften it. The last time I was in a marquee was when the circus came to Dunmoy, and the rain dripped through the canvas in several places making big dark circles on the sawdust floor.'

'You'd better not let her ladyship hear you say that. She might think you were comparing her venue to a circus,' Mary McLaughlin replied and they had a chuckle.

Just then, the smiling bride and groom made their entrance, stopping to talk to everyone before making their way to their seats.

At Tansy's insistence, the seating was informal. She'd confided in Phyllis that, because the two families came from such different backgrounds, it might be better to mix the guests, rather than have a 'them and us' situation. As she looked around, she was pleased that it seemed to be working.

She smiled at her new husband. 'I never realised I could be so happy. Thank you. I can hardly believe this is really happening.'

'Nor can I,' he said. 'And to think I almost let you get away.'

'You're stuck with me now, Prof.'

'And you with me, Mrs Pollard.'

'That makes me sound like your mother.'

'She seems to be getting on very well with your father.'

'I'm glad – he was so nervous about fitting in with all these highly educated folk. I had to tell him he wasn't sitting for an exam, he just had to be himself.'

The crystal glistened beneath the light of the chandeliers and countless candles gave off a warm light. Once everyone was seated, dinner was served.

Tackling some crab claws with gusto, Mary McLaughlin's verdict, which she offered to the man on her left, was, 'Well, they didn't disappoint. Sometimes these things have no substance to them at all.' The man was Ernest, Trevor's dad.

'You say that with such authority, you're obviously a woman of good taste. I'm very partial to seafood of all sorts, but I agree, sometimes they can be very bland.'

'Or overcooked until they become as tough as old boots.'

'My late wife used to make a wonderful fish pie. I have never tasted anything like it since she died.'

'Ah, fish pie, that's one of my favourite things. With hard-boiled eggs or without?'

'Without, definitely without.'

'I absolutely agree, but served on a bed of spinach.'

'That sounds mouth-watering.'

'I don't make it very often for myself any more. I live alone, and run my own business. Sometimes I just don't feel like cooking after a day's work,' she said.

'I'm on my own too and, as you can see, I love my food, but I'm not inclined to cook for myself sometimes either. There's a wonderful little bistro not far from where I live that benefits hugely from that. Perhaps we could have dinner together there sometime when you're in town.' Before she could accept or refuse he continued, 'Remind me, how do you know the bride?'

'Tansy's mother is my best friend; we've known each other

since we were children. We started school together, I was her bridesmaid, so I've known Tansy since she was born. I babysat her and was at her christening and pretty well all the important events in her life, and now, here I am at her wedding. What's your connection with them?'

'Mine is with Sean. I worked at the same university as him and was his predecessor as Head of Faculty. Lately I've come out of retirement to collaborate with him on his Spanish Civil War project. He was one of my students when he was a young buck. He stood out even then as a brilliant mind. It's good to see him settling down at last. We never thought we'd see this day.'

'It's nice to hear that. Don't they look good together? It happened in such a hurry that I had my doubts. We all thought she'd end up with her previous boyfriend, Jack, but that finished abruptly. A few days later she produced Sean and an engagement ring. I'll admit to you, but I wouldn't say it to anyone else' – she lowered her voice – 'frankly I was worried. You know what they say – marry in haste and repent at leisure, and all that. But maybe I'm wrong. I hope he's her Mr Right – if there's such a thing.'

'He's the lucky one. She's a very engaging and intelligent young lady. I thought that from the first time I met her. And what about you, am I allowed ask if you ever found your Mr Right?'

'No, I think I probably looked in the wrong places.'

'Obviously,' he replied.

'You know, I envy young people these days. They make their own choices and follow their dreams. I inherited a family business – a drapers and outfitters – and I was considered a "good catch" because of it. I didn't have the same opinion of my suitors, though.' She laughed.

'Owning a thriving shop had seemed like a wonderful opportunity. Don't get me wrong, it gave me a good life, but it's also stopped me from doing so many other things. In some ways instead of giving me independence, it did the very opposite. It shackled me to Dunmoy. If you've grown up and lived your whole life in a small place, your horizons are bound to become small too. Wouldn't you agree?'

'That's an interesting perspective, but you don't give me that impression.'

'Oh, I know the locals see me as a gossipy old woman. I was pigeonholed, like the aunts that I inherited from, who were both spinsters. They don't see the real woman trapped behind a shop counter.'

'I don't like the word "spinster", and it doesn't suit you. Tell me, who is the real Mary?'

'She's someone who lives her life through others, because their lives seem more exciting than hers. Does that make sense, or is it the wine talking?'

'It makes perfect sense. What would you like to do?'

'I'd love to travel. I've only been to London and Lourdes. I can't bear the thought of leaving this world without ever having seen so many other places. I fancy going on a safari, or up the Statue of Liberty to her torch. But what I'd love to do, above all else, is one of those great train journeys, the Orient Express, the Rocky Mountaineer ...'

'A woman after my own heart! I love trains; there's something romantic about them. I did the Blue Train from Cape Town to Pretoria in South Africa and that was an experience.'

'Oh, I've read all about that. That was the one that used to bring the royals and the wealthy down through France to the

Riviera and Monte Carlo. Did you have a butler, and brass taps on your bath, and sit outside on the last carriage watching the world go by?' she asked.

'All of the above.' He laughed. 'You do know all about it. I think you're a real romantic. Have you ever considered retiring and just taking off?'

'More and more, and having this conversation has made my mind up for me. I'm going to do it when I go home. I'll put the business on the market and start perusing brochures.'

'I'm delighted to hear that,' Ernest said. 'My wife and I travelled a lot. Since her demise, I haven't felt so inclined, but you've whetted my appetite for it. I'm afraid I've been monopolising you. Tansy's mother keeps looking over this way. I'm not sure if it's in disapproval or curiosity.'

'You're not! Pay no attention to her. I don't know when I've enjoyed a chat as much.'

'And that goes for me too. I usually hate weddings, but we've got to the speeches quite effortlessly and that's saying something.'

Although Tansy had tried to reassure her dad, who had been anxious about making a speech in front of those 'academic types', Peggy could sense his tension and tried to distract him.

'I see Mary is chatting away over there to that distinguished-looking chap. She's knocking back the red wine. I hope she doesn't let us down.'

'The poor fellow probably can't get a word in edgeways. She's probably giving him the third degree,' he said.

'He looks as though he's enjoying himself. So does everyone and I know I am too.'

◆

It was all over too quickly. Guests said their farewells, congratulations and thanks before leaving, and Tansy took her place between Sean and her mother-in-law to see them off.

'It was a wonderful day, Celia, one none of us will ever forget. You organised everything so quickly, and so beautifully for them, I can't thank you enough for everything,' Peggy said.

'It was my pleasure. I was beginning to think he'd never settle down.'

'And we certainly didn't think we'd have a wedding in the family for a long time yet.' Peggy told the girls, 'You all looked wonderful. What a special day it was. We'll never forget it.'

Phyllis said, 'Neither will we.'

Tansy's dad hugged her. 'I still can't believe my little girl is married. I hope you'll be very happy, love. Be sure and make space for your old man from time to time.'

'Always, Dad, and we'll see you in a few weeks, at Christmas.' She laughed.

Peggy, linking her husband with one arm, was clutching her daughter's bouquet in the other hand. The bridesmaids had insisted that she should have it to take home to Dunmoy with her and Peggy had shed a tear at the gesture. She called back, as they went down the granite steps, 'Send us lots of pictures of Vienna.'

Mary McLaughlin thanked Tansy for inviting her to share her special day and Ernest waited to give her his arm and escort her down behind them.

Sean closed and bolted the hall door after Trevor and the bridesmaids, who were the last to leave, had finally gone.

'You must be exhausted, Celia,' Tansy said. 'It's been a long but absolutely wonderful day.'

'I admit I am. I'll turn in now and leave you two to yourselves, but I'll see you in the morning, before you head off.'

She stood up and kissed them goodnight in turn.

'Thanks, Mum, for everything,' Sean said.

Celia replied, 'Make sure you're a good husband, like your father was.'

'I'll do my best,' he said and saw her to her room.

PART TWO

MARRIED LIFE

Chapter Thirty-nine

When, eventually, we were alone on our wedding night, Sean took me in his arms and started kissing me. I responded with every fibre of my being. I felt as though I had an electrical charge surging through me.

He turned me around and started opening the long row of little pearl buttons on my wedding dress. They ran from my neck to the upper curve of my buttocks. He said he'd been wanting to do that all day.

He cursed and laughed as his fingers fiddled and fumbled with them.

'I didn't think this through. If I had, I'd have opted for a Velcro fastening.' We ended up falling onto the bed laughing.

Finally, he opened enough of them for me to slip the dress over my head, revealing my sexy underwear and a lacy garter that Phyllis had given me. It had a little bow on it, for my 'something blue'. I had never felt so desirable or so desired and I was high on the feeling. The undies had cost a fortune, and I felt like a princess in them. I asked him if he liked them and he told me he'd prefer them on the floor.

'Do you remember you promised to love me forever, and that you're now my wife?'

'I have some vague recollection of saying something like that. And I seem to remember you making similar promises, didn't you, promises to make me happy forever?'

'Can I show you how I intend to fulfil some of those?'

'Yes, please. But I hope your mother won't hear us.'

'She's won't. This is a very solid house, her bedroom's downstairs now and she doesn't sleep with her hearing aids in.'

'So what's keeping you?' I asked.

We made love with a passion we had never reached before. I thought I'd burst with happiness. All the pain and heartache he'd caused me just vanished and I felt complete, absolutely and utterly complete.

Eventually, he fell asleep, his head on my shoulder. I didn't want him to move. My arm went dead and I had to try to extricate myself somehow. He moved and muttered something indistinguishable as he turned over. I studied the back of his head where a small band of paler skin showed around his hairline after his visit to the barber's for the wedding. There were a few grey hairs. I ran my hand over his shoulders, feeling his smooth, warm skin and he groaned.

I lay there, wide awake. Had this day really happened? I tried to conjure up every moment, from seeing him waiting for me at the registry office, to exchanging our rings. I couldn't remember one single word of the speeches, even though I know I had found them witty and entertaining and laughed at them.

It had all gone by too quickly. A whirlwind romance, a whirlwind wedding – I hoped that wasn't going to be a metaphor for our lives together. I wanted to slow it down and savour it all.

The post-mortem with Mam would have to wait until after the honeymoon. She'd have to content herself with Mary McLaughlin's observations meanwhile. I wondered what she had thought of it all, and of my new mother-in-law.

They took it hard that we didn't have the wedding in Dunmoy, but it was a master stroke getting Celia to ask Mam to make the cake. That had been Sean's idea. I know she was feeling a bit sidelined up to then. He'd said it'd be a way of including her, making her feel she was part of it all. And the cake was a triumph. But Mam's cakes always were. It not only looked good, it tasted wonderful. Everyone said so and she glowed from all the compliments.

Celia made a point of adding to them as well.

Peggy had whispered to me, 'I have to say she's growing on me. She not as hoity-toity as I first thought.'

'What did I tell you?' I replied. 'It's just that everything she surrounds herself with looks classy and refined, almost from an even older generation than hers. And she's certainly taken her duties seriously and made everyone feel really welcome, whether she knew them before the wedding or not.'

'I have to hand that to her too. That she certainly did.'

Sean had told me that Celia and his father loved entertaining, that this was a real party house before he died. If the wedding was a standard to measure this by, she must have been a sensational hostess.

I supposed she must miss all that too.

I remember that night, or rather early the next day, thinking how glad I was that we'd have photographs to remind me of everything, because right then, apart from the cake, I couldn't remember a single thing I'd eaten. When I told Sean that before we went down to breakfast, his reaction was, 'Well, that's lovely. We could have saved a fortune and gone to McDonald's.'

'That would have caused a bit of a stir, us traipsing in there in our finery and ordering burgers.'

'You looked fantastic in that finery,' he said. 'I was the envy of every man there. But I think I'd prefer you without it!'

I still couldn't quite believe this was all happening. I didn't think we could top yesterday, yet here we were, 'my professor and me', getting ready to set off on our honeymoon. It couldn't get much better than this. Could it?

Chapter Forty

Our flight wasn't until early afternoon. Maisie, who came in a few days a week to help out, had arrived early to oversee the clean-up. Celia breakfasted with us and we had a bit of a run-through of how well everything had gone. It was perfect. I felt I was getting to know her a bit better. There was a commotion of activity about the house and garden – the caterers arrived to dismantle the marquee and remove all traces of the celebrations. I felt a little sad looking at it disappear bit by bit, seeing the garden returning to its November blandness. Sean went to get our bags and have them ready for when the taxi arrived.

With all the to-ing and fro-ing I didn't notice the Garda coming up the steps to the hall door, until I heard one of the workmen shout, 'Oh, give us a break. We have to load the truck and there's yellow lines in front of all of these houses. I know you've a job to do, but so do we.'

I went to investigate what all the hullabaloo was about. I was going to pull the newly married card to appeal to his good nature, but they'd gone out into the porch before I had a chance, and I couldn't hear what they were saying.

Sean was on his way down with our bags and the fellow from

the caterers called him over. Honestly, when I think how naïve I was. I thought they were going to try to bribe the Garda to turn a blind eye, so I stayed where I was, just inside the drawing room door. I'd obviously been watching too many B-movies. I didn't even know if people did that in real life, bribed cops. When Sean came in and took me by the arm, I still thought he just wanted to keep me out of whatever had taken place.

It was only when he told me to sit down that I began to suspect something was up. I'm not sure if Celia was in the room or not, but my first thought was that she'd had another stroke, because everything seemed to go quiet. On some level I knew that didn't make any sense.

Sean sat down on the sofa and put his arm around me and the Gardaí came in. There were two of them now, a male and a female. The woman knelt beside me and told me there'd been an accident. I knew then, without being told, that it involved Mam and Dad. He hated to be away from the animals and would have wanted to be out of the city and on the road before daylight to get back to them.

She delivered the news as though it was a radio bulletin – 'a head-on crash between a car and an articulated truck on the dual carriageway, five miles from Dunmoy. There were three fatalities. The truck driver was among those who died. The only survivor was the back seat passenger in the car and she has been transferred to a Dublin hospital.' They hadn't been named until next of kin were notified.

Three fatalities. Who were the other two? No! No!

'Next of kin? Is that me? Am I being notified?'

It took a few seconds for what I had been told to make sense to me. Weirdly, part of me accepted that there wasn't a thing I could do to change anything. All I can remember is being pulled down into a deep, dark hole with no means of escape. I was drowning and there was no one to rescue me. Life would never be the same again.

'Did they say anything?'

'I gather it would have been instantaneous. They were both dead when the emergency services arrived. The other driver died on his way to hospital.'

'And Mary?'

I don't know why I asked. I didn't want to hear that the survivor was Mary McLaughlin.

I have no idea of time. I only remember people floating in and out. The taxi arrived to bring us to the airport and I saw Sean nod at one of the Gardaí. I knew from the hushed voices in the hall that he was explaining what had happened.

I don't think I cried then until Phyllis, Mags and Gina arrived.

'I wanted her to be dead, not Mam or Dad,' I blurted. 'What sort of person does that make me? I've just been told my mam and dad have been killed and the only thing I feel is anger that Mary McLaughlin is still alive.'

Mags said, 'Tansy, that's the most natural reaction in the world in the circumstances. You're in shock now. You'll feel differently when it's had time to sink in.'

I didn't want it to sink in. But it did. Sean was a rock over the next few days as it began to filter through at some level that I had lost my entire family.

'I'll never be able to substitute for them, but you have us now, Celia and me. We're your family and you're ours.'

'Home won't ever be home again. There's nothing in Dunmoy for me now.'

'It's where you grew up and where all your happy childhood memories are. Give it time and you'll feel differently.'

I wouldn't have got through those days without my friends, Phyllis in particular. When Mags suggested giving me something to calm me, she objected. I was pretending to be asleep, already worn out by the enormity of what had happened, but I heard them arguing softly.

'Some people think you shouldn't block out the reality with drugs but should let the grieving process start straight away.'

'I've heard that too, but can you just begin to imagine the immensity of this? Getting married one day, celebrating with your folks, waiting for the taxi to arrive to start your honeymoon and in a second your whole world implodes. I think I'd need something stronger than a Valium to help me see my way out the other side,' said Gina.

I think Phyllis was probably right. I needed to shout and to cry. I needed to feel the pain and the sense of utter loneliness, the blackness and despair. Logically, I knew that the sooner that happened, the sooner I'd learn to cope again, but I wasn't ready for any of that. I didn't know if I'd ever be. I just wanted Sean. I needed him to take the pain away.

Celia surprised me with her sensitivity. I don't know why that should have been; she was a doctor after all and was used to dealing with death. She hovered discreetly while Gina, Phyllis and Mags kept me company. The doorbell seemed to ring continuously. Ernest, Trevor and others called to offer sympathy or condolences. I never liked those words. They didn't belong to me. They had a heaviness about them.

I remember the looks of pity in people's eyes, but how I responded escapes me. All that registered was that Maisie seemed to be on hand at all hours, making tea and sandwiches as though on a loop. I don't know how many cups I drank that day, but it was a lot.

I actually felt sorry for Sean. This wasn't the way any marriage should begin. I opened my eyes when I heard his voice. He had on a heavy coat and I panicked and asked him not to leave me. I was terrified that anything would happen to him if I let him out of my sight.

He held me in his arms for a few moments and assured me he'd be safe – there were things he had to sort out – and he'd do that while the girls were with me.

Of course, he meant things to do with the funeral. A funeral – for the two of them. The phrase I'd read somewhere, probably seen it in a B-movie, sprung to mind in one of those serendipitous thoughts – together in life, and in death, together for ever.

But this was no movie. It was reality. My reality.

Sean told me he was going to visit Mary in hospital. It was only then I thought of how she must be feeling. She'd witnessed the accident, been part of it. I needed to talk to her. She must be distraught, and I needed to know more about what had happened.

'I'm not sure that's such a good idea. Why don't you try to rest? I'll take you in tomorrow.'

I argued. 'She has no one in Dublin and she may need some things – toiletries and the like – the things men don't think about.'

Phyllis agreed with me. 'Do you want me to put a few things together for her?'

'No. I'll do it,' I said, and I saw Celia nod in approval.

Sean didn't fool me. Toiletries were the last thing on his

mind and when I challenged him, he admitted that he hoped to find out if Mary and my mother had ever talked about their funeral wishes. He was sure it was something they might have discussed.

'I don't need to be shielded. I want to know what's happening,' I insisted.

I hadn't a clue if my parents had ever bought a plot in the local churchyard, or if they had a preferred undertaker. Ross's father did all the local burials, so that was more or less a given, although after the way he treated me, my mother might have had different ideas about that. It wasn't something we'd ever discussed around the stove. Nor was whether they preferred burial or cremation. It was then I suddenly realised I could never ask them these questions, or any others for that matter.

That was when I started to cry, and Phyllis offered to come with us to the hospital.

◆

Mary had suffered severe concussion, a deep cut on her forehead and other minor cuts and bruises. Against medical advice she was insisting on being discharged so that she could attend the funeral, no matter how soon it was going to be.

Phyllis tried to advise against that too, but Mary wasn't open to any such suggestion. She'd made her mind up. I could understand that.

'I can't believe this has happened, Tansy. I keep hoping someone will tell me that it's this concussion playing tricks with my imagination, but I know it's not. Your folks were so proud of you and yesterday was such a happy day for them. They had a wonderful time, and despite our early start – we were too early for breakfast in the hotel – they were in great form when we left this morning. I teased them about how long it would be until they'd hear the patter of tiny feet. And Peggy told me to give you a chance.

'We chatted about this one and that, and who had worn what. I was just telling them that I had decided to retire, sell the shop and go travelling, and Peggy's response, which was so typical of her, was "Are you mad, Mary? Go travelling? At your age?" That was the last thing she said to me, Tansy. "Are you mad, Mary? Go travelling? At your age?"

'Before I could answer, I saw these lights, lots of lights coming straight at us from across the carriageway. They didn't seem to slow down but just kept coming through the hedge. Your poor father let out some choice expletives, but he couldn't do anything to move out of the way. It all happened in a flash. I remember the impact, I was screaming, the sound of glass breaking, metal scraping against metal and a fierce jolt, then everything went black.' Her voice broke.

'Perhaps you'd rather not talk about it,' Sean suggested, but she insisted she wanted to, only she couldn't remember anything else.

'I keep trying to put the pieces together. But they won't join up,' she sobbed.

She didn't have any recollection of being put in an ambulance, or of being taken to Dublin to hospital. The doctors told her that often happened after a head injury. They explained that sometimes the brain blocked out horror forever.

I wished mine could do that. I didn't want to remember either. I tried to concentrate on what Mary was saying. Had I heard her correctly – she was going to sell her shop? I could hear

Dad's voice in my ear. *What will she do for gossip?* I felt the tears welling up again. Sean took my hand and squeezed it.

Phyllis asked Mary what made her come to the decision to sell and she simply told us, 'It was because of Ernest and something he said at the wedding.'

I thought I'd missed a bit of the conversation, but no, she repeated it.

'I never got to tell Peggy all about that, and I can't believe that I'll never have the chance now.' She broke down then.

Neither would I. I put my arms around her and we cried together. Words weren't necessary. Sean and Phyllis left us for a bit to let us begin to grieve for our collective loss. Those tears were only the beginning of the rivers that would follow. Grief is a curious thing. It allows you to laugh and be normal betimes, then it pulls you up and reminds you it's still there, lurking.

So much happened in those few days that my timeline has become confused. While I tried to shut it all out, Sean spent a lot of time on the phone making arrangements. To participate would have meant recognising the realties that I wasn't ready to acknowledge.

He talked to Patsy Maher, the solicitor in Dunmoy, who had the deeds of the farm and my parents' formal-sounding last will and testimony. Patsy later advised me against making any decisions about the property for at least a year. I told him I hated seeing my father's life's work being decimated, and he suggested that he'd be able to lease the farm out in the interim. That took the pressure off. He talked to Little Jim, and he mustered the help of some of the neighbours. Between them they took custody of the livestock and chickens. I was glad about that.

Dunmoy would never be my home again. Its heart and soul

had been ripped out of it for me. Perhaps in time it would come to represent a treasure chest of memories, but I wasn't ready to think like that.

♦

We got through the funeral. I did take a Valium on that day. Two coffins, two photographs of two people together, two people now gone. It was dramatic and surreal, listening to everyone speaking glowingly about my parents: about what an impact they had made on them. I had always considered their lives small but, too late, I realised how wrong I had been. It wasn't necessary to live life in the fast lane to make a difference. They had done that by being decent and caring and would always be remembered for these qualities.

I had to give a small eulogy. I couldn't let my parents go without telling everybody how much they had meant to me and how I would miss them. I was afraid I'd break down. Phyllis told me that didn't matter, just to be true to myself. And I was.

I held it together until I was walking back to my seat and I noticed a tall head above the mourners, an easily recognisable red head. Jack, dear kind Jack, had come to pay his respects to two people he had possibly thought could be his parents-in-law one day. I couldn't hold the tears back anymore. Sean put his arm around my heaving shoulders. I looked for Jack outside, but I couldn't see him anywhere. It was only a few days later that I wondered why he wasn't in Australia.

I don't know how many hands I shook outside the church and I was touched by the number who had turned up – neighbours, school and college friends, friends of Sean's and everyone who had been at the wedding.

'No one mentioned the wedding,' I said later, after we had had lunch in the local hotel – not a spread like Mam had put on for Gappy Jim. 'It's as though it hadn't ever happened.'

'Perhaps people avoided it out of kindness,' Mags said.

I could see that, but by then, all my memories were painful, especially the good ones; even the ones about our wedding night. Especially the ones about our wedding night, because with them came guilt for being so happy.

A few days after the funeral, Celia asked me if I felt up to going away to Spain so soon. 'I'd like you to consider this your home if you want to stay for a while. I know I'm not your mother, and I can't imagine how you must be feeling, but you might be happier for the moment here in Dublin, close to your friends rather than being lonely and far away. You can have them to stay over any time you like.'

I was speechless, humbled by her generosity. I stood up and hugged her and the tears came pouring out. When I could speak again, I told her I needed to be with Sean. I didn't tell her that I didn't want to let him out of my sight in case anything happened to him.

Chapter Forty-one

I was so lonely those first few weeks in Spain. I so badly wanted to be able to pick up my phone and talk to Mam. The realisation that I'd never be able to do that again was slowly filtering through on some level. In a perverse way I was glad that they had gone together. I don't know how Dad would have coped without her, and she'd have been lost without him. But that was no consolation to me. I had no choice but to get on with my life, with the two of them missing from it.

We had moved directly into a furnished farmhouse and I tried to fill my time by rearranging the bits and pieces. I still feel empty remembering it. Sean did his best to be with me. Because he had lost so much time, in trying to make it up he was sometimes away from early morning until late at night.

Christmas was looming and I wasn't looking forward to that. I wanted to run away and hide until it was over, but I'd discovered there was nowhere to escape from myself.

It was funny the thoughts that came into my mind during that time – unconnected, inconsequential things. Perhaps they were nature's way of giving me a break from being in the shadow of the darkest clouds I could have imagined. I thought I'd take the blue and white jugs that were always on the dresser in the kitchen in Dunmoy and put them on my own. They had come from Dad's mother's home, a grandmother I didn't remember, but somehow the connection seemed more important now.

But I had no dresser, no home – I was living in a rental in Spain and there was precious little space in Sean's flat in Dublin for anything else. We'd already dumped all my stuff from Rathmines there. Before any of the awfulness happened, we had decided that we wouldn't go house-hunting until he'd finished his project, and that we'd hold off starting a family until then.

During my early days staying with Rosa and Pedro, I used to tell her that she was my Spanish mother. Now she became one. When I reminded her, she smiled sadly.

'No one will ever replace your *madre*, but I can always be an honorary grandmother when that time comes, and you have your own family.'

'Rosa, I feel I've become two halves of a whole, one broken, waiting to be fixed, while the other one is out there somewhere, holding on to promises and hopes. I know they'll get back together someday. It's *when* that confounds me.'

'It's hard, but you have to let nature take its course.'

She invited us for dinner several times, but I made excuses not to go. She cooked the odd meal and brought it over. She suggested that we might like to spend Christmas with her and Pedro. Sean told her that Celia was expecting us. We hadn't discussed this, but where else would we go? And I'd get to see the girls again.

Rosa assured me that I'd feel better once the holiday season was out of the way, saying how both Christmas and New Year were such difficult times for anyone who had suffered loss of any kind. I didn't respond to platitudes. I'd heard too many by now. 'Time's a great healer' was the most popular. But it didn't seem to be doing anything to alleviate my losses.

No going home to Dunmoy on the crowded bus, bags and parcels digging into my legs and everyone talking to each other. No Dad to collect me and no tree to decorate with Mam. I wondered where Mary McLaughlin would eat her Christmas dinner this year. I rang her that night, as I often did, needing the connection. She sounded as lost as me. Celia suggested we invite her to join us, but she declined.

We flew back a few days before Christmas and took a taxi to Celia's house. The plan was to stay until after the New Year.

Her welcome was warm and genuine and, over coffee served in rose-sprigged bone china, her instructions were that I was family and as such, this was my home to come and go as I pleased and invite my friends when I chose.

'I need you to indulge me in one thing, if you don't mind,' she said. 'I'd prefer if you didn't walk around the house in your dressing gown, no matter how pretty it is.'

It crossed my mind that Sean had told her how sometimes I didn't feel like getting dressed at all and stayed in mine all day. Surely not. He didn't have those sorts of conversations with Celia. Perhaps, though, they had colluded to try to break my cycle of gloom, or even to prevent me slipping further into depression. Before I solved that riddle, she said, 'I'll see enough of that when Sean puts me in a home for the bewildered.'

'He'd never do that,' I assured her.

'Oh yes, he would. I've seen it happen countless times, and I understand that sometimes there's no choice, but despite the TIAs, or mini-strokes, I'm not ready for one yet.'

She consulted me about arrangements for Christmas Day. She wasn't religious but surprised me by saying that she and Sean would be happy to accompany me to a service, if I wanted to go to one.

I declined. Whatever vestige of belief or curiosity I had ever had about God was gone. What kind of creature could oversee a world with so much pain?

That afternoon Sean and I went out to buy our presents. I had intended getting some things for Phyllis, Gina and Mags in Spain, but somehow I hadn't got around to it. I had nothing for Sean either. I had to rectify that. Our first Christmas together. I couldn't let that pass.

He was a generous gifter and had bought much more than me. Passing a toy shop, he saw a wooden train set in the window and said, 'Perdita's little fellow would love that. It's not noisy. And although he sometimes makes a lot of it, he doesn't like noise. That seems to be a trait with his form of autism.'

After buying it, we split up and arranged to meet an hour later. He was laden down with bags when he reappeared. He was also five minutes late and I could feel myself panic. Had something happened to him? I tried to hide my distress. I don't think I succeeded. I declined his offer of a drink, all the Christmas music and the festive atmosphere was proving too much.

Over the next few days, the house and Maisie were busy. Celia had lots of friends who popped in for coffee and a chat. I don't know how I had ever thought of her as a lonely old woman. She wasn't.

She couldn't have been nicer, either. She didn't crowd me.

She had even put flowers on the table in our bedroom and made sure there was always a fire burning in the grate.

Christmas morning is a bit of a blur, or else my subconscious has chosen to block it out. We were twelve at the table. I was pleased to see Ernest was among them. I like him a lot and I was pleased for Sean that he was there. They always had such interesting things to talk about.

I had my moments that day, despite trying to keep busy, helping with serving and clearing up. I slipped away at one stage and Sean came to our bedroom to comfort me.

'Would you like me to keep you company?' I just wanted to be alone, but he lay on the bed beside me, his arms around me. The heat from his body comforted me and I fell asleep.

The St Stephen's Day Leopardstown meet was part of the Pollard Christmas tradition. Sean did his best to persuade me to go along and have a flutter on the horses. I waivered a few times, before finally deciding against it. It was a chilly day and the roaring fire won out. I insisted that he go and enjoy himself. Celia and I listened to music. There was always music playing softly in the background, classical and operatic, and I'd begun to like it.

Sean had to go back to Spain a few days ahead of me. I had papers to sign and a power of attorney to organise so that I could leave the legalities that death brought to the solicitor in my absence. I didn't want to go back to Dunmoy to do all that.

Phyllis and I were sitting by the fire one afternoon when I announced, 'There's no word for someone who is an orphan, an only child, and has no children. There should be.'

Pragmatic as always, Phyllis said, 'Two of those you can't change. One you can!'

'Yes, I can. I can!'

And she laughed at me.

We made love on that last night before Sean went back. He had been kind, considerate and patient, waiting until I was ready. I loved every fibre of the man, and I tried to ignite the passion we had experienced in that very bed on our wedding night. I really did. I'm not sure if he could tell that I was faking. It was too soon to be happy, but at the back of my mind those words of Phyllis's echoed. I would change the only thing I could. I'd stop taking the pill and let nature take its course.

'Are you worried about going away again? I know it was hard for you, but I'll be around more this time, I promise, and I'll keep you busy with my papers.'

'I'm fine. You keep ahead of your work. I'll be starting teaching in a few weeks, and I'm looking forward to that.'

'I'm going to miss you,' he told me.

'But it's only three days.'

'Three days too many,' he replied.

I knew I'd miss him too.

Chapter Forty-two

Sean flew back to Spain on New Year's Eve. I went to bed at about ten and talked to him for ages on the phone. I loved his voice.

Before I slept, I remembered other New Year's Eves. Being allowed stay up late. Opening the hall door with Mam and Dad on the stroke of midnight to let the old year out and to welcome the new one in. Making the first entry in a new diary when I was a teenager. That party at Ernest's and the falling-out with Phyllis. I couldn't believe it was only one year since Jack and I ate the grapes at Elena and Álvaro's wedding – the grapes that promised prosperity and good fortune. I wondered how Jack was doing. Had they delivered for him? Had he eventually managed to spend Christmas on Bondi Beach? I really hoped so. I fell asleep before midnight.

I was determined to spend as much time as possible with the girls before Gina headed back to her teaching job in Málaga. Trevor and Mags insisted that we all go out for drinks one night, for old time's sake. And it was good. We laughed and reminisced and talked of Mam's cakes. I told them I just wanted to go back to Rathmines with them and pretend nothing had changed.

'I can understand that, Tans,' Phyllis said, 'but you can't reverse time. You're an old married woman now – and a professor's wife, no less.'

'I'll miss our chats,' Celia told me as I was about to leave for the airport. 'And I've enjoyed having your friends call by too. It's too easy to get stuck in a rut, spending all one's time with one's peers. You young people have brightened the house up. Sean was never one for bringing his friends home much, but then that's men for you.'

He was waiting at the airport when I arrived, and my heart did a flip. It was our first time apart in our five-and-a-half-week-old marriage, and I still could hardly believe he was my husband. I ran forward to meet him and hugged him as though I'd never let him out of my sight again. This was the nearest thing to happy I'd been since our wedding night. I was determined to make it up to Sean. The last few weeks hadn't been much fun for him either. I had to keep these parts of my life separate. My grief and my happiness – our happiness.

I settled down more easily this time. Sean had put a lot of work into setting up a proper office where we could work side by side.

'This reminds me of my first morning working as your research assistant, everything stacked and categorised methodically. Except I was terrified of you then.'

'I'm glad that's changed,' he said, taking me in his arms.

'So am I. Who'd ever have thought?'

He had misplaced one folder and he spent two nights after dinner going through everything trying to find it, but with no success.

'I know I had a copy of it on my laptop, but that seems to be missing too. I can't figure it out.'

'Could you have done it on someone else's? Maybe Ernest's?'

'Tansy, you're a genius. I did it on Perdita's! I remember now, I'd lost my charger and hers wasn't compatible, so she lent me her laptop one day to write up the notes. I'll give her a ring.'

I offered to go and collect it, if it saved him a journey. It wasn't far and I needed the practice of driving on the other side of the road.

'She's not at home right now, and you wouldn't know where to look for it, but come along and keep me company on the drive.'

Her *casa* was in a village between Álvaro's family mansion and the one where Sean's Civil War studies were being conducted. I stayed in the car while he searched for his house key, opened the door and went inside. I followed his progress as he switched on lights in the dark house.

A few minutes later, a car pulled into the driveway and Perdita got out. I don't think she noticed me in the dark. I watched as she opened the back door to let Juan out of his child seat. On seeing Sean's car, he started shouting, 'Papa, Papa' and bolted for the house. A few seconds later through a window I saw the three of them together. Sean stooped down to lift the child up and give him a kiss. He held him and talked to him, stroking his blond hair. I tried to imagine him with children. Our children. Plural. We were both 'only's' and I didn't want that. I wanted my son or daughter to have at least one sibling, more if possible.

Perdita watched, and when he'd put the child down, he and

she embraced. Jealousy is a green-eyed monster, but I didn't much like to see this woman embrace my husband with such familiarity. In fact, I didn't like it at all. Then they seemed to be arguing, shouting at each other, even. They left that room and Sean emerged, a laptop in his hand, while Juan and Perdita stood in the doorway, the child clutching a wooden toy train, the one Sean had bought him. She turned and had gone inside before Sean got into our car.

'I got it,' he said as he reached behind and put the laptop on the back seat.

'I saw you arguing.'

'I know. She said she needed her laptop tomorrow, so I have to bring it back later when I've retrieved my files.'

'Couldn't you have emailed them to yourself?'

'No, apparently Juan smashed the router in one of his tantrums over Christmas. He doesn't like anything with lights that flash. She usually turns it off until he's in bed, but she forgot and he went berserk. He's broken a television in the past too.'

'That's awful. It must be very difficult to cope with a child like that.'

'It is. She has a cousin who stays with her a lot of the time and that keeps her sane. What gets to me are the noises he makes when he screams. They're almost animal-like.'

'I don't know how I'd cope with something like that. When he saw your car, he started squealing and calling, "Papa, Papa".'

'He thinks any man who comes to the house is his papa.'

'I figured that. Poor little mite.'

'Once I download these files, I'll get the computer back to her. You needn't stay up. Your classes start in the morning.'

'I've done the prep but I think I'll turn in. I don't want to show up on the first day with bags under my eyes.'

'You'll look as beautiful as ever.'

'Thank you, Professor.' I kissed him goodnight.

'I'll drop you off in the morning.'

Later, I heard Sean coming in and looked at the bedside clock. It was after two. He climbed in beside me and, when he realised I was awake, he whispered, 'Go back to sleep, Tansy. It's very late. Juan had a meltdown when I was leaving and I stayed to help Perdita settle him.'

I snuggled up beside him and went back to sleep again.

◆

I enjoyed being back in the classroom. The staff were friendly and helped me settle into the role. My pupils were twelve, thirteen and fourteen-year olds – who, if their grades allowed, would be going to Ireland for family stays during the summer.

And I'd be going back then to start my married life proper there.

Chapter Forty-three

'You seem to be settling in well,' Mags said when she phoned one evening. 'I'm sure it helps that you have some friends there already.'

'It does, although I'm still not very social. Ernest calls occasionally and he's come to dinner a few times. He's an easy guest to entertain, and it gives Sean a break from me,' Tansy said.

'I doubt he needs that. Trevor tells me that he and Mary McLaughlin keep in touch regularly. Who'd have thought?'

'Just goes to show – you never know.'

Tansy mailed Phyllis.

Elena and I meet for coffee occasionally and I'm coming under pressure from Sean to return some of the dinner invites we have accepted. Before I could organise anything, Álvaro pulled a stroke to get us to visit them again. Part of me is pleased that I don't have to be the hostess, but honestly I'm still not in the mood. I can't believe Mam and Dad are gone and keep imagining that when I come home, they'll be there like always.

Álvaro has invited his parents too. Apparently, his father is looking forward to hearing an update on the Civil War project from Sean, informally, of course. The Marqués is head of the foundation that's funding the research and Álvaro knew I was unlikely to do anything that might upset that. Consequently, we've accepted.

She replied:

'Good for Álvaro! I know it's hard, but you'll probably enjoy it.'

I wasn't so sure, but I owed it to Sean to make the effort.

◆

There were eight of us. I didn't know the other couple and I can't recall his name, but his wife was a guest professor too.

'Tansy, I think you have already met Perdita?' Álvaro said. I was surprised to find her waiting on the table.

'Yes, I did.' I smiled a hello. 'But I'm afraid my Galician is non-existent. How is your little boy?'

Elena translated and Perdita looked first at Sean. Then she gave me the strangest look. Her eyes filled up with tears and she excused herself and ran out of the room. Amid some confusion, Álvaro's mother followed her and we heard raised voices.

'Perhaps I shouldn't have mentioned Juan. I didn't mean to upset her. Maybe she doesn't like talking about him.'

'I'm sure that's not what's wrong,' Álvaro assured me and went out after them. He and his mother returned a few minutes later and she said, 'She's not feeling too well, so I've sent her home.' She began telling the others that I was teaching and they quizzed me about how that was going. I told them I loved it.

I was so proud of Sean. I loved listening to him tell his yarns. I still couldn't believe that of all the people he had met on his adventures and travels, he had picked me to marry. Sitting there, rubbing shoulders with the nobility and those in academia, he was totally at ease.

When I mentioned that to Phyllis, she laughed at me. 'And what do you think you were doing? Sitting there rubbing shoulders with the nobility and those in academia too, being totally at ease. And, woman, if I remember rightly, the nobility concerned were your friends before they met Sean. Just sayin'. Give yourself some credit, Tansy. You've arrived.'

The dinner discussion revolved around some aspects of the conflict that had divided Spain, and when it seemed to be getting very heavy, Álvaro's father said, 'Forgive us. We're becoming bores and hogging the limelight.'

He told us they were experimenting with some new organic wines. 'I'm letting Álvaro take the lead. But it's a slow process. Nothing in viniculture happens quickly. It can take years to know if these will pay dividends.'

'My father is not entirely convinced that our merchants or customers can tell the difference, or even if they are ready to embrace such drastic changes yet.'

'I don't entirely agree,' his father argued.

'We could put it to the test. The *bodega* is set up for a blind tasting tomorrow. We're expecting a group of wine writers from France. Let's see how discerning your palates are. Ladies, will you join us?'

Álvaro's mother cast her eyes skywards and laughed. 'Not unless we have to. You men are so competitive.'

'I'd rather stay here and chat. What do you think?' Elena suggested and we agreed.

When they had gone out, Álvaro's mother brought up the accident that had killed my parents. I hadn't been expecting anyone to mention it – the proverbial elephant in the room – but in a way, it opened up a new perspective.

Elena said, 'You never get over losing your mother. Even though it's been six years since mine died, I miss her every day. And I found it particularly sad planning my wedding. I kept wondering how she'd have done things. It was so emotional. I was lucky to have such a wonderful mother-in-law to step in and be there for me through all that though.'

The other female guest said, 'I know it's not the same, but I do understand grief a bit. I miscarried twice and I still find it hard to be around pregnant women and young mothers. We haven't managed to have our own baby yet.'

As I listened, I began to realise that others had gone through the same degree of pain and that they had survived. I will too. I know I will.

The last of whatever barriers had been between Elena and me fell that night. We had something in common over which to bond, painful and all as it was. The conversation moved on and I began to relax.

But not for long.

Coming back from the bathroom, I met Álvaro's mother. Without preamble she asked me if everything was all right with Sean. I didn't know how to answer. What sort of question was that? And what right had she to ask? Of course everything was all right, or as all right as it could be with a grieving wife.

'Make sure you always put your man first,' she told me, patting my arm. 'No matter what's going on, men can be like spoiled children – they need to feel they are the centre of your world. If you get my meaning.'

I was amazed. This was the twenty-first century, not the nineteenth. I actually resented her, and I had to try very hard not to give her a smart answer. After his father, Álvaro and Sean were the last to return from the cellar and I wasn't sure if I was just still smarting from my encounter, or if there really was an atmosphere in the air between them that hadn't been there before. I hoped that Álvaro hadn't broached the same subject with Sean. He mightn't have been as polite as me.

Our marriage was our affair and nobody else's. I knew we hadn't made love very often, even though I wanted to have a baby. Sean had been really understanding and assured me he didn't mind waiting. He'd never have told anyone that, surely.

Would he?

Men had their needs. I vowed to try harder to recapture those intimate feelings we'd shared, but something was still shut down inside me. It still felt wrong to be so happy. It felt as though we were both playing a waiting game until they returned, and I was certain they would.

Later I asked him about the wine tasting.

'They take the whole business so damned seriously. They had me don a blindfold, before tasting and spitting, tasting and spitting, and tasting again.'

'Why the blindfold?'

'So that I wouldn't be influenced by the colour or the legs.'

'The legs? I thought you were there for the wine!'

He laughed at me. 'Yep, the legs. They're the runs on the

inside of the glass. Apparently, they can have something to do with the alcohol level in the wine. Viscosity or some such. They love their terminology. It was all pretty fine to me – it just seemed a shame to spit it out.'

'I suppose they'd all be alcoholics if they had to drink glasses of the stuff every day.'

He laughed again. 'I could think of worse ways to go. I think I may be tipsy already anyway.'

I thought he was. I reached for him and put my hand on his face. He took it and held it.

'I do love you,' I told him. 'I really do.'

'I know you do,' he replied.

That night we got a little closer, but I was still nowhere near providing the intimacy he was seeking. Things in that department did improve, but as his research progressed, I saw less and less of him. He often came home after I'd gone to bed, sometimes the worse for too much drink. This dining at ten o'clock at night made the evenings seem endless and very lonely. To pass the time, I immersed myself in his notes, photos and papers. I began counting the weeks till we'd be packing up and going home. In my mind I felt that our normal life would begin when we were back in Ireland. We'd have the summer to house-hunt, and start a family. And by then I'd have come to some sort of terms with the loss of my parents. I felt I couldn't really do that here in Spain – I needed to be nearer to them. I could hear my mother saying, 'Don't waste time on what might have been – enjoy the what is.' There were also lots of little bits of unfinished business that needed my attention at home too, but I was beginning to look ahead and that in itself was progress.

We flew back to Dublin for a weekend. Sean had a meeting

with the authorities in the university about resuming his position as Dean of the Faculty in the coming autumn. He was excited at the prospect.

Celia had had another TIA since we'd seen her.

'You should have let us know,' Sean told her.

'And have a load of fuss over nothing? Maisie was here when it happened, and she called the ambulance. They've changed my blood pressure tablets and I'm fine. I could have done that myself. I know how this goes. I just have to hope when my time's up, there'll be a massive power failure and whoof – the end. I didn't spend my whole life in medicine to bury my head in the sand.'

'Don't talk like that, Celia,' I told her.

She laughed. 'Don't worry about me. I'm not being morbid, just realistic. And even though that time in a home for the bewildered is fast approaching, I'm still nowhere near being ready to sit staring at walls, trying to make sense of things that once did.'

'No one can predict things like that. I'd give anything to have my parents here to look after, whatever their condition. Besides, we'll be back here soon, so you won't be on your own.'

'I'm sorry. That was insensitive of me, Tansy. I don't like this getting old business. I've been independent all my life and I resent losing that. I don't want to be a burden on anyone.'

'Don't look at it like that. Think of it as a time to be looked after. Something you've done for others all your life.'

She laughed. 'Then, Sean, you can begin by getting me some tea, please. I think Maisie left the tray ready.'

When he left the room, she said, 'You're wise beyond your years. Sean is lucky to have you in his life.'

'And I to have him in mine.' Celia didn't answer. Sometimes I got the impression that she was about to confide in me about something but thought better of it. We had our tea and he headed off to his meeting.

I had never seen Sean in a foul mood before that day. The hall door slamming shook the porch windows and announced his return.

'I take it your meeting didn't go well,' his mother said, looking up from her book.

'I'll take them to the Labour Court. They can't treat me like this. I was given an understanding that I'd go back in as Head of Faculty and now they tell me I can't.'

'Perhaps they didn't expect you back for another year,' I said, and he jumped at me.

'I don't need your stupid excuses. You haven't a clue about the politics in that place. What would you know about how these things work?'

'Maybe not a lot, Sean, but I do know that's there no need to take your anger out on me,' I replied.

He said nothing.

Celia put her book down purposefully on the side table and said, 'I agree with Tansy. That's not the way you were brought up, and I'm not comfortable with you talking to anyone like that in my home, much less your wife. If you'll both excuse me, I'm going to lie down for a bit before dinner.'

He poured a whiskey from the decanter on the sideboard and, after he'd taken a sip, he said, 'Want one?'

I declined but I suggested perhaps he might like to enlighten me as to how these things did work.

He said nothing and I pushed. 'What happened?'

'They fired me,' he shouted. 'They're out to get me. I've seen this happen before. I'll show them. They'll be sorry they messed with Sean Pollard. They won't walk over me. And now I have my mother treating me like a naughty schoolboy and you looking at me like a whipped pup.'

I was shocked. Why would they fire him? I knew he was one of their highly regarded professors, both by his peers and his students. As well as being the recipient of many awards, both national and international, he was acclaimed for his publications and contributions to journals.

They must have given him a reason, but I was still smarting from the vitriol in the way he had spoken to me. I needed to talk to someone. I needed my mother. Oh, how I needed my mother. Not that I would ever have been tempted to tell her what had just happened.

When he fell asleep in an armchair after several more whiskies, I went upstairs and rang Phyllis. She knew by my voice how upset I was. She offered to come over, but I put her off. She wasn't Sean's favourite person and I thought having her around would probably set him off again. I didn't tell her he had been fired, just that he'd had some serious disagreement with the college authorities.

'So, you've had a tiff. It'll blow over and it'll be worth it all when you make up. I can see why he's upset, but good on you for standing up for yourself, and to Celia for having your back.'

'You always cheer me up, and although we can't catch up this time, it's only a few weeks to Easter.'

'I'm already looking forward to that.'

Sean tried to offer a drunken apology later that evening, but I shrugged it off and told him to go to bed.

The next day I heard him on the phone. In fact, he was on the phone all morning, ranting and raving. Several times he stopped talking when I came into the room, but I caught snatches of those conversations.

I only half listened. I knew he was disappointed, angry, even, but he was going on and on about it, and about who was going to pay for this travesty.

'… That's all in the past … How can they keep raking these things up? … I'm not the only lecturer to have had whisperings … bloody rumour machine … someone over there has obviously been talking, trying to sully my reputation … I feel I'm trapped in a net.'

I didn't know what he was going on about but encouraged him to go out that afternoon, to meet a few of his colleagues.

'Maybe the Board will have reconsidered their decision. Perhaps your friends could put in a good word,' I suggested.

'That's not the way things are done.'

'It won't do any harm to keep a clear head, just in case. You don't want to bad-mouth anyone when you're drunk.'

'Are you turning into my mother? I'm a grown man and can make my own decisions.'

'I'm concerned for you, Sean. I love you and don't like to see you so disappointed.' I went to kiss him, but he didn't come any closer.

Celia obviously knew her son far better than I did. She told me later it was best to ignore him.

'Let him fume. He'll eventually burn himself out like a volcano, then he'll be all apologies. He always had a fiery temper.'

'I hope our children won't inherit that trait when we have them.'

There was that look again. I wished that just sometimes she'd be a little disloyal and tell me what she was thinking, although I supposed that's what mothers did. Was I being a disloyal wife having such thoughts?

I decided to attempt a reprise of our wedding night, in the same bedroom where I had experienced passion like I never had before. I bathed, shaved, plucked and preened, scented and moisturised and fell asleep, on my own.

I couldn't say what time my husband came home, but either his snoring or the alcoholic fumes, or both, woke me at around four o'clock and I couldn't go back to sleep.

We flew to Spain the next day and, on the flight, I tried to be cheerful, pretending there was nothing wrong.

'When you've finished up in June, we'll have time to get the apartment ready for sale. And we can start looking for our own place. You could use your father's study to work on your research. That way we'll be able to complete the project with far less pressure than if you were spending all your time at the university.'

He never answered, just sat in his seat staring ahead. I didn't know this Sean. And I remembered that's what Mam, Phyllis and Álvaro had all worried about. They had all asked me if we knew each other well enough to marry in such haste. I was certain that we did.

'Let's look on it as a fresh start. The one we should have had when we got married. We might even have time to take our honeymoon. By this time next year, we could be in our own home, living out our dreams. I'm sorry everything's been so awful. But I'll make it up to you. I promise.'

He took my hand and held it to his lips, then folded it

between his two. 'None of that was your fault, Tansy. Don't blame yourself.'

'Thank you.'

'Don't thank me, either. I don't deserve it.'

The 'Fasten your seatbelt' sign came on and we began our descent to Madrid.

I felt happier than I had done all weekend.

Chapter Forty-four

As soon as the schools broke up for Easter, Phyllis flew over to join us. I knew she was anxious about me, and, if I'm truthful, I was a bit anxious about how she would get on with Sean. He was quite unpredictable these days, and I was finding it hard to deal with his moods. He greeted her with politeness, a wariness even. I could see it unsettled her. Watching this unsettled me. My two favourite people in the whole world and they seemed incapable of seeing eye to eye on anything.

I brought her into Alcalá de Henares to meet Rosa, who insisted she see the stick man statue and the ones of Don Quixote and Sancho Panza outside Cervantes' home. 'They're all around the Plaza – we can see those when we finish our coffee,' Rosa said, 'and you'll be here for the *Santa Semana* processions. They're special.'

'So I've heard, but I want to see the place where the King and Queen met Tansy.'

'I think that should be the other way around.' I laughed.

'Definitely not – did no one tell them what a privilege it was for them to be granted an introduction to my friend?' Phyllis replied.

'I absolutely agree,' said Rosa.

Before we finished, I had fixed a date to host my overdue dinner.

'I've never done anything like this before. Whereas it's second nature to Elena, I'm not even sure if we have enough serving dishes and glasses in the house we're renting.'

'And you can borrow anything you need from ours,' said Rosa.

'But I want you and Pedro to be there, as our guests, and meet the people who are important in my life. Mags and Trevor are coming over tomorrow to spend Easter with his dad, Ernest, and you both know him. I'll ask Elena and Álvaro. Neither of you have met her, but she's been really kind to me.'

◆

I can't describe how happy I was to have Phyllis with me for those ten days. With her I was free to talk about anything and everything, except Sean's dismissal. We cried a little and we laughed a lot. I could see the relief on Sean's face. Slowly he was getting the real me back again. But I wasn't getting my professor back. Something had changed, seismically. He was tense and irritable, and I knew he was still grappling with the shock of losing his job and trying to sort things out. It probably wasn't the best time to have a houseguest, but I put on a brave face.

I told Phyllis, 'We may all be moving on, but I feel there's a bond that will always be there to hold us together. It's cemented in friendships that will endure, no matter what distance separates us. Don't you agree?'

'I do,' she said, before adding, 'Sean seems to be very stressed.'

'He is. He's furious over the Dean of Faculty business, which hasn't yet been resolved, and is concerned about meeting his June deadline for the field work on the current project. He wants to have that completed before losing his research students.'

'Did he tell you why he's not being reinstated? Surely they gave him some explanation.'

'How did you find that out?'

'Mags told me.'

Of course, Ernest would have told Trevor ...

'He won't talk about it. I've asked and cajoled, but he's adamant that he's being wronged.'

'They must have some serious reasons.'

'I'm sure they have, and he's not helping his cause by refusing to talk to them.'

I needed to know what had happened. I cornered Ernest and asked him if he had any idea. He sidestepped the question, muttering something about them having their own agenda. 'There are always policy differences within departments from time to time, and personalities sometimes get in the way too.'

I wasn't sure that was entirely true. It didn't seem like a sacking offence, not agreeing with each other. Sean was drinking an awful lot, something was weighing him down and he was trying to drown it out with alcohol, copious amounts of alcohol. I couldn't mention it again. The last time I did that, he accused me of claiming he had a drink problem.

Reluctantly, Ernest agreed to talk to him for me.

I was a little apprehensive about the dinner party. 'I think Sean may have had some sort of disagreement with Álvaro,' I told Phyllis. 'Something's changed since the night we were at their villa with his parents. He's certainly not quite as enthusiastic about him as he used to be.'

'That's men for you, Tans. He's probably jealous of your friendship with him.'

I dismissed that. 'So tell me, have you not met anyone yet to take your fancy, Phyllis?'

'No. And I'm not in any hurry.'

'I could hear Mary McLaughlin in myself as I said that,' I told her. We laughed.

'How is she doing? She must miss your mam.'

'She does, terribly. She's put the shop on the market as a going concern, but with the new shopping centre outside Dunmoy, I'm not sure how that will work out. When we were talking the other evening, she asked if I was looking forward to the patter of little feet any time soon. She's the only person who has the nerve to ask questions like that in this day and age, and before you ask, no I'm not expecting them yet!'

'I wasn't going to ask that. I just wanted to tell you I expect to be a godmother to your first!'

We spent the next day making lists – the things I needed to borrow. There were tablecloths and napkins, cutlery and dishes, and all sorts of kitchen gadgets. I wasn't so sure about the food, and how I'd be able to serve everyone and keep the dishes hot at the same time.

Phyllis suggested getting a local woman in to help and I thought of Perdita. She could probably use some extra money. I asked Sean for her phone number and he nearly went into orbit. His reasoning made no sense to me.

'Do you want Álvaro and Elena to think we are trying to be their equals, poaching their domestic staff?'

I thought it was highly unlikely that it would be construed like that. I didn't like Perdita being referred to as a domestic either.

He was totally inflexible and insisted I ask one of the women from the village. Not wanting to create a bad atmosphere while Phyllis was with us, I acquiesced.

Ours was a real party house over that period, three flatmates and Trevor of course, reunited in reminiscences of our college days. They regaled me with tales of their teaching experiences and wanted to know if I'd be looking for a job for the coming autumn.

'It's unlikely. I still have some sorting out to do concerning the house and land in Dunmoy. And although I hate the thought of having to go through everything and clear it out, it'll have to be done.'

'We'll come down and give you a hand,' said Phyllis, 'won't we, Mags? That way it won't take as long and you'll have some company.'

'That would be great. Friends like you are worth your weight in any precious metal!'

Sean joined in the chatter when he was there, and he came with us to the *Santa Semana* processions. It was his first time seeing them too, and he was his perfectly charming, generous self and a model host. I felt much more at ease than I had been.

Despite it being Easter time, I felt Sean could have been around a little more. Or perhaps he was just giving me time with my friends, allowing me a little space. Perhaps he needed some for himself. Had I been too clingy, too demanding? He had his work and his students. Apart from my few hours' teaching, a couple of days each week, he was my everything. Note to self – try not to be so needy.

One evening he went to bed before the others had left. We

had been enjoying the wines that Álvaro had very generously brought over for us to try, and I pretended not to hear Gina saying to Álvaro, 'I suppose it's an age thing. He probably thinks we're too immature for him.'

'Oh, I doubt that's the reason,' he replied. 'Sean is a complex man.'

Complex. I thought that was an interesting way to describe him.

◆

The dinner party went much better than I could have hoped. Trevor and Mags, who had missed out on the summer trips to Spain with the rest of us, got to meet Álvaro and Elena, and Rosa and Pedro.

'Now that we know you all, we can match the names and faces,' said Mags.

'How is Jack, or is anyone in touch with him?' Álvaro asked Phyllis. 'I often wonder if Australia is living up to his expectations.'

'He never went,' Phyllis replied. 'He decided to do a master's instead. He pops in to see us sometimes, and we all meet up for a drink occasionally.'

That was news to me. None of them had mentioned that before, but I supposed it was only natural that they'd avoid telling me anything about him, after the way I'd behaved.

'I always thought he was keen on you, Phyllis.'

'I know you did, Tans, but he only ever had you in his sights.'

'Do send him our best. I really liked him, and his ginger hair,' Elena said. Rosa and Pedro agreed.

I was pleased with the way the evening went. It had been

worth all the effort. Everyone mixed well and Maria from the village served and cleared away like a true professional. At one point I saw Ernest, Trevor and Sean in deep conversation in the garden. It wasn't really warm enough to be outside, but they were all grown men, and whatever they were discussing looked serious, so I left them to it.

Phyllis stayed on for a few days after the others had gone and we went to Madrid. I gave her the grand tour, even taking her to the little restaurant at the back of the *charcutería*, where Sean had brought me on my first visit. That was where he'd taken a *pimiento* olive from a little dish and held it up to my mouth. I remembered that as he did so, he looked straight into my eyes and I knew for certain that that moment of intimacy had been what had made me so certain that he returned my feelings.

'You've had an awful lot to cope with in the last six months, Tansy. I don't know how you've kept sane. And although he's not who I would have chosen for you, I'm glad to see that your eyes light up when you talk about Sean. You deserve to be happy, and I'm happy for you.'

'It has been very tough at times, especially leaving you all behind so soon after the funeral. I miss you and the others so much. Much as I like being here, I'm counting the weeks till we leave.'

'Are you moving back to Sean's apartment?'

'No, we're going to move in with Celia initially.'

'Are you happy about that?'

'I don't mind. It won't be forever and she's actually very nice. When I met her first, I thought she'd be the mother-in-law from hell, and she's anything but.'

'I agree. You've got an unlikely ally there, and you never know when it might come in useful. Keep your hair on, Tans, I'm just sayin'. That's all!'

'You don't have to elaborate and, Phyllis, don't ever change. I need you to keep me grounded.'

'Delighted to oblige.'

'You've no idea how much I needed you here.'

'I think I have,' she said, giving me a hug.

Chapter Forty-five

As the weeks went by, I was faced with the prospect of going back. Being away from Ireland meant I was able to hide from certain realities, from the knowledge that my parents were now gone. But I wouldn't be able to run away from them forever. Despite this, I was getting excited at the prospect of being able to meet the girls any time we wanted to, instead of talking to them on devices that distorted their faces, enlarged their teeth and elongated their noses.

Sean was the very opposite. He got more and more morose as the days passed. He seldom made it home in time for his dinner and, when he did, he usually came in reeking of whiskey. I worried about him driving like that. He ate little and said less.

One evening he shouted at me.

'I don't know what's got you so chirpy. We're not exactly going to be the toast of society when we go home. Your professor's got no job. The funding for the completion of the current project is in doubt and I'll have to endure the silent, disapproving treatment of my mother, and now of my wife too.'

I laughed. 'Oh Sean, you really are feeling sorry for yourself. Look on this as an opportunity. You can take up a post abroad somewhere. We can travel together, like we planned, maybe go to South America. You'll be free to attend the conferences you've had to miss. All those awards you have, and the academic reputation you've earned over the years, are a sure-fire guarantee that whatever you want to publish will be snapped up. Look on—'

He shut me down with a sharp, 'Just leave it, will you? All these cheerful banalities. You don't know what you're talking about.'

'Maybe not,' I told him as I watched him pour from the whiskey bottle. 'But you've no right to take your frustrations out on me, Sean. I'm on your side.'

'I wonder for how much longer.'

'That's nonsense. You're not making any sense. And you won't find what you're looking for at the bottom of a glass.'

I went to bed.

Something was wrong, very wrong. I needed to talk to someone, although it felt disloyal to think like that. I dismissed the idea of Phyllis on the grounds that she didn't have a high opinion of Sean anyway, and when it blew over, whatever it was, I would prefer she didn't know I'd been so concerned.

I considered ringing Ernest, but Sean would never forgive me if he found out that I'd spoken to a colleague about him. I decided on Álvaro. I could trust him. And when we were back in Ireland, we wouldn't be bumping into him every day.

He came to the house the next day after lunch and I blurted out my worries as soon as he was through the door. It was obvious he was uncomfortable talking about Sean, and I had a strong inkling that he knew more than he was prepared to admit.

I challenged him about their relationship and he assured me that they had argued over the politics of the Civil War that night in the *bodega*, nothing more.

'Are you sure there isn't something you're not telling me?' I asked.

'We're both strong-willed and stubborn. Neither of us wanted to back down and let the other think he was right. Understandably, he's gutted about his job, but drinking won't help that.' He smiled at me and took my hand. 'Try not to stress. You'll get through this, but it's not me you should be having this conversation with, Tansy. It's Sean. He needs to know how you are feeling.'

'Álvaro …'

'Talk to him, Tansy. And just remember, whatever happens, I'll always be here for you. Elena too.'

Instead of reassurance, that promise held foreboding.

The next few weeks were busy, packing up and getting Sean's papers and books ready for shipping. My classes gave me lots of small gifts and cards. He didn't want to do drinks with the people he had worked with for the past two years and declined Rosa and Pedro's invitation to dinner on our last night. I would miss my Alcalá friends.

Our departure was very low-key. It wasn't the farewell I had expected. We just seemed to slip unobtrusively from our Spanish world back into an Irish one, where we had yet to establish any routine or structure.

I urged Sean to go and see the Board in the university. Perhaps they'd had a change of heart. But he adamantly refused. He would see them in court when he sued for breach of contract, not before.

It was hard to tell if Celia really welcomed us into her ordered life. I sensed there was some new tension between mother and son, but I couldn't ask her, and he would tell me I was paranoid.

We had everything except our clothes and personal effects delivered to Sean's apartment. He'd decided he could work better there and I could go over when needed. I was happy about that as it meant we wouldn't get too cosy in his mother's house.

I met the girls, Trevor too, and would see Gina when she brought Gonzalo home to meet her family in July.

When not at his apartment, Sean spent a lot of time those first weeks talking about organising his life: about unpacking the documents and books he'd brought back. He didn't, though. I offered to help and was told that when he needed it, he'd ask.

In some ways I welcomed this break from his papers. It had been a bit intense before we came home. Now I had the time to pop into some estate agents and explore the properties that were available.

'Is it a house or an apartment you're after? A period property or a new build?'

I didn't know. That was something else we needed to discuss, but it could wait until Sean sorted out his work situation. I took a fistful of brochures, thought better of bringing them home and put them in a litter bin around the corner.

A few weeks after returning, Celia summoned me to her sitting room, the one at the front of the house where we had been first introduced. When she indicated where I should sit, I felt I was about to be interviewed.

'Tansy, we don't know each other very well or for very long, and you may feel it's not my place to discuss certain things with you. But I'm a straight talker and I feel obliged to have this chat, however disagreeable.'

I didn't know what was coming next, so I held my peace.

'Dublin is a small place and people talk. I have discovered why my son has not been reinstated in his previous post, nor, I regret to say, will he be.'

'Oh.' What she had just said sank in slowly.

'Can't we wait a bit, Celia? I'm not happy discussing Sean when he's not here.'

'I understand that, Tansy, but I don't think he'll give you the real reason. He has no one to blame but himself for the current situation. He's always had an eye for young women and he has been cautioned on several occasions about his liaisons and indiscretions with various students.'

'He told me about his marriage and the baby they lost.'

'I'm glad to hear that. But she wasn't the only one. He's been censured on numerous occasions, and I've discovered that when he took this last sabbatical, it was to remove himself from another scandalous and unethical situation.'

I couldn't believe what I was hearing. He had told me he'd gone away because he knew he loved me and couldn't trust being around me.

'Was the girl pregnant?'

'Not this one. That was another one, some years ago. She probably would have been if he hadn't had the vasectomy. Her parents are friends of the Provost and they went right to the top in making an official complaint. That's why he's been dismissed.'

I couldn't talk. Phyllis had tried to tell me and I wouldn't listen. Had Sean's mother just told me that my husband had

had a vasectomy … and that he had been dismissed? Dismissed from the university in disgrace?

I felt the blood drain from my face. I thought I'd pass out.

'A vasectomy. Sean had a vasectomy?'

I started to cry and I couldn't stop.

Celia tried her best to comfort me, telling me that the operation could often be successfully reversed. I realised that was why she had acted so strangely when I mentioned having babies. That wasn't the point, though. It was the fact that he'd deceived me. And all the times I had talked about us starting a family …

That he had had several other affairs and dalliances, had been dismissed and was possibly now unemployable didn't seem so important at all in comparison with that bombshell.

'It pains me greatly to tell you this, Tansy. I'm very ashamed of my son. He may be highly intelligent but, when it comes to women, he doesn't use his brain to think. He lacks morality and has always been a disappointment to me and his father. I'm just glad that he is not around for this latest development.'

'Why didn't anyone tell me?' I asked, but I already knew the answer. They had tried. 'People said he had a bit of a reputation, but I hadn't wanted to hear that. My friends tried. And Phyllis – she must have known when she challenged him head on at the party in Ernest's house. No wonder he doesn't like her.'

Celia said, 'I wanted to warn you when he brought you home to meet me, but he'd already put a ring on your finger, and I was wrong-footed. I'm sorry now that I didn't. I feel I have let you down. You deserve much better than him, Tansy. And that's not an easy thing for a mother to say.'

I didn't feel sorry for her then. I was too gutted to think about anyone but myself. Later I realised how difficult it must have been for her to have that conversation with me.

The older woman began to cry.

'I'm so sorry you've got caught up in this mess … in his mess,' she said.

'So am I,' I replied.

I went to our bedroom, curled up on the bed and cried like I hadn't done since Mam and Dad died. This nightmare had to end, soon. If it had been anyone other than Celia who'd told me these things, I wouldn't have believed them.

There were bits of our whirlwind romance that were making no sense to me as I looked back over them. Other thoughts were filling the gaps. His disappearance from campus that autumn, without any mention of the fact beforehand. That surely hadn't been organised overnight. He had to have been planning that for some time to have funding, etc. in place.

The manic speed at which Sean declared his love for me and insisted we become engaged and get married. I had been used as a pawn; a diversionary tactic to add respectability to some other dubious aspect of his life and to save face. I had been the cover-up for the affair that was to be his downfall.

And the vasectomy. Why hadn't he told me about that?

I needed time to think, but I didn't want to think.

I needed to talk to Álvaro. He'd know what to do. I rang him. He knew from my voice that I'd found out something.

Before I could explain what, he said, 'So you talked to Sean. I suppose he had to come clean. There's no arguing with the DNA results.'

'DNA results? What do you mean?'

There was an awkward silence.

'Álvaro, what DNA results? What are you talking about?'

'Don't mind me. I have my wires crossed.'

'What did you mean – whose DNA results? Tell me, Álvaro. I'm going mad here.'

'Tansy, this is very awkward and not the sort of conversation we should be having over the phone.'

'I can assure you, you're not going to shatter any illusions I have about my lying husband. His mother, the poor old woman, has just told me everything. At least, I thought she did. I'm not sure now.'

I wasn't prepared for the next shock. Álvaro asked me if I remembered the dinner in his home when Perdita was waiting on the table and she got upset.

Of course I remembered. I had thought it had been because I had asked about her little boy.

'It wasn't that at all. Juan is Sean's child. I believe he never doubted that, yet he always denied it. Anyone could see that from Juan's colouring, his blue eyes and floppy hair, he wasn't her husband's. They both grew up on farms on our estates. Perdita is one of several Galician families we have here. My grandfather suspected what had happened. He's a tough businessman, and whatever people think of him, he really cares about his estate families. When he heard Perdita's husband left after finding out about their relationship, he was determined to make Sean support his son. He confronted him and of course Sean denied everything.'

'But how did he get him to do a DNA test?'

'He didn't.'

'I don't understand any of this.'

'Sean was still living in Perdita's house, and still carrying on with her, when he met up with you again. He'd never mentioned you to her. She was already under the impression that he was going to marry her and make a real family of the three of them. When she met you, she thought you were just another research assistant or doctoral student who had come to Spain for a few months.'

I couldn't talk. I couldn't find the words. I'd wake up any minute.

'Are you sure you want to hear all this, Tansy?'

'No, Álvaro, I don't want to hear it. Any of it, but I have to.'

'That night when you both came to dinner with my parents was when Perdita realised that Sean had actually married you. When you asked about Juan, she couldn't take it and fled.'

'My God, I don't believe it. The poor woman. She must hate me, but I didn't know. Honestly, I didn't. I'd never have ...'

'I don't doubt that, Tansy. That night she told my mother and me that Sean was Juan's father. My father and grandfather needed proof and they'd set a trap for him. I knew nothing of this and you were certainly never meant to find out. Juan is going to need a lot of special attention as he grows. His autism is pretty bad, and Sean doesn't contribute anything. My grandfather just wanted to make sure the child's future would be secure and that Sean took some responsibility.'

'What did they do?'

'Do you remember we left you ladies and went to taste some wines in the cellar? Well, they got a saliva sample of Sean's from the spittoon and sent it off. Of course it was a match. Conclusive proof.'

'Do you know Sean never told me that he'd had a vasectomy?

How could he do that to me? He knows I have no family and
how badly I want a child of my own.'

'Perhaps he was afraid you wouldn't marry him and time was
running out, because of his affair with the student in Dublin.'

'You know something, Álvaro, I was so besotted with him
that I'd probably have accepted that. We could have adopted.'

'I'm so sorry, Tansy. I wish I hadn't been the one to tell you
any of this.'

'What did he do when he found out about the DNA test?'

'You don't need to know that, Tansy. He never had any
doubts about Juan. He just didn't want to acknowledge that
he could have fathered a defective child, as he sees it. That's
probably why he had the vasectomy.'

'He's a lying, cheating, bastard. And he's a coward too. I'll
never forgive him. It's no wonder he's drinking himself into
oblivion.'

'If you want to come over and stay with us at any stage, you
know you're always welcome in our home.'

'You're a great friend, Álvaro, and I will take you up on that
offer sometime, thank you, but not now.'

'What will you do?'

'I haven't an idea.'

And I hadn't. I didn't know where to turn.

'Does Elena know?'

'She does. She's in the room here with me and has heard
everything. She wants a word, if you're up to it.'

She was so kind that I broke down and cried, again. 'We're
devastated for you. I had no idea that night what was going on.
We never wanted to get involved in your marriage. Believe me,

Juan's welfare was all anyone had at heart. I'm so sorry, Tansy, and so sorry you had to find out like this.'

'There was never going to be an easy way.'

Sean was incoherent when he returned that night. His inebriated state prevented me from having any sort of discussion with him. It was just as well, because I had no idea how I'd have handled the situation.

If I'd had a gun, I'd probably have been tempted to use it.

Chapter Forty-six

I got up very early the next morning. Sean was still in a post-binge sleep. After showering, I stood looking at him in the bed, sweaty and tossed. He seemed to have shrunk.

The magic had died.

I wanted to thump him, to make him realise what he'd done to me. He'd taken my hopes and my heart and broken them into pieces, yet there he was, oblivious. He didn't give a damn about anyone, only himself. I made up my mind there and then that he wasn't going to destroy me.

I went downstairs to find Celia. I told her I was going to go to Dunmoy for a few days, to see Mary McLaughlin, and to sort out a few legal bits and pieces with the solicitor, Patsy Maher.

She nodded.

'I think that's a good idea, Tansy. I heard Sean come in last night, the worse for drink again. I'll see if I can talk some sense into him while you're away.'

It wasn't the time to tell her that no matter what she said, it would make no difference. Perhaps she already knew that.

I woke Phyllis when I rang.

'God, woman, it was for these long holidays and lie-ins

that I became a teacher. It's half-past eight, Tans! What's the emergency?'

'I have to go to Dunmoy, this morning.'

Without hesitation she said she'd come with me.

The next few days were the strangest and also the most decisive of my life. Phyllis uncharacteristically held her counsel and didn't question me at all on the drive. I didn't talk much either.

We stopped at the churchyard at the top of the town. It was my first time back. The soil had sunk and the plot looked abandoned. I was glad my parents couldn't see me now, standing there feeling lost and alone, despite Phyllis's arm linking mine. There was a weird sense of solace in knowing that they'd never find out what had happened.

In the town large billboards on each corner of Mary McLaughlin's shop declared 'Sale Agreed'. We didn't stop to go in, but kept on for home, although it didn't feel like that any more.

It was tough turning in through the gates of the farmyard. Little Jim's car was there, so too was my mam's. For a second, I wondered where my dad's was. Then I remembered it had been written off in the accident.

Little Jim appeared from behind the house.

'I thought I heard an engine. It's great to see you back, Tansy, you're a sight for sore eyes.' He hugged me solidly and the earthy smell of the farm on his tee-shirt brought me right back to childhood. I wept openly.

'You have the place looking very well.'

'Sure I feel obliged to look after it not just for your folks' sake, but for Gappy Jim's too. This farm has always been part of our lives. I don't suppose you'll be coming home to live here, now that you're a married lady in the city.'

I forced a smile. 'I've made no decisions about anything yet, that's partly why I'm here. I'll know more after I've had a chat with Patsy Maher.'

Despite the warmth of the day, the house felt cold. No smell of baking greeted us as we walked into the kitchen, my mam's kitchen. There was no warm glow from the stove. Apart from that, nothing much had changed. The oilcloth covered the big wooden table. Bills and letters still stuck out on the second shelf of the dresser, alongside my grandmother's never-used collection of blue and white crockery jugs. The framed picture of me with the Spanish royals was still proudly displayed on the centre shelf. I went over and turned it face down. Perhaps in time I'd be able to look at it again.

Phyllis followed me as I walked from room to room. I didn't know why I did that. Was I trying to reconnect with my existence before Sean, or harness the essence of me, attempting to make sense of the mess that was now my life?

'Do you ever see Jack?' I asked Phyllis.

'Yes. I had a drink with him the other night. What made you think of him?'

'The last time I was in this bedroom was when Jack stayed over two Christmases ago, before we went to Spain. Mam had bought the new duvet set and those lamps, and she let me know in no uncertain terms that there'd be no hanky-panky under her roof.'

Phyllis laughed. 'I can just imagine that. He always asks after you.'

Little Jim came back an hour later. He'd been to the local

shop and bought us tea, bread, butter and milk, cooked ham, tomatoes, a tub of coleslaw and a Swiss roll.

'An Irish picnic,' he joked. 'That'll keep you going for a few hours, although Mrs N would kill me if she saw that on her table. It's probably the first time ever that there was a shop-bought cake on it.'

I didn't allow myself time to dwell on the situation I was pretending hadn't happened. That afternoon I signed numerous documents. I handed over the farm to Patsy Maher to sell, either as one parcel of land with the house and outhouses included or as two separate properties. The only proviso was that Little Jim had first refusal on any transaction. He was also entitled to take possession of any machinery, goods or chattels that he wanted from the farm.

I got the balances on my parents' bank accounts. Mam's was modest, Dad's surprisingly not. Their life policies had been credited to my account too.

I insured Mam's car in my name and put Phyllis on Sean's car insurance. Dad had taught me to drive at seventeen, after I'd had one lesson with Mam and we'd ended up shouting at each other.

I rang Mary McLaughlin and arranged to meet her in the village pub the next day for lunch, after I'd seen the undertaker and made final arrangements about finishing the grave and the wording for my parents' headstone.

'I don't know about you, but I'm exhausted,' Phyllis said, 'and not just from the driving. Let's get some food and a bottle of wine and go home and you can tell me what's going on. I know you're hurting, and you haven't mentioned Sean once all day.'

'I don't know where to begin.'

'At the beginning, woman. At the beginning.'

◆

After hours of what-if, if-only and why-didn't I, she asked me, 'What are you going to do? You have to file for divorce.'

'No, I don't.'

'Of course you do. Tansy! You can't let him get away with it.'

'I've no intention of letting him away with anything. I'm going to find a solicitor who specialises in family law and see if I can get an annulment. I think I have a good case.'

'Good woman, and I'm right here beside you.'

'I don't know what I'd do without you, Phyllis. You're a true mate.'

'You've got a good ally in Celia, too. I was very wrong about her. It looks as though she was on your side all along.'

'So was I. It just goes to show how wrong first impressions can be.'

◆

Mary McLaughlin told us, with delight, that she had managed to find a buyer for her shop.

'A young Polish couple bought it and they're going to clear the old storerooms and live above it. He's an electrician and she's a seamstress. She wants to do alterations and soft furnishings. They have two little boys. One of them will be starting school in September. They were living in Dublin but found it far too expensive. They didn't like city life, so this is ideal for them.'

She paused for a breath. How my dad would have laughed

at how much information she'd managed to fit into that intro. 'Seed, breed and generation,' he'd have said.

'Now, what's happening in your world? How's that lovely husband of yours?'

Phyllis saved me by suggesting we order some food first. There was no stopping Mary, though.

'How is Sean?' she asked again when we'd chosen.

'He's great altogether. What else would you expect, being married to this one?' Phyllis answered. 'And it looks like you've all become property speculators in the last year, and here's me still rentin' and sharin' in flatland. Do you know anyone who might buy the farm from Tansy?'

'I'd have thought Little Jim might show an interest in the place, but I'll spread the word. It should fetch a good price. Land values have been on the up and up since the recession ended, so you should do well out of it, Tansy.'

'What'll be your first great adventure when your shop deal has been closed?' I asked her. Her reply surprised me.

'Iceland. Sean's friend Ernest has been telling me all about the Icelandic ponies, the hot spring geysers, and the geothermal spa at the Blue Lagoon, of course. He's such a kind man. He's kept an eye on me since the accident and helped me greatly with negotiations for the sale of the shop.'

I saw Phyllis's eyebrows shoot up and knew she was thinking the same as me. What did Ernest know about Sean's activities, and had he told Mary anything? I hoped not. I didn't need my business touted around Dunmoy.

Phyllis and I spent the next few days going through my parents' personal effects, sorting clothes for the charity shops and burning papers that were no longer relevant. Mags came down at the weekend and lent her weight. To save me having to go into all the sordid details, Phyllis took her for a walk and filled her in. When they came back, she hugged me and confessed that she and Trevor had had misgivings when I got engaged.

'You didn't think to warn her off,' Phyllis said.

'How could you tell someone who was so obviously happy that you thought they were making a huge mistake? Trevor and I talked about this. In fact, we argued about it with Jack. Yes, with Jack. He thought you should know the stories behind Sean's reputation. Unfortunately, we disagreed. In the end, we felt that Sean should be given the benefit of the doubt. After all, he could have changed – you could have changed him.'

'A leopard, spots and all that.'

'I know, Phyllis, and when Ernest told Trevor there were rumours about Sean's inglorious dismissal, we were racked with guilt.'

'There's no need to feel guilty. If anyone should, it's me,' I told them. I wouldn't have listened to any of you. I went into it with my eyes open, and I walked over Jack in doing so. Maybe what's happened is karma.'

'That's ridiculous. You couldn't have stayed with Jack when you had such strong feelings for someone else. That would have been wrong,' Phyllis argued, and I supposed she was right about that.

Sean never tried to contact me while I was in Dunmoy and I was glad. I didn't know how I'd react if he did call me or, worse still, turn up on my doorstep.

'Clearing out someone else's house has to be one of the most awful things anyone ever has to do,' I told the girls. 'I'm going around in circles here, dithering over photos, many faded and of people whose faces I don't recognise. I'm shifting letters and papers from one pile to another, and all I've managed to do is create several more piles and the largest of these is the "undecided" one.'

'You've got to be ruthless, Tans. Will you wake up one day and think, I must have this or this? If not, bin it now,' Phyllis said, 'or give it away.'

'Yes, Ma'am, Sergeant Major, Ma'am.' I laughed, but she was right.

'There's enough bed linen and towels here to start a boarding house. And they're all perfect,' Mags said.

'Take anything you want, except the blue and white jugs on the dresser. I'm keeping those. They were my grandmother's.'

'Don't be so hasty, Tansy, you might regret the clean sweep later.'

'I won't, Mags. I've had plenty of time to think about these things. And that's all they are, things. They may have had some significance to my parents, but I'm not sentimentally attached to them except that shoebox on the table. Remember? I'm moving on.'

'What's in the box?'

'A tiny Babygro that I came home from the hospital in, and my first pair of shoes. Those things were precious to Mam. She kept them all these years, and so will I.'

We ploughed on. Phyllis agreed to stay until the following week, but Mags had to go back that Sunday.

I was surprised to see Celia's number come up on my phone.

'I just thought I should let you know that Sean has gone away.'

I stopped myself from saying, 'To rehab?'

'He's gone to a conference in Mexico, in the Yucatán. Some

friend of his, a professor from Alcalá, I believe, persuaded him the break would be a good idea and that perhaps he could get some lecturing out of it, somewhere that his reputation hasn't preceded him.'

'He had talked about going to that,' I said, not knowing how I should reply. 'When is he due back?'

'In two weeks. I know you've been keeping out of his way, and I understand why, but I want you to know that you mustn't stay away on my account. You've no other home in the city and you're welcome back here any time, Tansy. I'm not going to interfere between the two of you, but I'd like you to know that you have my support whatever you decide.'

She really did care.

'Celia, you don't know how much that means to me. Thank you.'

'How's the clear-out going?'

'Slowly, but we're getting through it. I'll be back midweek, if that's OK. We can talk then.'

Chapter Forty-seven

We drove back separately, Phyllis ahead of me in Sean's car. I could still smell Mam's perfume. She loved this car, her first ever brand spanking new one and, despite the country roads and farmyard puddles and splashes, she always kept it pristine. In the glove compartment I found her sunglasses and her spare pair of readers.

Celia was true to her word. She welcomed me back lovingly and, again, had fresh flowers in my bedroom. I could see this business of Sean's was taking its toll on her. She had dark circles around her eyes.

There were no questions and no recriminations. We'd talk when she was ready. She told me she'd ask Ernest to dinner that evening.

He was discretion itself, but I knew when Celia left the room 'to whip cream' that this had been a concerted act. Maisie would never have left anything for Celia to do in the kitchen, never mind when she had guests.

I didn't wait for Ernest to talk. I just came straight out with it.

'I'm going to get my marriage annulled. I haven't told him yet, or Celia, and I'd prefer if Mary McLaughlin didn't hear about this until it's a *fait accompli*.'

'My dear Tansy, I assure you she'll hear nothing about that from me, and for what it's worth, I think you are probably taking the right course of action. This is a terrible business altogether. I told Sean nothing good would come out of it and advised him against marrying you. But his ego was too big. In his mind, I think he thought that he could still have his mistress and his wife and keep both of them apart and happy.'

'Surely Perdita didn't want to have anything to do with him after the way he treated her and Juan?'

'Oh no, dear, not Perdita. And she was treated abominably by Sean. It's that professor at the University in Alcalá.'

Once again the alignment of my world wobbled.

'Professor Cortez, the one he got my Erasmus placement through, was his mistress?'

'Yes. That's who he's gone to the Yucatán conference with. She's a heavy drinker too, and I'll be surprised if she manages to hold on to that position, if she keeps that up.'

'Does Celia know about this?'

'Regrettably, yes, and I think she'll understand perfectly your decision to look for an annulment.'

I nodded. I was losing count of Sean's conquests. How many lives did that man have?

'Tansy, you must feel free to come and stay in my house if it's uncomfortable living here. You've been there and seen it. It's far too big for an old fellow on his own like me, and Mags probably told you that she and Trevor are going to move in before school term begins in September.

'You need a good lawyer. I can recommend a friend to act for you,' he said, and even offered to contact him and make the introductions.

I didn't tell Phyllis about this until the next afternoon. She told me to come over and to bring doughnuts. Rags was reclining on the windowsill. If he recognised me, he wasn't going to give me the satisfaction of letting me know. I tickled him under his chin and he reluctantly purred. I bent down and kissed his warm fur.

If I could hardly get my head around this latest revelation, Phyllis went ballistic, although her expletives were much more creative than mine.

'I wouldn't let him off with an annulment, hit him where it hurts – in his pocket. Go for a divorce and take him for every penny.'

'I don't want anything from him – only my freedom.'

'I know what I'd do to him if I got him,' she replied.

'I still don't know how I'll react when I have to confront him.'

'Why do you need to put yourself through that? For all you know, they've probably done a runner. Don't you think it's a bit suspicious that they're over on the other side of the world, together?'

'Not really. He's written a lot about the Mayans, so in a way it makes sense, but then what do I know about that man?'

'No more than any of us do.'

'If Trevor and Mags are moving out, do you think I could move back in with you here? I have enough savings to pay the extra rent and more than enough to live on until probate and the sale go through.'

'That would be amazing, Tans. I'd love that. And we'd have our own rooms, but no Mags to borrow our fashion from. I'd have to go frock fishing from you instead!'

I would never have believed it if anyone had told me that the flat would become the nearest thing to home I'd possess.

Chapter Forty-eight

Neither Celia nor I had had any communication with Sean since he'd left for Mexico. Nothing since he'd left the house, eight days earlier, yet I still jumped when my phone rang in case it was him.

Celia was wonderful. She minded and cosseted me, even buying agapanthus for my room because she remembered me telling her on my first visit that they were my favourite flowers.

She talked to me about her late husband, and how successful he had been in the world of pioneering cardiac surgery. She told me how they'd met and how he always put her first. She reminisced about being pregnant with Sean and how they had big dreams for him, and how devastated they were when their little grandson died, despite being furious with Sean for getting his eighteen-year-old girlfriend pregnant. She told me again and again what a disappointment he had turned out to be.

I still didn't know if she knew she had a beautiful blond, blue-eyed, autistic grandson in Spain. Somehow, I didn't feel it was my place to tell her. Sean had brought enough sadness to her life.

'I sometimes wonder if he resented me for being a career

mother. Is he acting out his spite on the women he professes to love? If he really cared for any of them, he would never have treated them as he does.'

'I don't think you can blame yourself in any way. From my perspective, he had a charmed life, Celia, and he reaped the benefits of your hard work, with his education and trips all over the world, to places most of us only see on a map.'

'You're young, Tansy, and you must promise me that you'll put this awful period in your life behind you and move on. Don't stop following your dreams. You're a kind, caring young woman, and I hope that when you can see clearly again you'll meet someone who deserves you.'

I crossed the room and gave her a hug. She smiled and said, 'I'm becoming too sentimental, so I'd better go off to bed now. You have a good night.'

The house phone woke me when it rang out at five-thirty the following morning. The birds were trying to out-sing each other and the dawn sky promised a clear day. I didn't think Celia would hear it. She always took her hearing aids out when she went to bed. I was sure it was Sean, probably drunk and feeling guilty about leaving me with his mother, or her with me.

By the time I got downstairs to the hall, it had stopped ringing. I was just back upstairs on the landing when it started again. This time I got to it in time.

It wasn't Sean. A woman's voice asked if she could speak to Mrs Pollard.

'I'm afraid she's in bed, asleep. May I give her a message? It's very early.'

'*Es muy urgente* – very urgent – it's about her husband.'

I was about to say, 'But he's dead' when I remembered I was

Mrs Pollard too. Stupidly, I asked, 'Which Mrs Pollard did you want?'

'The *mujer*, the wife of Sean Pollard.'

'That's me. Who is this?' I suspected it was probably another lover claiming part entitlement to my Lothario.

'It's the Policía Federal in Mexico. Is there someone there with you?'

Was this a cruel joke?

'No, yes, but she's asleep. It's the middle of the night here. What do you want?'

'I'm afraid your husband was taken to hospital.'

'What happened? Was he in an accident?' My heart nearly stopped – this couldn't be happening again.

'He was found in the street. He had been robbed and stabbed. I regret to tell you, he did not survive his injuries.'

My God, no. Not Sean. Dead. It had to be a mistake. I took a deep breath and heard myself say thank you. I hung up and sat on the stairs for a long, long time.

Was I sad? Yes. Was I shocked? Yes. Yet a part of me felt I had been released from something I couldn't describe.

Sean, whom I had once loved with all my heart, would have walked through fire for, gone anywhere with. He'd been murdered in a foreign country. No matter how awful he was, even he didn't deserve this.

How was I going to tell his mother?

He'd already put that poor woman through so much.

I hadn't even asked where the call had come from, got a name or a number. All I knew was that I had to get someone to be with her when I broke the news.

The minutes ticked by and I stayed on the stairs. Once the

time on the grandfather clock showed seven, I texted Maisie and asked her to contact me. As I sat there I was glad Sean had given me her number – 'in case of emergencies', he'd said. We could never have imagined that the emergency would be one like this. I texted Ernest and Phyllis too. Ernest arrived before Celia had surfaced and, with a calm authority, contacted a friend in Foreign Affairs to deal with Mexico.

I'm still not sure if Celia's medical training was what got her to the stage of acceptance so quickly. Or if, as I did, she experienced a sense of relief that our torture and humiliation had ended. We had both loved the same man, and he had broken our hearts.

I got used to being referred to as 'the widow', and hearing words like 'tragic' and 'tragedy' being coupled with my name. I learned to smile acceptance when people offered condolences, and when they told me how wonderful my husband had been. It was just a pity that the memories I'd carry with me would not reflect similar experiences.

Out of a sense of loyalty I couldn't really explain, I tried to hold on to some of the good memories and willed them to eclipse the more recent revelations, knowing they'd never erase them.

As the widow, I was expected to make decisions: wording for the death notices; did I want to fly over and accompany his body back home? Did I want his body repatriated?

'I can't do this, any of it, Celia. I'm too hurt and angry. I can't stand at a coffin and listen to words of regret and loss, knowing the way I feel. I'm sorry. He was your son, and I'd prefer those decisions were made by you.'

'I understand perfectly, Tansy. I feel much the same myself. I was thinking perhaps we should have him cremated in Mexico and his ashes scattered at one of the Mayan sites he was so interested in. I'll have his name added to his father's headstone too. What do you think of that?'

It sounded like the perfect solution.

A few weeks later, one of his former colleagues wrote to me suggesting a memorial service for him. I declined, saying this was not my wish. I don't know what they thought of my reply, but at least it was honest, unlike anything else about Sean Pollard's life.

I stayed with Celia until September and then moved back to Rathmines with Phyllis.

Chapter Forty-nine

My friends, my real friends, were there every step of the way. They didn't feel the need to utter banalities, to tell me things would get better; that I'd forget all about Sean in time; or that I'd meet someone else. They were just there for me.

Álvaro and Elena flew over to Dublin one weekend shortly after we got the news of Sean's demise and we had a bittersweet reunion.

Gina and Gonzalo came home for a few weeks before the end of the summer. They were excited because they had found a premises to rent, outside Málaga, and they were going to start giving their own language courses.

Trevor and Mags moved in with Ernest, and Trevor got his master's, with distinction.

'No more books for you now, lad,' Phyllis said, when we all went out celebrating.

'That's what you'd think, wouldn't you, but no – he's decided to go for a doctorate! Haven't you, Trevor? My eternal student!'

'There's a proviso, though. I'll only go for it if I can persuade Mags to do her master's.' He laughed.

'I always knew you pair were headed for academia,' I said, and the others agreed.

Phyllis had a spring in her step and I suspected she was seeing someone and probably didn't want to make too much of it in front of me.

'I don't want you all pussyfooting around me. I am coping, much better than I thought I would, so I want to be included in everything. Even your love life, Phyllis.' She just threw her eyes towards heaven.

I missed her when she went out to teach every day, but I had too much to do to be able to hold down a job just then. I gave myself that academic year to sort out my affairs.

Not only was I dealing with the sale and disposal of my parents' house and farm, but as Sean's widow I discovered I had not only inherited his Dublin 4 apartment, but a holiday home in Connemara too.

'The paperwork involved is unbelievable. I can't tell you how many forms have to be filled out and signed. Every one of them worth a fee to the legal eagles, no doubt. I go to bed with terms like "inheritance taxes", "death duties" and "annuities" swimming in front of my eyes. And it seems to be endless.'

'It'll be worth it all when you've got it sorted,' Álvaro said.

'Are you sure you don't mind taking on responsibility for Juan's trust fund for me? I feel I foisted that on you, but I'd just feel happier having it managed in Spain. It would also mean that my name can be kept off the paperwork and Perdita need never find out.'

'I told you, Tansy. It's no problem at all.'

Inheriting Sean's apartment meant I had the unenviable task of emptying that too. I hated going in there, and the girls often came with me at weekends. Ernest and Trevor kindly offered to take all the research papers and books and rehouse them where appropriate. Even I recognised that there was valuable material there.

'You ought to invest in a property or two yourself,' Ernest suggested.

'I will,' I told him, 'just not yet. It's still too soon.'

My first wedding anniversary came and went. It was impossible to ignore it, because no matter how I went about avoiding it, it would always be the eve of my parents' anniversaries.

Phyllis, no filters as always, said, 'You need to erase the whole damned experience and start again, Tans.'

'I'm not a computer with an erase button, Phyllis, although I wish I were! It would make life an awful lot easier.'

Elena and Rosa both invited me to spend Christmas with them, but I opted to go to Celia. I didn't like to think of her on her own. Even though I visited her every week, I could see that life was taking its toll on her.

We became very close, and once she told me, 'Sean may have tarnished too many good years on me, but I have to give him credit for one thing, and that's for bringing you into my life.'

'And you into mine,' I replied and I really meant it.

I was determined to be in bed before midnight on New Year's Eve. I needed to bury my head. Looking back was still physically painful and I wasn't really ready to look forward yet. I was in a kind of holding pattern. It would pass. I had no doubt about that, but I also knew there was no way I could hurry it along.

'For old time's sake, let's order in a pizza,' I said, weary of all the rich seasonal fare.

'You're payin',' Phyllis said. 'I'm broke.'

'Was it ever any other way?' I laughed.

When the doorbell rang, I went to open it with the money in my hand, but instead of the delivery guy, Jack stood there.

Like an idiot, I just stared up at him. He seemed much taller. I remembered the look of hurt in his eyes the last time we were together, but it wasn't there. He reached out and hugged me. 'It's great to see you, Tansy.'

'I thought you were our pizza.'

'Sorry to disappoint. I just wanted to be the first redhead across Phyllis's doorstep to bring good luck for the new year.'

'You're a bit early,' I replied.

'I can come back again if it's bad timing.'

'Don't be mad, come in,' Phyllis called, coming up behind me, just as the pizza delivery arrived. 'There'll be enough for the three of us. Go on through. I'm just heating the plates.'

'I hear you've had a rough time, Tansy. With your parents and the Sean business. I'm sorry. You must miss your folks terribly. I really liked them a lot.'

'Thank you, and I do. They liked you too. I saw you at their funeral, but you were gone before I could talk to you. Can I just say something before Phyllis comes back? I'm glad to get this chance to tell you how much I regret the way I treated you. I never set out to hurt you, or to mess with your plans. And I'm sorry you didn't get to go to Australia. I know how much you wanted to.'

'It wouldn't have been the same without you,' he said quietly. 'And I was no competition for Sean.'

'I was blinded by Sean, and he used me. Oh, I don't doubt for one minute that there was some level of mad attraction between us. But if he hadn't been pressured into presenting the façade of a happily married man, instead of a philandering professor playing out his midlife fantasies on unsuspecting females, would he have come back into my life? Probably not!'

'You weren't to know that.'

'But he did. In fact, I think he was banking on it. He knew I'd be there, waiting in the wings, love-struck and flattered by his attentions. I'd fallen hook, line and sinker to become living proof of Mary McLaughlin's prophecy – if you marry in haste, you'll repent at your leisure. Those six months of our engagement, right up to the wedding, were a whirlwind. I was intoxicated and blinkered.'

'I'd like to think someone would love me like that sometime,' Jack said.

'And don't they?' said Phyllis, coming in, balancing three plates of pizza and garlic bread. 'You were right about one thing, though, Tansy, and I think it's time we told you – Jack and I are an item now. You always said you thought he fancied me, so I waited patiently in the wings until he decided he did.'

'That's great news. I'm really pleased for you both.'

'You don't mind?' Phyllis asked. 'I didn't know how to tell you.'

'Mind? How could I mind – my two favourite people – it's great news. I'm genuinely delighted.'

'What are your plans now?' Jack asked.

'I haven't made any yet. I'm a bit of a disaster. I can't seem to think ahead just yet. I'm still in no man's land until all this legal stuff is ironed out.'

'You're being very hard on yourself,' said Jack.

'I keep telling her that. Whoever would have thought she'd

graduate, be married, orphaned, widowed and become a property mogul all in the same year?'

'When you put it like that, it's a heck of a lot of living, and a heck of life-learning too in a short time,' he agreed.

'Most of which I would have preferred to have avoided.'

'You can't force grieving. It has a pace of its own,' Jack said, 'but you'll know when you're ready to move on.'

'That's exactly what Celia told me too. What about you two? Have you plans?'

'I hope to finish my master's this summer and, who knows, we may even head Down Under after that.'

'You weren't expecting that, were you, Tans?' Phyllis laughed.

'Definitely not.'

♦

They had been right, my friends. Grieving had a pace and a pattern of its own. It hit me randomly – when I was busy or idle, happy or sad, in traffic or at home. I realised that you can grieve for so many other reasons than death. You can grieve for love and lost dreams, for abandonment and betrayal and for the loss of a future.

I did all the things they told me to do: keep busy, keep in touch and keep healthy.

I didn't give myself goals. I wasn't ready for those, but as the year rolled on, I found I was achieving them, little by little. When Patsy Maher contacted me to tell me that he had an offer for the farm and homestead, I was delighted.

'It's from a local – Ross Doyle – who has been living abroad, out in the Emirates, I believe, for a few years. He has a young family and says he knows the property well.'

When he told me, I immediately thought, hell yes! I could hear my father say, 'It'll be in good hands there – that lad always loved his horses and the land. He'll look after the place.' Mam might have had a few words about this, but it was me who was making the decisions now.

'Go ahead and sign the deal,' I told Patsy Maher, 'and give my regards to Ross.'

It felt good. I hadn't realised I'd need to invest so much time and energy in bureaucracy, form-filling and red tape, but by my parents' second anniversary it was done. Properties sold. Taxes paid. All that was left was for me to get myself sorted and start getting on with my life.

Epilogue

It wasn't her favourite time of the year. Tansy didn't need any reminding that there were just eleven shopping days to go to Christmas. She was well aware of the fact, but it made no difference. She hadn't an idea what to buy anyone. This was her second tour of the shops and inspiration continued to evade her. It was definitely time for a break.

After queuing and navigating the crowded café she managed to find a seat at a tiny table. The warm aroma of wet clothes and hot coffee clung to the air around her. These shoppers all looked as though their present-buying was going better than hers. The previous customer had left the morning paper in disarray on the table and, as the waitress went to gather up the sections, Tansy stopped her. Having something to read always made her feel a little less conspicuous eating or drinking alone, although logically she knew no one paid the slightest bit of attention.

'May I have a look at those?' she asked. The disinterested girl handed the bundle to her with one hand, as she swiped a discoloured cloth across the table top, leaving streaks on its surface. Sections of the paper fell on the floor and the youngster made no attempt to help rescue them for her.

Tansy re-assembled them as best she could in the confined space. She glanced through the news. There was nothing she hadn't heard on 'What It Says in the Papers' that morning.

The cover of the Saturday supplement had an inviting ad for winter sunshine in Morocco. It jumped out at her. She had always wanted to go there. Some ditty her nan used to recite to her had a line 'Morocco, Mauritius and Malta' in it. She couldn't remember anything else, apart from her nan telling her, 'I've never seen any of those places so you must go for me instead.' She made her recite their names and show them to her on the globe she'd given her. Tansy always agreed. The front-page spread of a camel on a beach, the sun setting in the distance and palm trees in the foreground jogged those memories. On impulse she downed her mediocre coffee, squeezed between chair backs and stepped over carrier bags to make her way out into Grafton Street. She headed straight to the travel agent, visions of souks and lamb tagines impelling her through the jostling Christmas shoppers, obliterating the conflicting cacophony from buskers and carol singers.

Within a half an hour she'd done it. She'd booked a holiday. It was so much more than that, though: so much more.

'I just have to get Christmas out of the way now,' she told the travel agent, putting her credit card back in her purse.

'A lot of people feel like that about this time of year. Cheer up, there are only eleven shopping days left.'

'And not a present bought.' She laughed. 'And do you know something? I don't give a damn. Whose idea was it that we need gifts and tinsel and dates on a calendar to make any time special?'

'That's the spirit. Have a good one,' he said, handing her the paperwork.

She walked towards Marks & Spencer and bought vouchers for everyone on her list and left with a smile on her face and a lightness of spirit that had been missing for longer than she could remember.

She took out her phone and rang Phyllis. 'Guess what I've done!'

'Surprise me,' her friend said, and she did.

Phyllis shouted into the phone. 'Thanks be to Jaysus, Tansy – you're back!'

'I am. Watch out, Phyllis. I'm definitely back!'

◆

I could feel the heat through my jumper as I came down the steps of the plane, alone. Alone, but definitely not feeling lonely. Instead, I had a sense of freedom and optimism.

As I stood in line at the airport, queueing for security clearance, I knew I was ready to move on, at last. A man with a young boy stood behind me chatting away in Arabic. The little fellow was jumping up and down with impatience.

'He's excited to be coming back to see his grandparents,' the man told me. 'Is this your first time in Morocco?'

'Yes.'

'It's changed an awful lot since I left, sixteen years ago. We didn't have many tourists and the airport was tiny then.'

I picked up the immigration document and started answering

the questions, while officials with oversized uniform caps observed those who were streaming across the tarmac behind me.

As the queue wended its way slowly through the security points, I found myself speculating on what sort of people I'd meet. I might have given the impression of being a seasoned solo traveller. Only I knew how untrue that was.

I got some dirhams at the bank while I waited for my bags and then went in search of the company guide. It was easy to spot him, holding a placard with the hotel names on it. Once we were ticked off a list, a group of porters surged forward, jostling to carry my bags.

'I'm afraid I have no Arabic,' I confessed as the one who'd succeeded thanked me profusely for the tip. '*Suchran* – thank you – *suchran*,' he told me. I tried saying '*suchran*', and he bowed slightly, showing his toothy smile again, before hurrying back to capitalise on the other new arrivals. I was relieved that no one sat beside me as we set off through the surprisingly fertile landscape for the half-hour journey to the hotel.

I wanted to absorb everything. The guide outlined the excursion options and I felt free, free to do as I liked. To go or not – it was for me to decide.

The guide's announcement, 'I have seven people for this hotel,' broke my reverie. 'Buckley by two. Black by two. Nugent by one and O'Beirne by two.'

A sleek ginger cat strolled about, looking disdainfully at this invasion as we picked up our bags and checked in. I reached down to stroke him as he passed and he paused for a moment in acknowledgement before continuing his tour of inspection.

Djellaba-clad males stood at various points about the spacious vestibule. 'Some mint tea to refresh you, lady?' one of them enquired as he decanted a golden liquid into a glass and pointed to a curved sofa where some of the new arrivals were already seated.

A couple, who said they were the Blacks, were already sitting there. 'Is it your first time in Agadir?' the woman asked.

'Yes.'

I told Phyllis later on, 'They were both Trump orange, with peroxide bleached hair and Argos catalogue jewellery.'

'They sound awful.'

'They're probably OK, if a bit enthusiastic. I think they feel I'm a poor damsel in need of rescuing. When she discovered I was on my own, they exchanged looks of pity. Within minutes I knew everything about them. They come here every winter to avoid the cold at home and save on their heating bills. His father's gaga and goes into respite while they're here. He thinks they're in Monaco, not Morocco, visiting Princess Grace. Yes, he thinks she's still alive. They won't be doing the tours: they've seen it all before – the knock-off handbags and the duty-free booze allowance are mega!'

'You could learn a lot from them.' Phyllis laughed.

'She then went on to tell me that I needn't worry about being lonely, because – wait for it! – because I'd be sure to meet someone while I'm here. Apparently last year their friend met a gorgeous waiter, who made the best cocktails in Morocco and, I quote, "they had a mad, lustful, fling". The orange husband agreed. "Aye, they had." He then told me they know all the good bars and that they'll keep their eyes open for me.'

'What did you say?'

'What could I say? I didn't want to sound churlish, so I just smiled, downed my mint tea in a few gulps and headed to my room, which is lovely by the way, and there's a plate of some interesting-looking almond cakes tempting me.'

'Enjoy every morsel. You deserve it all.'

'Thanks, Phyllis, I'll do my best.'

I walked out onto the balcony and looked across the pedestrian esplanade to the beach where the mighty Atlantic was finding land, gently on the Moroccan sands. I sat down to enjoy the view and sighed.

I was here. I was really here.

Morocco, Mauritius and Malta ... I still couldn't remember where that chant had come from. Except that it was in a childhood story or a poem my nan used to read to me, but for whatever reason, it had made an impression. It had become a symbol of adventure and excitement, a doorway to the future. And that future was just beginning.

I unpacked my case, changed into something lighter and set off to explore the complex. After wandering through the flower-filled gardens I decided to go a little further afield. I loved the smell of the warm air, the birdsong, the smiling Senegalese vendors who tried to sell me collages made from pieces of soft drinks cans and jewellery made from coloured beads. I felt invigorated and alive.

Here I was, finally making it to Morocco, as I had promised my nan all those years ago. I had not come here to find a man, no matter how enticing his cocktails or his bartending skills might be.

I had just found Tansy Nugent again.

It had been a long, difficult and painful search to get to this point.

Now, what I needed to do was take the time to get to know who she was before embarking on any other quest.

Acknowledgements

I have to acknowledge Team Hachette, yet again, for their support.

A Degree of Truth is my seventh novel to be published with them, and they make it all seem so effortless, despite my editor, Ciara Doorley, going on maternity leave without my permission!

A special mention has to go to Joanna Smyth, again, for her cheerful and efficient attention to detail and her gentle nudges as deadlines loom.

And a shout out to all those involved in editing, cover design and distribution.

And finally, but by no means least of all, to my readers.

Muriel Bolger
April 2019

From the bestselling author of The Captain's Table

MURIEL
BOLGER
Family Business

Can she have
it all?

Family Business

Young, clever, and accomplished, Anne is fully committed to her career at her father's law practice – much to the delight of her parents and the not-so-hidden resentment of her younger sister Gabby. She doesn't have time to think of her dreams of art college or, indeed, the lack of love in her life.

Then Anne finds herself facing charismatic barrister Daniel Hassett in court. Equally ambitious, they seem to be the perfect match. But just as Anne and Daniel's relationship heats up, a series of shocking events force Anne to question what she really wants.

Will an unexpected French inheritance be just the thing to help her decide a way forward – in law and in love?

Also available as an ebook